A THIRST FOR MURDER

C. R. Koons

CAVEL
PRESS
Kenmore, WA

CAMEL PRESS

Camel Press books published by Epicenter Press

Epicenter Press
6524 NE 181st St. Suite 2
Kenmore, WA 98028.
www.Epicenterpress.com
www.Coffeetownpress.com
www.Camelpress.com

For more information go to: www.Epicenterpress.com
Author's website: www.cedarkoons.com

A Thirst for Murder
Copyright © 2024 by C. R. Koons

ISBN: 9781684921539 (trade paper)
ISBN: 9781684921546 (ebook)

LOC: 202345704

Cover photo by Edward Scheps.

Dedication

For Phoebe and Bee Siegel

Acknowledgments

The author wishes to acknowledge Sharon Stewart for reading the manuscript and offering her sensitive understanding of the people of Mora County before and after the catastrophic fires of 2022 as well as numerous other insights, and Rena Pyne of Picuris Pueblo who has warmly welcomed me into her home at Pueblo dances and feast days helping me to know more about the Picuris people. The author would also like to acknowledge her husband, Edward Scheps, for his plot advice, emotional support, delicious meals and beautiful cover photo.

Dear Reader,

This book revolves around surface water rights in New Mexico where water is all-important. The region gets only about thirteen inches of rain per year. However, northern New Mexico, which includes the southernmost Rocky Mountains, receives abundant snow in the high elevations. Because of spring run-off from the melting mountain snowpack, small scale agriculture has been possible here, due to an ancient system of irrigation ditches called "acequias." Snowmelt fills the rivers and streams each spring with the extra water necessary to irrigate orchards, pastures, and gardens in the typically dry springs until the annual monsoon rains arrive in early July.

Acequias are a treasured part of New Mexican culture. These hand-dug gravity flow channels deliver water to adjacent landowners with rights, who are called "parciantes." Acequias date to the Spanish settlers who, beginning in the seventeenth century, brought the practice from Spain. Some Native American tribes, including the Picuris and Taos Pueblo Indians, also established acequia-type irrigation prior to the Spanish conquest.

Individual acequias are governed by a local "comisión," volunteers elected from among the parciantes to distribute water fairly, oversee the acequia infrastructure, and collect dues. The comisión hires a "mayordomo," a parciante who manages the delivery of the water in amounts prescribed by tradition and law.

When several acequias use the same river for irrigation, conflicts sometimes arise during times of scarce water. A traditional practice of water sharing, called "repartimiento," brings the acequia comisionados who share the water source together to discuss how to distribute scarce water equitably.

In New Mexico, surface water rights are governed by a state bureaucracy called the Interstate Stream Commission, headed by a State Engineer who is appointed by the governor. The State Engineer operates with broad discretion to make policy in accordance with state statutes on surface water.

Water rights are traditionally tied to the land to which they were originally assigned and cannot be sold separately except under rare circumstances. The oldest water rights are called priority rights because their preservation takes precedence over newer rights. But if water rights are not used for agriculture over many years, the rights can be removed. And, when a party has used surface water for agriculture for many years, even if they had no right to take it in the first place, they can claim the right according to law. This practice is called "perfecting the right."

Today, acequias are facing many threats to their very existence. Climate change is causing warmer winters with less snowfall and earlier, faster spring run-off. Subsistence agriculture, the underlying reason for acequias, still exists in modern New Mexico, but it is being replaced by other uses for surface water. Government pressure to provide water for downstream interests—including municipalities, manufacturing, mining, large scale commercial agriculture, and interstate compacts made in more recent times—creates conflicts with users like small farmers, who are dependent on acequias. And finally, developers are increasingly looking to buy unused water rights, using legal, quasi-legal, and illegal methods to acquire water for projects like ski resorts, golf courses, and housing developments.

When water rights are somehow separated from the land, they can be bought and sold as "paper rights" and transferred miles away from their source. Paper rights, through complicated legal agreements, allow developers to acquire the required amount of water for their projects even when it is not available to them in their immediate vicinity. Those downstream on watercourses from where rights are sold may not be able to recover what they have lost in these arrangements.

There is an old saying in the West: "Whiskey is for drinking; water is for fighting." Many a battle has been fought over water rights in New Mexico, both in the courts and in the villages, over hundreds of years. There is another old saying in New Mexico, "El agua es la vida," meaning water is life. Sadly, fights over water can sometimes lead to murder.

This book is a work of fiction. All people, events and interpretations of the law are the creation of the author. Any resemblance to persons, living or dead, is coincidental.

There is a glossary of terms at the back of the book.

Yours Sincerely,
C.R. Koons

Chapter 1

Just before dusk on an evening in late May, Antonio Valdez, a comisionado on Acequia San Lorenzo, walked a path downstream along Rio Pueblo between the river and the acequia. Antonio had examined the presa to confirm that it was set at the appropriate level, just enough to send water into his acequia for its parciantes to irrigate their gardens and orchards, while leaving enough in the Rio Pueblo for the Acequia de los Patos downstream. While checking the presa, Antonio had hidden a lock box inside the seldom used tool storage shed that stood nearby.

The river flowed high and loud and turbulent on one side of the path with the last of the spring run-off. On the other side, the acequia it fed was full. Acequia San Lorenzo currently had no mayordomo. Jacinto Ramirez, the mayordomo hired the year before, had quit suddenly after a dispute with the comisión. As a result, Antonio, as one of the three comisionados, had to take his turn managing the ditch until a new mayordomo was hired.

Willows and cottonwoods were leafing out on both sides of the river and Antonio heard the song of the yellow-breasted chat, a night singer familiar to the bosques in summer. He remembered the song from his boyhood, when he listened from his bedroom in the old adobe he'd inherited from his parents and where he and his wife had raised their daughter. It was lonely now at home without Reina, his wife of forty years, who had died of cancer the previous September, especially since their only child, Delilah, had taken a job as a staff attorney at a major water rights law firm in Santa Fe, about fifty miles from his home in Vadito.

As he walked on the mayordomo's path, Antonio mused on how the small accumulation of snow from a mild winter in the Sangre de Cristo Mountains was melting far too fast and the month of May, usually cool, had been unseasonably warm and windy, even here at 7,500 feet. Water from the river, though plentiful now, might not last until the monsoon rains came. Already he'd had words with mayordomos from the other acequias that shared the Rio Pueblo.

Just two days ago, Jeremy Diggs, the mayordomo of Acequia de los Patos, had loudly accused Antonio at the Village Market of taking more water than he should. Then yesterday Antonio had an unpleasant interaction with Carlos Gutierrez, mayordomo of the acequia upstream from him, when he asked for repartimiento early to avoid stress on his parciantes' young seedlings. Carlos shook his head and said, darkly, "It won't matter, Antonio. Look at that mountain. It's nearly bare already. The run-off will be finished in a week. No one should even consider planting this spring." *No one but those on upstream acequias like yours, Carlos,* Antonio had thought.

If only our watershed was not being depleted by those old diversions that transfer water into Mora County, we'd all have much more water, Antonio thought. The Mora transfers were a series of ditches and concrete structures hidden high in the mountains that funneled water from some of the Rio Pueblo's watershed over a series of passes and into the next basin in Mora County. The ditches were dug by Mora County farmers in the early to middle nineteenth century, supposedly with the permission of Picuris Pueblo, to whom the water actually belonged. Antonio, a retired professor of New Mexico history, was familiar with this story of permission giving. He'd also heard Picuris tribal members object that they had never agreed to giving up their water. Still, in 1907, with help from members of the notorious Santa Fe Ring, Mora had received permanent and perfected rights to the water over the objections of the Picuris tribe. The water they'd sent to Mora County diminished the entire Rio Pueblo watershed.

Antonio fervently believed that water which had fallen as snow and rain in their watershed rightfully belonged on their side of the mountain. Mora residents believed as passionately that water delivered by ditches laboriously dug by their ancestors belonged to them. Recently, an important court ruling, the Rimrock decision, had established that Native American tribes had priority rights to water flowing to their lands because they had been on their lands longer than anyone else. The Rimrock decision meant that the Mora transfers could be relitigated, restoring water to Picuris Pueblo and the Rio Pueblo watershed. Antonio hoped he could get his daughter Delilah's firm to take the case. But recently she'd been working long hours at her new job or spending time with her new fiancé. Antonio and Delilah had been playing phone tag for a week.

But tonight, something else, something dangerous, was on Antonio's mind. Earlier that afternoon Antonio had visited his late wife Reina's brother, Delfino Mondragon, at Taos Pueblo. The Pueblo, about twenty-five miles away, was closely related to Picuris Pueblo, speaking the same language and sharing the same religion. Del was a renowned sculptor and an influential member of the tribal council, but he had gotten himself mired in tribal politics which had recently become heated over a proposed sale of water rights to a golf developer. Del had obtained something that could get a lot of powerful people in trouble and he'd given it to Antonio for safekeeping. This evening Antonio had again called Delilah for her advice about what to do, but she didn't pick up. What he had to tell her was far too sensitive to leave in a voice mail message. In the meantime, Antonio had stowed the item in a safe hiding place out of the house, at least for now.

The long day was coming to an end and darkness obscured the rough trail. *I'd better get home before I fall and hurt myself,* Antonio thought. Just then he heard a rustling in the willows between the path and the river. *A bear? No, not at this time of year,* he thought. Bears were more likely to come down from the mountains in the fall.

"Hello?" he called out and the rustling stopped. *That's a person,* he thought. Again, he heard the rustling and called out, "Is someone there?" He continued walking, feeling afraid. Someone was just below him on the riverbank, moving through the willows. Antonio had begun to run when the man climbed suddenly onto the bank in front of him. He was carrying a shovel. In the dark, Antonio couldn't make out his identity.

"Who are you?" he asked. "What do you want?"

The man ran at him, swung the shovel at his head and struck him hard on his left temple. Antonio fell to the ground, unconscious.

Taos County Sheriff Ulysses Walker stood at his front porch watching the sun peek over the mountains. The spring morning was especially beautiful with a deep blue, cloudless sky and the green of new aspen leaves beginning to creep up the lower slopes of the Sangre de Cristo range. Ulysses had slept soundly the night before, with no dreams to trouble him for a change. He took a sip of hot coffee, enjoying his morning of relative ease.

In a little more than a week it would be the primary election day and Ulysses was on the ballot for his second term. Early voting had just started. In Taos County, whoever won the Democratic primary often ran unopposed in November. Ulysses was ahead in the polls and was also favored as the incumbent. If he won the primary against his opponent, former Deputy Ernesto Ruiz, Ulysses would have another four-year term as sheriff. He stretched his long, lean frame and thought about going for a run before breakfast.

Rosemary, Ulysses' wife of ten years, came out on the porch and sat in one of the rocking chairs. Tall and curvy with red, curly hair and freckles, Rosemary had been up early and had already milked the goats, fed the chickens and taken her allotted acequia time to irrigate her market garden and orchard. Rosemary grew herbs and vegetables for the Taos Farmer's Market and was famous for the chutneys, jams and goat cheeses she sold there.

"Ready for some pancakes, Ulys? I've got batter made."

Just then the cellphone in his pocket rang. It was Angela Romero, his deputy sheriff. Ulysses put aside the idea of a run. While weekend mornings were sometimes low-key at the Walker household, one phone call could bring an end to the peace and quiet.

"Yes, Deputy?" Ulysses said. "What's up?"

"Sheriff, a man named Antonio Valdez has been found dead behind his house over at Vadito."

"How did he die?" Ulysses asked. He was trying to remember if he knew Antonio Valdez.

"Rescue says it looks like he drowned. It definitely sounds suspicious."

"Was he in the river?"

"No, he was in the acequia," Deputy Sheriff Romero said. "Rescue is there, but they are waiting on us before they move the body."

Ulysses remembered how he knew the victim. Antonio was Delilah Valdez's father's name and Delilah had grown up in Vadito. Ulysses had met Delilah at UNM where she was two years behind him. Her father had been a history professor and he remembered her mother was a Taos Pueblo member. Delilah was pretty as well as smart and Ulysses had once asked her out. She'd told him she had to study on the night in question and he'd never tried to date her again.

"Listen, I'll get a move on and pick you up. Call them back and tell them we are on the way."

"Yes, Sheriff. I'll wait for you here at Headquarters." She had just finished the night shift and had hoped to go home to get some sleep.

"Will you be gone long?" Rosemary asked when Ulysses got off the phone. She was making pancakes for their two children.

"Hard to say. How about I meet you at Headquarters for Lorraine's goodbye party?" Lorraine Baca, Ulysses' secretary, was retiring.

"At 1:30?"

"Yeah. And we've got that meet and greet at the Women's Shelter at 3:00. Are you coming?"

"I'll be there," Rosemary said. She wrapped a warm tortilla around scrambled eggs, potatoes and greenchile for Ulysses to take on the road.

"Daddy," Amelia said, "I wanted us to play Wordle today!" At nine, Amelia loved to read and was good at all sorts of word games.

"We'll do it when we get home," Ulysses said.

"Promise?"

"I promise."

Monty, seven, made a face but didn't say anything. Ulysses could tell the boy was really disappointed.

"I know we were supposed to go on a bike ride, son," Ulysses said.

Monty got up from the table and started to leave the room.

"Take your plate to the sink, Monty," Rosemary said.

"We'll get a bike ride in later," Ulysses said.

"Here's your breakfast," Rosemary said, handing Ulysses the burrito in a napkin and a thermos of coffee. "Be careful out there. Are you having lunch with Stephanie?"

"Oh, thanks for reminding me. Yes, we have a campaign meeting at Mateo's." Rosemary shook her head and smiled. "That should be fun." Stephanie Gold was Ulysses' old girlfriend from high school. Rosemary was possessive of Ulysses around Stephanie, who in addition to being an attractive blonde, owned a successful real estate brokerage. Rosemary also liked to tease Ulysses about Stephanie even though she insisted she wasn't really threatened.

Ulysses drove down his long dirt driveway, crossed a cattle guard and turned onto the main road to Taos. As he passed through the sleepy village of Arroyo Hondo he thought about the newly dead man. Antonio Valdez was a respected local elder from an old, established family in Vadito, a small town founded in the late eighteenth century at a ford of the Rio Pueblo. Ulysses thought he was an acequia commissioner and also involved in regional water politics.

He stopped at Headquarters to pick up Deputy Romero, a slender young woman with large brown eyes and long hair she wore in a tight bun. Ulysses had come to rely on his deputy and hoped to promote her at his earliest opportunity. The state legislature had appropriated money for an undersheriff in Taos County for the next fiscal year, less than a month after the election.

"How was it last night?" Ulysses asked.

"Quiet for a Saturday," Angela said. "Mark and I broke up a fight at the Local, but we didn't have to make an arrest. That was about it."

Ulysses turned off the main road and headed into the high country. They drove in silence following the GPS directions until they turned onto a tree-lined driveway that led to the Valdez property, a sprawling old adobe hacienda flanked by majestic cottonwood trees. The Peñasco Fire and Rescue truck was parked near the path to the river with its lights flashing. Sheriff Walker got out and spoke to the two EMTs who'd been waiting.

"Who found the body?" he asked.

"A woman named Barbara Salazar," the lead EMT answered. "She lives just downstream. She was out at dawn walking her dog."

"Did she touch anything?"

"No, but she was pretty shook up by what she saw."

"How long do you think he's been dead?"

"Twelve hours maybe. Rigor mortis is pronounced."

"Have you contacted next of kin?" Ulysses asked.

"No. I'd rather you did that if you don't mind."

"That's my job," he said, dreading the call to Delilah. "Deputy, let's go take a look." He and Angela started down the path to the river.

When they got to the acequia they crossed on a footbridge and walked upstream with the loud river on one side of them and the full acequia on the other. Before long they came upon a man's body lying prone across the path. He was wearing blue jeans, a flannel shirt and boots. Ulysses felt sick to his stomach, as he always did when seeing a murder victim. He breathed deeply for a few moments. Angela, aware of her boss's reaction to murder victims, stood quietly while he recovered himself.

"Did you know Mr. Valdez, Sheriff?" Angela asked.

"I met him once. He seemed like a nice man. I think he was a comisionado on this acequia. Did you know him?"

"No, but I've heard of him and his family. I'll get some pictures." The victim lay on his stomach, head and shoulders in the water, arms and legs splayed on dry ground. The dirt around his body was disturbed but no clear footprints were visible. On the bank, willows were mashed flat and a thick poison ivy vine had been pulled loose from a tree and hung across the path. Ulysses bent down and lifted the man's head from the water. The side of his face had a dark contusion from the temple to the jaw. It bore an expression of horror, mouth and eyes open. Ulysses placed the head back into the water.

He stood up from the body and wiped his hands on his handkerchief. He had some knowledge about acequias because his father, Monty, had been a mayordomo for a few years when Ulysses was a teenager and he sometimes went along to help him. "Valdez must have been walking the ditch to check the presa. I think it is just upstream from here. His attacker might have been someone he knew. Let's go down to the riverbank. We might see more there."

Angela took pictures of the bank where broken willows and mashed grasses showed someone had climbed up from the river, maybe in a hurry.

"What do you think these are?" Angela asked.

Ulysses looked closely at some fresh slices in the bank. "I think the killer got up to the path using a shovel and maybe grabbed that poison ivy vine." He pointed to the thick vine swinging across the acequia path. "Once he got up from the river, he could have hit Valdez on the head with the shovel, knocked him unconscious and then drowned him in the acequia." Ulysses paused. "Whew, that's ugly."

In the mud beside the river, they found several footprints that appeared to come from upstream. Angela took a few photos of a man's boot with pointed toes and what appeared to be a large nick in one boot heel. She took a little tape from her pocket and measured the prints, making a note in her phone. "Size 10 and ½" she said. They followed the prints until they came to a place where they disappeared, alongside the presa.

"I think the killer came down that hill from the road." He pointed to a steep bank where the grasses were also pressed down.

Angela photographed some more shovel cuts. "That looks right. Then he headed downstream, maybe following the victim?"

"Yes. Then, when the time was right, he came up the bank and surprised Valdez."

Angela took more pictures of the cuts in the bank. "That's ironic that he was hit with a shovel," Angela said. "The saying is 'Pala Power' for acequieros. Meaning shovel power."

"I know," Ulysses said. "That's a dark twist to a good saying. Let's get back to the EMTs."

As they walked back, Angela said, "Isn't Delilah Valdez an attorney?"

"Yes, she's with Brown and Bronstein in Santa Fe. I'll have to call her when we are done here."

"That must be the worst part of your job."

"It definitely is."

"Do you have any ideas about who might have done this?"

"Nope," Ulysses said. "But there are people I want to interview."

"I can help, Sheriff. If you like."

"Call Joseph Maes, the new deputy, to come. You two can review and tape the scene. Then go home and rest until Lorraine's party. It isn't good to get overtired in this job."

"Yes, Sheriff."

"I'm going to have a look in the house and call Delilah to tell her about her father. If I have the time, I'll visit Barbara Salazar."

After the Rescue left with Valdez's body, Sheriff Walker went in the unlocked back door of the Valdez home and pulled on some latex gloves. He called Delilah from a landline on the counter and sat down at the kitchen table. Delilah Valdez answered the phone on the first ring.

"Daddy?" she said.

"Ms. Valdez, this is Sheriff Ulysses Walker."

There was a pause; then she said, "Is something wrong, Ulys?"

"I am terribly sorry to tell you this, Delilah, but your father is dead."

"He's dead?"

"He was killed last night. We think he was murdered."

After a long pause, Delilah asked in a whisper, "Who killed him?"

"I don't know. But I will find out, I promise you."

"Oh, my God," she said. "Where is his body?"

"He'll be taken to the morgue in Taos."

"What do I need to do?" Delilah said, starting to cry.

"Someone will have to identify the body. The coroner will call you when he's ready for you to come. When he's finished with the postmortem a funeral director can take over. Do you have anyone who can support you through this? There will be a lot to do in the next few days."

"My fiancé, Arthur Davenport, is here. Listen, Sheriff, I have to tell you something. My father had been trying to reach me for a couple of days. Last evening, he left me a message about something he said was really important. He told me he had to speak with me in person. Daddy wasn't one to exaggerate. I tried to call him back but," she paused and held back sobs. "I have no idea what it was he wanted to tell me! Oh, God, I wish I knew," she said, choking back more sobs.

"Ms. Valdez, don't worry about this just now. You've had a terrible shock. When you've taken care of the basics you and I will talk, okay? In the meantime, if you recall anything that could be helpful, give me a call." He gave her his cellphone number and she hung up.

Ulysses sat for a few moments to settle his mind, then proceeded to search the house for clues to help him understand this murder.

The large, old-fashioned kitchen where he sat had been ransacked, and the refrigerator had been left standing open, with food placed on the floor and counter beside it. The cupboards above the stove had been emptied and broken dishes and glassware littered the floor. Only the table, with a dinner plate and glass of milk, were undisturbed. Beside the plate was a pencil and notepad, the top sheet of which looked blank at first. Ulysses picked up the pencil and traced over indentations in the paper. The tracings showed the number 1797. Ulysses tore off the sheet, folded it, and put it in his pocket.

In the living room the cushions on two slipcovered couches had been sliced open, as had the leather on a big armchair. Books and journals had been rifled through and thrown to the floor. The television and other electronics were askew, as if they'd been searched. Ulysses looked into the main bedroom, where the bed was stripped and the mattress and pillows sliced open. Bureaus had their drawers emptied on the floor and clothes had been dumped in a pile. The bed was upended in Delilah's mostly bare old bedroom with its fading posters from a pow-wow at Taos Pueblo in the 1990s. In the bathroom the medicine cabinet was pulled from the wall and lay on the floor with its contents strewn.

The room Valdez had used as an office had also been torn apart. Desk drawers were open with contents spilling out. The file cabinet was overturned. From the way the desk was arranged, Ulysses suspected a computer was missing. The cords to charge a computer were there, but whatever they plugged into was gone. *The murderer was motivated to find something he thought would be easy to locate,* Ulysses thought. *My guess from the way this place looks is that he didn't find it. But this could be a clue.* He patted his pocket with its piece of notebook paper where he'd traced the number 1797.

Chapter 2

The Corn Maiden Gallery, Taos's oldest and most prestigious gallery, was an old two-story brick house on a quiet street off a pedestrian mall near Taos Plaza. Behind the gallery in a grassy yard, surrounded by a tall coyote fence, was Delfino Mondragon's studio. FBI Agent LizBethTallichet parked in the lot and walked through a gate to a yard that held several large, completed sculptures and a south-facing shed that housed tools, blocks of uncarved stone, and a large worktable. The garage door that made up the shed's fourth wall was open. A huge old ponderosa pine towered over the studio, providing welcome shade.

Mondragon greeted her at the gate and offered her a camp chair near the worktable, where he was carefully sanding a bust of a young Indian woman with double braids. He was tall and fit-looking, in his fifties, with shiny, black hair he wore short and a handsome, weathered face. LizBeth noticed that he barely looked at her when he greeted her but that his expression was guarded and his body language betrayed tension.

"This is a portrait of my niece, Delilah Valdez," he said. "I need to have it ready for her wedding. I hope you don't mind if I work while we talk?" Mondragon looked through a box and found a finer sandpaper to smooth the face of the bust.

"Not at all," Agent Tallichet said. "What was it you wanted to tell me?"

Mondragon sanded in silence for a few moments, then stopped and sighed. "I called because I finally got fed up with the influence of one individual on our council, State Senator Ramón

Trujillo. I work closely with the tribal governor. We've been in negotiations to sell some of our water rights to a developer, Trey Cameron, who wants to build a fancy golf resort. Senator Trujillo is involved with Cameron and the project. Senator Trujillo has many friends on the council," Mondragon said, putting down the sandpaper and looking at LizBeth for the first time. "It's gotten very complicated. My apprentice, Raven Sandoval, kept pressuring me to call you, but I wasn't ready." *I'm not sure you are ready now,* LizBeth thought.

"Why was he pressuring you?" she asked.

"Raven is a very idealistic young man. He and some of the younger men in the tribe feel pretty strongly about protecting our water rights."

"Did this Senator offer you a bribe?"

"No. But he threatened me if I didn't agree to the water rights sale. It's coming up for a vote by the tribal council very soon."

"Who is this guy, Senator Trujillo?" LizBeth asked.

"He's the state senator for most of Taos County. Some tribal members really like him. He's gotten us capital outlay from the state legislature and has helped us avoid problems at our casino with the State Gaming Commission. He's become the go-to person when a tribal business gets snarled up in any permitting process. I don't think most people realize there is a cost to his help."

Mondragon picked up a small, delicate chisel to work on the bust's neck and shoulder. LizBeth watched his skilled hands as he worked. She could tell he was debating how much to tell her.

Finally, he put down the chisel and resumed talking.

"Trujillo did something big for me a few years ago, before I knew better than to trust him. He recommended me to a gallery, Mountain Spirit Native Arts, in Jackson Hole. They were eager to show my larger pieces and offered to pay for the shipping. Those works are hard to place and expensive to ship. The Jackson Hole market is lucrative and I sold a lot of pieces for good prices. Later I realized that the people who owned that gallery were kind of like an art mafia. When they want something in return, you can't refuse, or they'll demand you ship your art home immediately at your expense, and then blackball you with other galleries in the region."

Mondragon wiped his hands and covered the bust with a cloth. "That is all I'm going to do on her today," he said. "Would you like a cup of tea? I have regular black tea or red willow bark."

"Is the red willow from around here?" Agent Tallichet asked. She knew that Taos Pueblo were called "the people of the red willow."

Mondragon laughed. "No, it's from Germany—a customer gave it to me. I'm going to have Earl Grey."

"That works for me."

Mondragon turned on an electric kettle and put out cups, milk, and sugar. He sat down across from her.

"You still haven't told me how Trujillo threatened you," Agent Tallichet said.

"Last year, after I was elected to the tribal council, Trujillo suggested I enter Native Artist Showcase, a national contest run out of Jackson Hole that brings people from all over the U.S. for juried shows. The Mountain Spirit Gallery owner sponsored me and paid for all the sculptures I entered to be shipped. I won the grand prize in January. It's called 'Native Artist of the Year' and includes $50,000 in prize money and lots of publicity. It means my work can get into virtually any gallery. But after the awards ceremony, the gallery manager told me in a roundabout way that a few bribes had been strategically placed with the judges on my behalf." Mondragon poured boiling water over their teabags and sat back down.

"What did you do?"

Mondragon dunked his teabag in the hot water until it was fully steeped.

"I didn't know what to do, so I did nothing," he said at last. "Big mistake. Later, when Trujillo was seeking votes in the council, he threatened to make Showcase bribes public and say I had placed them, unless I voted to sell water rights to his friend, the developer. That's when I found out that Trey Cameron, Trujillo's friend or possibly his boss, is a silent partner to the owner of Mountain Spirit Gallery."

LizBeth prepared her tea and took a sip. "So, what are you going to do?"

"I've been stalling for time to figure it out. I've acted like I'm going to vote yes to sell, just to keep Trujillo happy and buy time. I've thought about exposing the Showcase bribes myself. That's most likely what I'll do. And, of course, I've considered just voting to sell our water rights and being done with it." Mondragon shook his head and smiled ruefully. "Frankly, I wish I could do that, but I don't think I could live with myself."

"Tell me a little more about Taos's history with water rights," Agent Tallichet said.

"We've always had our river coming right down to us from the mountain, pure enough to drink. We've had enough water to grow our corn, beans and pumpkins and to have pasture for our livestock. Even with this drought," Mondragon said, "we have water."

He sipped his mug of tea. "Fifteen years ago, an outfit from California wanted to buy water from us for a senior living complex across NM 64 from tribal lands. Some in the tribe were really hoping that we could get money for things like affordable housing, urgent care, a nursing home, all of that. Others were worried that the people from California would somehow screw us and we'd end up without our rights or the money. A few of us, myself included, didn't want to threaten our traditional way of life by selling our water. It got pretty heated for a while, but finally the Hondo acequieros downstream from the project fought it in the courts and they succeeded in blocking the sale."

Mondragon stood up, stretched, and started to put away his tools. LizBeth carried the teacups to a basin and put the milk in a small refrigerator. She wondered if he was trusting her with this information but holding back something else.

Mondragon continued, his back to LizBeth. "Since the Rimrock decision people think we can sell water rights and there will be no consequences to us. All on the upside, no downside. The water would be transferred on paper, not like real water. Sure, the amount would be taken out of the total water allocated to our watershed, but we'd never miss it, supposedly because we have so much. First of all, I don't believe that we'd never miss it, what with climate change and all. But also, this sale is different. It involves a cross-basin transfer out of the Rio Grande basin and into the Arkansas River basin. It is very rare to do that and I'm not sure it is even legal. Okay, they have permission from the new State Engineer. But if the sale went through and then was overturned in court, it could hurt us."

"How could it hurt you?"

Mondragon chuckled. "We have a long history of being lied to in just this kind of way—'this will have no consequences to your people.'" He turned around and looked at LizBeth intently. "Just knowing some of the people who are eager to make this deal convinces me it's a bad idea."

"So, what are you going to do?"

Mondragon's cellphone rang and he looked at the caller ID. "It's my niece," he said, "I have to take it."

LizBeth listened while Mondragon heard what the apparently bad news was. Mondragon tried to console his niece but LizBeth could tell he was deeply alarmed. "Let me call you back," he said, "I'm not alone. I'll call you in half an hour."

When he got off the phone he said, "I just got word that my sister's husband, Antonio Valdez, was murdered last night in Vadito. I have to go. Please keep what I've told you confidential, for now." Mondragon looked deeply shaken.

"Do you have any ideas as to who might have killed your brother-in-law?"

Mondragon was rapidly packing away his tools and getting ready to leave. "No. But I'm going to go up on our mountain, do a little fishing and a lot of thinking. When I come down, I'll be ready to take the next steps."

What steps? LizBeth wondered. *And why the hurry?*

"Are you going to go alone?"

"I will ask Raven to go with me."

"Are you worried these people might hurt you?" Agent Tallichet asked.

"Not Trujillo himself, nor Cameron. They are both old men who aren't that strong. But I think they have some rough characters working for them."

"Have you met any of their operatives?"

"I saw two men in the Wyoming gallery one time who looked like Cameron's security. One was white and one was mixed race. I wouldn't want to tangle with either one of them. What will the FBI do about this situation?"

"Nothing just yet," she answered. "The murder is in the county's jurisdiction. When you are ready to make your statement about the extortion and bribery, the FBI will investigate further and maybe bring an indictment. What will it mean for you to come forward?"

"I can't be sure," Mondragon said. "I'll be pretty unpopular for a while. And that is an understatement. We don't usually take our council business off the pueblo, if you know what I mean. Given how damning the Showcase bribes could be, I'll probably lose this space and maybe my other galleries." He shrugged. "But you got to do what you got to do." He shook his head sadly.

"When will you come back down?"

"I don't know. I'd like to help my niece... but I have to get clear first."

"Call me at this number just as soon as you get back, will you?"

"Okay, Agent Tallichet. Thanks." He closed and locked the studio and together they walked out to the parking lot. Mondragon got into his car and sped away, talking on his cellphone.

LizBeth walked across the parking lot to her car. There were several more cars parked than when she arrived, including a new grey truck with tinted windows and temporary tags. Its engine was running and LizBeth noticed two men sitting inside.

When Ulysses left the Valdez home, he drove to the next-door neighbors, Barbara and John Salazar. Their newish two-story stucco house and attached garage were flanked by tall Colorado blue spruce trees. The lawn and adjacent hayfield had clearly benefited from lots of irrigation. Ulysses got out and knocked on the front door. A woman in her sixties wearing blue jeans and a sweatshirt answered the door, holding a big, brindled pit bull by the collar. The dog barked ferociously when he entered, then started wagging from head to toe and licked his hand.

"Don't mind Dixie, Sheriff," Barbara Salazar said. "She's still wound up from this morning. We've been expecting you to come by. Have a seat. Can I get you anything?" She indicated a leather chair by the door.

"No, thank you," Sheriff Walker said, sitting down. "Please tell me what happened."

"It's pretty straightforward," Salazar said. "I took the dog out at the crack of dawn. I usually walk her on the road, but I decided to go down by the river so she could run off leash. We hadn't gotten far on the path when Dixie started barking. That's when I saw Antonio's body. I knew right away he was dead because, well you know, his head was in the water. I had to go close to him to leash Dixie so I saw more than I wanted to see. It was horrible. I ran all the way home. John called the Rescue."

"Did you see anything unusual either on the way or on the way back?"

"No, nothing. But you know, I've been thinking a lot about something I saw on Saturday."

"What was that?"

"I was at the Village Market just outside of Peñasco one day last week and I heard Jeremy Diggs, the mayordomo of Patos, downstream from us, yelling at Antonio about our acequia taking too much water. Lots of people must have heard it. The store was busy at the time. Antonio didn't say anything at first, but I could tell he was getting pretty angry. Antonio said, 'you have no right to talk to me like that.' Then Diggs said, 'you have no right to steal our water.'" I thought they would start to fight, but the manager came and told Diggs to leave."

"Have you had contact with Mr. Diggs before?"

"Oh, yes, Sheriff. He goes to our church. His wife is a sweet woman and we were friends when her first husband was alive,

Ruben Tafoya. But Jeremy Diggs is not someone we've been friendly with. My husband thinks something is wrong with him."

"Did I hear my name invoked?" John Salazar, a fit-looking man with white hair and glasses came into the room from the kitchen. "Hello, Sheriff, I guess Barbara has pulled me into this."

"Hello, Mr. Salazar. Do you have any information to offer?"

"Not about Jeremy Diggs, no. But last night on my way home from my poker game—I play with some men I used to work with at the Lab—I saw a vehicle parked near the property line we share with the Valdez place."

"What time was that?"

"A little after nine o'clock," John Salazar said.

"What kind of vehicle was it?"

"A truck, but I couldn't tell what kind. Late model I think, dark, not sure of the color. It wasn't Jeremy Digg's truck."

"Did you see any lights on at the Valdez home?"

"No, not as I drove by, but it is hard to see lights over there from the road with the trees all leafed out."

"Well, thank you both for the information. Here's how you can contact me if you think of anything else."

Ulysses decided to interview Jeremy Diggs as long as he was in the neighborhood.

The Diggs place was also on the river, two miles downstream from the Salazar place. The land had once belonged to Ruben Tafoya, a friend of Ulysses' father Monty, who had served with him in Vietnam. Tafoya's widow, Brenda, had remarried a younger man, Diggs, who arrived in their neighborhood from Texas about seven years after Ruben died. Brenda's property included some of the best farmland in the area. Diggs raised Herefords on improved pasture, and grew an acre of alfalfa, a crop that needed a lot of water. Their well-kept, double-wide mobile home stood on a permanent foundation down a gravel driveway. Diggs had served as mayordomo of the Patos, an acequia downstream from Acequia San Lorenzo, where Valdez's body had been found, for three years. He used every drop and more of his 1 "peon," the traditional designation for an acre foot of water rights.

When Ulysses pulled into the driveway, he saw Diggs was irrigating. His cattle were penned in a loading chute area, and Diggs, his plaid flannel shirt open to his white belly, was pitching them hay. He paused and jumped down from the back of his pickup when he saw the sheriff get out of the car.

"Good morning, Mr. Diggs," Sheriff Walker said, shielding his eyes from the sun. The day was turning hot and a breeze was picking up.

"What can I do for you, Sheriff?" Diggs asked, approaching the fence.

"I'm making some inquiries regarding a homicide in the vicinity," Ulysses said. Out of the corner of his eye, he saw the front door of the double wide open. Brenda Diggs came down the steps and walked toward them.

"Who is dead?" Diggs asked.

"Antonio Valdez."

Diggs said nothing. He pulled a bandana out of his pocket and mopped his brow.

"Do you know him?" Ulysses asked.

"Yeah, I know him." He scratched some pink welts on his hand.

Brenda had arrived and stood beside her husband, a little out of breath. "Know who?" she asked.

"Antonio Valdez was killed last night, Mrs. Diggs," Ulysses said.

"Oh, that's terrible! Who would do such a thing?" Brenda looked timidly at her husband. *She looks more like his mother than his wife*, Ulysses thought.

"Mr. Diggs, where were you last night between 6 and midnight?"

"He was here," Brenda said. Diggs said nothing. He looked over his shoulder at the progress of the irrigation water flowing down the gentle slope into his pasture.

"Sheriff, if that answers your questions do you mind if I get back to work? Brenda, go back to the house."

"Just a minute, Mrs. Diggs," Ulysses said. "Are you sure your husband was at home all that time? Were you awake?"

"I go to bed early, but he was there when I went to bed and when I woke up to use the toilet he was in his bed. We sleep in separate rooms. He is such a light sleeper." Again, Brenda looked furtively at her husband.

"What time did you go to bed?" Ulysses asked. Diggs bent down and picked up the pitchfork he'd been using and put it in the bed of his truck beside a long-handled shovel. A pair of cowboy boots were also in the truck bed.

"About eight or eight-thirty."

"And when did you wake up to go to the toilet?"

"I don't know for sure. Around midnight, I think."

"Mr. Diggs, you and Mr. Valdez had an argument at the Village Market, correct? What was that about?"

"How much water Acequia San Lorenzo was taking from the Rio. He wasn't leaving enough for Patos. Jacinto Ramirez, their former mayordomo, will confirm this."

"Did it get heated?"

"Not for me."

"Did you have a reason to dislike Mr. Valdez?"

"I didn't dislike him." Diggs cleared his throat and spat.

"What size shoe do you wear?"

"Why are you asking? Am I a suspect?"

"Do you refuse to answer?"

"Size 10 or 10 ½ depending on the shoe. Can we be done now? I need to go close my head gate. My irrigating time is over." Brenda was gripping her hands tightly in front of her apron. "Go get my lunch ready, Brenda," Diggs said.

Brenda turned and walked back toward the house, looking over her shoulder several times.

"I'd like to take a look in the back of your truck," Sheriff Walker said.

"Not without a search warrant," Diggs said.

"Suit yourself, Mr. Diggs. I'll be back."

"Anytime, Sheriff. Just let me know so I can get my attorney here."

Ulysses got back in his car and texted Stephanie that he would be a few minutes late for their meeting. Then he drove off reflecting on what he'd learned. Diggs had an alibi but it wasn't solid. His shoe size was about right. And was that poison ivy on his hand maybe from the vine near the body? None of these factors were enough to charge him, but if he could get DNA off that shovel or find a nick in the heel of one of those boots, he would have probable cause to arrest the man. Would Diggs really kill Valdez only because of too little water in the acequia? To Ulysses, that seemed pretty unlikely. And why would he tear up the Valdez house?

Ulysses arrived at lunch twenty minutes late and found his campaign manager, Stephanie Gold, sitting at an outdoor table sipping iced tea and talking on her phone.

"I know, it *is* important," she said, "and we'll take care of it right away. I'll make sure he gets the extra servers also. Okay, listen, Sheriff's here, finally. Bye, Kitty." She placed her phone in her purse and looked at him with shrewd, hazel eyes. "Where have you been?" she asked.

"Sorry I'm late, Stephanie. It's been one hell of a morning."

"I ordered you a greenchile cheeseburger—I hope that's okay?"

"Sure, fine."

"So, what happened this morning?"

"Somebody killed a man over in Vadito last night. Antonio Valdez. I got the call around 6 this morning."

"Is he the one who always gives the talks on the history of acequias? I heard him once at the New Mexico History Museum in Santa Fe. Good speaker."

"That's the one. He was Delilah Valdez's father. Do you know her?"

"Yes, I do. Lovely woman. I'm really sad for her." Stephanie frowned. "Could this have an effect on the election?"

"Your guess is as good as mine. Depends on how the media spins it. But it won't make the run up any easier for me. I'll have a lot more demands on my time."

Their food arrived. Stephanie poked at a beet salad with feta and Ulysses tucked into his cheeseburger. The waiter brought him water and refilled Stephanie's iced tea.

"That was Kitty Austerlitz I was talking with just now," Stephanie said. "She's my neighbor who's hosting us at her beautiful home for our fundraiser, you remember? She wants you to bring some of your employees to act as servers. She's having trouble rounding up enough waitstaff."

"I will if it doesn't violate the Hatch Act," Ulysses said.

"It doesn't. I checked with Dan." Dan was Stephanie's ex-husband, a successful lawyer in Albuquerque. They'd been divorced for several years but remained good friends.

"The fundraiser is this coming Saturday, remember?"

"Oh, damn, it's Monty's birthday," Ulysses objected. "My mother and sister are coming for the weekend."

"Ulys, get real. Between now and election day consider every minute fully booked."

"You're right. But I'm feeling the squeeze on all sides."

"That's how campaigns go, Ulys. That's why you hired me. You should appreciate me." Stephanie pinched his cheek and gave him the radiant smile that graced her billboards in town, which read, "The Gold Standard for Real Estate."

"Stephanie, I do appreciate you," he said. *But I wish you wouldn't flirt with me*, he thought.

"You'd better," she said, taking a final sip of iced tea, then applying lipstick. "Listen, Kitty said that we have a yard sign problem in her neighborhood. I hadn't noticed because I rarely get home before dark."

"A yard sign problem?"

"More yard signs for Ernesto Ruiz than for you," Stephanie explained.

"What should we do about it?"

"We, meaning *you*, need to get more signs out there. I have plenty at my office. Get some volunteers to go door to door..."

"Stephanie, I have a high-profile murder to solve...plus, you have the volunteer names and numbers."

"Okay, okay. So much for the nap I was planning for this afternoon."

"How is the money holding up?" Ulysses asked. He did not want to have campaign debt when this was all over.

"We have a lot riding on this fundraiser. We have about seventy-five attendees so far and we need twice that. But it's still early. Another big invitation will go out tomorrow. Luckily there are lots of high rollers on Kitty's list."

"And if we don't get a big turnout?"

"We'll have some debt. Not much, maybe ten thousand."

Ulysses was silent a moment as he thought about the unpleasant prospect of campaign debt. "I understand Kitty is pretty important to us. But tell me, why is she supportive? What is in it for her?" Ulysses asked.

"Kitty's a big advocate for women. She likes that you opened the women's shelter and she likes your emphasis on reducing domestic violence. The rich aren't all bad people."

"I never said they were." Ulysses finished his burger and took a big drink of water. "By the way, how are your real estate sales?"

"Blazing," Stephanie said. She had weathered several real estate busts and consistently appeared at or near the top of the "Best of Taos" list. Ulysses guessed she was worth a small fortune. "I actually wouldn't mind if they slowed down a little. And this is just the beginning of the season."

"How do my polls look?"

"You are consistently about five points ahead of Ruiz, just out of the margin of error. I'd be more comfortable if it were ten points." She looked at her watch. "I've got to run. I have a showing around the corner. I paid for lunch already. I'll see you at the Shelter at three." Stephanie stood up and straightened her flattering red pencil skirt and white silk blouse. Ulysses stood up and gave her a hug. She smelled like the fragrance she'd worn for years. He'd once given her a bottle of it but he'd forgotten its name. Stephanie turned around just before walking out to the sidewalk. "Remember to chat up the director," she said. "Her name is Holly." As he often did when he left Stephanie's company, Ulysses felt a mix of sadness and relief. He still cared for Stephanie as a friend, but he knew she wanted something from him he could never give her.

Joseph Maes, a new deputy sheriff hired by Taos County in April, dropped Deputy Romero at her house in town, a one-story bungalow with a wide front porch on a shady street near the Taos Plaza. Mr. T, Angela's big Siamese cat, had left an eviscerated mouse on the doormat and was sitting in his favorite sunny spot on the back of the living room couch when she came in. He gave a complaining meow that Angela interpreted as his dismay at her being late coming home to feed him. "You should have eaten all your mouse, T," she said, dutifully scooping some wet food into his bowl. Angela took off her belt and boots and pulled her uniform shirt loose from her pants. She took down her bun and poured some cereal and milk into a bowl.

Angela sat on the big comfy sofa in the living room and ate her breakfast slowly. Her father had bought this house before she was born and she inherited it when he died. Frank Romero was from a wealthy family by Taos County standards at the time. He married her mother, Catalina, when he was forty and she was eighteen, taking her away from an impoverished home in Mora County. Angela was born a year later.

Angela looked at the fine oil portrait of her mother that hung over the fireplace. It was one of the last paintings by the famous portraitist Clarence Madrid, and probably valuable. Angela would never part with it. She had only a few photographs of her mother and this painting captured best how she remembered her, with dark curls falling around fragile shoulders and a sad look in her wide-spaced brown eyes. People said Angela looked like her mother but she couldn't see it. She prided herself on an absence of fragility.

Catalina had disappeared when Angela was twelve and no trace of her had ever been found. Some thought she had run away with a lover and others believed she'd been kidnapped and was probably dead. Angela had hoped and prayed every day for her mother's return until she was sixteen, when she realized she no longer believed her mother was alive. After Catalina's disappearance, Frank Romero never spoke of her again. He died from a heart attack before Angela graduated high school, leaving her in the care of his parents. The memories she had of her parents were often painful and Angela refused to dwell on them.

She set a timer on her phone for an hour and stretched out on the couch. Mr. T curled his bulk on her legs, purring loudly as she fell into a deep sleep. When she awoke there was just enough time to shower and dress in a fresh uniform for Lorraine's party. The nap had refreshed her, especially since she knew she'd have the night off also, unless the Sheriff had other plans for her.

Angela knew she was up for a promotion to undersheriff. She had fantasies of being sheriff herself one day, after Sheriff Walker retired, of course. She was a hard worker, rarely saying no to any demand the job placed on her. She had almost no social engagements, no romance and often went without sleep and meals to fulfill the highest standards she set for herself.

Angela drove the few miles to Taos County Sheriff's Headquarters, an older but well-kept stucco building near the Judicial Complex east of the Plaza. The building had a large front office for the secretary's desk, a waiting area and the deputies' cubicles, a public bathroom, the comfortable Sheriff's office with its private bathroom, and the 911 dispatch office next to the break room. At the end of a hall were three seldom-used holding cells behind a locked door. Angela carried in a boxed red velvet cake she'd bought for Lorraine's party. In the big front room Rosemary Walker greeted her by the table set up for the food, cards and gifts. Angela put the cake on a stand and arranged paper plates and napkins around it. Rosemary had already put out bowls of chips, guacamole and salsa, and cheese and crackers, and made sure the cooler was stocked with drinks. The Walker children, Amelia and Monty, Deputy Zach Wright and his wife and baby, Deputy Mark Shea and his two sons, and a handful of Lorraine's relatives, milled around waiting for the party to begin. The children ran up and down the halls making noise but staying mostly out of trouble. At one the sheriff arrived along with the new deputy, Joseph Maes, and the 911 phone staff, Megan Atencio, Dakota Wilson and Michael Jaramillo. With characteristic good timing, Lorraine Baca arrived when everything was ready, but she looked frail and nervous. Ulysses wondered what it must be like for her, single with no children, to have received a diagnosis of stage four pancreatic cancer and now be facing a poor prognosis.

"Come sit down," Ulysses said, taking Lorraine by the elbow and leading her to the "throne" deputies Mark and Zach had made for her with a fake ermine coverlet thrown over a wing chair in the middle of the room. They piled the gifts at her feet. Lorraine smiled and started to compose herself. Rosemary brought her a plate of snacks and her favorite soda.

"I hope I can get through this without breaking down," Lorraine said.

People approached one by one to speak with her in an informal receiving line. Ulysses put a chair behind her and spoke in her ear. "Remember how we didn't get along at first?" he said.

"I sure do, Sheriff. I didn't know if you could do the job in those days."

"I didn't know if you'd ever accept me. I thought it was because I was young and Anglo."

Lorraine shook her head. "You were very young, or so it seemed then. And very Anglo. Still are!" She laughed. "But you grew on me!" She turned to pat his arm affectionately.

"I never thought I'd be able to match Sheriff Trujillo in your mind."

"Well, we know how that turned out. It took me too long to figure out what a rat he was!"

"It's hard to believe he was sheriff for five years."

"Yes, elected twice and gone before his second term was up."

"I guess law enforcement wasn't his thing," Ulysses said.

"That is for sure, Sheriff. He was more of a law breaker," Lorraine said. "But we'll save that for another time."

"Speak of the devil," Ulysses said. Former Sheriff, now State Senator Ramón Trujillo swept in the front door with a grocery store bouquet that had seen better days. A tall man of about sixty with a head of thick, white hair, Trujillo wore a well-cut white linen jacket and expensive cowboy boots. He came right over to Lorraine, took her hand and kissed it.

"My dear," he said, "How are you?" He handed her the flowers, which Lorraine held awkwardly until Rosemary took them from her to put in a vase.

"I've been better, Ramón," Lorraine said. She gestured toward Ulysses and the rest of the staff. "I'm going to miss this job."

"I'm sure you will," Trujillo said, looking around the room to see who was paying attention. "And they will miss you!" He winked at Ulysses. Then he stood up and prepared to give a little speech.

"Everyone," he said, "what an occasion this is! Lorraine has been the heart and soul of this department for now, how many years is it, Lorraine?"

"Twenty-seven," she said.

"When my wife died and I was out of the office so much with all the arrangements, Lorraine covered everything, didn't you, my dear?" Trujillo continued, "She even made me dinner on more than one occasion." Lorraine looked surprised.

"I never made him dinner!" she whispered to Ulysses. "You know I hate to cook!"

Trujillo chuckled and turned to Ulysses. "It must be hard for you to lose her now, right before this big election?"

Ulysses nodded but didn't say anything. *I can't stand this man,* he thought.

"I'm sure her shoes will be very hard to fill." People began to talk among themselves and move toward the refreshment table. Trujillo recognized that his moment in the limelight had passed.

"Well," he said loudly. "I must go. I just wanted to drop in to acknowledge the best secretary ever, Lorraine Baca. Good luck, Ulysses." He applauded himself, kissed Lorraine again and went out to his Lincoln which was parked in a handicap spot.

"That scoundrel," Lorraine said.

"What a showboat that man is," Lorraine's niece said.

"He used to be a real ladies man," her nephew said.

"That was a long time ago," the niece quipped.

Angela put a CD of Los Coyotes in a boom box and she and Rosemary cut the cake and gave out pieces. The party was back on. When Lorraine had finished her cake, she opened the gifts. The deputies had contributed to buy a down robe and slippers. The entire staff bought a beautiful Nambè silver platter engraved with "Lorraine Baca, the Power behind the Throne," with the dates of her tenure.

Lorraine told Ulysses she was feeling tired and asked her nephew to bring the car around. As she stood up to go, Ulysses slipped a small box into her hand. "This is from Rosemary and me. We hope you like them." She opened the box to find a pair of classic diamond stud earrings. Lorraine looked delighted. She had lost one of her diamond earrings at the office six months earlier. The staff tore the office apart looking for it but no one could find it even after invoking St. Anthony, the patron saint of lost items. "I will cherish these, Sheriff," she said as her nephew helped her out of her chair.

"It's going to be chaos without her," Ulysses said to Angela after Lorraine was gone. "We'd better get someone in here right away."

"We'll find someone, Sheriff," Angela said. "In the meantime, the deputies can handle it."

"I wish I were that confident," Ulysses said. He looked at his watch. "I have to go to a meet and greet at the Women's Shelter," he said. "You should get some rest so you'll be ready for tomorrow!"

As the only elected law enforcement in Taos County, Sheriff Walker enjoyed being accountable to the voters for his performance. He relished his independence from other authorities including the Taos police, the city mayor and the county commission. Able to set his own agenda, he had applied for state money midway through his first term to address the county's problems with domestic violence and homelessness. The result was the Su Casa, a women's shelter which occupied a newer building south of town. Previously there had been no beds in the county for homeless women.

Ulysses and Rosemary had long been advocates for reducing violence against women. Because of the shelter, Ulysses hoped that incidences of those crimes would continue to trend down in Taos County. Su Casa also provided longer-term beds for victims of domestic violence and their children. The director, a social worker originally from Lubbock, had added vocational rehabilitation, access to health care, AA and NA meetings and even short-term therapy. The project brought the community a lot of pride by winning a national award.

The meet-and-greet was to take place in the multipurpose room where a podium with a microphone and rows of chairs had been set out. Rosemary was already there with Monty and Amelia, who both looked cranky. A refreshment table featured store-bought cookies, bottled water and bowls of M&Ms.

Stephanie was up at the podium with the director when Sheriff Walker arrived. He strode up and shook the director's hand. *Her name is Holly, he remembered.* "Hello, Holly," he said.

"Hello, Sheriff," she said, looking pleased. She was a casually dressed, middle-aged white woman with short brown hair and a Texas accent. "Let's get this mike adjusted for you. There are also a couple of roving mikes for the audience in case anyone wants to ask a question."

Meanwhile, the room was filling with women, children and a few men. Ulysses started walking around, introducing himself and talking with the attendees. Rosemary was clearly getting impatient with the children, who were trying to steal M&Ms though they'd expressly been told not to touch them.

Finally, Holly took a microphone and introduced the sheriff. He walked to the podium amid polite applause. Just then, the door opened and in came a reporter, a cameraman, and Jazmine Ruiz, his opponent Ernesto Ruiz's wife and the daughter of Senator Ramón Trujillo. She was a heavy-set blonde who wore lots of make-up, leather pants, and a cowboy hat.

"Hello, everyone," Sheriff Walker said, taking index cards out of his pocket. He gave a prepared speech about his commitment to women's safety and briefly discussed street crime, drug addiction and homelessness. He spoke about the increase in domestic violence during the pandemic and the steps he'd taken to bring it back down, including a warm line staffed by social work interns that women could call if they needed support to leave an abusive relationship. He felt that the audience was receptive, so when he finished, he called for questions. Immediately, Jazmine Ruiz raised her hand and one of the rovers handed her a microphone.

"Mr. Walker," she said, dispensing with his sheriff title. "Why has crime increased so dramatically under your administration?" All heads in the auditorium turned toward Jazmine.

"Mrs. Ruiz," Ulysses said, surprised by the question, "Uh, folks, let me introduce my opponent's wife..."

"I am a candidate myself for County Commission. Perhaps you don't want to acknowledge that since I'm a woman?" Ulysses noticed Rosemary walking toward Jazmine.

"No, indeed," Ulysses said, "I'm always glad when women go for more leadership..."

"So why don't you answer my question?" Jazmine asked. A few in the audience murmured in discomfort or disapproval. The camera man continued to film the scene. Ulysses felt himself getting flustered.

"Crime has not increased dramatically under my administration," he began. "There has been..."

"Domestic violence has increased..."

"Can you let me finish, please?" Ulysses said. He took a deep breath. "Yes, domestic violence increased during the pandemic, but..."

"So that's your excuse?" Jazmine began again, but before she could finish, Rosemary stepped up to her and took the microphone from her hand. Ruiz, surprised by the bold move, let go of the mike.

"Jazmine," Rosemary said in a calm voice, "you've interrupted Sheriff Walker three times. I think there are some other people here who'd like to ask him some questions and actually want to hear his answers." The camera turned to Rosemary, who was smiling with confidence. Hands went up all over the auditorium. The camera turned away from Jazmine and toward a young woman holding a baby. Jazmine looked furious. Rosemary, handing the microphone back to Holly, sat down.

"Sheriff, I want to thank you for providing housing for me and my daughter," the woman said. "Before this place opened I had nowhere to go when my husband came home drunk and beat me. Now I have this place and also my dreams of independence. It is safe and clean here and I am never going back. Thank you, also, Holly." She sat down to a round of applause.

Another woman asked if there could be GED classes added to the program. A third woman described being homeless in Taos before the Shelter opened and how much harassment she faced as an addict living on the street. "Now I have a job and an apartment I share with two other women. I've been clean for six months." When Ulysses finished answering questions, he noticed that Jazmine Ruiz was gone but the reporter was still taking notes and the cameraman continued filming. *I wonder how this will shake out on the late-night news, he thought.*

When everyone who wanted to had met him and shook his hand, Ulysses went over to where Rosemary and Stephanie were chatting with Holly.

"That was intense," he said and the women laughed.

"You are too polite, Ulys," Stephanie said.

"It's a good thing your wife was here," Holly said. "Jazmine Ruiz is a piece of work."

"She was completely unprepared for me to snatch that microphone," Rosemary said, laughing. "The look on her face was priceless."

"I just hope the media doesn't spin it as me having to be rescued by my feisty wife," Ulysses said.

"Are you kidding, Ulys?" Stephanie said. "People love seeing a strong woman stand up to a heckler, especially another woman. And imagine if you'd had to smack down on her. I don't think Jazmine did herself or her husband any favors."

"Depends on how they slice and dice the footage," Holly said. "But honestly, I thought you handled it well, Sheriff. And Rosemary, you were masterful!"

"Thanks, Holly," Rosemary said with the smile that brought out her dimples. "Got anything else going on Ulys, or are you coming home?"

"Looks like I'm headed home, thank God. Kids, want to ride with me?" he asked. "There's still time to have a bike ride *and* play Wordle!" The children, excited and high on M&Ms, ran out and got into the Expedition.

Chapter 3

The morning after Lorraine's party, Sheriff Walker came into the office early to survey the situation. Lorraine's former desk was already covered with messages and as senior deputy, Angela was showing Joseph how to handle the phones. Michael was covering 911 and was set to pull a double shift since the supervisor, Dakota, had a bad cold and Megan couldn't come in before three to relieve him. Deputies Mark and Zach were finishing up paperwork from the night before and about to head home. *We are way too short-staffed to run this place effectively without Lorraine,* Ulysses thought. *I have to hire someone today or get a temp.*

"Good morning, Sheriff," Deputy Romero said. "You've had a bunch of calls already this morning. I left the messages on your desk. And I made some coffee so it would feel normal around here. It's almost ready."

Before he could say anything to Angela, his old friend, Picuris Pueblo tribal council member Ray Pando walked in the office. "I've got to talk with you, Ulys," he said. "Rosemary told me you had come in early."

"Ray, good to see you. Want some coffee? Joseph, can you bring us two cups into my office? Mr. Pando likes his black."

They went into the office and Ray took the chair beside Ulysses' desk.

"Are you here about the Valdez murder?" Ulysses asked. Valdez lived near to Picuris.

"Yeah, Delilah called me," Ray said. "I just saw Antonio last Friday. What happened?"

"Somebody killed him when he was walking the ditch late in the evening on Saturday. We haven't got the postmortem yet. I have at least one person of interest but the motive is weak."

"That's so brutal," Ray said. "I'm glad his wife isn't alive to have to go through this. So, you have no idea who killed him?"

"He had no real enemies as far as I can tell."

"I might have an idea about a motive. Are you familiar with the Mora transfers?" Ray asked.

"I've probably heard of them, but, no, I don't know much about them, really."

"Sometime beginning in the 1820s, a bunch of people from Mora County decided to divert the creeks high on the western slope of the Sangre de Cristo mountains so that the water would flow over to the eastern slope out of the Rio Grande basin and into the Arkansas River basin. They made use of the contours to get a considerable amount of water to cross the divide. It's been flowing out of the Rio Pueblo watershed and into Mora's ever since. And about twenty years ago they built a big concrete presa up there to increase the efficiency of the flow."

"How much water are we talking about?" Ulysses asked, wondering what this had to do with Antonio's murder.

"It amounts to about ten percent of the watershed, give or take."

"That's a lot of water. But doesn't Mora own the water now that they've been using it for 200 years?"

"According to the Rimrock decision, Picuris' priority rights now take precedence."

"But didn't Picuris give Mora that water?"

"That's a myth, Ulys. We never approved the transfers and weren't given our due process, either."

"What can you do about it?"

"I'm not sure yet. I've spent a lot of time with Antonio talking about what we can do. Antonio specialized in the history of Taos County. That's how I met him, because of his interest in Picuris Pueblo, and we've been friends since. Clarice and I used to socialize with him and Reina. My son Matt, and his daughter Delilah more or less grew up together. Anyway, last winter

Antonio got me to go with him down to Santa Fe to the State Records Center and Archives to see what we could find about the Mora transfers. That is where I first learned of the existence of a letter from one of our governors opposed to the transfers. It was written by an ancestor of mine."

"How did Antonio rope you into rooting through old records?" Ulysses asked. "That doesn't sound like your thing."

"Oh, Ulys, like you warned me, retirement doesn't suit me. I quit being war chief and sat around the house getting fat and bothering Clarice. Matt's wife, Sarah, was working from home and had me and Clarice taking care of the baby all the time. I love that baby but I'm no babysitter. Then I ended up being elected to the tribal council last year, kind of against my better judgment. But after Rimrock came down I actually got interested in this water issue. We have a chance to right a wrong."

"So, tell me about this letter you found."

"State Archives had documents that referenced the letter but no copies of the letter itself. Then about six weeks ago I actually found the original at the Pueblo in some files stored in the tribal secretary's filing room.

"Right before the pandemic the feds told us that if we built a secure museum facility of our own, they would help us get back some of the artifacts of our people. A lot were bought by white people for next to nothing and then sold to museums. We've been in the planning stages of building a facility. We're collecting archeological and historical artifacts from our members, the kind of family treasures people have in their attics, including old papers. I did an inventory of about forty boxes of materials and that's when I struck gold—an original letter from Governor Juan Pando, in his handwriting." Ray sat back in his chair and crossed his arms.

Ulysses said, "That's an amazing find. But what does it prove?"

"The letter dates to 1878, well before the transfers were put into law on Mora's behalf in 1907. It clearly states that Picuris never gave permission for the water to be diverted to Mora, which pretty successfully debunks the myth."

"I see. But what about the water war you will start?" Ulysses asked. "People are already hurting in Mora after the terrible fires over there last summer. If you try to take their water on top of that, it could get ugly."

"Ulys, it isn't *their* water. It's ours. It is a lot of water *and* a cross-basin transfer. It would be illegal now to do what they are doing. I think it should be illegal now to keep doing it."

"What would Picuris do with the water?"

"We could grow cannabis with it or make more pasture and raise more bison. Hell, we could double the size of our fishing lake. Plus, a lot of water would flow down to the Embudo Creek area, which has really suffered from the most recent drought, to recharge their aquifers and refresh their bosques. That was what motivated Antonio, to keep the water on this side of the mountain for all our communities. With Rimrock I think we have a fighting chance."

"Okay, I get it Ray. It's a reasonable cause. But do you think someone would kill Antonio over this? Seems more likely they'd come after you. Although, somebody ransacked Antonio's entire house looking for something. Did you give him the letter?"

"No, of course not. I gave him a copy only. Don't worry about me, Ulys. I know how to take care of myself and the pueblo is well-armed and secure. And no one will ever find that original, I guarantee it!"

"So, who would kill over this? Some Mora acequiero or land grant advocate? I can't see that happening."

"I wouldn't rule it out, Ulys. But listen, there is more. After the fires, some people in Mora started selling their land. The fires destroyed so much that some people don't want to try to rebuild and FEMA has been really slow with distributing relief money. Matt told me a developer is going around buying up parcels near Chacón, one of the three places where our water was diverted to."

"What kind of developer?" Ulysses asked.

"This guy who wants to build a world class golf course, luxury second homes, a heliport, and a hotel."

"I heard a rumor about this," Ulysses said. "I just wrote it off as nonsense. Isn't Chacón a tiny hamlet at 8500 feet? Do they even have services nearby?"

"No, they have almost no services. But the land around it is beautiful, green and lush with spectacular views. It was spared the worst of the fires. They want to put a heliport there so people can fly in from Dallas or L.A. and take a helicopter from Santa Fe. Rich people love that kind of thing."

"Who is the developer?" Ulysses asked.

"The project is called something I can't remember, but the company is Wild West Development. The owner is a Texan with very deep pockets named Trey Cameron. He has a kind of checkered past, turns out. He was almost busted for racketeering in 2012."

"You've done a lot of research, Ray."

"Antonio did most of it. I just found the letter."

There was a knock on the door and Deputy Romero stuck her head in. "Stephanie Gold is calling. What should I tell her?"

"Did she say it was urgent?" Ulysses asked.

"No, Sheriff."

"Tell her I'll call her back in thirty minutes."

Ray said, "You've got your top deputy working the phones, Ulys? That's not going to work."

"No, it isn't, but I've interviewed a dozen people for the job and can't find anyone. I don't know what to do. I'm going to have to get a temp."

"Listen, I know somebody who could do this job with one hand tied behind his back. And he's looking for work."

"Seriously? Who?"

"My daughter-in-law Sarah's brother, Eli Martinez. He's a computer wizard and also good with people. Smart as they come. Used to be a river guide for Far Out Adventures. He's a Taos Pueblo member."

"Is he related to Mabel Martinez? We've gone to her house on feast days off and on for years."

"He's her grandson. Debra's child."

"I thought Debra had two girls, Sarah and Halona?"

"Halona is Eli now. He's now a man." Ray smiled and watched Ulysses' reaction.

"Okay..." Ulysses said. "Trans?"

"That's right. But don't worry, he's quite the dude now."

"Look, I don't care about that, Ray. I believe in live and let live. If he's as good as you say, tell him to call me. The sooner the better. And thanks! You might have solved my situation."

After Ray left, Ulysses called Stephanie back.

"U, I wanted to let you know we got the yard signs out but I think we have another problem."

"Thanks for doing that, Steph. What's the new problem?" "Evidently social media and talk radio are hammering you for not protecting Archbishop Sullivan from a murderer a few years back. They are saying you aren't a Christian and that you hate the Catholic Church."

Ulysses started to laugh but then he realized this was deadly serious. A number of his constituents identified as Catholic. Rumors like this, in addition to being false, could definitely hurt his re-election.

"I am not religious," Ulysses said. "But that is no one's business, right?"

"I'm not sure about that these days. But you don't hate the Catholic Church, do you?"

"Definitely not. I like it as much as any church. But what can I do about these rumors?"

"I think we are going to have to work on some media angles. I'd like to get you on Stu Wishard's call-in show. Have you heard of him? It's on AM radio and has a huge listenership."

"I've heard enough to think he's a bully."

"He is a bully," Stephanie said. "That's what people like about him. But I've seen how you handle bullies, Ulys, and I think you can change the narrative."

"I'll think about it. I'd have to be sure the show is live so he can't do an editing hatchet job on me just for fun."

"I agree. I'll see if it can be live. By the way, Rosemary knocked it out of the park on the evening news last night. They showed the clip of her taking the microphone and it was a big hit. Taos News is interviewing her today for an article on you."

"Today? Why didn't you tell me?"

"Rosemary was game and I thought it was a good idea, so we went for it."

"As long as they don't give out my address or take pictures of my kids," Ulysses said.

"Don't be paranoid, U."

Ulysses laughed. "I am a little paranoid these days. Things have gotten so hostile."

"That's politics," Stephanie said. "By the way, what is a constitutional sheriff?"

"It's a notion that sheriffs are the ultimate authority in their districts and don't have to enforce laws they don't like. It's cockamamie. The sheriff in Colfax County, Phil Hogg, was big into it until he got beaten last election by a sane person. Why?"

"Ruiz has put that on his new yard signs."

"Great! I hate the Catholic Church and my opponent is a constitutional sheriff? It sounds like the opposition is going off the deep end. I'm going to go ahead and say yes to that Stu Wishard spot. Let's do this."

"Good! I'll try to set it up for Thursday. You got those servers yet for the fundraiser?"

"I spoke to Dakota and Angela and they are good to go. I just need to get one more."

"Okay, good. Over and out." Stephanie hung up.

Ulysses noticed he felt really rattled by the talk about the election. He had thought it would be smooth sailing to victory but he realized he was being overly optimistic.

It was nearly lunchtime. Ulysses went out to the front office and saw that Deputy Angela Romero wasn't there.

"Have you had lunch, Deputy Maes?" he asked Joseph.

"I had a shake and a protein bar," Joseph answered. "I'm good."

"Where is Angela?"

"She's in the break room eating lunch."

"Hold my calls for about forty-five minutes, will you?" Ulysses closed the door to his office and ate the lunch Rosemary had packed for him. He knew it would be good to meditate but the pull of a nap was too strong. He stretched out on the couch and began counting his breaths, a way he was able to fall asleep quickly.

Ulysses began to dream that he was in a canoe on a quiet river. At first, he was just being carried along by calm water. Then he noticed the river was running faster and he could hear the roar of falling water not far away. Ahead he saw the river drop away in froth and foam indicating a mighty falls. Ulysses desperately tried to paddle away from the falls' precipice but could not escape. The boat hit a rock and broke apart and Ulysses, swimming for his life, was about to go over the falls when he woke up. He'd been trying to scream.

Ulysses had been paying close attention to his dreams for a few years now. In his thirties he had started having occasional dreams that he interpreted as warnings. Some of them were just forebodings and some took on the heart-racing feel of nightmares. All were related somehow to his work and the dangers associated with law enforcement. Many proved oddly prescient. Ulysses spoke to Rosemary and once to his mother about the dreams, but generally kept quiet about them. He was afraid if word got out people would think he wasn't fit to be sheriff. His mother pointed out that his father had nightmares for years about his service in Vietnam. But that was different. That was PTSD.

Once, after a particularly dangerous and frightening line of duty encounter with a delusional psychopath, Ulysses consulted with a psychologist. She tested him for PTSD and told him he didn't really meet the criteria. About the dreams she said, "You're not dreaming about events that have already happened to you. These dreams seem more like premonitions than re-experiencing." She smiled wryly and said, "Maybe you are psychic. Or maybe you are just anxious. That would make sense given your work." Ulysses never went back for a second appointment.

With ten minutes left to his break, Ulysses woke up and decided to try to settle himself with a short meditation. He set a timer on his phone and sat on a straight-backed chair with his feet flat on the floor and his hands in his lap, allowing his body to become still. He began with deep breathing and then used his favorite mantra, "Just this," on the inbreath, and "moment" on the outbreath, spoken inwardly. His thoughts came and went including images from his dream, but Ulysses stayed with the mantra until the chimes rang on his phone. He stood up and stretched, feeling better.

Ulysses looked over the messages on his desk and delegated most of the calls to his deputies, Angela and Joseph. One call was from Delilah who was headed out to the Valdez home to pick out clothing for her father to wear in his casket. She said she wanted to speak with him about some things, so Ulysses decided to drive out there.

Outside it was hot and the UV had become intense. A wind blowing steadily from the west made Ulysses remember the Hermit Peak Fire of the previous summer. Even though very little of Taos County was burned, the fires had most of the people in the high country on alert for the entire month of June. The fire had burned more acres than ever before in Mora and San Miguel Counties. Day after day, ominous pyrocumulous clouds formed over the mountains south of town and whenever the wind shifted, smoke filled the air. Now fire weather was again threatening, putting everyone on edge.

When he arrived at the Valdez place, Ulysses saw Delilah's blue truck parked out front. He knocked on the screen door and Delilah came to let him in. A blonde man in a grey suit stood up from the couch and introduced himself as Arthur Davenport.

Delilah said, "Sheriff, Arthur is my fiancé. He works as an advisor to Governor Montaño."

"Nice to meet you, Mr. Davenport. I know Delilah must be glad to have your support now."

"Call me Arthur," the man said. He put his arm around Delilah. "Thank you for coming."

"How're you doing?" Ulysses asked Delilah. The small-framed woman with shoulder-length black hair had facial features that looked both Latino and Indian. She seemed on the verge of crying.

"I'm in shock, I think. Are you sure my father was murdered?"

"Yes, pretty sure. But we'll know more when Dr. Vigil gives us his report. We just don't know who would have murdered your father or why. Were you aware of him having any enemies?"

Delilah shook her head. "Daddy was always dealing with water controversies but I don't think he had enemies. Things might get heated during a drought but people made up after the rains came. Even when the mayordomo quit I don't think it got that acrimonious."

"Did you know about his work with Ray Pando regarding the Mora transfers?"

"I knew he and Ray were working on something about Picuris's priority rights. My new firm does water rights litigation almost exclusively. I told Daddy I would look at anything he found if he wanted."

"The night your father died someone tore through this house looking for something. Do you have any idea what that could be?"

Delilah's eyes filled with tears. "No, and I've been wracking my brain. His voicemail sounded so urgent. When he called, Arthur and I were at a wedding in Pecos. When I finally called him back, he was already dead." She shook her head and covered her face with her hands. "I feel so bad that I never got to speak with him again. I wonder if I could have saved him?"

"None of this is your fault, Delilah," Arthur said softly.

Ulysses cleared his throat. "Do you know anything about a development company wanting to build a golf course near Chacón?"

Delilah looked puzzled. "No, I've not heard about that."

"I've heard of it, Sheriff Walker," Arthur said. "They want to build a high-end golf course on some property the developer has acquired up there."

"What can you tell me about it?" Ulysses asked.

"The man, Trey Cameron, has already bought a lot of land around Chacón," Davenport said. "He asked the governor to take a look at his plans for a boutique hotel, luxury condos, and a heliport. The Forest Service is on board. Of course, he'll need additional water rights."

"What do the local people think of the plan?" Ulysses asked.

"The people in Mora are still trying to adjust to the damage from the fires. Some think the golf course could bring jobs. Others are angry at what they're calling a land grab. You know Governor Montaño is from Mora County herself."

"Yes, I did know that somewhere in the back of my mind. What does the governor think of the plan?"

"I can't really say, Sheriff," Davenport said. "Honestly, I don't think she's made up her mind. The developer has a great deal of money and connections backing him, including Taos' Senator Ramón Trujillo."

"What about Mora County's Senator Ortiz y Muniz?"

"He's opposed. He is a former land grant activist. The loss of the Mora community land grants is still a fighting matter over there."

"So, you are saying that the feelings are mixed about this project?"

"I'd say that's fair. Not too many folks in Mora play golf. And some people are suspicious of the company, Wild West. The project is called 'Highland Fling,'" Davenport said.

"And do you know where they are looking to get the water rights?"

"They are saying that a lot of the water will come directly from the rights connected to the land they've purchased, all of which comes from the Mora transfers. But they may try to get some paper rights also." Davenport paused and looked at Delilah who sat staring out the window. "They are looking to Taos Pueblo for some of the water." Delilah turned, looking shocked. Arthur nodded to her. "Sorry, Honey, if you didn't know this," he said.

"Hmm," Ulysses said. "I wonder just how many acre feet they plan to use?"

"That I do know because I had to research it for the governor. They are saying they need 60 additional acre feet. But my research says it will be much more like 100. Golf courses are thirsty. And there are complications to the deal, also. It's up to the State Engineer."

"Do you think this development has anything to do with Daddy's death?" Delilah asked.

"I don't know. I'm just trying to check out as many angles as I can," Ulysses said. "Did you find what you needed for the visitation?"

Delilah took a deep breath and blew her nose into a tissue. "I got his clothes and some photos, but I couldn't go into the office because Deputy Romero said not to. I'd like to get some of his awards to go with the pictures."

"I'll let you into the office," Ulysses said, handing her some plastic gloves. "Be prepared, though, it is really a mess. And I think they took his laptop."

Delilah took a deep breath. "That's terrible," she said. "He had files on everything and everybody."

Ulysses cut the tape and opened the door to Valdez's office. Delilah stood and surveyed the damage for a few moments in silence. "I need to talk with Ray," she said. "Maybe he can help me figure out what Daddy wanted to talk to me about."

Delilah started collecting things for the funeral home display.

"When is the visitation?" Ulysses asked.

"Tuesday and also Wednesday from 5–7."

"Does the number 1797 mean anything to you?" Ulysses asked, pulling the sheet of notebook paper out of his pocket.

Delilah took the paper and looked at it. "What is this?" she asked, looking puzzled. "That's Daddy's handwriting, I think. He always scored his sevens like that."

"There was a notepad on the kitchen table when I first came into the house. It looked blank, but as I looked closer I saw the indentation of writing from the page that had been torn off. I traced it as you can see. Is that number familiar?"

Delilah took a deep breath and thought for a few minutes. "I don't know what it could be. Do you think it's a date?"

Ulysses said, "I have no idea. Does it ring any bells for you?"

Delilah shook her head. "No, nothing. Daddy was a historian so it might be a date. Vadito was settled in 1798. I just don't know." She sighed deeply. "But there is one other thing I wanted to mention. I don't know if I am being paranoid but I've had the feeling I was being watched since the day after Daddy's death."

"Tell me about it."

"Day before yesterday, from about 3 pm until dark there was someone sitting in a car across the street from my condo. Mine is the only unit that faces that direction. It was really creepy. I put down the shades and locked the doors and windows. Arthur saw someone again this morning. A grey truck, looked new. It had dealer tags in the back window but I couldn't read them."

"What did they look like?"

"I couldn't see because of the tinted windows. I took a picture on my cellphone." She showed Ulysses a picture that revealed the driver's side of the truck but next to nothing about the figure in the cab.

"Send that to me at this email," he said handing her his card. "At least it gives us a good image of the vehicle. Maybe it's not such a good idea for you to stay alone, Delilah."

"She's going to stay with me from now on," Davenport said. "This situation definitely feels sketchy."

When the sheriff got back to Headquarters there was a man waiting for him in the front office. Deputy Maes stood up when Ulysses entered and said, awkwardly, "This guy wants to talk to you, sir."

A slender young Indian man with a long braid, a goatee and wire-rim glasses stood up and introduced himself. "I'm Eli Martinez," he said, offering a handshake. "Ray Pando said you might be looking for a secretary." He was dressed in blue jeans, a white shirt, suit jacket and a tie.

Sheriff Walker stood up and shook Eli's hand. "That was quick. Come on in."

He closed his door and they both sat down. "So, Eli, here is the situation. Our secretary for many years had to leave suddenly for health reasons and we have to replace her quickly. Have you ever done secretarial work?"

"Before college I worked at our casino at Taos Pueblo—using Office applications, filing and a little bookkeeping."

"Ray said you used to be a river guide for Far Out Adventures. How long did you do that?"

"I did it every summer when I was at New Mexico Tech and then for the first couple of years after I graduated. I still fill in for them when I can."

"That sure puts you in contact with the public," the sheriff said and Eli laughed.

"Yes. You might have ten people of all ages on a raft and another six in kayaks and you have to teach them what to do, keep all of them safe, feed them lunch and everything. Of course, you have a team—usually." Eli smiled for the first time, a nice smile, Ulysses thought. "It's a lot like being a Boy Scout leader for adults, but with plenty of genuine danger."

"Eli, the secretary deals with the public a lot. People come in and want to pay fines, need someone to listen to their concerns, have all sorts of questions. And the secretary handles all the phones, except 911, of course. We pride ourselves on having good customer service. There are also some computer programs to learn."

"I understand," Eli said. "Did Ray tell you I own a small business as a computer consultant?"

"He did. What do you do in that capacity?"

"I help individuals with software and hardware problems, install apps, do a little data recovery and set up networks."

"Why do you want to take another job?"

"I'd like to have a more predictable income. I can give up the consulting if the pay is enough."

"That's not necessary. But this job can be stressful. There is a lot of detail to keep track of which is tedious. Would you get bored working here full time?"

"I don't think so, Sheriff. Not for a good while, anyway. I'd like to learn your flow, update stuff and improve your systems. I bet there is a lot of that to do."

"There is. Do you have any questions for me?"

"Is this a tolerant work environment?"

"Yes, I can guarantee that. But I can't promise you won't experience some prejudice from the public. I will stand up for you if that happens, however."

Eli nodded.

"Can you make a commitment up front? Six weeks for starters, then a year? Can you do that?"

"Yes. I can do that."

"Okay, then. Let's give ourselves six weeks to see how it's going and for me to get you on the state jobs register. If all goes well, then you can go permanent and I'll expect a year of work with the possibility of renewal. The pay and benefits are pretty good and the hours are mostly predictable. Sound good?"

"Sounds good to me."

"When can you start?"

"How about tomorrow?" Eli said.

I think I'm going to like this guy, Ulysses thought.

Chapter 4

After Deputy Romero got Deputy Maes oriented to handling phones and walk-ins, she was ready to go on patrol when a 911 call came in from Carson. A woman reported being beaten and robbed by her boyfriend who had then fled. The victim and her toddler lived near Carson, off the grid. Deputy Romero asked Deputy Maes to tell the Sheriff and took the keys to one of the deputy vehicles.

Angela drove north out of town and crossed the Rio Grande gorge bridge, then turned left on a dirt road. Below her, the river had taken on the beautiful teal color of more settled waters as its spring turbulence decreased. The wind on the llano blew with surprising ferocity, buffeting her truck. Angela followed the GPS directions based on the address dispatch had given her.

The llano west of the Rio Grande held signs of human habitation from the past: historic buildings including an early twentieth-century stone one-room schoolhouse, an old clapboard church, antique homesteads with falling down barns, a few decrepit trailer homes and dilapidated shacks surrounded by mesquite and sagebrush. The place had an expansive view of the mountains that towered over Taos above the dark, jagged slash of the Rio Grande gorge. Angela always thought the area was perfect for a certain type of Anglo survivalist who needed the wide-open spaces and didn't mind the isolation and incessant wind. She found the area unnerving. While she liked to drive through it on her way to soak in the ancient hot springs at Ojo Caliente, she wasn't keen to stop here on official duties. She suspected most folks around were armed to the teeth and maybe a little crazy.

Angela felt a sense of dread related to any domestic violence call. In her mind, not only were the calls potentially dangerous; they were also depressing. She tended to judge the women as hapless victims, clueless about how to protect themselves and too duped and dependent to file charges against their abusers. They were fearful of striking out on their own, she thought, and it was understandable. Their partners often came after them with a vengeance. On the other hand, some of the women were almost as ready to pick fights as their partners. They usually just ended up on the losing side. The whole thing made her sick to her stomach and angry.

It didn't help that she'd seen her father strike her mother on more than one occasion, usually after her mother had "talked back" to him. Was her mother hapless? Angela had to admit she always thought she was. But recently, she'd started to think differently about Catalina's submission to her father. Perhaps because of the poverty and isolation of Catalina's childhood, she'd never learned to stand up for herself. And it wasn't like she had the means to leave her husband, especially with a child in tow. Until she did, of course, leaving Angela without a mother. And where had she gone? *I'll never know the answer to that question.* Angela had never told anyone about the violence in her parents' relationship. But she knew it was why she hadn't wanted to marry.

When she came to what accounted for an intersection she turned right, scattering a small flock of bighorn sheep ewes led by a fearsome-looking ram with huge, coiled horns. She headed due west toward the town of Carson, which had a post office and a restaurant but little else in the way of services. When the road curved to the south and went downhill, she looked for another dirt road on her left. This road, hardly more than a track, led her for another mile past a ruined geodesic dome, an abandoned trailer, and a modern one-room church with a white steeple. At last, she came to her destination, a newish yurt on a wooden platform reached by rickety-looking wooden stairs. Smoke tumbled down over the top of the structure from a metal stove pipe. The deputy pulled up beside the yurt, tooted her horn, and got out. She looked east at the mountain view that inspired awe but also gave her a lonesome feeling. "Deputy Angela Romero to see Maddy Smith," she yelled but the wind seemed to blow her words away like plastic bags, the "witches britches" that blew across the mesa until they became ensnared in the cholla. No one came to the door.

Under the yurt was an older white compact car, locked. In the backseat were several full black plastic garbage bags, some toys, and a basket of neatly folded laundry. Angela walked up the stairs. When she reached the yurt's decking she looked all around. There were no trees to break the ferocious wind. *This place is so desolate,* she thought, *how could anyone live here?*

The front door had a window that bore a spiderweb of cracks. Angela knocked on the door and again yelled her name, but it was clear no one was inside the one-room structure. She peered into the window and saw a large stove in the middle of a big room, a mattress to one side and a makeshift kitchen and toilet on the other. She tried the door. It was unlocked, so she went in. The room smelled of canvas, creosote and burned food. Someone had been cooking rice on top of the wood stove and it had scorched the pan. Clothes were strewn about the bed and spilled out of a cardboard chest of drawers. There were several diarrhea filled diapers in the open kitchen garbage can along with some bloody rags on the kitchen table. Where were Maddy Smith and her child? Angela took pictures of the yurt interior. *This place feels like a fresh crime scene,* she thought. Then, realizing it wasn't safe for her to be there without back-up, she turned and walked out of the yurt, ran down the stairs, got into her truck and drove back the way to the main road.

In Carson, she pulled into the post office parking lot where two young women were talking near their cars.

"Excuse me, ladies," Angela said, "I'm Deputy Romero from the Taos County Sheriff's Office. I wonder if you have a moment for me to ask you a few questions?"

Both women looked Anglo. One had long dreadlocks and a pierced septum and the other had pink hair and black lipstick and was smoking a cigarette. They stopped talking and turned to look at her with guarded expressions. Neither said anything.

"Do either of you know Maddy Smith?" she asked.

The women exchanged furtive looks and then the one with pink hair said, "I know her."

"She's not in trouble," Angela said. "I'm trying to make sure she is okay. She called in a domestic violence report."

The woman with the dreadlocks pointed in the direction of the yurt and said, "She lives down that road…"

"I've just been to her house," Angela said. "She wasn't there."

The women exchanged another look. The woman with the dreadlocks said, "I have to go. I don't know anything." She got in her car and drove off.

The other woman, more of a girl, said, "Maddy's baby has been kind of sick. Maybe she took her to Urgent Care."

"How old is the baby?" Angela asked.

"About sixteen months," she answered. Then, as if she wanted to help, she said, "Maddy has a mean boyfriend. I don't know his name or anything about him except his reputation."

"What kind of car does he drive?"

"I'm not sure."

"Okay, well, thank you," Angela said. "Here is how to reach me if you see or hear anything about her." She handed the young woman her card.

The woman stubbed out her cigarette. "I hope you find her," she said.

Angela called into the office but the Sheriff was not available. Joseph said he was in his office talking to "some Indian guy." She drove back to town to file her report. It appeared that the boyfriend had come back to prevent Maddy Smith from reporting the beating he'd given her.

When Angela got back into the office it was almost time for shift change. The sheriff was in his office on the phone and Zach and Mark were debriefing Joseph from his day covering the secretary's job. He'd filed his first paperwork for a search warrant for the home and vehicles of Jeremy Diggs but was unsure why the warrant itself hadn't come through yet. Zach and Mark knew Sheriff would not be happy about it.

Deputy Romero looked at the 911 report and then completed her own paperwork. Michael Jaramillo, who was covering 911 when Maddy Smith's call came through, indicated in his report that she had sounded quite distressed. Jaramillo said she was in her twenties, born in Silver City and had no priors. Deputy Romero continued to worry about the young woman. As Deputy Maes packed up to leave for the day, Deputy Zach Wright took over the phones. Ulysses came out of his office and asked Maes for the search warrant.

"Sheriff," Maes said, "I filed all the information as requested before 1 o'clock but for some reason the clerk is saying I got it in too late to get a stamped warrant today." He looked sheepish.

"Deputy Romero, call over to Judge Esposito's clerk and see if you can get an override," he said. "If we don't search this afternoon, we are not going to find anything."

She was already dialing the clerk's direct line and leaving her a voicemail. "I think they close up in thirty minutes."

"Deputy Maes, run over there and see if the clerk can help you get that warrant. Call me when you find out." The sheriff sounded stern.

Maes ran out the door toward the district court office.

"How did the 911 call go?" Ulysses asked Deputy Romero. He decided not to bring up the policy of taking two deputies to every DV call. It couldn't be helped today because they were so short-staffed.

"She called from a yurt out on the mesa south of Carson," Romero said. "But she was already gone when I got there. Her car was still at the scene. Two women at the post office knew her. One said Smith's baby had been sick and that she had a "bad boyfriend." Angela made quotes with her fingers. "I didn't feel good about it, Sheriff. I found some bloody rags at the scene. I took pictures." Angela showed him the pictures on her phone.

"Poor girl," Ulysses said, "and poor baby, too."

Just then Deputy Maes called to say that the judge's clerk was out sick and the office was closed. Ulysses thought: *I'm sure that*

*shovel has been wiped clean and those boots are long gone by now. I
should have taken him into custody earlier. Why didn't I?*

Sheriff Walker said, "Hey everybody, listen up. I've hired
someone to take Lorraine's job. His name is Eli Martinez and he's
a Taos Pueblo tribal member. He came highly recommended and
he's got a lot of skills. He starts tomorrow. I want Deputy Romero
to orient him and everybody else to play nice and help out as much
as you can until he gets acclimated." The staff looked at him with
poker faces and nodded. "You got it, Sheriff," Romero said.

Ulysses kept thinking about how Diggs had said that Jacinto
Ramirez, the former mayordomo of Acequia San Lorenzo, had
agreed with his negative assessment of Antonio Valdez. He
decided to interview Ramirez before heading home. Ulysses
drove into the high country looking for the address he had found
for the man, down a dirt road that ran into the woods not far from
the boundary of Picuris Pueblo. His house sat well back from the
road among big Pondarosa pines alongside the Rio Pueblo. A new
green mini-excavator was parked in the driveway. Ulysses noted
a rusted truck without tires and an ancient-looking cement mixer
as well as a pile of beehive parts littering the front yard. A baby's
swing was hanging from a beam nailed to two trees. The stiff wind
whipped the trees. When Ulysses pulled up in the Expedition,
Ramirez was sitting on his front porch stoop with a black and
white cattle dog at his feet. The man said nothing as the sheriff
approached him. The dog gave a low growl.

"Mr. Ramirez?" Sheriff Walker asked. The man stood up. He
looked to be about sixty, five foot eight and thin, with sinewy
arms, a handlebar mustache and grey hair he wore in a ponytail.

"Why are you here?" the man asked. The dog barked and
showed his teeth. Ramirez spoke to him in Spanish and he
became quiet.

"I am looking for the former mayordomo…"

"You found him. What do you want, Sheriff?"

"Where were you on Saturday night, Mr. Ramirez?"

"This past Saturday night?" Ramirez took out a pack of
tobacco and started to roll a cigarette.

"That's right. Where were you between 6 pm and 11 pm?"

"I was right here."

"Were you alone?"

"I was with my grandson until my daughter-in-law came by to bring me dinner. I watch my grandson on Saturdays when she has to work."

"What time was that, Mr. Ramirez?"

"She left him with me about six and picked him up at around nine. After that I was alone."

"What was your relationship like with Mr. Antonio Valdez?"

"Fine."

"What caused the two of you to fall out?"

Ramirez took a lighter out of his pocket then sat back down on the step, placing the cigarette he'd rolled behind his ear. "The parciantes were prejudiced against me. They said I wasn't fair with the water. The comisión didn't stand up for me. So, I quit. Now they can't get anyone to do their job and they have to do it themselves." *This guy has motive,* Ulysses thought.

"Were you over at the presa on Saturday late?" Ulysses asked. He looked at the man's feet. He was wearing lace-up leather boots with Vibram soles, maybe a size 10.

"No, I don't work there anymore," Ramirez said. "I was here. My truck is broke down and I am waiting on the parts to fix it."

"Where'd you get that new mini-excavator?"

Ramirez looked surprised at the question, then his face resumed its sullen expression. "What's it to you?"

He could have driven that to the San Lorenzo presa, Ulysses thought. *But someone would have seen it parked there. And what would he have done with the child?*

Ulysses looked around the front of the cabin. In the shady yard there was a fenced dog run with a doghouse, a yellow plastic tricycle, and a sandbox. Against the side of the porch stood a pair of rubber waders, several empty beer cans, and a long-handled shovel.

"Can I take a look at your shovel, Mr. Ramirez?"

"Help yourself."

Ulysses noticed that the shovel had blood stains on the back of it. "How did this shovel get bloody?" he asked.

"I killed a rat with it this morning."

Ulysses picked up the shovel and sure enough there was a large dead rat under it. Ramirez came over and picked up the rat by its tail and flung it into the brush.

"Listen to me," Ramirez said. "I don't like the way you are treating me. You come here to accuse me of killing someone..."

"I'm not accusing you, Mr. Ramirez," Ulysses said. "I am just asking you about your whereabouts when a man you had a dispute with was killed."

"I'm not the only one who had a dispute with Antonio," Ramirez said. He lit his cigarette and drew in a lung full of smoke. "Valdez acted all high and mighty. He looked down on people, like he was better than them. Valdez was disrespectful. He was condescending. But I didn't kill him."

"Who else might have had a grudge against Valdez?" Ulysses asked.

"Jeremy Diggs didn't like him. Some of the San Lorenzo parciantes, too. My relatives in Mora said he was delving into things better left alone."

"What kind of things?"

"Water rights disputes," Ramirez said.

"Who told you that?"

"I used to live over in Mora. I was born there. A few years ago, I moved here to be closer to my daughter. People over there don't take kindly to anyone threatening their water."

"Can you give me any names?" Ulysses asked.

"No, I won't give you any names." Ramirez drew on his cigarette and looked at Ulysses belligerently.

The sun was low and the wind had quieted. *I'm not going to pick this fight,* Ulysses thought. *Not right now, anyway.* He gave his card to Ramirez and said, "Call me if you think of anything else that will help us find the killer." Ramirez coughed up phlegm and spit. Then he went into his house without a further word.

On the way home Ulysses thought about the encounter. Ramirez had a motive and an incomplete alibi. But he didn't have a working vehicle, apparently. Of course he could have walked, but if his daughter left at nine it would have been pitch dark by the time he arrived at the San Lorenzo presa. But he had a strong motive. *This man has wounded pride from losing a job that gave him some prestige,* Ulysses thought. *That could be enough to prompt a murder.*

After the sheriff left, Ramirez texted Senator Ramón Trujillo. "The Taos Sheriff was here nosing around. He asked about the backhoe. I thought you'd want to know."

Ulysses arrived home in time to say goodnight to Monty and Amelia, who had already brushed their teeth, put on pajamas, and listened to their mother read bedtime stories. Amelia was lying on her side looking out the window at the crescent moon when Ulysses went into the room to kiss her goodnight. "Daddy," she said, "I can see the outline of the whole moon now, even though only part of it is lit up! It looks so pretty." Ulysses stood at the open window and gazed at the distant mesa where the waxing moon stood bright in the clear sky near the horizon. "It sure does, Bean," Ulysses said. "There is a saying about that. It goes, 'The new moon holds the old moon in its arms.'"

"I learned today that light from the earth makes us see the whole moon when it's a crescent. They call it 'earthshine,'" Amelia said.

"Daddy, Daddy," Monty yelled from his room. "Come say goodnight to me too!"

"Pipe down, Monty," Rosemary said from the bottom of the steps. "Lights out, Amelia." She came upstairs and into Amelia's room, closed her window and tucked the down comforter around her. "Goodnight, Beano," Rosemary said, kissing her daughter.

In Monty's room, Ulysses was treated to a blow-by-blow account of how he caught a young wether for his mother when the goat got loose from his pen at milking time. "He went this way and I went that way, and then I just grabbed him! Mom was real happy," he said. From the other room, Amelia said, "Monty, you are the one who let him out in the first place!"

"Yeah, but I caught him too!"

"Hush, you two," Rosemary said.

Ulysses roughed the boy's curly hair and kissed his forehead. "Goodnight, son," he said.

Ulysses went downstairs to where Rosemary was putting their dinner on the table. She'd waited to eat with him. "Tell me about your day," she said. After dinner they both went to bed.

Just before dawn, Ulysses had a dream that he was swimming in a river at night and came upon a huge beaver dam with a lodge. A large aggressive-looking beaver slipped into the water and swam rapidly toward him. As it got closer, he realized the beaver was actually Jeremy Diggs, his face lurid in the moonlight. Ulysses woke up, shivering. The night had turned chilly but Rosemary was sleeping soundly. He got up to close the windows and put another blanket on the bed, wondering at his brief but vivid dream.

Chapter 5

When Ulysses arrived at the office the next morning, he was pleased to see Eli Martinez already installed at Lorraine's old mahogany desk taking cash from a man paying a fine. A fresh pot of coffee was percolating and Eli had brought in some banana bread. Zach was sitting at his desk going over the call list from the night before and chatting with Megan Atencio who was just about to clock out from covering 911 for the night shift. Angela was filing the last of the paperwork that had cluttered Lorraine's desk while keeping an ear out to make sure Eli handled the transaction correctly.

Ulysses took a deep breath and felt a sense of relief. The Sheriff's Headquarters felt like it might return to normal. He poured himself a cup of coffee, took a piece of banana bread, went into his office and shut the door. He began to make his to-do list for the day.

His priority was to create a training plan for Eli and make sure he knew enough to do his job if he was left alone in the office. But first he had to call Stephanie and find out what was planned for the fundraising event. He should also call his mother and let her know the weekend might not be exactly as discussed. Yes, it was Monty's birthday but the party had been moved to earlier in the day because of the fundraiser. Rosemary was in charge of Monty's party so Ulysses had no worries there. His mother, Diana, an easy-going woman, wouldn't be upset by the changes, but it was only a courtesy to let her know beforehand that he would have other duties beyond visiting with family.

Angela knocked on the door and came in. "Sheriff, did you see them?" she asked.

"See what?"

"The billboards?"

"No, I haven't seen them." *So much for feeling relieved,* Ulysses thought.

"Ernie Ruiz has put up billboards all over town. One on 68 coming in from Santa Fe, one near the turnoff to the pueblo, one in Carson, and at least two more."

"Damn, he must have some cash," Ulysses said. "What do they say?"

"Something about 'take back our county' and then 'Ernesto Ruiz, Constitutional Sheriff?' What on earth is that?"

"That is some bull from the lunatic fringe," Ulysses said. "How many did you say there are?"

"Five as of this morning."

"Okay, I'll call Stephanie. Could you write a list of everything you can think of that you can train Eli on? And while you're at it add anything you think I should train him for. Oh, and ask him if he can be a server at the fundraiser on Saturday, will you?"

"I will, Sheriff. By the way, Eli seems really nice *and* competent. Where did you find him?"

"Ray recommended him."

"He already knows his way around Lorraine's desk and he made some good coffee too. Plus he fixed Zach's computer keyboard!"

"Well, something is going well."

Ulysses called Rosemary and asked her to tell his mother about the weekend. "Babe, I already called her. She's fine with it. Your sister can't come, by the way. Gabe is moving out of the dorm for the summer and she has to help him."

Ulysses felt it was just as well Paloma wasn't coming. She'd be irritated that part of the visit had to be devoted to a political fundraiser. Still, it had been too long since he'd seen her. *Once I get through the election, I'll plan a day to go see her and Gabe.* His job had become so demanding Ulysses often felt guilty about not spending time with the extended family. *I bet I do better than some folks in law enforcement though,* he thought.

"Oh, Ulys, have you seen the billboards, yet?" Rosemary asked.

"No, but I heard about them. Have you seen them?"

"I actually drove into town to take a look. I'll text you a picture."

"Jeez, that is awful," Ulysses said when he received the picture.

Rosemary took a deep breath. "I wouldn't say they are good. But honestly, I don't think most Taoseños know what a constitutional sheriff is."

"I wouldn't know about it either if not for Sheriff Phil Hogg of Colfax County," Ulysses said. "He was a true believer in all manner of nonsense."

"Yeah, and he lost his election, didn't he? Doesn't he work at a gas station in Wagon Mound now?"

No sooner had Ulysses hung up from speaking with Rosemary than Stephanie called. "We've got to get out ahead of this, Ulys."

"The billboards? How are we going to do that?"

"This constitutional sheriff stuff is really big in Texas and Florida," Stephanie said.

"Well, this is New Mexico and people have a little more sense."

"Wish I had your confidence. But we need to find out who these 'New Mexicans for Freedoms' people are. They've got some deep pockets. Billboards are expensive."

"Can you look into that?" Ulysses asked.

"I'll see what I can do but I've got two closings today and an open house this evening. Plus I have some things to do for the fundraiser."

"Do you get the angle on the billboards? Take back our County? What the hell?"

"Ulys, politics these days is all about fear, division and extremes. You know that. Make people afraid, make it about us and them, make up a few hare-brained conspiracies and you are off to the races. Maybe he's trying to work the Anglo/Hispanic divide."

"Call me naïve but I never thought this level of crap would play here in Taos."

"It won't. But we have some built-in divisions and Ruiz must think it's to his advantage to exploit them. It's our job to tell the truth, point out the misinformation and run on your record."

"And get some billboards of our own?" Ulysses asked.

"I've got a better idea," Stephanie said. "Press conferences and TV spots."

"Can we afford TV?"

"Not ads, interviews."

"Okay, but I don't think it's ever been done in a sheriff race."

"There's always a first time," Stephanie said.

There was a knock on his door. It was Eli, and behind him Ulysses saw Brenda Diggs, sitting in the waiting area looking anxious. "Sheriff, Ms. Diggs is here to see you. And I will be happy to see what I can find on the people funding those billboards Angela saw."

Ulysses was surprised at this offer but decided to accept it, even though technically that kind of research might be campaign business. "Send Mrs. Diggs in," he said.

Brenda Diggs had a bruise on her left cheek. "Sheriff, Jeremy didn't come home last night," she said in a voice barely above a whisper. "And he didn't take his cellphone with him."

"When did you last see him, Brenda?"

"He left to meet someone right after dinner. A man who was going to help him with a culvert, he said. I asked him where they were meeting and he wouldn't say. He can be like that. Sheriff, I'm really worried."

"Brenda, how did you get that bruise? Did the two of you fight?"

Brenda looked down. "No, Sheriff. I fell coming down the steps from the porch."

"Have you called the comisión president? He would know if someone was going to help who wasn't a parciante. Wouldn't Jeremy have to get permission to hire someone?"

"I don't know anything about the ditch," Brenda said, wringing her hands. "I don't meddle in Jeremy's business. He'd be very angry if I did that."

"Did you drive along the ditch to see if you could see his ATV parked anywhere?"

Brenda began to cry. "I don't drive anymore, Sheriff. Not since I had a heart attack two years ago."

"Who brought you here today?"

"My sister Loretta," Brenda said. "She's waiting in the car."

"Okay, Brenda, I will look into it. In the meantime, you go home and wait to hear from me. And if you hear from Jeremy let me know, will you?" He handed her a card. "And what is the name and number of the comisión president?"

After Brenda left Ulysses called José Maestas, a comisionado from Patos.

"Hello, Sheriff, what can I do for you?" the old man asked.

"Can you tell me where your mayordomo was having a culvert problem?" Sheriff Walker asked.

"I'm not aware of any culvert problem," Maestas said. "We had a beaver last season near Ben Romero's in that big culvert just below the desagüe. But we've installed grates since so no beavers can get in. Why do you ask?"

"Jeremy Diggs didn't come home last night and his wife is worried about him. She last saw him at dinner yesterday. He said he was going to meet a man to help him with a culvert. She thought the man was not a parciante but an outside worker."

"That is very odd, Sheriff. I haven't heard a thing about it. If we were going to hire someone, I am supposed to know about it."

"How many culverts do you have on Patos?"

"Just that one above ground, Sheriff. The others are all buried."

"I'm going to take a look at that culvert..."

"It is just off the drive to Ben Romero's house, kind of in the woods. If he's there, you'll see his red ATV. Let me know if you need anything else."

Ulysses went out to the front office and told Angela to get ready to go with him to find Jeremy Diggs. "Eli, are you okay to cover for a couple of hours on your own? If you need help,

Michael is in the back with 911 and he might be able to lend a hand."

"I'm good, sir," Eli said. "I think I've got the basics."

Angela led the way to her great-uncle Ben Romero's property, which was less than a mile from the Diggs property. From the road, the acequia looked overfull with irrigation water, straining the bordos. They turned into the driveway to Ben Romero's property, a fine apple orchard and vineyard that had been in the family for a century. "There is the desagüe," Deputy Romero said, indicating a concrete supported iron gate that could be raised to let water flow out from the acequia back into the Rio Pueblo. Mayordomos used desagües, or drains, to empty water from the ditch below them in order to make repairs, flush debris and regulate flow. "Water is still running full into the ditch," Romero said. "The desagüe must be closed." Below the desagüe was a raised flume, a culvert that spanned a small arroyo. Water flowed in a ditch past the closed desagüe and into the flume to cross the arroyo and then emptied back into the ditch.

"I wonder if he was here last night?" Angela said. "I don't see his ATV anywhere."

"Let's imagine first that he was telling the truth," Sheriff said, getting out of the cruiser. "Do you see any problems with this structure that Diggs might have needed help with?"

Romero walked the forty feet of twenty-four-inch corrugated metal pipe that was supported on concrete struts. Water was flowing through it at a high, almost dangerous volume. "Maybe a beaver? They love to build dams in culverts, especially big ones like this," she said.

"Mr. Maestas said they had a beaver in this culvert last year, but they installed grates on this one," Ulysses said. "The grate is in place and there don't seem to be any leaks."

"I wonder why the water volume is so high?" Angela said. "It could definitely cause a blow-out."

Ulysses walked down to the outflow end. "There is a grate here, too." He tested it. "It's a little bent. It looks like it could come out pretty easily."

"Do we think Diggs was even here?" Angela asked. "Maybe that was just a story he told his wife?"

"I have a bad feeling about this," Ulysses said. He shone his flashlight into the culvert. Water poured through, filling almost the entire circumference of the metal tube. Against the grate he saw a dark hairy orb bobbing in the rushing water. At first, he thought was an animal. But when the flashlight illuminated the entire area, he realized it was the head of a man. When the blue-white face rolled up, he recognized Jeremy Diggs. He was dead, drowned in the flume. Ulysses felt a chill run down his spine as he remembered his dream from the morning.

Deputy Romero took pictures before Sheriff Walker pulled off the grate and he and Angela maneuvered Digg's body onto the acequia bank. Ulysses stood still for a few moments to breathe, feeling nauseated. He slowly recovered and was able to examine the body. Diggs had a wound from a blow to the head. It looked to Ulysses as if he'd been dead many hours. The corpse was limp, blue and bloated. He was wearing blue jeans and the same flannel shirt he wore when Ulysses last saw him. The left bootheel of his cowboy boots had a sizable nick in it. "Looks like the boot that made the prints we saw at the Valdez murder site," Sheriff said. "Call Deputy Wright and the Rescue," he told Romero. "I'm going to look around." Ulysses examined the ground around the flume and also around Digg's ATV, where he saw Digg's shovel; he put it in the Expedition to have it examined for evidence. The rest of the site was offered no clues, not even footprints.

After the Penasco Rescue drove off with Digg's body, Sheriff left Romero and Wright to go over the scene, and went to give Brenda Diggs the bad news about her husband. As he pulled up and got out of the cruiser, Brenda's sister Loretta Sanchez opened the front door. Brenda, pale and nervous, stood behind her. Ulysses took off his hat and went inside the spotless house with its wall-to-wall plush carpet.

"I'm so sorry to tell you this, Brenda," Sheriff Walker said, speaking slowly to allow Brenda to brace herself for the news. "Your husband is dead. We found him in a big culvert over at Ben

Romero's." Brenda cried out and sat down in a slump. Tears began to stream down her face and she made little choking sobs. Her sister Loretta, younger by about seven years, held her sister's hand, looking stoic. "I knew something was bad wrong," Loretta said.

Sheriff and Loretta sat in silence for a few minutes while Brenda cried.

"How could this have happened?" Brenda asked. "He was always so careful in that culvert!"

"Brenda, it might not have been an accident," Sheriff Walker said.

Brenda gasped. "You mean someone killed him?"

"Looks like it."

Brenda stopped weeping and swallowed several times. "Oh, Jesus," she said, "Oh my Lord God." Loretta rubbed her back and shoulders.

"Sheriff, I have to tell you something," Brenda said at last.

"Okay, go ahead."

"On Friday, the day Jeremy got into it with Antonio at the market, he saw someone..."

Brenda had started crying again and seemed to lose her focus.

"It's okay, Brenda. Take your time," Ulysses said. Loretta brought Brenda a glass of water and more tissues. She blew her nose and took a drink of water.

"That day, in the post office parking lot, Jeremy saw a man he had worked for in Texas. The man who had caused him to go to prison, years ago. He was waiting for Jeremy. When Jeremy pulled up on his ATV, the man called him over. Jeremy said he offered him a job that would make him a lot of money but Jeremy said no, he never wanted to see his face again. When he came home he was really shook up."

"What kind of job?" Ulysses asked. "What was the man's name?"

"He wouldn't tell me," Brenda said, "and I knew better than to ask." She took another drink of water. Loretta sat with her arms folded and a frown on her face. *She never approved of her brother-in-law,* Ulysses thought.

"Why was he so shook up? Was he angry or afraid?"

Brenda shook her head. "I think he was afraid."

"Tell me about Jeremy's life in Texas."

"It wasn't a good life, Sheriff. His father beat his mother and then ran off. She drank. Jeremy was in and out of foster care and dropped out of high school. Then he got friendly with some people in the oil business. He never would say what it was he did, but the company was called Big Hat, I think. When he was only twenty-one he was arrested for beating a man so bad he nearly died. He went to prison for ten years. When he got out he moved here. I met him when he started coming to my church. I was a widow and he started helping me out here, you know. He turned his life over to Jesus and we got married not long after that."

"He took advantage of Brenda," Loretta said quietly.

"No, he did not," Brenda said. "Sheriff, he was a good man. He was faithful and he protected me. I loved him."

"He bullied you, Brenda," Loretta said.

"Loretta, he's not even in the ground! If you can't speak well of him, you shouldn't say anything."

"Do you have any reason to believe your husband could have killed Antonio Valdez?"

Brenda took a deep breath and wiped away her tears. "He never liked Antonio. But I wouldn't think he would kill him."

"You seem to have some doubt, Brenda."

There was a long pause.

"Sheriff, I didn't tell you the whole truth about the night Antonio Valdez died," she said.

"What didn't you tell me?"

"I went to bed pretty early, before dark, but I didn't fall asleep right away. I heard someone come in the house and I heard him and Jeremy talking. I heard the man say, 'You will do as you are told or you will regret it.'"

"What did Jeremy say?"

"He said, 'What are you going to do, send me to prison?'" Brenda choked back a sob. "After that the man left and not long after, Jeremy left too. Jeremy was gone for about two hours."

"So you lied to me about that?" Sheriff said.

Brenda nodded, looking at the floor. After a few moments she said, "The next morning I asked Jeremy about what I'd heard, and that's when he gave me this," she said, indicating her black eye.

Loretta, who had been looking on disapprovingly, stood up and went into the kitchen.

Ulysses let the new information sink in. "Do you have any idea who this man was?"

"No, I didn't recognize the voice. I never met anyone from his past before, but it could have been the man he saw at the post office," Brenda said.

"Did you see or hear anything that might help us identify him?"

Brenda thought for few minutes. "Jeremy let him smoke in the house. He left two cigarette butts."

"Do you still have them?"

"They are in the garbage," Brenda said.

"I'll look for them," Loretta said from the kitchen.

"Here, use these," Ulysses said, getting up to hand her a pair of latex gloves. When she'd found the two cigarette butts, Ulysses put them into an evidence bag.

"Did Jeremy do anything else unusual?"

"He wasn't acting like himself at all. He seemed afraid. I saw that he had put his guns in his ATV."

"Brenda, it is pretty likely that Jeremy killed Antonio Valdez. We have pictures of a boot print from the murder scene that match the boots Jeremy was wearing when he died."

Brenda sobbed and shook her head. "No, I can't believe he'd kill anyone. I can't believe it," she said. Loretta sat down beside her sister, looking disgusted.

"Maybe this man forced him to do it," Ulysses said. "Loretta, can you take care of your sister tonight?"

"Yes, Sheriff, I'll bring her to my house."

"Okay, well, call me if you think of anything you want to tell me. We'll find out who killed Jeremy." He left his card by the door on an antique table with a statue of Jesus holding a lamb.

Ulysses drove back to the office thinking about his dream from the morning. Was it just a coincidence that he dreamed about Jeremy Diggs? It made him wonder more about his dream from the day before. Was he about to head over a waterfall in a rickety boat? Was the dream a metaphor or was it a literal warning? *These dreams are not helping me. They are just stressing me out,* he thought.

And what should he make of Brenda's revelations about a man from Jeremy's past? Who was this man? Had he made Diggs kill Antonio Valdez, and if so, why? He kept thinking about the number he traced from the notepad, 1797. It was probably nothing, but he decided to call Delilah to ask if she'd had any thoughts about what it might mean.

Chapter 6

Back at Headquarters, Eli, the new secretary, was helping a woman file a complaint and Michael was covering 911. Megan was still out sick and Dakota wasn't expected to come in for about an hour. Deputies Mark and Joseph had gone to respond to a 911 call. Aware of how thin the coverage was, Sheriff was pleased to see everyone coping well.

In his office, Ulysses found three messages on his desk. One from Ray asking him to call back as soon as possible, one from FBI Agent LizBeth Tallichet who said she'd like to drop by around 2:30, and one from Rosemary reminding him of the visitation for Antonio Valdez from 5 to 7. Ulysses looked at his watch. He called Ray first.

"How's it working out with Eli?" Ray asked.

"Good so far. He's been here half a day and already seems comfortable. Hey, I just got back from another murder scene."

"Really? Who was killed?"

"A mayordomo on the acequia below Valdez's, named Jeremy Diggs. Same M.O. for the killer—a hard knock to the head, then drowned."

"Wasn't he your prime suspect in Antonio's murder?" Ray asked.

"I was planning to bring him in, but his killer got there first. When I went to the house to tell his widow, she told me there was a man at the house with him the night Valdez was killed, someone from his past. It sounds like the man was trying to pressure him to do something.

"Do you know who that person is?"

"Nope, nothing yet. How are things over your way?"

"We had an unauthorized drive-by last night, late."

"What is an unauthorized drive-by?"

"Since the pandemic, we've had signs posted to keep people from driving through the pueblo except during daylight hours on official business. But some guy in a truck, late model, maybe dark grey, drove into the plaza about midnight and idled there for about ten minutes. The sound of the engine woke Clarice up and she called Matt. When Matt came, the guy took off. Matt followed him, but he couldn't get plates. The guy had dealer plates on the inside back window, but the windows were tinted."

"That's the description Delilah gave of a man who was watching her house. Late model truck, dealer plates, tinted windows."

"When did she see him?"

"Sunday and yesterday."

Ray said nothing for a few moments, then he said, "I guess the guy knows where to find us. I wonder who he works for?"

"We need to find that out as soon as possible. If it's the same guy as killed Jeremy Diggs, I'm worried for your safety."

Ray shook his head. "Don't worry about me, Ulys. But make sure Delilah is safe."

While Ulysses was waiting for FBI Agent LizBeth Tallichet to arrive, Dr. Vigil showed up with the postmortem on Antonio Valdez.

"Good afternoon, Sheriff," he said, strolling in through Ulysses' open door. "I can tell you that your surmise about the cause of death was correct."

"Hello, Dr. Vigil," he said to the man Rosemary called, 'the courtly coroner' and he dubbed 'the smiling mortician.' "So he was knocked on the head and then drowned?"

"Precisely. The victim was hit on the side of his head with a large object, perhaps a shovel, and then forced into the acequia where he was held down until he drowned. I do not think he was knocked unconscious, merely stunned, because he fought his attacker. The killer restrained him by placing his knee on the middle of his back and held down the victim's upper body until he succumbed to the water. There was considerable bruising under his shoulders and on his neck. There was also bruising on his legs. Do you think there could have been two killers?"

"It's possible," Ulysses said, "why do you ask?"

"Señor Valdez had a large frame and was pretty strong for an older gentleman. A second assailant could have provided some assistance during the drowning."

And could have helped clean up the crime scene, Ulysses thought, thinking of Jeremy Diggs' evening visitor. "Anything else, Dr. Vigil?" he asked.

"No, nothing, except that the time of death was between nine pm and two am."

Dr. Vigil put his report on Ulysses' desk. "Zach told me there is another suspicious death?"

"Yes, another drowning. A man named Jeremy Diggs."

"I do not know him," Dr. Vigil said. "You are keeping me busier that I like to be, Sheriff. It isn't good for you, especially not during election season."

"Sad but true," Ulysses said and paused. "I hope I can count on your vote, Doctor," he asked, a bit awkwardly.

"I would never vote for a Trujillo protégé, Sheriff. You will get my vote."

"Thank you, sir."

"It's not the same around here without Lorraine, is it?" the older gentleman mused.

"No, but be sure to introduce yourself to the new guy, Eli."

"I already did. Seems like a nice young fellow."

When Ulysses said goodbye to the coroner at his office door, he saw Agent LizBeth Tallichet come in the front door. He was glad to see his old friend who had worked with him on his biggest case a few years ago.

"How are you doing, Ulys?" LizBeth asked. "I can't believe I haven't seen you since Dawa and I got married."

"Yeah, it's been too long. I'm good," Ulysses said. "Though I can't wait for this election to be over."

LizBeth smiled, "You've got this one, Ulys, don't you worry!"

"Thanks, LizBeth, I hope you are right. What's been going on?"

"A lot. Dawa and I just moved into our new house in Placitas. Dawa got a position at UNM Hospital in Albuquerque. And I got a new boss." They went into Ulysses' office and closed the door.

"Is that good? I remember you liked your old boss."

"I did like the old one. I'm still trying to get used to the new guy. He's from Oklahoma and very old school. He's really changed the atmosphere at work." Ulysses could tell from her face that the atmospheric change wasn't a welcome one.

"I'm sorry to hear that, LizBeth."

"The good news is I'll be up here a lot more than I have been. Evidently, Taos, Colfax and Rio Arriba Counties are generally considered backwaters you don't want to be assigned to. My boss put me in charge up here and reassigned my cases in Albuquerque to two agents he brought with him from OKC."

Ulysses said, "I'll be glad to have you around in our little backwater. What brings you up here today, LizBeth?"

"I hear you've had a murder up here?"

"Yes, two actually, and I think they are connected. Why do you ask?"

"Oh, just keeping up with the local doings in case they have any bearings on my business. Have you heard anything about what is going on at Taos Pueblo?"

"No."

"About three weeks ago we got an anonymous tip about a high profile person passing bribes on an issue before the tribal council."

"What's the issue?"

"Someone with deep pockets has made an offer to buy 60 acre feet of their water, which I'm told is a whole lot of water, even though its so-called 'paper rights' only. The vote goes before the council soon."

"Who made the offer?" Ulysses asked.

"A company called Wild West Development for a project called Highland Fling. The principal dude is a guy named Trey Cameron. He's from Texas but has a house here in Taos County."

"I've heard of this, LizBeth. Is the water for a golf course in Mora County?"

"That's the one. And the sale is complicated because it's a cross-basin transfer. But evidently Cameron has permission from the State Engineer. He is a well-connected, very rich man."

"So is he trying to bribe council members?"

"That is a very interesting story. So the other day I went to talk with a Taos tribal council member about it. I found out the bribes are being offered by a Cameron surrogate, your old nemesis Senator Ramón Trujillo."

"Really?" Ulysses said, surprised. "Who is your source on the Taos tribal council?"

"Delfino Mondragon. He's a well-known artist who has gotten caught up in the whole mess. Sounds like he's being extorted for his vote on the transfer."

"Mondragon is the brother-in-law of Antonio Valdez, one of my homicide victims. Is he willing to make a statement?"

"Well, it's complicated. When I was speaking with Mondragon he got a call from his niece about Antonio's murder."

"Delilah Valdez," Ulysses said.

"That's right. Mondragon was exceedingly spooked by the news of Antonio's death. He was close to making a statement, but he decided he needed to think on it, so he's gone on a little retreat."

Ulysses whistled under his breath. "Did Mondragon seem afraid for his life?"

"I would say so," LizBeth said. "He's hiding out now on Taos Mountain with his apprentice Raven Sandoval. Said he'd be back for Antonio's funeral."

"I hope he's safe up there," Ulysses said.

"So tell me what you know about Highland Fling and the Mora transfers," LizBeth said.

"Ray Pando and Antonio Valdez had been interested for some time in trying to reverse a deal, the Mora transfers, where water is taken out of the Picuris watershed and sent over the mountain to Mora County. They've got some good evidence plus a recent favorable court decision and Delilah's expertise and connections. They were considering a lawsuit to reverse the transfers. But in addition to opposition from farmers and ranchers in Mora, one of the places where the transferred water goes is Chacón, the village near where Trey Cameron wants his luxury development and Cameron needs that diverted water."

"How long have these water transfers been going on?" LizBeth asked.

"About two hundred years. They divert this water every spring and summer from creeks on this side of the mountain and deliver it over the mountain into Mora. Highland Fling would use a lot of that water but they'd also need more, which is why they must be courting Taos Pueblo."

"Let the water games commence," LizBeth said.

"More like the water wars. The Mora transfers are old cross basin transfers. Maybe Cameron hopes to capitalize on them as precedent for his project. Of course Valdez and Picuris Pueblo would be some strong opposition. Ray thinks somebody might have found that kind of inquiry threatening."

"What do the people of Mora think of Picuris trying to take their water back? Could one of them be responsible for Valdez's murder?" LizBeth asked.

"It's possible," Ulysses replied. "I'm not sure the acequieros over there are organized enough to pull off a murder."

"If they are at risk of losing water they've had for 200 years, don't you think they'd get organized?"

"Again, it's possible. From what I hear they are pretty demoralized after the fires last summer. But you are right, a big rancher in the know about the risk of losing their water, could have motive." Ulysses stood up, stretched and walked to the window that looked out toward the mountains. "So, who tipped you off to the troubles at Taos Pueblo?"

"Mondragon, but I think he remains profoundly ambivalent. He has a lot to lose if he votes against the water rights sale and I don't think he was telling me the whole story."

"What do you mean?"

"Just a hunch I had that he was holding back something important."

"Where did you meet him?"

"At his studio in town. He didn't want me to go to the pueblo, for obvious reasons."

"When are you going to talk to him again?"

"I asked him to call me when he gets back from his retreat."

"Did he tell anyone else he was going?" Ulysses asked.

"I think I heard him tell Delilah," LizBeth said.

"Well, keep me posted on any developments. Information relevant to what I'm investigating would be especially appreciated," Ulysses said.

"I'll see what I can do, but this new boss is solidly anti-share with any other law enforcement agency. He's always got an eye on who he needs to protect and I have a hunch this case has some high-profile people involved. This Cameron guy is a very influential in Texas and Oklahoma, which is where Special Agent Barkley comes from. I don't want to be on Barkley's shit list."

"What kind of protection are you talking about?" Ulysses said.

"The kind given to well-connected, rich people. Not the protection of the public that I signed on for." Ulysses noticed LizBeth looked worried and burdened.

"Yeah," Ulysses said, turning away from the window, "this situation could be bigger and more complicated than either of us originally thought. I think you and I should stay in close touch with what we discover."

Sheriff Ulysses Walker walked into the crowded funeral home for the visitation just as the people were finishing reciting the rosary. It was stuffy in the brightly lit, crowded room. Large sprays of pink gladioli stood at each side of Antonio Valdez's casket. The casket was open to show a corpse dressed in a brown suit, white shirt, and a turquoise tie, hands crossed on top of the blue satin casket coverlet. Delilah stood to the right of the casket holding a mother of pearl rosary in one hand, looking fragile. Arthur Davenport, watching the room with a composed, respectful demeanor, held her other hand. The visitors were approaching the casket to pay their respects. There was a hum of low, reverential conversation.

Ulysses knew many of the people in the room, including Antonio's younger sister and brother-in-law, the Garcías, and some of Reina's relatives from Taos Pueblo. Also present were his former colleagues from UNM Taos and a sizeable contingent from the Watershed Guardians, an environmental group that counted Antonio among its founders. Standing in the parlor doorway, he greeted many by name. There were two Anglo men in expensive suits that Ulysses didn't recognize but thought must be the partners at Delilah's firm.

The deputies, Angela, Zach and Joseph were standing in the hall near the front door in a crowd of young people. He looked around for Mark but didn't see him. As he surveyed the rooms, Ulysses thought he felt more discomfort than is usual in such familiar circumstances—the extra discomfort people always feel at a sudden death, compounded by the horror of a murder.

Senator Ramón Trujillo came in the front door with his daughter, Jazmine Ruiz on his arm. A burly dark-skinned man in a tight-fitting suit with a shaved head and a pencil mustache stood behind Senator Trujillo. *Since when does Trujillo travel with security?* Ulysses wondered. *And what is the Senator doing here?* Then he remembered that Antonio and Ramón attended the same church. The young African parish priest walked over to Trujillo and the two men conversed warmly. Jazmine moved around the room, talking a little too loudly, shaking hands, and mentioning her campaign for county commissioner.

Ulysses looked at Delilah to see how she was taking this display of poor taste. Delilah walked away from the casket dabbing her eyes with a handkerchief. She asked Ulysses to step outside with her.

"How are you holding up?" Ulysses asked when they got outside. Wind was steady out of the north and the evening had turned chilly. Delilah directed them away from the front door and into a dark corner of the front lawn. She hunched her shoulders against the cold. "Not great. Everything is a blur. I heard someone killed your prime suspect in Daddy's death."

"Yeah, yesterday. Was there something you wanted to talk with me about?"

"Yes. A man, the one I told you has been watching me, was outside the courthouse early this morning. I was coming out with some friends and it looked like he was waiting for me. Once he saw that I wasn't alone he quickly turned his back and started walking toward the Plaza."

"What did he look like?"

"About six feet, medium build, dark hair in a pony tail. Anglo, I think."

"Did he speak to you?"

"No."

"How do you know he is following you?"

"Ulys, I just know. Trust me." Delilah pulled out a cigarette and lit it.

"I didn't know you smoked," Ulysses said.

"I don't. It has been one hell of a week."

"I know, I'm sorry. What about the guy scared you?"

"Everything about him. He was so brazen."

"Listen, Delilah, I'll call the police in Santa Fe and get some protection for you."

"Yes, please. Just until Saturday. After that Arthur and I are going to stay at Daddy's."

"What makes you think that will be safer?" Ulysses asked.

"I'll just feel safer there. There is a security system and my uncle Del will come too if I need him."

"By the way, did you come up with any thoughts about that number I traced on the notepad?"

"Not really," Delilah said. "But I think the Valdez family came here around that time, in the 1790's. So I'm guessing it was a date.

Daddy was all about history, you know. And he seemed really preoccupied with the Mora transfers, but they were twenty-five years later. So I just don't know. We should ask Ray." She took another drag on her cigarette and blew the smoke toward the sky.

"I will," Ulysses said. "Hey, I didn't see your uncle in there. Where is he?"

"Del wanted to go up on the mountain for a couple of days. He said he'd be back for the funeral."

"Why was he going on the mountain?"

"Hell if I know, Ulys. Del is a world unto himself."

Delilah shrugged and stubbed out her cigarette. "You saw Senator Trujillo here tonight, right?" Delilah asked disgustedly. "Rumor is he is involved in passing bribes over water rights. And some on the council are taking the money. The whole situation has everybody up in arms. Did you see that character he has doing security? Scary."

A voice called from the top of the stairs. "Delilah? Are you out there?" It was Delilah's aunt, Antonio's younger sister Edna García, calling Delilah back to her duty at the casket.

"I'm here, Auntie, I'll be there in a minute."

"People are asking for you," the older woman said.

"I know. I'm coming." She turned to the Sheriff. "Can you call the Santa Fe police right away, Ulys? I don't want to go home until I hear I'll have someone watching over me."

"You got it. I'll text you the plan." Later that evening the Santa Fe police sent a patrol car to park outside Delilah's condo with a plan to stay until Saturday morning.

Chapter 7

Ulysses arrived home after the children were already in bed. He came in, flicked off the front porch light, locked the door, and put his gun in the safe. The house was warm and smelled of herbs and goat milk. Racks of fresh farmhouse goat cheese rounds filled the kitchen counters ready to go to market on Friday. Rosemary came in from the bedroom in her nightgown. She set his dinner on the table, part of a goat cheese with crackers and a bowl of white bean soup with kale from the garden.

"How'd it go with the *Taos News* reporter?" Ulysses asked.

"She was friendly. She took pictures of the house and farm and asked a lot of questions about what it was like to be your wife."

"What is it like to be my wife?"

"You'll have to read about it in the article. It comes out tomorrow. I told her about your commitment to women's safety, and all your achievements, like saving people at Picuris Pueblo from a psychopath. I sent her home with two chutneys and my best aged chèvre. She said she'd seen me at the Farmer's Market. Trust me, it'll be good."

"Okay, I trust you. But you didn't let them take pictures of the children, did you?"

Rosemary scoffed. "This is trust? No, I'm not an idiot, Ulys. One thing was weird though. She asked if you were religious. Can you believe it?"

"What did you tell her?"

"I said you meditated daily."

"You didn't!"

Rosemary laughed. "No, I didn't. I said you were a man of faith but that your faith was deeply personal."

"Well done."

"Stephanie gave me my talking points. Hey, don't you have that interview with Stu Wishard, the radio bully, tomorrow?"

"Thursday. In the afternoon. I better get prepared."

"You'll be great, Ulys," Rosemary said. "I made some chamomile tea if you want some." She poured herself a cup.

"I'll just have a cookie," he said, finishing his soup. He'd noticed that the cookie jar was full of his favorites, oatmeal raisin.

"I had a nightmare yesterday when I grabbed a nap after lunch," he said.

"You are under a lot of stress, Ulys," Rosemary said. "Don't you think?"

"Yes, definitely. Today we discovered another murder. My dream last night was kind of a premonition, but it wasn't a nightmare, just a series of images."

"Who was killed and how?"

"The mayordomo on Acequia de los Patos was hit on the head and then drowned in a culvert. He had been my prime suspect in the Valdez murder. I think he probably did kill Valdez, but I don't know why someone would kill him."

"Whew. Another murder, especially now," Rosemary said, shaking her head, "not good. What was your other dream, the one you called a nightmare?"

"I was about to go over a waterfall in a rickety boat. Kind of standard nightmare stuff."

"You are under too much pressure," Rosemary said, putting her hand on his shoulder. "The murders and also the election. Are you worried about the vote?"

"A little, but I think I'm going to win. I'm wondering about these dreams. Why do they keep happening? Do you think I should talk to another shrink?"

"If you want to," Rosemary answered. "But the last time you did, nothing came of it. Do you want to stop having them?"

"Not if I have to take a medication," Ulysses said. "I wish I could find a way to have them be useful instead of just disturbing."

Rosemary dried her hands on a towel and then put lotion on them. "Maybe they are there to give you important information. You know the Bible is full of prophetic dreams. I just don't think we pay as much attention to dreams as we probably should. Maybe if you took the dreams more seriously, they could guide you."

Ulysses laughed. "My father used to say he remembered past lives. I always thought that was a crock but he wasn't one to make things up."

"Whether you believe the dreams or not, you do keep having them," Rosemary said. "Just try to be as careful as you can around rivers!"

"I will," Ulysses said. "Hey, I'm going to turn in, want to join me?" He was surprised when Rosemary gave him a big, wet kiss and led him into the bedroom by the hand.

The next morning Rosemary was up early looking at the Taos News online. The feature article about her was on the front page with a flattering photo and the headline, "Sheriff Walker's Secret Weapon, his Wife, Rosemary Walker." Rosemary was pleased that the article referred to her Best of Taos Market Stand three years running and that the photo showed her with her favorite milk goat, a lovely Nubian named Dolly. Ulysses scanned the article and noticed a reference to Rosemary "rescuing her husband from his opponent's wife at a campaign event."

"I knew that angle would come out eventually," he said. "Did the reporter ask you about that?"

"No, she didn't. She was the reporter who was there that day! It's a small town, Ulys." Rosemary went out to do the chores while Ulysses dished up bowls of granola for Monty and Amelia.

Amelia came to the table dressed for school and in a chipper mood. "I get to go to Bea's house after school to play," she said. "Bea is my best friend."

Monty was dressed but he was grumpy. "I hate school," he said. "Why do I have to go to school?"

"Why do you hate school, Son?" Ulysses asked. A truck he didn't recognize was pulling up to the goat shed where Rosemary was milking.

"I hate my desk. It's so uncomfortable! And I don't like my teacher either." Ulysses poured milk into Monty's bowl.

"Be sure to change that shirt after you eat," Ulysses said. "I think you wore it yesterday and it's dirty."

"I don't care," Monty said.

Ulysses saw a man get out of the truck and he felt a protective twinge. Then he realized it was their acequia's mayordomo, Bill Sykes, a man in his forties who raised turkeys. "Eat up and then put your bowls in the sink and brush your teeth," Ulysses said. "And change that shirt, Monty. I'm going out to check on something."

Outside, he heard Rosemary say, "I took water yesterday from 1 to 3 like you said I could, Bill."

"We got a complaint that you were watering well after 4," Sykes said with an accusatory tone. Sykes had only been mayordomo of Acequia de Torreon for a year and the general agreement was that he "lacked people skills."

"Well, I wasn't," Rosemary said flatly. "Who complained?"

"I can't tell you. My wife took the call and she didn't ask."

Ulysses walked up and greeted the mayordomo. He put his arm around his wife and said nothing.

"Sheriff, water is scarce these days and everybody either has seedlings or is getting ready to plant," Sykes said. "Maybe Rosemary could get away with taking a little extra when there's plenty, but..."

"Bill, I didn't take extra. I never do." Rosemary picked up her milk bucket. "If you'll excuse me, I have to take the children to school."

"Okay, Mrs. Walker. Have a good day," he said. The expression on his bland, round face registered his disbelief of Rosemary. He got in his truck and drove off.

"Who might have complained about me?" Rosemary said. "I left a full ditch at 3 on the dot."

"I know you did, honey," Ulysses said. "Sykes ought to know better than to pass on an anonymous complaint. Listen, I've got to run. I'll see you this evening."

"It's going to be another hot, windy day," Rosemary said. "Stay safe out there. It's a perfect day for a wildfire."

On the way into town Ulysses noticed yet another new billboard in El Prado for his opponent, Ernesto Ruiz. "Protect Our Values" it proclaimed over a picture of Ruiz looking down a rifle sight. Underneath the picture it said, "Constitutional Sheriff" and "Paid for by New Mexicans for Freedoms." The billboard made Ulysses angry (*protect whose values?*) but he pushed the emotion aside and made a mental note to look into "New Mexicans for Freedoms" which he thought sounded like a goofy, astroturf political action group.

When he got to headquarters, Angela and Eli were sitting together at Eli's desk looking at Eli's computer screen.

"Good morning, Sheriff," Angela said, standing up. "Both Mr. Pando and Agent Tallichet called and wanted you to call back asap."

"What are you two looking at?" Ulysses asked.

"We've been looking at the people responsible for the new billboard," Angela said. "Eli found this." Eli turned his monitor so Ulysses could see a website. Under a banner that said, "Prosperity for New Mexico" were photographs of oil rigs near Hobbs, a golf course in Ruidoso, a big dairy farm near Edgewood, and a Four Seasons resort in Santa Fe. Around the edges were photographs of children playing, traditional families going to church, and men in suits and hard hats standing next to "shovel-ready" projects. In several of those pictures Ulysses saw Ramón Trujillo and Ernie and Jazmine Ruiz.

There were some other pictures that didn't look familiar to Ulysses. "Where is that?" he asked, pointing to a western scene.

"Palo Duro State Park in Texas," Eli said. "Look at this." He opened another website called "Wild West Development." The website's banner said "Bringing prosperity and progress to West Texas since 1971."

"The same pictures of Palo Duro, same children playing, same families going to church, the whole spiel. And look at this guy." Standing beside Senator Ramón Trujillo was an older white man in a tailored suit and fawn-colored cowboy hat carrying a cane with a silver head.

"Who is that?" Ulysses asked.

"That's Trey Cameron," Eli said, "CEO of Wild West Development and very rich dude. Look at this." Eli opened an article from the *Texas Bee* called "Texas Plutocrats Exposed" and there was a better picture of Mr. Cameron with his much younger, very tall, Hungarian-born wife, Cili, and their two blonde children standing beside their Gulfstream airplane. "The article says he got his start with money from his father, who ran an oil lease outfit called 'Big Hat', founded in 1965." The quote under the picture said, "From wildcatter to Wild West fat cat."

"Jeremy Diggs worked for a company called Big Hat," Ulysses said.

"Angela told me that. Let me show you one more." Eli opened a website called "Constitutional Sheriffs of America." There, under a banner that read, "Join our People's Posse! End Federal Overreach!" was a picture of a Texas sheriff addressing over a hundred other sheriffs at some kind of convention. On the stage, in the front row to the right of the speaker sat Trey Cameron.

Ulysses whistled under his breath. "Man, you have been busy to find all this."

"It didn't take long, Sheriff. I got in here fifteen minutes early and found all this pretty quickly. And I got everything filed, learned how to operate the radios and 911 equipment too."

"We have to be careful not to mix work and campaign, Eli."

Angela spoke up. "Sheriff, isn't it kind of complicated? I mean, isn't there a connection between Cameron and our two cases?"

Ulysses scratched his chin. "You could make that argument. *And* you can't be doing campaign research on the county's dime."

"Sir," Eli said, "that's why I came in early. Also, I've seen this man at Taos Pueblo." Eli indicated Ramón Trujillo. "I'm pretty sure he is trying to make friends on the tribal council." Eli pointed to a large man behind Trujillo who was wearing a black cap with "Security" in white letters and a bullet proof vest; he was carrying a semi-automatic rifle. It was the man Ulysses had seen at the funeral home visitation. "That's his body guard, Cody Parker," Eli said. "He is not a good guy."

"Well, thank you for this," Ulysses said.

"Anytime, Sheriff," Eli replied.

Ulysses went into his office and called Ray. "Hey, man," he said. "What's up?"

"Something is happening over in Mora that might interest you."

"Oh, yeah, what?"

"A group of land grant activists and farmers met last night in Chacón to talk about the renewed Picuris interest in ending the Mora transfers. The letter came up, you know, the one from my ancestor that Antonio Valdez had a copy of. I heard they were pretty riled up. They are forming a group to fight us."

"That didn't take long," Ulysses said. "Who told you about it?"

"A journalist I know, Rita Wainwright. I met her when she did a story on how the pueblos handled the pandemic. She also covers the land grants and other cultural issues in Mora. She lives in Chacón."

"How did the people get a copy of the letter?"

"Rita said several of them received copies in the mail in a plain envelope with no return address. I'm thinking that whoever broke into the Valdez household found that letter on his laptop and took it right to the people in Mora."

"Who would benefit from riling these folks?" Ulysses asked.

"Either acequieros or the developers of the golf course, you know, Wild West. Both have a lot to lose if the water transfers are overturned in court."

"My money would be on Wild West."

"Mine too, Ulys."

"What else might be on Antonio's laptop, Ray? You know it's missing, right?"

"Yeah. All his contacts, his data, and probably a few legal arguments he's sketched out. The guy was a historian, a scientist and very good writer. Plus, he knew everybody. I'm sure whoever has the laptop has a trove of information. But Antonio was not one to put really sensitive information on his laptop. He was a little paranoid about getting hacked."

"What did he do with the really sensitive stuff?"

Ray shrugged his shoulders. "I would imagine he hid it in various ways."

"Are you going to meet with the activists in Mora?" Ulysses asked.

"Eventually maybe. But not yet. We need things need to simmer down first. But I wanted you to know about the leak of the letter."

When Ulysses called Agent Tallichet, she said she was on the way there. She came into his office a few minutes later with a cup of coffee and a breakfast burrito. "Mind if I eat while we talk?"

"Not at all," Ulysses said. He opened his drawer and got out a paper plate, some salt and pepper, and a napkin. "Want a fork and knife?"

"No thanks, unless you want to share some?"

"I already ate. I hope you have some information to share with me."

"I do indeed. You can't tell anyone where it came from, though. My boss, Don Barkley, would not be pleased. Since he came on board he's made it clear that sharing the wrong information can lead to termination."

"My lips are sealed. I have a little info for you also."

"Cool, you go first."

Ulysses told LizBeth all Ray had told her about the leak of the letter and the heated meeting in Mora. She ate her burrito and made no comment on his news.

"By the way," LizBeth said, putting down her burrito and wiping her mouth. "If I can get Mondragon to make a statement about Trujillo engaging in extortion and bribery, what will you do?"

"I probably can't do anything before the election. But, I'll talk to the county attorney and get some advice about how to proceed with a big fish like Trujillo. Where are you headed this morning?"

"I'm going to visit a woman named Mabel Martinez at the Taos Pueblo. She asked me to come by to discuss something she was unwilling to bring up on the phone."

"Give Mabel my regards," Ulysses said. "Maybe she'll have some of her pineapple upside down cake for you. We used to always get some on Pueblo feast days. She's an amazing cook. That's her grandson at the front desk. He took over from Lorraine."

"Everyone is related up here," LizBeth said. "Here is what I brought you." She put a folder on Ulysses's desk full of photocopies and put her finger to her lips. "A synopsis of the Cameron RICO case that went nowhere. Handle with care. It looks like this case was nipped in the bud by powers that be well over my pay grade. I'm surprised it's still in the system."

After LizBeth left, Ulysses covered the file and opened his door. In the main office he heard Mark and Zach telling Angela and Eli about their domestic violence call where they'd arrested both partners.

"They're in the cells in back for now but I'm taking them to the Adult Detention Center in a few minutes. I just have to fax this paperwork," Zach said. There were muffled sounds coming from the cells behind a closed door at the end of the hall.

"We had to take their poor dogs to the shelter," Mark said.

"Good thing they don't have children," Angela said.

"Did you guys eat lunch?" Eli asked. "Go ahead and when you get done you can cover for me and Angela." The two deputies left to transport the prisoners and then eat at the Chuck Wagon, their favorite haunt.

The talk about domestic violence set Angela to thinking about Maddy Smith, the woman in Carson who'd called 911. She knocked on Ulysses' door.

"Sheriff, do you have a moment?"

Ulysses had started to peruse the RICO file. He looked up.

"I've been thinking about that woman who called us from Carson on a DV complaint. You know, I never got a chance to actually talk with her and I've been worried about it. Should I do a wellness check?"

"Usually a wellness check is called in by a family member or a neighbor, not something we do on our own, Angela." He looked back at the file.

"I know, Sheriff. But I had a bad feeling about her situation and there's a young child involved."

"We can't be babysitting the population, you know that." Ulysses looked up from the file and noticed his deputy looking at him with an irritated expression. "Why don't you call her?" Ulysses said. "That would be more in keeping with protocol."

"Okay, Sheriff, I'll do that," Angela said. She went to the 911 call log, found the number and placed the call. It rang and rang until voicemail picked up. A young woman's voice answered and asked the caller to leave a message. But when Angela tried, the mailbox was full and not accepting messages.

Agent Tallichet drove to Taos Pueblo to meet with Mabel Martinez, Eli Martinez's grandmother and a good friend of Delfino Mondragon. Mabel lived in an adobe house down a long drive surrounded by fenced pasture where several horses grazed. To the east of the house the Sangre de Cristo Mountains towered, green and forested, unencumbered by roads, development or powerlines. Mabel was hanging sheets on a clothes line near a chicken house. She wore a denim shirtwaist dress and her long salt-and-pepper hair was loose. The sheets were flapping in a stiff wind.

Mabel looked to be about seventy. She greeted LizBeth with a warm smile and said, "Just let me finish this and we can go inside. Would you like some coffee? I have cake left from Sunday, pineapple upside down. It's always better two or three days after it's made."

"Yes," LizBeth said, "I would."

"Good. My poor husband can hardly eat more than a bite or two these days and I don't want it to go to waste." She finished hanging a pair of pillowcases and picked up her basket. "With this wind and sun the clothes will dry fast. Let's get inside."

They walked into a living room where an old man slept in a recliner with the television on at low volume. Mabel invited LizBeth into the kitchen where she'd already set out plates, napkins, forks and coffee cups. She closed the kitchen door and said, "Sam has mesothelioma. He worked many years up at the Lab and before that he was on a Navy submarine. He's not doing so well, but at least he's at home with me. We've had a good life. You can't have everything." Mabel lifted the lid off a cake stand and cut LizBeth a generous piece of cake, then poured them both some coffee. "I can't eat this anymore because of my blood sugar," she said. "Cream for your coffee?"

As LizBeth ate, Mabel talked rapidly in a low voice. "I'm worried about Del. Del is my best friend Gayle's son. Gayle died eight years ago, suddenly. I've never gotten over it." She took a sip of coffee. "People are very divided over the water rights sale. Some people became angry when he came out in support of the sale. Others say he is actually working against the sale. They say that he's made so much money from his art that he doesn't care about the tribe. That isn't true."

"Are you worried that someone will harm Del?"

Mabel waved away the question. "No, it's just gossip. At least I hope it is. But the people behind this, the money people, they seem like they would do anything to get the water for their project."

"When you say 'the money people,' who are you referring to?"

"There's a bunch of them. Senator Ramón Trujillo is one. He tried to get me to talk to Del, at the beginning, to change his mind. Imagine that! He doesn't know Del very well if he thinks I could change his mind! There is a man who follows Trujillo around, Cody Parker. A bodyguard I guess, a big guy, bald, says he's part Comanche, but no one believes him," she said. "I think he's Mexican but he doesn't have an accent. I don't like the look of him. The big boss, drives a Mercedes, has been here to meet with our tribal governor a time or two. My sister has seen him. He walks with a cane." LizBeth heard Mabel's husband call out from the other room. "Let me check on Sam," she said and got up to go to him.

LizBeth looked out the kitchen window and noticed Mabel's back yard contained several large, beautiful sculptures that looked like Mondragon's work. Mabel came back in and got a glass of water for her husband. LizBeth finished the moist, delicious cake and took a sip of coffee, wondering about Mabel's relationship to Mondragon and how she got her information. So far, it seemed mostly like what she had to share was gossip, but LizBeth knew from experience that gossip in a small, close-knit community could carry valuable information.

Mabel came back in and sat down. "He wanted the television off and was thirsty," Mabel said. "Now he sleeps most of the time. Anyway, what was I saying? Oh yes, did I tell you our governor has been wrapped up in this too? I'm pretty sure he's received some bribes because he and his wife just got a brand new Land Rover and redid their kitchen."

Mabel paused and took another sip of coffee.

"Mrs. Martinez, you've told me Del was your best friend's son. Was there anything else special about your relationship?"

Mabel sighed. "Since Gayle died, he's been like a son to me. He's always been a bachelor, you know. I cook for him and he's had meals with Sam and me several nights a week for years. He does odd jobs around here and keeps me up to date on everything that goes on in the council. The only other news I get is from my sister, Rowena; she lives behind the South House, you know, in the old historic part of the pueblo, up against the mountain. We talk a couple of times a day." She paused as if losing her train of thought. "Would you like more coffee?"

"No thank you," LizBeth said. "Mrs. Martinez, there was something you especially wanted to tell me. What was it?"

Mabel paused as if trying to remember. "Oh, yes," she said after a moment. "Did I tell you that Del went up on the mountain for a retreat? He took Raven with him. That's his apprentice, Raven Sandoval."

"Yes, I know," LizBeth said.

"Not that Raven could protect him from anyone. He's such a little thing, he couldn't even protect himself. But at least there will be two of them. Raven is my sister's nephew by marriage…"

"You were going to tell me something, ma'am," LizBeth said, interrupting the distracted woman.

Mabel paused again. "Oh, yes, my goodness. Rowena told me that early this morning she saw that big guy, the bodyguard, headed up the mountain with a pack. Cody Parker."

"How could Parker get permission to go up the mountain unless he's a tribal member?"

Mabel shook her head. "Probably he didn't. But Rowena is certain she saw him. About 5:45 this morning, before full light, she said."

"Would he know his way around up there?" LizBeth asked.

"I don't know," Mabel said. "The trails are pretty well marked, I think. I don't go up to the ceremonials anymore, these last years, what with Sam and all."

LizBeth asked, "How long did Del tell you he'd be up there?"

"He said he'd be back for the funeral, his sister Reina's husband, the one who was killed," Mabel replied.

LizBeth finished her coffee and put her napkin on the table. "Thank you for the information, Mrs. Martinez, and for the delicious cake. Sheriff Walker told me about your pineapple upside down cake. He sent his regards."

"Oh, you know little Ulys? I guess he's not so little anymore, is he? What a sweet child he was. So helpful and always had a big appetite on feast days. I haven't seen him in quite a few years."

"I believe your grandson, Eli, is working for him now?"

Mabel looked confused for a minute. "Yes," she said, "Eli. Used to be Halona, but I always knew that child had a man's spirit. She'll do a good job for Ulys. She's…he's smart as a whip! First in the family to go to college." She chuckled. "It's good for children to grow up to be who they are. Try to keep Del safe, will you?"

The Sheriff's Department was quiet in the midafternoon lull, not long before shift change. Eli was replenishing office supplies from the supply closet to his desk. Zach and Mark were completing their shift paperwork and Angela had just tried to reach Maddy Smith again with no success.

"Did you bring lunch?" Angela asked Eli.

"No, but.."

"Want to share my chef's salad? It's big enough for two."

Angela forwarded the phones to Dakota while she and Eli went into the small break room. Angela split the salad on two plates and filled their glasses with water. Eli found forks and napkins. He closed the door and they both sat at the room's only table.

"How did you become a deputy?" Eli asked.

"I applied for the job four years ago, right after Sheriff was elected. The former sheriff, Trujillo, lost a lot of staff there at the end and there were openings he needed filled fast."

"What kind of qualifications did you have for the job?"

"Are you thinking you'd rather be a deputy than the secretary?"

"Well, not exactly," Eli answered, smiling at Angela's question. "I'm just trying to understand stuff. You know, what makes this place work."

"I got my B.A. in criminal justice from New Mexico State. This was my first real job out of college."

"So you've always been interested in law enforcement?'

"Pretty much," Angela answered, looking closely at Eli. *Can I trust him?* she wondered. Angela tended to avoid close relationships with men and didn't typically trust other women. But she was drawn to Eli's soft-spoken manner. She took another bite of salad and chewed thoughtfully. "My mother disappeared when I was twelve. The police looked for her for about three months, then more or less gave up. I always thought somebody should do a better job."

"It must have been hard to lose your mother like that," he said at last. "How was it for your father?"

"He passed when I was sixteen. My mother's disappearance was hard for him but he never talked about it. At least not to me. His parents thought she'd run off with another man. Lots of people thought she'd been murdered. I kept hoping she'd come home, but eventually I had to accept that I'd probably never see her again."

"Wow, so you are an orphan?" Eli asked in a soft voice.

Angela nodded. "After my father's death, my grandparents took care of me until I was ready for college. My father left me our house and a little money. I went to college on the lottery scholarship."

Eli got up and took their paper plates to the trash, then rinsed the forks and glasses and put them in the dishwasher. "Are you satisfied you found the right job?"

Angela wiped down the table. "Pretty satisfied, yes. Sheriff runs a good team. He doesn't discriminate because I'm female."

"He does seem fair," Eli said. "Hey, thanks for lunch. I'm liking getting to know you."

"Next time I get to ask the questions," Angela said.

Dakota, the 911 operator, ducked into the room when they were finished and said, "Angela, a woman called you about someone named Maddy Smith. She left a phone number for a call back. I put it on your desk."

Angela called the woman back and she picked up on the first ring.

"This is Deputy Romero," Angela said, "you wanted to speak with me?"

"I met you at the Carson Post Office when you were looking for Maddy Smith. I'm Cicely Duncan. Can you meet me at the Springs Hotel in Ojo Caliente? I get off my shift at 4."

"Yes, I can meet you. Where will you be?"

"I'll be in the parking lot."

"Do you have information about Maddy?" Angela asked, but the woman had already hung up.

The drive to Ojo Caliente took about forty minutes. Angela told Eli and Sheriff where she was going. The afternoon was hot and windy, and the UV was intense, but she was happy to see the first large cumulous clouds towering over the mountains, indicating a possible change in the weather. Those huge puffy white clouds tended to gather when the monsoons were approaching, but it was early for that. Still, they might bring an afternoon thundershower, a relief from a spell of dry, windy days. Angela refilled her water bottle and checked her weapon, then got into the department's unmarked car to make the drive across the mesa, through Carson and beyond to the village of Ojo Caliente, the site of a natural hot springs which had been a popular spa for almost one hundred years. Around 4 she pulled into the Springs property and crossed the Ojo River, then came into a gravel parking lot shaded by large cottonwoods. The pink-haired girl was standing outside the Ojo Caliente historic hotel near a beater car, smoking a cigarette. She was dressed in a maid's uniform. As soon as she saw Angela, she put her cigarette out and came up to her car.

"Can I get in?" she asked and quickly climbed inside the car. "Let's go over to the RV area. There's hardly anyone there."

The RV area along the river bank was thick with trees and shrubs. Angela parked where the girl indicated, in a secluded spot near the end of the lot.

"I don't want anyone to see us talking," she said.

"How do you know Maddy?" Angela asked.

"Before she had her baby she used to wait tables here. Sometimes she drove me to work. Then she got involved with the scary guy." "Why do you call him that?" Angela asked.

"He's mean and he's an abuser. Yesterday he came by here on my lunch break to threaten me," Cicely said. "He said if I spoke with the cops again, he'd 'fuck me up.' Those were the words he used. My mom said I should tell you right away."

"How did he find out you had spoken to the cops?"

"It might have been Jolie who told him, the girl I was with when you saw us at the post office. She's friends with him."

"What is this guy's name?" Angela asked.

"Maddy called him Las. I don't really know. He has L.K. tattooed on his hand and I think those might be his initials."

"What does he look like?"

"He's Anglo, in his thirties. About six feet tall. Black hair he wears in a ponytail. Clean shaven, blue eyes. Lean and muscley. I used to think he was handsome."

"Do you know where he lives?"

"Somewhere over in Tres Piedras in a travel trailer," Cicely said. "But I don't know where, exactly."

"What does he drive?"

"He has a new truck. Grey Dodge Ram. Still has the temporary tags."

"Where does he work?"

"I don't know if he has a job but Maddy said he has plenty of money."

Cicely took out another cigarette and her lighter. "Mind if I smoke?" Without her black lipstick she looked much younger and more vulnerable. Her nails were bitten down to the quick.

"Not in here," Angela said, "but we can go sit at that picnic table over there near the river."

"No, someone might see us. I'll just wait," Cicely said. "I don't want to take any chances."

"Is this man Maddy's baby's father?" Angela asked.

"No. She only met him about six months ago. The baby's father lives in Rinconada."

"What is his name?"

"Jared Renfro."

"Does she have any relatives in the area that you know of?"

"Not that I know of."

"Have you seen Maddy since we talked the first time?"

"No. But Mom and I drove by her place and it was completely trashed. The front door was standing open and her car was gone. That's when I started to get really worried."

"Cicely, do you live alone?" Angela asked. She was starting to worry not only about Maddy but also about Cicely.

"No, I live with my mother and my brother."

"What do they think about these threats?"

"My brother is only twelve. But my mother takes this stuff seriously. She has a pistol and a Bushmaster and is a pretty good shot."

"Okay, well, you be careful. You are really brave to come forward. I wouldn't want anything to happen to you."

"Thank you. I am tougher than I look. Me and my family, we've been through a lot. We don't take too well to getting threatened."

"Good for you," Angela said.

"I'd love to have a job like yours," Cicely said. "Helping people and all. Cleaning hotel rooms is all I've ever done."

"Did you finish high school?" Angela asked.

"No. We had to leave Alamosa when I was in tenth grade. My dad got injured at work. He was addicted to oxy and kind of went crazy. He beat up my mom bad so we came down here where he can't find us. Anyway, I got a job then and I been working ever since."

"Well, if you ever want to talk about how to get a GED, call me and I'll put you in touch with a program. From there it isn't too hard to get an associate's degree. That's all you need to get into law enforcement at a basic level."

"Thanks."

"Call me if you see that man again."

"I will."

Angela took Cicely back to her car just as thunder rolled. The sky was now fully overcast and a few fat drops of rain fell on her windshield as she drove back across the empty llano. Due to the dryness of the air, some of the clouds were shedding rain that failed to reach the ground.

Angela was relieved to find Sheriff in his office looking at his computer when she came in. "I just came back from an interesting meeting," she said. "I wanted to tell you about it."

"You drove over to Ojo Caliente to meet the friend of the missing girl?" Ulysses asked.

"Yes, but it may have links to our murder case, too. One of the young women I spoke with on my first visit to Carson called me.

She works as a maid at The Springs Hotel. Maddy's boyfriend came by her house and threatened her if she spoke to law enforcement again. That was why she wanted to meet me at her work."

"Did she know anything about Smith's whereabouts?"

"No, nothing. But she told me some things about Maddy's boyfriend. For one, he drives a late model grey truck, a Dodge, with dealer tags and tinted windows."

Ulysses scooted back in his chair and stood up. "Did she describe the guy?"

"Late thirties, about six feet tall, black hair, pony tail, clean shaven. Tattoo of L.K. on his hand."

"That's the guy who was stalking Delilah," Ulysses said. "Same car, dark hair and a ponytail. What is his name?"

"She thought Maddy called him Las, or Les. She didn't know more than that. She also said she went by Smith's yurt and it was trashed. Her car was also gone. I confirmed this. Doesn't Smith qualify as a missing person now?"

"Yeah, it's been long enough. Does she have any next of kin?"

"Her baby's father lives in Rinconada. Named Jared Renfro. Cicely didn't know of anyone else."

"Where does Cicely live?"

"With her mother and brother somewhere near Carson. Cicely said they are armed and used to protecting themselves."

"That's what a lot of people think," Ulysses said. "Maybe we can catch up with this man so they don't have to. See if you can locate Jared Renfro and pay him a visit, will you?"

"Yes, Sheriff."

"Good work, Deputy. I'm studying for my interview with Stu Wishard tomorrow."

"That sounds like fun," Angela said.

Chapter 8

Trey Cameron sat outside enjoying his breakfast in the cool spring morning at his expansive home on the llano west of Taos. His table was laid under the grape arbor by the pool. He rested his bad leg on an ottoman.

Cameron had lost his leg below the knee in a car accident twenty years ago. He was lucky to have survived the accident. His former girlfriend, who was driving, had been killed. The stump was sore this morning after Cameron overexerted playing golf. The pain made him irritable.

The butler, Ron, had brought Cameron coffee and freshly squeezed orange juice which he sipped waiting for his steak and eggs that were soon to follow. He briefly scanned *The Wall Street Journal* on his computer, annoyed by the headlines. He had a long, busy day ahead full of appointments made by his chief of staff.

Just as he finished his coffee, Ron arrived with two eggs scrambled and the petite filet Cameron ate most mornings. Ron tucked a napkin into the collar of his boss's white shirt and made sure it covered his expensive tie. In a few minutes Cameron had a meeting with Gilbert Herrera, the State Engineer, to check on plans for the cross-basin water transfer paperwork. He noted that Ron had placed Herrera's fat envelope of money on the table. An installment of $10,000 on his $100,000 commitment. Herrera was a useful fool to Cameron's mind, greedy and stupid. The business with him could be quickly dispatched.

After Herrera, Cameron had a scheduled phone call with his CFO about a problem with a large loan he was trying to obtain.

He didn't look forward to that call. His CFO was "insufficiently subordinate" in his opinion, and lately he'd been thinking of replacing her with someone more compliant. This loan should never have become a problem for him.

After lunch he would be driven to Santa Fe to meet with Governor Montaño and some representatives of the Mora land grant to discuss sensitive cultural aspects of Highland Fling. Gilbert Herrera, the State Engineer, would also attend this meeting. Cameron's valet and bodyguard, Rowdy, would chauffeur him.

These cultural sensitivity meetings were so tiresome to Cameron, but he knew he had to tread carefully in New Mexico. The governor was purported to be favorable toward the project, but the state was rife with tension and political divisions. One false move could endanger his investment. He needn't worry about cultural sensitivity when he met with James Halloran, Forest Supervisor for the Carson National Forest for a drink before dinner. Halloran, an ambitious man, was fully on board. Finally, this evening, he'd have dinner with his old fraternity brother, FBI Field Office Director Don Barkley, at Geronimo's in Santa Fe.

Cameron liked to eat his breakfast alone. He had instructed his wife, Cili to bring his seven-year-old daughters for his inspection once they were fully dressed and ready to go to their fully outfitted home classroom. The twins, who were fraternal, were both blonde and blue-eyed like his wife. At eight-thirty they would go upstairs to be instructed by the Taiwanese governess/tutor who lived on the property. Cili would join him for a second cup of coffee before she headed into Taos for a Pilates class, followed by her tennis lesson at the club, lunch and a massage. Cili's assistant provided Cameron with his wife's schedule and updated him daily on any changes. Cameron knew Cili chaffed at the limitations to her lifestyle posed by their location. Cili was an obedient wife for the most part and fulfilled all her obligations. Cameron was glad he had a solid prenuptial agreement in place that would cause her to reconsider any impulse toward misbehavior.

Cameron had promised his wife that once all the contracts on Highland Fling had been signed and the primary election was over, he would fly her and the children for a long visit with her family and friends in Budapest and Vienna. She wanted to relocate to their house in Texas and keep this place as a weekend escape, but Cameron found the heat in his home state all but unbearable. Maybe they could move to Budapest instead.

Right on time, the girls, suitably dressed for school in plaid skirts and weskits, came to kiss their father before being hurried away by their governess. Cili, already wearing her Pilates clothes, put down her handbag, racket and tennis dress and sat down next to her husband. Cameron noticed with satisfaction that his wife was looking slim and fit this morning. Most people would never guess she had recently turned forty. Ron brought a French press on a tray and Cili served her husband his second cup of coffee while Ron took away the breakfast dishes.

"Good morning, dear," Cili said. "Did you sleep well?" She spoke with a heavy Hungarian accent that Cameron loved and associated with his parents, who immigrated to the United States before their only child was born.

"Not well, but enough," Cameron answered. "Who will you be having lunch with today?" Cameron disliked that his wife sometimes ate with a tennis pro, a Mexican man he both disdained and distrusted who was his wife's age and considered to be handsome.

Cili looked out to the northwest where the solitary volcanic dome called Ute Mountain shimmered from across the mesa. "I'm lunching with Emily," she said, not meeting her husband's eye.

"Just the two of you?" he asked.

Cili nodded. Cameron thought, *she's not a very good liar. I'll make sure Parker checks on her.* Rowdy Eustace was the security staffer who Cameron usually favored for discreet jobs like this one. He was clean-cut and a churchgoer. But Rowdy would be unavailable today.

His other staff were considerably rougher, but then he had also chosen them for activities compatible with those traits. "I am meeting with the governor this afternoon," Cameron said. "She could be quite valuable in getting the final approvals for Highland Fling."

"Yes, that will be good," Cili said, looking at her varnished pink fingernails.

"Then I'm having dinner with Don Barkley."

"I've heard you mention him," she said, looking at the distant horizon. Cameron regarded her beautiful profile and found it still enchanted him. It was her prettiest angle by far. No sagging yet under the lovely chin.

"Don is my old fraternity brother from UT," Cameron said. "He recently took a job as director of the FBI field office in Albuquerque."

Cili's eyes flickered over to her husband's with a slight frown. "FBI?" she asked.

"Don is a friend. He might prove to be useful."

"I hope your meetings are successful," she said. "Will you be wanting to see me before I go to bed?"

Cameron looked at his watch. *Where was Herrera? He should be here by now.* "Wait for me until ten o'clock tonight. If I arrive after that I will be too tired to desire your company." He smiled and took her hand briefly. She smiled back, also briefly, then leaned over and kissed him on the cheek. "I will see you later, then," she said, then stood and collected her things.

"Be good!" he said, wagging a finger at her.

Ron came to collect the coffee tray and brought Cameron the cane with a silver head of a griffin that he'd bought in Inverness on his first visit, when he'd first come up with the idea of building a Scottish style golf course. Cameron's father had changed the family name from Nagy before Cameron was born. In spite of his Eastern European heritage, Cameron, like his father before him, admired all things Scottish, except for their liberal politics and assertive women.

Cili crossed the pool area and opened the sliding glass door to Gilbert Herrera, a small man in his fifties with greying hair and hunched shoulders, wearing a bolo tie and a cowboy hat. Ron escorted Herrera to the table where Cameron was sitting.

"Good morning, sir," he said. "I'm sorry I'm late."

"Sit down, Gilbert," Cameron said. "What caused the delay?"

"I just received a call from Senator Ramón Trujillo. He said it was urgent."

"What did the good Senator want?"

"He wanted to discuss the Taos Pueblo project."

"What specifically, Gil?" Cameron asked.

"Senator Trujillo believes that opposition to the plan is building both in Mora and at Taos Pueblo." Herrera cleared his throat and adjusted his hat. Ron offered him coffee, but he said, "Just water please."

Cameron felt irritated by this man whom he'd known since childhood. Herrera's father had been a hard-working employee of his father's company, Big Hat. Gilbert, the son, after attending college paid for by Cameron's father, was still beholden to the family. But Cameron thought of Gil as weak and on the lazy side. It was the way he felt about most Hispanic people.

"Gil, what you are telling me is none of your concern. You just need to make sure that approval for the cross-basin transfer is finalized. That is the sum total of your duties and why you were hired for this position. Do you understand?" Cameron pushed the envelope of cash toward Herrera, who picked it up and put it in his suit jacket pocket.

"If Trujillo contacts you again, redirect him to me, is that clear?"

"Yes, Mr. Cameron."

"So, how is the deal progressing?"

"I signed the papers your lawyers drew up yesterday. They've been sent to the governor. If you are correct that the governor is on board, we should be okay unless someone files suit."

"Don't worry about lawsuits. I have that covered. You focus on keeping the governor in our camp."

"Sir, I can't figure her out. I'm not sure where she stands..."

Cameron said, "Gilbert, that is the problem you must solve. Solve it, please."

Stephanie Gold arrived at Ulysses' office early to help him prepare for his big interview.

Ulysses was going over the notes he'd made on what he expected to be asked in what was supposed to be a radio interview.

"Good morning, Sheriff Walker, are you ready for prime time?" Stephanie had come from her morning ride at the barn and was dressed in riding pants, a denim shirt and cowboy boots, her blonde hair in a single thick braid. "Did I tell you the visuals are going to be livestreamed?"

"No, you did not," Ulysses said. He looked around at his office and noticed what a mess it was. *Had Lorraine tidied up his office? Probably she did, and I never even noticed. That explains why it's been such a mess since she left.*

"We better get this place looking a little better for your audience. How about I get Eli to help?"

Eli came in and surveyed the situation. "Sheriff, shall I arrange your desk so it looks neater and less cluttered? Mind if I move these pictures of your family and your award from the Governor so they are behind you and on camera?"

"Let's put the flags behind him also," Stephanie said. "Off to his right." She looked at Ulysses. "Did you bring a tie?" she asked.

"I never wear a tie," Ulysses answered, opening his desk drawer, "but Rosemary put one in here about year ago." He rooted around in his drawer and pulled out a leather bolo tie with a turquoise slide and silver tips. "What do you think?"

"Perfect," Stephanie said. "It will bring out your eyes. Here, let me," she said smiling at him. She stepped in close, lifted up his tan collar, widened the slide and slipped the tie over his head, coming so close Ulysses felt she might kiss him. Stephanie smelled of sweat, horse and her perfume. Ulysses felt her erotic energy and felt aroused for a moment. He stepped back abruptly. "I can do it," he said, too sharply.

Stephanie gave him a puzzled look.

Eli, arranging the pictures and awards on the credenza, appeared not to notice the interaction. Ulysses went into the bathroom and splashed cold water on his face. When he came out Eli was cleaning his computer monitor. He had installed a clip-on lamp to improve the lighting. Stephanie was going over his notes and making edits. She handed her edits to Ulysses without a word and slipped out of the office while Ulysses was getting settled for the interview. *I hurt her feelings,* Ulysses thought. *Was she coming on to me or am I imagining she was?*

Suddenly his computer came to life and he saw a balding white man in his fifties wearing a navy suit and a bright pink tie.

"Good morning, Sheriff Ulysses Walker of Taos County! Welcome to a live show of Battlelines with Stu Wishard." The man gave a broad, wolfish smile.

"Hello, Stu, thank you for having me." Ulysses put on his game face—sincere and somewhat stern with unrelenting eye contact.

"Let's get right down to it, Sheriff Walker. You are in a tough bid for re-election against native son, Ernesto Ruiz, who has surged in recent weeks because of rumors that you are anti-Catholic."

"Stu, I want our listeners to understand that these rumors are false and are spread to distract voters. I respect all religions and faiths. Religion is an important part of our culture here in New Mexico. And also, just FYI, I also was born and raised in Taos County."

"Well, many voters are upset that Archbishop Sullivan, who was much beloved, was murdered on your watch, Sheriff. What do you have to say about that?"

"Archbishop Sullivan was murdered by a psychopath who had a personal vendetta related to abuse of minors by priests."

"So are you saying Archbishop Sullivan was guilty of child abuse?"

"I'm not saying that, but the Governor's Task Force on Clergy Abuse determined that the Archbishop knew that child sexual abuse was going on and did nothing to stop it."

"This is a line of reasoning that anti-Catholics use to discredit the clergy," Wishard said in a belligerent tone.

"Those are the facts, Stu. The Governor formed the task force and a full report has been issued. I encourage you to read it if you haven't. The rest is politics. I think the voters of Taos County understand this."

Ulysses looked up from his monitor. Angela had slipped into the room to listen. She gave him a thumbs up.

"Ernesto Ruiz says if elected he will be a constitutional sheriff. Do you also subscribe to this type of law enforcement?"

"No, I do not. And I will tell you why. Perhaps you don't know this, but sheriffs are not mentioned even once in the Constitution of the United States. If I am re-elected I will do as I have done in my first term, which is to enforce all of the laws of New Mexico without fear or favor."

"Does that mean you won't respect the Second Amendment?" Wishard asked.

"Certainly not. New Mexico currently has strong second amendment protections. We are an open carry state. I will uphold all of our laws, even ones I personally disagree with."

"Can you give me an example of a gun law you don't agree with, Sheriff?"

"I'm not stepping into that trap, Stu," Ulysses said and laughed. "Look, my personal views are irrelevant when it comes to the law. The law is the law and in my administration that is all there is to it."

"It's been said that domestic violence has had a big spike on your watch. What is your explanation for that?"

"Domestic violence spiked all over this country during the pandemic. Numbers have actually come down in the past six months, but they are still too high. I have dedicated a great deal of effort to increasing safety for the women of Taos by opening the Women's Shelter to get homeless women off the street and provide beds for victims of domestic violence. We've also started a "warm line" so that women considering leaving an abusive relationship can talk to a trained volunteer. Over time these efforts will continue to reduce violence against women."

"With the ongoing drought and the lack of snowpack in the mountains, it seems like water squabbles are picking up around your county. As sheriff, will you be taking a firmer hand with the misuse of water resources within acequias and domestic mutual water systems?"

"Water use in acequias and domestic mutual water systems very rarely comes into the purview of the sheriff, Stu. The only time it does is when there is some kind of violence. New Mexico acequias are governed by their commissions, who are elected by their parciantes. Domestic water systems are governed by their boards. As sheriff I will continue to respect the laws in place around these entities and only step in if and when a crime has been committed."

"What if someone is stealing water during a drought, robbing farmers and ranchers of what they are due?"

"I would only intervene if there was an actual crime, Stu. The mayordomos handle misbehavior like stealing water on their acequias with fines and the like."

"Sheriff Walker, we have a few callers on the phones who want to ask you some questions, are you ready for that?"

"Of course. Go ahead," Ulysses said. *So far so good*, he thought.

A woman's voice came on the line. "Sheriff Walker," the woman said. "I've heard that your wife has been cited for stealing water. Is that true, and if it is what are you going to do about it?" Angela and Eli looked alarmed and Ulysses felt his heartrate spike.

"Ma'am, I don't know where you heard that information, but it is not true. My wife has never been cited for stealing water," Ulysses said. *Where the hell does this stuff come from?* he wondered.

"That's not what I heard. I live in your area and everyone says Rosemary Walker takes water out of turn and people downstream from her don't get any."

"I won't listen to these falsehoods," Ulysses said firmly. "Ma'am, what is your name?" The woman hung up the phone. "Stu, that woman was not telling the truth and your call screeners should have picked up that she was planning on smearing my wife."

"Sir, on Battlelines I want to hear from any citizen about their concerns, whatever they are. Do you have time for one more caller?" Before Ulysses could reply, another woman came on the line.

"Hello, Sheriff Walker," another woman said. "Three years ago my son tried to jump off the Rio Grande Gorge Bridge during a psychotic depression episode. You and your deputy talked him down from the railing and saved his life. My husband and I wanted to thank you. Because of you, he's still alive and he's doing much better."

"Ma'am, I really appreciate you telling me that. Suicide continues to be a leading cause of death for our young people and we need to do more to help. It's really good news that he is feeling so much better."

"That's all the time we have, folks," Wishard said in his booming radio voice. "Thank you for being on the call, Mr. Walker. That was Ulysses Walker, running against Ernesto Ruiz for Sheriff of Taos County." Wishard ended the call.

"Whew, I'm glad that's over," Ulysses said. "You did great, sir," Eli said. "You really sounded in control."

"I thought you handled that first caller so well," Angela said. "I hate that she attacked Mrs. Walker like that."

"I really hope Rosemary didn't hear it," Ulysses said.

Just then Ulysses' cellphone rang and it was Rosemary. "You were awesome, Ulys," she said, "and don't worry about that first caller. You put her right in her place. I actually recognized her voice."

"Who was it?" Ulysses asked.

"I'll tell you when you get home," Rosemary said.

After Ulysses hung up with Rosemary, he found Agent Tallichet knocking on his door. "I need a favor," she said.

"What can I do?"

"I have a dog team meeting me at Taos Pueblo tomorrow at dawn. We are going up on the mountain to look for Mondragon."

"How come?"

"Mabel Martinez told me yesterday that her sister saw a man going up the trail toward Blue Lake with a backpack at dawn. Her sister said it was Cody Parker, a man with a bad reputation who sometimes works for Ramón Trujillo. So, I decided to go check on the situation right away."

"But won't Mondragon be back this evening for Antonio's funeral?"

"He's already missed it. The funeral was at eleven o'clock."

Ulysses looked at his watch and then at the calendar on his desk. Sure enough, he'd missed the time of the funeral. *This damn election,* he thought, *it's interfering with my job.* "Didn't Mondragon leave word as to where he'd be?"

"No, he didn't, and that part of the pueblo is tens of thousands of acres of mountain wilderness. I wouldn't dream of going there without trackers. Plus many of the men who run the teams are Native so they won't run afoul of the rules," she said.

"How hard is it to get permission from the tribe to go up on Taos Mountain?" Ulysses asked.

"A lot harder that I thought."

"Why is that?"

"Barkley, my boss, started off saying a search was unnecessary and intrusive, which is complete bull. So we argued for a while and eventually he said I needed to get a tribal member to accompany me. I don't really know any tribal members who could make it up that trail, so I went to the tribal chief of police to ask him. Turns out he is the tribal governor's younger brother and the governor is cozy with Trujillo. Surprise, surprise, the chief of police said he couldn't spare anyone from force to go with me. Then I remembered Eli!"

"Have you talked with him?"

"Of course not. I wanted to get your permission."

"How long will you be gone?"

"All day tomorrow. I have the team from 7 am to 7 pm."

"I'd have to get coverage for him, but other than that I have no objection. Why don't you go ahead and see if he's willing to do it, and I'll see if one of my deputies can cover the desk."

"I'll owe you, Ulys. Big time. Thanks."

When LizBeth spoke with Eli, she found he had already talked to his grandmother, who knew through the granny grapevine about the FBI agent's need for a tribal member to accompany her up the mountain on a search. Eli had already asked Zach to cover in case he got tapped to go.

"I'll meet you at the Pueblo at 6:00 am," LizBeth said. "Bring a pack with food and water and everything you think you'll need."

"You got it, Agent Tallichet. I'll see you in the morning."

When LizBeth left, Ulysses called Eli into the office.

"I appreciate you being willing to help out on this case, Eli. But I want you to be clear that you are not going as law enforcement," Ulysses said.

"I understand, Sheriff. But is it okay if I bring my gun?"

Ulysses was surprised at the request. "Why are you thinking you need to be armed?"

"Sir, my grandmother gave me to understand that Cody Parker is involved. I know him a little and I don't trust him to be, shall we say, friendly."

"I can't stop you from carrying a gun for self-defense, Eli. But again, you need to understand that you are to do exactly what Agent Tallichet tells you to do and nothing else."

"I understand, Sheriff."

"How do you know Cody Parker?" Ulysses asked.

"I've seen him around the pueblo from time to time over a few years. I once saw him shoot a dog just because she growled at him. She had puppies. Anyway, everyone is a little afraid of him."

"Well, be careful. I wouldn't want you to get hurt on this outing."

"Thanks, Sheriff. I'll be careful."

Ulysses planned to meet Ray for lunch at the brand new Picuris Travel Center and then pay a visit to John and Barbara Salazar.

After the light rain the day before, the air was cooler and the wind was blessedly still. When he came out of the office, Ulysses noticed that the climbing rose that Lorraine cared for over the years was covered in crimson blooms and wet from a recent watering. He felt grateful that someone, probably Angela, had attended to this detail in the dry weather. Ulysses took a deep breath and climbed into the Expedition. It would be good to get out of the office.

Ray was waiting for him outside the Travel Center and the two men went in, ordered sub sandwiches, iced tea from the deli, and sat in a booth near the door. "Pretty nice place you have here," Ulysses said looking around the store and restaurant. "How is it going?"

"Good, so far," Ray said, biting into his turkey club sandwich. "A lot of the community comes here of course, and we attract business from people going camping in Santa Barbara campground. Clarice is happy to be able to be able to buy some staples close to home. And, as expected, we are selling a lot of gas with low reservation prices."

"Have you had any further unauthorized people coming to the pueblo?"

"No. Just that one time."

Ulysses showed Ray the picture Delilah took of the truck outside her house. "Does this look familiar?"

Ray put on reading glasses and looked closely at the image on Ulysses' phone. "Yes, that looks like the truck I saw at the pueblo. I'd like to show this to Matt."

"I'll send it to you," Ulysses said. "Our friend LizBeth Tallichet stopped by to tell me that she's taking a dog team up on Taos Mountain tomorrow to look for Delfino Mondragon, you know, Delilah's uncle."

"He wasn't at Antonio's funeral this morning," Ray said. "He was expected but Delilah didn't seem to be worried about him."

"LizBeth said a man might have been sent up there to apply some persuasion."

Ray whistled under his breath. He wiped his mouth with his napkin and took a drink of iced tea. "Who?" he asked.

"A man named Cody Parker. Works for Ramón Trujillo. Eli says he's a bad actor."

"I know Cody Parker," Ray said. "He's definitely bad news. I arrested him in Albuquerque when he was a juvenile, and I know he's spent some time in the State Pen for aggravated assault and battery. Why in hell would Trujillo employ him?"

"They call it security. Racketeers always have thugs on the payroll. Brenda Diggs told me Jeremy worked as muscle for Cameron years ago back in Texas."

"This is way out of hand, Ulys. These guys act like mobsters."

"And they're backing my opponent in the election," Ulysses

said ruefully. "Have you spoken with Delilah about the letter from your ancestor you found?"

"No, not at a funeral."

"Do you think the Picuris tribe will hire her to restore your water?"

"I have to get our tribal council and governor on board first. We have to pay for her services and that law firm is expensive."

Ulysses finished his sandwich and they sat in silence for a while. The sunny restaurant was starting to empty out after the lunch rush.

"Can you tell me more about that meeting in Mora?" Ulysses asked.

"I wasn't there, you know. My contact is a journalist named Rita Wainwright who lives in Chacón. She and I became acquainted two years ago. Rita comes to our dances and she and Sarah, my daughter-in-law are friends. She called me after the meeting to tell me about it."

"Did the meeting get heated?" Ulysses asked.

"It did. According to Rita, the people in Mora are on a hair trigger since the fires destroyed their homes. A lot of folks just want to sell. They don't want to wait on FEMA. They're demoralized and they don't want to rebuild." Ray took a breath mint from a roll and started to suck on it. He shook his head. "Other people, like the land grant folks, are angry. They see all this land changing hands. An influx of rich Anglos threatens their culture."

"It's like a replay from the days of old Santa Fe Ring where rich Anglo lawyers stole land from the land grants and got richer," Ulysses said, shaking his head about a dark period of New Mexico history. "But how does it involve the transfers of water?"

"Ulys, the developers, Cameron and his bunch, want this land *because of water. Our water.* There won't be a golf course and luxury condos if they can't irrigate their greens and flush their toilets. So they turn the local guys, the acequieros, ranchers and land grant activists in Mora against some other local guys, the Picuris tribe. It's a big distraction from what is really going on."

"Does that mean that Picuris fighting the transfers has become even more inflammatory?" Ulysses asked.

"Probably," Ray said. "I don't think the folks in Mora would be agreeable to ending the transfers on a good day. And this definitely isn't a good day for them."

"Okay, so, Cameron distracts the Mora people's attention from all the land being bought out from under them by stoking fears that Picuris is going to take their water, right?"

"Right," Ray said. "And Trujillo works Taos Pueblo by dividing the tribe with bribes and threats to win the tribal council vote."

"Do you think you could try to explain this to the Mora people?"

"Are you crazy? This old Indian doesn't want to poke a hornet's nest. I mean why would they trust me?"

"That makes sense. But what about explaining it to Taos? Aren't they a sister tribe, sort of?"

"Ulys, you are full of good ideas today," Ray chuckled. "Man, it's not my job to convince Taos not to sell their water to these racketeers."

"True enough," Ulysses said. "I just thought I'd try. So now what do you do?"

"There is another meeting tonight at the fire station. Rita promised to give me a report."

"Let me know how it goes."

"Bottom line, we don't want a water war. If we're going to win back our water, it is going to be in court. I'm counting on Delilah to run with this ball if we can work out the financing. But she's got to get her feet back under her after her father's murder."

Ulysses dropped in at the Salazar residence where John was working in his garage. He showed Salazar the picture Delilah sent him of the truck that had parked outside her house. Salazar said he thought the vehicle in the photo could be the truck he'd seen parked on the side of the road in front of Antonio Valdez's house the night he was killed. It was the right age and color. "Those big trucks all look alike to me, so I can't vouch for the make and model," he said. Ulysses noticed Salazar was charging a new electric car. "I hope you catch Antonio's killer," Salazar said. "You should have seen how many people came to his funeral. It's a huge loss for this community."

Ulysses pulled out of the Salazar driveway and decided to pay a visit to Dr. Vigil. Without the make, model, and license plate number, there wasn't much he could do to trace this truck, but he had something else he could look into. He reached into the center console of the Expedition and found the evidence bag with the cigarette butts he'd taken from the home of Brenda Diggs.

Dr. Vigil was alone in his windowless office at the Taos County Medical Examiners Building, a rambling one-story stucco building near the courthouse complex that housed a room of cadaver coolers, an exam room, and three offices. It served as a satellite to the larger main morgue established in Santa Fe several years back. Dr. Vigil was sitting at his desk typing on his computer and looked surprised when Ulysses knocked on his open door.

"I was just thinking of coming to see you, Sheriff," the coroner said. "I have the report on Jeremy Diggs for you."

"What's the story?" Ulysses asked.

"Death was by drowning. And as you thought, Diggs was hit in the back of the head with a shovel and knocked unconscious, in a sequence quite similar to Mr. Valdez. The difference though is that it appears to have been a struggle prior to that blow. No element of surprise. Diggs had bruises on his knuckles probably from blows he landed. I think Diggs put up quite a fight. But he was wearing gloves, so I've got nothing from his fingernails. There may be something on the shovel though."

Ulysses pulled the evidence bag with the butts out of his pocket. "I wonder if you see if any DNA from whoever was smoking these cigarettes?"

Vigil adjusted his readers on his nose and looked in the evidence bag. "Where did you get these?" he asked.

"Brenda Diggs's sister Loretta found them. Brenda said a man was at her house the night Antonio Valdez was killed and he left these butts."

"I'll send them off. We'll see what comes back," Dr. Vigil said.

"Have you released the body yet?"

"No, it is still here," Vigil answered. "Would you like to look at anything?"

"Did he have a case of poison ivy?" Ulysses asked. He'd rather not look at the corpse of Jeremy Diggs unless he had to.

"Funny you should ask," Vigil said. "He did. Of course, he was a mayordomo and that is kind of an occupational hazard. But yes, he had a bad case on his arms and his right hand. Like he'd grabbed a plant or something."

"He might have grabbed a poison ivy vine. Anything else I should know about Digg's body?" Ulysses asked.

"A small tattoo on the underside of his left wrist. 'L. K.' Looked like a jailhouse-type tattoo. I see them a lot. Sometimes the inmates do them to themselves, sometimes gang members do it for them, to point out who is in charge."

"I guess I better look at that," Ulysses said.

Vigil pulled on rubber gloves and took Ulysses into the cooler room where two rows of six coolers rumbled under a rack of fluorescent lights. "All of these are empty right now except this one," Vigil said, opening a door and pulling out the stretcher inside. The earthly remains of Jeremy Diggs, blue-white and unpleasant-smelling, filled Ulysses with disgust and the urge to vomit which he effectively hid. The chest, neck and right arm were covered with reddish blisters. Ulysses managed to look at Digg's face without really seeing it. But when Dr. Vigil lifted his left arm and exposed the underside of his wrist, Ulysses noted a long, jagged scar running from his wrist to the inside of his elbow. On one side of the scar was a crude tattoo of a knife dripping blood and the initials L. K.

"It looks like he might have tried to cut his wrist at some point," Ulysses said.

"Yes, I was going to mention that. It's an old scar and possibly evidence of a serious suicide attempt." Ulysses took a picture of the arm with its scar and tattoo.

"Strange," he said.

"No, it's common, actually. The underside of the wrist is actually a popular place for tattoos. I've seen them on many suicides and the occasional homicide victim."

"Okay, that should do it," Ulysses said. *Let me out of here,* he thought.

Vigil rolled the cadaver back into its temporary grave. "I'll release the body to the family this afternoon," he said.

"Thanks for the report. Let me know what you hear about the DNA," Ulysses said. He was relieved when he walked down the long hallway and out into the sunstruck parking lot.

Back in his office, Ulysses pulled a rolling whiteboard out of the closet in his office and took a pack of colored markers out of his desk. He flipped up the cover on the white board and wiped the board clean. In the center of the whiteboard he wrote Trey Cameron, trying him out as the hub of the current investigation. He drew another circle and wrote L. K. in red with a question mark. Who was L.K.? He'd never been directly associated with State Senator Trujillo so far as Ulysses knew. Ulysses drew a line from L.K to Jeremy Diggs in black and one to Antonio Valdez, also in black. Was L.K. Maddy Smith's boyfriend and possibly her kidnapper? Ulysses wrote her name, circled it and drew a dotted line to L.K.. Ulysses hypothesized that L.K. was involved in the murder of Antonio Valdez and might have killed Jeremy Diggs. But why did Diggs have L.K. tattooed on his arm? Was L.K. the man who caused him to go to prison? Then he would be connected to Trey Cameron's racket. A prison enforcer might have tattooed him as a threat. Ulysses drew a line from Trey Cameron to a circle for Ramón Trujillo. Was Trey Cameron Ramón Trujillo's boss or was it the other way around? Ulysses thought for a moment. No question, he said to himself, Trujillo was the hired hand. Cameron pulled the strings on all these threads. Ulysses drew a line from Cameron to Trujillo.

Ulysses made another circle and wrote in Cody Parker's name. Cody Parker worked for Trujillo. Did he also work for Cameron? What was Parker's relationship to L.K, if any? Ulysses connected Parker to Trujillo. Parker was currently trespassing on Taos sacred land, possibly hunting Delfino Mondragon, but that was Agent Tallichet's domain. Ulysses stepped back from his creation and stared at it for a few minutes. His next priority was to identify and apprehend L.K.

Trey Cameron settled into the plush leather backseat of his Mercedes limousine as his chauffeur pulled out of the restaurant parking lot toward home. He took a toothpick out of a silver case and set about removing pieces of meat from his teeth and spitting them into the paper cup Rowdy had provided. As the car carried him north in the night he reflected on what he had accomplished.

The meeting with the governor of New Mexico had been disappointing. He was ushered into her office by a young, well-dressed blonde man who introduced himself as "Arthur Davenport, aide to Governor Montaño" and seated next to two Hispanic men in front of her massive desk. The men were introduced by name, but Cameron paid no attention until Davenport said they were representatives of the Mora Land Grant, an activist group he knew might oppose his plans. He noticed with irritation that Gilbert Herrera hadn't showed.

Governor Montaño, a trim, energetic woman wearing a tasteful dark suit and turquoise jewelry, appeared right on time. Cameron thought she must be about sixty. She smiled too much, Cameron thought, in the way of women when they are trying to manipulate you. Montaño acted as if she'd never heard of his project. She asked to hear all about it but Cameron noticed she didn't ask the follow-up questions he'd expected. While he sat in the uncomfortable chair in front of her desk talking, she walked around the room clicking her high heels on the marble floor or stood looking out the window. Cameron wasn't accustomed to being made to feel subordinate, especially by a woman, and he didn't like it.

Cameron knew that the Governor had been raised in Mora County and knew its people intimately, but she didn't allude to it. When she spoke, it was in generalities about respecting "Mora's traditional culture" and "preserving the commons." Then she gently reminded Cameron of his newcomer status. "New Mexico still clings to its Spanish roots," she said with the smile that continued to annoy him. *Yeah,* he thought, *so does Texas, but real Americans run things there.* Meanwhile, Davenport and the two older gentlemen from Mora said nothing.

Cameron tried to sell her on how Highland Fling would bring good jobs to the very poor region, but he could tell she wasn't buying. Governor Montaño implied she knew he'd be importing all the high wage work. He'd bring his own management team, his chefs and pros. The project would employ local maids and groundskeepers, waiters and busboys and line cooks, most at minimum wage or less. Tips might be good but not the wages. The governor listened politely until he was finished. "Mr. Cameron," she said at last, "Mr. Ben Ramirez and State Senator Roberto Ortiz y Muniz here," indicating the two land grant activists, "have some important questions for you." Immediately they began to ask him about how their land use rights would be respected at Highland Fling. Would they still be able to use their water, hunt and fish, cut firewood and Christmas trees?

One of the activists, Mr. Ramirez, had a weathered face and farmer's hands and spoke with the heavy New Mexico accent of persons for whom Spanish was their first language. Ramirez insinuated that Cameron was engaged in a massive land grab and planned to exploit the people of Mora with service work. "You want my grandson to be a caddy for your rich friends," Ramirez said. "The land and water you want have belonged to us for three hundred years!" *Yeah, and you stole it from the Indians,* Cameron thought. Cameron had masked his pique with feigned surprise, as if he'd never realized that his development might be seen as anything other than a boon to the remote region. Inwardly he was seething. He tried to pander to Ramirez by rhapsodizing about introducing New Mexico's unique and marvelous culture to the hoi polloi who would come to Highland Fling. Ramirez wasn't impressed. "We want to be left alone to live with our traditions on our land, without interference, Señor," he said. "You and your Anglo friends have nothing we want!"

"You want your water from over the mountain, don't you?" Cameron said, his anger only thinly veiled. "I can make sure you get to keep that water."

Ramirez said something under his breath in Spanish to his companion. He stood up, bowed to the governor, and left the room.

Ortiz y Muniz , who was younger than Ramirez and wore a suit said, "I know you are working closely with my Senate colleague from Taos County, Mr. Trujillo." Ortiz y Muniz spoke in a soft, polite tone. "You should know he has been under investigation by my committee for ethics violations."

"I believe that has been put to rest, Senator Ortiz y Muniz, has it not?" Cameron thought how glad he was Trujillo hadn't accompanied him to this meeting as originally planned.

"Not entirely, Mr. Cameron. New information has come to light about conflicts of interest between his work on the environment committee and his consulting contract with you. This may adversely affect your project."

"What kind of new information, Senator?" Cameron asked, surprised and not liking the feeling.

Ortiz y Muniz said, "I cannot say just now, Mr. Cameron. But the main thing is that you and your associates at Wild West should be aware that here in New Mexico we are very concerned that land sales and leases, especially in the historic land grants, are all completely above board and according to our laws. It has not always been the case in our history and feelings run high about these matters."

Governor Montaño listened from behind her desk with a noncommittal expression. "Your plan to log hundreds of acres of forest in roadless areas will come under serious protest from some of the old enviros in the area, Mr. Cameron," she said. "How do you plan to deal with that?"

"When people see how careful we are with the development, I think they will welcome us. We will take better care of our leased Forest land than the US government ever has. We will thin the forest to reduce the risk of fire. And Wild West will post a large bond to cover any problems that arise. We will be a boon to the region, you'll see!" Cameron smiled ingratiatingly.

A young man in a slim fitting suit wearing rimless glasses came into the room and introduced himself. "Hello, Mr. Cameron, I'm Josh Griegos, assistant to the State Engineer. I'm sorry to be late. Mr. Herrera regrets that he was unable to make this meeting. But he told me to tell you that you are fully on track to be approved for your water transfers."

"That's some good news, finally," Cameron said.

Governor Montaño frowned at Griegos and said something to Davenport that Cameron didn't catch. She took that moment to say her goodbyes, shaking hands with Ortiz y Muniz and Cameron. Cameron now realized the meeting was essentially over and nothing was really accomplished. *These people*, he thought, *are keeping themselves poor with all their traditions. They should see how we do things in Texas!*

After leaving the Governor's office, Cameron met with the contact he'd been cultivating at the US Forest Service. James Halloran owed Cameron a favor for the recommendation that landed Halloran a promotion to Supervisor at Carson National Forest. The two men sat in a booth in the quiet bar at the Eldorado Hotel.

"How are you settling in to your new job, Jim? Did you find a place for your family in Taos?"

Halloran, a paunchy man with a combover; small, close-set blue eyes; and a nervous manner, scanned the empty room and sipped his beer. "It's been quite an adjustment after a lifetime in Oklahoma," Halloran said. "My wife and kids don't like New Mexico. They hated Taos. Christy insisted on living in Santa Fe so the children can go to a better school. But they don't much like Santa Fe either and now I have this huge commute. All Christy does is complain about the dryness and the altitude. But I'm settling in okay at work. Seems like Carson National Forest is a pretty laid back. Since the fires, everyone tries to stay under the radar. People mind their own business for the most part." Halloran unwrapped a stick of gum.

"I guess initiating a 'controlled burn' that turned into the state's biggest wildfire ever didn't go over that well," Cameron said, chuckling.

"Hell, no," Halloran said. "Everybody in Mora County hates us."

"Is everything set with my leases?"

"So far as I know, Trey," Halloran said. "We've got a little pushback on logging the roadless area." He popped his gum into his mouth. "I'm trying to quit smoking," Halloran said.

"What kind of pushback? On the building sites or the golf greens?"

"The greens, mainly," Halloran said, chewing his gum. "Aren't those the areas where you plan to cut the forest?"

"Yes," Cameron said. "We can move the hotel out of the woods and use low-impact methods to log the roadless areas for the greens and fairways. It's only a few hundred acres, maybe 500 tops."

"What kind of low-impact methods do you have in mind?"

Cameron smiled. "Helicopters. We'll going to log with helicopters."

Halloran shook his head and smiled, "Trey, you are amazing. You never let anything get in your way, do you? I'm impressed."

"This is how money is made," Cameron said, handing an envelope of cash to Halloran.

Cameron met his old fraternity brother, Don Barkley, Director of the FBI field office in Albuquerque, at Geronimo's that night, for dinner. He'd invited the tall, broad, red-haired former college football star to the most renowned restaurant in Santa Fe, housed in a small, tastefully appointed historic building at the end of Canyon Road in the town's gallery district. They'd enjoyed aged, well-marbled steaks and a fine Cabernet suggested by the sommelier. Cameron and Barkley had finished off two bottles of wine and were starting on a third while they brought each other up to date on their personal lives. Cameron bragged about his twin daughters and his wife's fitness regime. Blakely, who was twice divorced with grown children, mentioned his new girlfriend,

Laura, a successful and connected political pollster who lived in Austin. Then Cameron told Barkley in detail about his plans for Highland Fling.

"It's literally a fire sale, Don," Cameron said.

Don finished his wine and winked at his friend. "You've always been good at sealing these kinds of deals, Trey," he said.

"It will bring employment, of course. These people should be grateful. But they won't be, I'm pretty sure of that."

"So many of those people up there are drug addicts," Barkley said, refilling his wine glass. "It's why this state is so poor. And it's a wasteland, except for the southeast where the oil is. I would never have come to Albuquerque if I hadn't been promoted two grades. As soon as I can I'm going to transfer to Texas. That's where it's happening in law enforcement. In everything, actually."

"You just arrived here," Cameron said, chuckling. "You should come up north, enjoy some of the peace and quiet. I actually like the place. It's beautiful and remote. I agree about the people, though."

"Not me," Barkley said, putting his napkin on the table. "I'm itching to get out. If I don't make any waves I'm in line to go to Austin in two years when the director there retires."

"What kind of waves?" Cameron asked.

"Any waves," Don answered. "My sponsors want nothing that upsets any members of the club, if you know what I mean. Prosecute drugs dealers and deviants of all kinds. Crack down on the riffraff."

"Well, luckily, there is plenty of that." *Just what I wanted to hear,* Cameron thought. *Leave businessmen like me alone!*

"And keep my head down," Don said. "Reign in the agents, slow walk everything."

"You should be pretty good at that," Cameron said. "Take a page out of Greene's book."

"The lawyer who pulled your RICO case?" "The very one. She's in DC now, at the DOJ. The new administration loves her. I can put you in touch if you'd like to get some pointers."

The two men parted ways with a plan to meet again at a party Barkley planned for the Balloon Fiesta in October. Barkley said, "All my friends in oil and gas will be there."

Cameron's Mercedes purred through the Rio Grande canyon with Rowdy driving and arrived in Taos about ten o'clock. The town was already asleep. Cameron pondered what he'd learned about Ramón Trujillo being again under suspicion in the Senate for ethics violations. Trujillo had brought a lot of pressure to get those leases so soon after the fires. Had he gone too far and alerted opposition? The man could be so clumsy. Cameron needed those leases. Three thousand acres of woods, right where the water came over the mountain. It was crucial to the development plan and where he'd build the fine dining restaurant and boutique hotel, because it had the best views. If that lease was in jeopardy, Cameron would have more aggravation and he was getting sick of being aggravated. *I should never have trusted that buffoon to handle such an important lease,* he thought. *Good thing I have Halloran.*

Chapter 9

Early the next morning, Ulysses met with his old friend Lex
Sisneros in the Taos County Attorney's sunny corner office at
the Judicial Complex. Ulysses and Lex had known each other
in high school but became friends when both were studying
criminal justice at UNM. They'd bonded during a kayaking trip
on the lower Rio Grande one spring break. Since graduation Lex
had attended UNM Law, then joined a prestigious firm, and their
social paths had diverged. Lex was serving his second term as
County Attorney. He stood up when Ulysses came into the office,
a handsome if overweight man with a ready smile.

"How is the campaign going?" Sisneros, who wore a dark,
conservative suit, a red tie and wingtips, asked by way of greeting.

"I can't wait for it to be over," Ulysses said.

"You'll win by a mile," his old friend said. "Don't worry! What
can I do for you?"

"I've got a tricky situation I wanted to run by you."

"Shoot."

"As you know, my opponent in the election is Ernie...uh,
Ernesto Ruiz. He is married to Jazmine Trujillo Ruiz, daughter of
Senator Ramón Trujillo."

"Ah, yes, your esteemed predecessor."

Ulysses nodded. "Right. With the election less than a week
away, I can't afford to misstep. But I have reason to believe that
Trujillo is involved in some criminal activities."

"What kind of criminal activity?" Lex asked, leaning back in
his swivel desk chair.

"Bribery and extortion," Ulysses said. "And maybe more. He's connected with an outfit called Wild West Development, owned by a guy named Trey Cameron. Do you know him?"

"I know him, yes. My wife plays tennis with Mrs. Cameron. We've been out to their house for parties. How is Trujillo involved with Cameron?"

"Trujillo is liaison for Cameron to purchase water rights from Taos Pueblo for a luxury golf development in Mora."

"Taking water from Taos over to Mora? Those kinds of transfers are complicated as hell and hard to achieve. Does Cameron need more acre feet than what they can get from the land he's buying?"

"Quite a bit more from what I understand. Even with rights from the land, which is water from the Mora transfers, they still need more. People are saying Cameron is bribing the tribal governor and threatening council members who don't want to vote yes."

"'People are saying'? Do you have anything more than that?" Sisneros made a tent with his fingers and peered through it at Ulysses.

"The FBI has someone who may testify to being extorted himself," Ulysses said. "And this same man may have witnessed a bribe being passed to the Taos tribal governor."

"May have?" Sisneros sat up in his chair. "Listen, Ulysses, you better let the FBI nail that witness down. To bring a man like Senator Ramón Trujillo in for questioning now would be very unwise, even if you have probable cause, which you don't. It would look like a political witch hunt and backfire on you in a big way. And you can't do anything before the election, you know that, right?"

"That's what I suspected," Ulysses said. "Still, this Wild West bunch have a lot of money riding on this golf abomination, Highland Fling. We have had two murders I think could be related to Cameron's need for water and I'm worried more people might get hurt."

"Well, get your facts solid before you proceed, my friend. Let's hope you are re-elected! And don't forget that some of us like golf!"

Agent LizBeth Tallichet was up before dawn the same day getting ready for her trip up the mountain to look for Delfino Mondragon. She'd staged all her gear in her motel room the night before and planned to pick up breakfast at a drive-through on the way to meet Eli Martinez and the Bureau of Indian Affairs (BIA) dog crew at the Pueblo. The morning was chilly and clear with sunrise still twenty minutes away. LizBeth checked her kit and got into the rental car. Before driving off, she texted her wife and suggested they have a good long talk on the phone that evening. She had a fantasy of a quiet weekend at their home in Placitas with no plans. She hoped that wasn't just a fantasy.

Eli was standing with the two BIA canine officers near the entrance to the historic pueblo when LizBeth parked her car. Eli introduced her to the two officers, Juanito and Bella, both from the Okay Owingeh Pueblo. They couldn't be expected to know the terrain they were searching, but both were in their twenties, fit and armed. They'd already gotten a glove belonging to Del and a shirt from Raven to give a scent for the dogs, three beagles in vests standing placidly beside their handlers, tails wagging. LizBeth finished her breakfast and the crew headed across the plaza toward the trail head just as the sun rose. She walked at the back of the line. She noticed Eli was also armed, a holstered pistol showing beneath a vest. She decided not to say anything until they were alone.

Juanito and Bella set a fast pace from the beginning, even with the dogs on leash. Eli and LizBeth struggled a bit to keep up as the rocky trail rose though piñon and juniper along the river. When they came to a fork where one trail led away from the river and up a series of switchbacks, Bella let the dogs sniff Mondragon's glove and the dogs, after a few minutes of running in circles their noses to the ground, took off on the river path. Everyone had to pick up the pace to keep up. The morning light fell through the ponderosa pines and illuminated the mountain stream below them, which was running full and loud.

"Have you spent a lot of time on this mountain?" LizBeth asked Eli.

"My Dad used to take us camping and fishing up here. And I've gone to the ceremonies up at Blue Lake. That fork we passed back there was the trail up to the Lake. I've been all over this mountain but this is the first time I went looking for someone."

"You know Mr. Mondragon?"

"Yes, but not well. He is close with my grandmother, but he and I never spent a lot of time together. Raven, though, he and I were good friends until I transitioned."

"When was that?" LizBeth asked.

"It's been about six years now. Raven and I dated when I was in high school and I think it makes him kind of uncomfortable that I'm a man."

"That's hard. I lost a few friends when I came out in high school. I wasn't really dating. I'd known I was gay since I was probably seven or eight years old."

"It was a little more complicated for me," Eli said.

They walked along in silence for a few minutes. The trail was steep and the river, still below them, was a long way down. The floor of the forest was dotted with delicate white and yellow wildflowers that trembled in the small breezes coming up from the river. LizBeth heard a woodpecker drumming on a tree below them. The dogs and their handlers were far ahead of them.

LizBeth said, "I noticed you have a gun. Don't draw it without my permission, hear?"

"I won't," Eli said. "Sheriff Walker spoke to me about it."

"You're his secretary, right? Not a deputy."

"That's right."

"Do you know how to shoot?"

"Sure do," Eli said. "Dad taught me. He took me to the shooting range from when I was twelve. It was the one time he was happy I didn't dress like a girl." He smiled, then asked, "How did you get into the FBI?"

"I was in law school and realized I wasn't cut out for office work. Law enforcement was a reasonable path but I wanted something more than police work. To be honest I'm amazed I made the cut.

Being a gay woman and small in stature, I didn't think they'd want me." LizBeth paused to catch her breath.

"What is it like working for the Feds?" Eli asked.

"I generally like my job. It's exciting and I feel like I'm making a contribution. You know, doing some good," LizBeth gave a rueful laugh and they climbed on. "But lately the atmosphere has been a little tense at work. We've had a leadership change." LizBeth decided this was all she would say. She felt inclined to mentor Eli but she didn't know how appropriate that would be. Better to keep her business to herself.

They hiked on until the trail descended and again ran close to the river. They forded the river and the trail led them into a boggy meadow full of yellow wildflowers. Eli took a drink from his canteen. "I'd like to get into law enforcement," he said. "I'm a secretary now, but I'd like to be a deputy. I think the sheriff might be open to it since he's so shorthanded."

They heard a series of distant gunshots.

"Let's go," LizBeth said. The two started to run toward the sound. They crossed the meadow and the trail quickly gained altitude. Before long both LizBeth and Eli were out of breath. They heard more gunshots and resumed jogging uphill, but the progress was slow. Below them the river descended into a series of small, frothy waterfalls. Then they heard shouts.

"Active shooter!" Bella yelled. They came to a place where an unmarked trail led down to the river. At the bottom of the trail the dogs stood, alert. LizBeth led the way, gun drawn, crouching, with Eli behind her. The trail descended rapidly. Ahead of them she could see that the dogs were standing over a body that was partially buried. "Take cover!" Bella yelled. The two officers were behind a large boulder. LizBeth and Eli came around the last bend of the trail and joined them, but there were no more shots.

"What happened?" LizBeth asked.

"We came upon guy trying bury a body," Juanito said. "He shot at us and we returned fire. Then he took off."

"Is either of you hurt?" LizBeth asked.

"No. I don't think we hit him either."

"Is the body Mondragon's?" LizBeth asked.

"From how the dogs are signaling I'd say yes," the Juanito said. He holstered his weapon.

"Did you get a good look at the assailant?"

"Yes, I'd recognize him. A big guy, shaved head, small mustache." Bella nodded.

"Cover me," LizBeth said and walked down the hill to where Mondragon lay, his legs and feet already in a shallow, crudely dug grave. Eli, gun in hand, came behind her. The two canine officers leashed the dogs. Eli crouched over the crumpled body and whispered a prayer. LizBeth looked at Mondragon's corpse and felt the peculiar detachment she'd come to associate with this part of her job. In her mind she heard the words of a Buddhist sutra her wife, Dawa, often quoted, "Gone, gone, gone beyond, Soul awaken." To Dawa this man was on another shore. To LizBeth he was just dead, even though she'd had a conversation with him only a few days before. She began to examine his remains.

Delfino Mondragon looked to have been hit hard on the side of the head. His forehead was covered in bruising and he had a jagged cut to his temple and dried blood streaked that side of his face. He had no other wounds to his body. His eyes had rolled back in his head so that only the whites showed and flies buzzed around his bluish face. Rigor had already passed. He looked to have been dead perhaps twenty-four hours. "Leave him like he is," she said. "I don't want to interfere with the forensic team."

LizBeth texted the FBI forensic team with a GPS marker and sent them further instructions.

"How do you think he died?" Eli asked.

"I would guess a blow to the head did the job." LizBeth took pictures with her phone. "Let's see if we can find Raven."

Juanito gave the dogs Raven's shirt to smell. Again, the beagles circled around, sniffing the ground and air. They ran up and down the riverbank before running to the main trail and taking off back toward the pueblo, occasionally stopping to run off trail or give a low howl. The canine officers ran after the dogs and LizBeth and Eli did their best to keep up. Luckily it was now downhill. They jogged after the dogs for about two miles before the dogs seemed to lose the trail. For about fifteen minutes they ran off the trail in all directions sniffing. Then they came back to their handlers and sat down panting.

"They've lost the scent," Bella said. She leashed the dogs and walked with them along the trail, but they never seemed to pick it up again.

"Why would this be?" LizBeth asked.

"No way to know," Juanito said. "But it happens. It makes me wonder if they picked up a false trail somehow."

The team rested, taking in food and water before resuming the search by returning to the spot where the dogs had lost the scent. "Give me a few minutes," Eli said, crossing the river and bushwhacking up a rocky slope to a ridge. The dogs nosed around in a leisurely fashion and LizBeth responded to a text about a location where the forensic team might be able to land a helicopter. "There is no such place," she responded. "Use an ATV."

Eli came back across the river holding a backpack. The dogs yelped around his feet. "I think this is Raven's," he said. Inside there was a sweater, a sketchpad and pencils, a candy bar, and a small medicine bundle. "It was dropped up on that ridge. People used to camp up there. It's level and there's a view. Let's take the dogs up there and see what we can find." The dogs were eager, but when they reached the top, they didn't find any further scent.

They searched in vain for the rest of the afternoon and into the early evening, before heading down the mountain. The handlers and their dogs left for home. When LizBeth and Eli arrived at the plaza, Mabel Martinez was waiting for them under a ramada. The sun had just set.

"Did you find him?" Mabel asked in a whisper.

LizBeth shook her head yes, then no, indicating he wasn't alive.

Mabel said, "I knew he was gone. I heard an owl." The old woman began to cry.

"Come on Grandma, I'll take you home." Eli embraced his grandmother and the two of them walked toward his car.

"I'm going to speak with Lt. Quintana of the Tribal Police," LizBeth said. "Maybe he can help."

While LizBeth and Eli were up on the mountain, Deputy Sheriff Angela Romero went to see Jared Renfro, the father of Maddy Smith's daughter. He worked at his uncle's garage in Rinconada, a small village along highway 68 in the Rio Grande canyon. Jared, a man in his twenties with a shaved head, a full beard, and a jumble of tattoos on his right arm, had a car up on the lift when Angela arrived. Jared's uncle was talking with a customer in the doorway of the ramshackle adobe building. When she introduced herself, Renfro wiped his hands on a cloth and stepped out of the garage into the sun.

"What this is about?" he asked, lighting a cigarette.

"Maddy Smith has been missing for three days along with her child. Have you seen them?"

Renfro took a drag off his cigarette. "No," he said. "She has a restraining order against me. I haven't seen her or Willa in four months." Renfro shaded his eyes with his hand. "Who reported her as missing?"

"She called 911 on Monday and reported domestic abuse. When I went looking for her, she wasn't there. Friends have also reported her being gone."

Renfro finished his cigarette and scratched his shaved pate. "Maddy moved out six months ago. For a couple of months, she lived in Dixon with some old lady, but then suddenly she was gone. I didn't even know where until I heard from one of her friends at the Springs that she moved to a yurt in Carson. She was hanging out with some dude named Lassiter Kane."

Angela asked for a spelling of the name and wrote down what Renfro gave her. "What do you know about him?"

"I've heard he deals drugs."

"If Kane isn't at the yurt in Carson, where else might he be?"

"I don't know. He drives a brand new truck, apparently always has lots of cash."

"Where do you live?" Angela asked.

"Over there," Renfro said, indicating a trailer across the highway, set back among some pines. "My uncle let me move in because Maddy and I had the baby. I never touched Maddy but she's accused me of abuse twice. Maddy has issues. Now she's with somebody a whole lot worse than me." Renfro whistled under his breath, "I'd like to get my kid away from Maddy especially because of that man. But she has full custody."

"Why did Maddy leave?"

"She was going through some stuff after the baby and relapsed on oxy. I always thought that was maybe how she met that guy, Kane. Anyway, I told her she needed to get clean for Willa's sake and the next day she was gone. I've only seen Willa once since." Renfro dug his toe in the dirt. "So much for fatherhood." He shrugged. Renfro's uncle came to the door and shouted across the parking lot to him.

"What's up, Jared?" the older man said, "have you pulled those brakes?"

"He'll have to replace them," Renfro yelled back.

"What do the police want?"

"Maddy is missing," Renfro said.

"Where is Willa?" the man asked.

"Missing too."

"Okay, well, wrap it up, will you?" The man went back inside the office and closed the door.

"Deputy," Renfro said, "I got to get back to work."

Back at the office, Angela ran a report on Lassiter Kane. Born in Oklahoma, he was forty years old. Last known employment was with Wild West Development. No current address on record. He had two priors: assault with a deadly weapon, for which he'd been given probation, and soliciting of a prostitute, for which he'd paid a fine. A mugshot showed a clean-shaven man with dark hair and light eyes who smiled confidently at the camera. *Sheriff will be glad to finally have a name for this man,* Angela thought.

Ulysses drove to the Double Rainbow in Penasco to meet Rita Wainwright, Ray Pando's journalist friend, for a late lunch.

Rita, a widow in her fifties, published the *High Country Beacon*, a newsletter that covered environmental issues in northern New Mexico. They sat on the patio of the restaurant under an arbor laden with windblown red roses. Ernest Charley, the proprietor, took their order. "It's just me and Millie in the kitchen today so you'll have to be patient." Ulysses ordered a BLT and Rita ordered yak tacos.

"You know I'm meeting you as a favor to Ray Pando," Rita said. "And because you offered to buy me lunch. Why did you want to meet with me?"

"I want to find out as much as I can about what the reaction is in Mora County to Highland Fling, you know, the golf development near Chacón."

"I know that, but why?" Rita asked.

"It might be relevant to the death of Antonio Valdez."

"Okay. I know Valdez was friends with Ray Pando. And he was Delilah Valdez's father. She's a friend. Do you have any clue as to who killed him?"

"I do. Antonio was looking into the Mora transfers and I think he ruffled some feathers. Possibly acequieros from Mora, or possibly employees of a developer named Trey Cameron."

"Of Highland Fling?"

"Yes. He needs the water from the Chacón diversion for his golf course. Plus more water from Taos Pueblo."

"So he wouldn't want Picuris to dismantle the transfers, right?"

"That's right. If he lost access to that water, his project would fail."

"How long have you lived in New Mexico?" Rita asked while they waited on their food.

"All my life. I was born near Taos and went to high school there. I graduated UNM and then lived for about twelve years in Santa Fe."

"What did you do there?"

"I was a police detective. First narcotics, then homicide before I ran for sheriff up here."

"So you know a little about this place, right? The history of land and water grabs in the state?"

"I vaguely remember my New Mexico history."

"Well, then you've probably heard of the Santa Fe Ring?"

"Yes, but refresh my memory," Ulysses said.

"It was an organized crime outfit of American gilded age lawyers and politicians," Rita said, happy to share her knowledge. "They got rich by buying land cheap from Spanish settlers for so-called back taxes and then selling it to unsuspecting people, who eventually lost it themselves because their deeds were bogus. The Mora people, whose families had been here for hundreds of years, lost their land and also lost the common lands given to their ancestors in Spanish land grants. The Ring also stole water and land from Native people. Their favorite tools were extortion and bribes, assassination, corrupt judges, rigged elections and "laws" that they made up. Because of them, New Mexico almost didn't become a state—too many people thought of the territory as lawless and of course too Mexican. The Ring were the people who made the Mora transfers legal in 1907, toward the end of their reign."

"Sounds like what is going on right now," Ulysses said.

"People in Mora are struggling with catastrophic changes since the fires last summer," Rita said. "Now this dude, Trey Cameron, is buying up distressed land to build a golf resort for rich people he wants to fly in on helicopters. It reminds people of the bad old days."

"Is there any public land involved or is it all private land?" Ulysses asked.

"Wild West has leased three thousand acres of public land, forest above Chacón, part of the old commons land grant, from the Forest Service, who manages it. This is where they plan to build first, but it's in a roadless area designated for wilderness and above 8,500 feet. The people of Mora feel the public land belongs to them as part of their heritage. And the Anglo people, mostly old hippies and environmentalists, don't want the development or the forest logged either. So they are all up in arms. And I agree with them. They are my readership, largely."

"What about the private individuals who sold land to Wild West? Are people angry at them?"

"Yes, some people are angry at neighbors selling family land. But others understand why they would want to sell. What little economic base there is around here is really depressed since the fires. Small farmers and ranchers have been devastated and FEMA has responded slowly. A lot of these people are poor and have little or no savings. They just want out. So far, Cameron has bought about two thousand acres of private land. They keep trying to buy the Ben Ramirez property, which is another five hundred acres. But Ramirez doesn't plan to sell."

"Do you know Ben Ramirez?" Ulysses asked.

"Yes, a little. He's a cattle rancher and land grant activist. His property is watered by the Mora transfer that comes into Chacón. He'd have reason to oppose ending the Mora transfers, obviously, but he's also opposed to Highland Fling."

"Why is that?" Ulysses asked.

"Highland Fling would be in direct competition with him for access to water. And it would be upstream from him as well."

"Do you know Jacinto Ramirez?"

"I met him at the meeting. He's Ben's cousin. But I don't think they get along. Ben is a land grant activist and very old school traditional Hispanic. He believes in being completely above board. Jacinto is sort of a ne'er do well."

Their food arrived and Ernest brought them a couple of pieces of carrot cake they hadn't ordered. "Millie sent this for you, Ulys. She remembered how you love her carrot cake."

Ulysses looked at the thick piece of cake with its raisins and walnuts and sweet cream cheese icing. *That's about five hundred calories I don't need*, he thought. "Tell Millie I said thanks. It's the best carrot cake ever!"

"Take it home and share it with Rosemary," Ernest said. "Rita, you eat yours for dinner. It's nutritious and you only had two small tacos."

"Thank you, Ernest. I will!"

The old man chuckled as he walked back to the kitchen.

"What do people think about Highland Fling?" Ulysses asked.

"A range of things. Some in the building trades see opportunity. But the people who live near the project, like me, see herbicides, noise pollution, light pollution, a decrease in bio-diversity and an influx of people not from around here…and most of all an abundance of wasted water. Most people think the employment that it brings will be low wage jobs. I heard one local woman say, 'if I wanted to be a hotel maid I would move to Santa Fe.' People prize their dignity and independence over there."

"What do people say about the Mora transfers?" Ulysses asked.

Rita took a bite of carrot cake. "Acequieros are afraid that with the Rimrock decision the transfers will become illegal because Picuris has priority rights. Rumors have been flying about the letter Ray Pando found from his ancestor that makes a mockery of the claim that the Picuris gave that water to Mora willingly. And now, people are saying 'there's no point taking water from the Picuris if it's just going to go to rich Texans.' So people are all stirred up."

"Can you tell what narrative is dominant in all of this?" Ulysses asked.

"It's hard to tell just yet. But what I hear most is, 'it's hopeless to fight the developers. We'll never win. But we can't let Picuris win, either.'"

"Interesting," Ulysses said. "So you don't think the acequieros will acquiesce to Picuris getting their water back?"

"Not on your life," Rita said. "It would be too much of a defeat. Neither will Wild West Development. They need every bit of the water in the transfer above Chacón. And they have the money and the lawyers to take it," Rita said.

"Just like the Santa Fe Ring," Ulysses said.

"That's right," Rita said. "Money and lawyers over people."

When Ulysses got back in the car after lunch he received a phone call from Ray. "Where are you?" Ray asked.

"At the Double Rainbow; I just met with Rita Wainwright."

"Stay put, I'm just a few minutes away. I want to show you something."

Ray arrived, parked his truck, and got into the Expedition. "Got time to go to the diversion presa above Chacón?"

Ray parked at the Double Rainbow and he and Ulysses got in the cruiser. Ulysses drove from Peñasco to Tres Ritos and then took a rocky Forest Service Road that climbed up along the fast flowing Rito la Presa to a ridge crest above Chacón. When they came to the end of that road, they got out of the car and walked a few hundred yards into the woods. There Ulysses could see that the huge, partially cemented berm built to direct the water toward Mora and away from its natural downhill course toward Picuris had been bulldozed. The broken piece of concrete now blocked the presa. Beyond the presa, the hand-dug acequia from 1865 held no water, though the bottom of the ditch was still wet. Someone had effectively ended the Chacón diversion with a guerrilla action and it looked to have been done quite recently.

"No wonder the water was flowing so full as we came up here. That little creek is usually almost dry," Ulysses said. "I never realized there would be so much water in it."

"Yeah, because usually all that water has been going to Mora to grow hay," Ray said, shaking his head. "Some enterprising vandal had some equipment over here."

"Well, this is still Taos County so I'll have to investigate," Ulysses said. "Do you think it was someone from Picuris?"

"I'm minding my own business, Ulys. You remember I said I thought the only way Picuris would get our water back is in the courts? I'm opposed to this kind of action."

"I get it. But do you think some tribal members did this?"

"It's possible. We have a few hotheads who might, but I don't know. I can't get involved in it one way or the other. If we're going to court on this I want to keep my nose clean."

"Makes sense. When did you find out about it?"

"This morning I got an anonymous tip on my phone. I drove up here about an hour ago to check it out."

A pickup truck was coming up the road with two men in it.

"That's Jacinto Ramirez," Ray said. "This could get ugly. Who is the other guy?"

"It could be his son-in-law. Not sure."

Ramirez got out of his truck and walked toward Ulysses and Ray. "What the hell is going on here, Sheriff?" he said. The other man, who was younger and bigger stood back and said nothing. He was holding a shovel. The two men looked at the damaged presa and talked in Spanish to each other.

"We just got here a few minutes ago, Mr. Ramirez. Looks like somebody vandalized this presa."

Ray said hello to the two men, but neither one replied. "What's he doing here, Sheriff?" Ramirez asked, indicating Ray.

"Mr. Pando told me about it," Ulysses said.

"That's 'cause he knows who did it, right, Pando?"

"Take it easy," Ulysses said. "We'll figure out who did this and what to do about it."

"What do you mean, what to do about it? Farmers have got grass that needs watering if they're going to make hay this season. You see how hot and dry it is. You can't take our water away now, our whole crop will be damaged!"

"Well, it's a crime scene so nobody can go near it for now. I was just about to tape it."

"Everybody knows who the fuck did this. You people," Jacinto said, pointing at Ray.

"You're going to be sorry you picked this fight," Ramirez said. He and the younger man got back in his truck and drove off.

"Friendly guy," Ray said. "You can see why I don't want to go to any of those meetings."

"Let's get out of here before more of them show up," Ulysses said. "Here, help me put up some tape." As they taped the site, Ulysses took pictures of the treads of a big front-end loader, the truck that brought it and smaller tracks of a backhoe. One ponderosa pine had a deep scrape in the bark where the backhoe had collided with it, leaving a trace of green paint. Ulysses took a picture of it. "I think this paint will match with a newer mini-excavator that was parked in Ramirez's front yard," he said.

Ulysses and Ray got back in Ray's truck to drive back to the Double Rainbow. The sun was intensely hot in the lacquered, turquoise sky, though the air was cool. Intermittent gusts of wind tossed the pines and the air smelled like their resin. "Does the number 1797 mean anything to you?" Ulysses asked Ray.

"Delilah asked me about it. She's been unable to come up with any ideas as to what it would mean. She's been working on the date angle. Poor thing, she's really suffering about how her father died. She keeps thinking she could have stopped his murder if she'd only had a chance to talk with him."

"'If only.' That kind of thinking will make you crazy," Ulysses said. "The number could be a date but it could also be a PIN, right?"

"Or a combination to one of those small locks people use, something like that," Ray said. They pulled up at the Double Rainbow and Ulysses got out of Ray's truck.

"Usually it's the simplest answer. Like a PIN to a bank account or a combination of some sort."

"Maybe you will have a dream about it," Ray said, chuckling.

"I wish," Ulysses said.

After Eli and Mabel Martinez left in the gathering darkness, LizBeth found Lt. Manuel Quintana, head of the Taos Tribal Police (and brother of the Taos governor, Jerry Quintana), alone in the police facility just off the historic Taos Pueblo. He was sitting as his desk eating a plate of chili rellenos with beans and rice and drinking a soda.

"What did you find up there?" Lt. Quintana asked.

"Delfino Mondragon's body," LizBeth answered. Quintana looked up, shocked. He sat back down, pushed his plate away and wiped his mouth. A few moments passed before Quintana collected himself.

"How was he killed?"

"He took a hard hit to the head. Someone was trying to bury him when the dog team came up. They came under fire but the perp escaped."

"Did you see the killer?"

"No. The dog team saw a guy trying to bury his body."

"What about Raven?"

"No sign of him, except we found his backpack up on the ridge."

"I'll need to get the guys to help me get Del's body out," Quintana said.

"You don't need to worry about that. I have my forensic team on it," LizBeth said. "I just want you to make sure no one else goes up on that mountain. And I need you to help me find Raven."

"Do you think Raven got away from the killer?" Quintana asked.

"Either that or someone was with the killer and maybe that person took him. But I think they mainly wanted Mondragon."

"If Raven got away, he might be hiding in Del's place in the North House," Quintana said, referring to the ancient multistory structure at the north of the plaza. "But knowing Raven I think he'd get on his motorcycle and ride as far as he could get away from here."

"Where's his motorcycle?" LizBeth asked.

"He parks it behind one of the houses not far from the cemetery. Let's go look for him. We'll go to Del's first."

They walked out into a night which was now full dark with the first quarter moon over the sacred mountain and Venus glowing near the western horizon. First they went by the North House to the rooms that were held by the Mondragon family. Quintana climbed the steps to the door and shone his flashlight into the windows. LizBeth could see a small, almost bare room with a kitchen area, a desk and some stairs to a sleeping loft. Quintana knocked on the door and called out. "Raven, are you in there? It's me, Lt. Quintana. Let me in." After a few moments he knocked again. Then he said, "I don't think he's in there. Let's go look for his bike."

When Quintana and LizBeth went to look for Raven's motorcycle, they found it locked up in a shed behind an empty old adobe. "This makes me think he never made it down the mountain," Quintana said.

"Maybe they took him hostage," LizBeth said.

Quintana said, "Or worse. I'm going to call his family and other contacts to see if they've heard from him. Was there a cellphone in the backpack? He has one, I think."

"Not in the pack," LizBeth said.

Ulysses got back to the office just before dark. Joseph and Mark had locked up and gone out on patrol. There was a note on his desk to call Angela.

"Sheriff, I have some information I thought you'd want," Angela said. "I spoke with Jared Renfro, Maddy's baby's father, and he told me the name of her abuser. It's Lassiter Kane."

"L. K., right?"

"That's right. I ran background on him. No current address, but he has two priors, one aggravated assault with a deadly weapon that he got probation for…"

"That's the plea deal that Jeremy Diggs did time for," Ulysses said.

"And solicitation of a prostitute, for which he paid a fine."

"That's it?"

"Yeah, that was the extent of it. But now we have a name and a mug shot. And confirmation he's been employed by Wild West. Renfro thought Kane was also a drug dealer."

"Where is Eli?" Ulysses asked.

"He wasn't back yet from the pueblo when I clocked out."

"Okay, Deputy, take some rest. See you tomorrow."

Ulysses pulled the whiteboard out of the closet and wrote Lassiter Kane's name where L.K. had been. Then he jotted down some notes about Jacinto Ramirez. Could he also be working secretly for Trey Cameron?

Ulysses drove home, arriving just as Rosemary was cleaning up from dinner. The children were already in bed. Tomorrow, Friday, was Rosemary's market day and also the children's last day of school for the year. Rosemary had her van already loaded and would leave to set up the moment she put the children on the bus. She came over and put her arms around Ulysses. "I'm exhausted," she said.

"I'll get my dinner and finish cleaning up the kitchen," Ulysses said. "You go lie down."

"Thanks, Ulys, but I want to hear about your day. Here's your dinner plate. You might want to warm it up." Rosemary sat down at the table and sipped a cup of chamomile tea.

Ulysses put his plate of goat carne adovada with posole in the microwave. He filled a bowl with mesclun salad and got himself a beer out of the refrigerator. "It was a pretty eventful day, I guess," he said, sitting down to eat. "I spoke with Lex Sisneros and he confirmed my suspicions that I don't have enough to bring charges on Trujillo. I had lunch with a journalist named Rita Wainwright and found out more about what's going on in Mora that might have bearing on this case. Then Ray and I drove up past Tres Ritos to where a Mora transfers diversion dam has been vandalized. We had a pretty unpleasant interaction there with Jacinto Ramirez, the mayordomo that got fired from Acequia San Lorenzo, you know, the one Antonio Valdez was a commissioner on."

"Who damaged the diversion dam past Tres Ritos?"

"We don't know, but I wouldn't be surprised if it was Ramirez himself, trying to stir things up. At any rate it's a bad time for the farmers in Mora not to get their irrigation water."

"I didn't get my water today," Rosemary said. "Bill Sykes said he'd had more complaints about me. Then when I came back into the house I had a voice message from Jean McNulty. I'll play it for you." Rosemary reached over to the phone machine and turned up the volume as the message played. "If you don't stop stealing my water, they're going to call the law on you, or worse, Rosemary! You better watch your back!"

"That's the woman who called in to Stu Wishard's show!"

"I told you I recognized her voice. She isn't even a parciante on our ditch! She's the woman who rents one of those trailers behind the library and has all the cats. Bill's got to know she's the one complaining. It's unmistakable."

"Somebody must be paying her to do this; either that or she's lost her mind. I'll drop in on her tomorrow."

"That's not all, Ulys. A woman from *The Albuquerque Journal* called me to ask about allegations of water stealing." Rosemary ran her fingers through her hair and then finished her tea and yawned. "I didn't pick up, but I can call her tomorrow if you want me to."

"That was smart that you didn't take that call," Ulysses said. "You don't need to call her back. Honey, you really look tired. Go on to bed. You have a big day tomorrow." He ate the last bite of savory meat, finished his beer and got up from the table. Rosemary left her cup on the table and went to bed. While Ulysses was cleaning up he saw Rosemary's almanac open on the counter. The almanac where she wrote down the dates she planted seeds and also recorded what she called her "moon time," her periods. *Maybe she started her flow and that's why she's so exhausted,* he thought. But when he looked for the numbers she wrote to calculate the days since her last period, he found the count was up to 60 days. *She's missed two periods,* he thought.

Chapter 10

Ulysses decided to go by Jean McNulty's on his way into work to confront her about the threatening call to Rosemary. He drove into Arroyo Hondo and down a dirt road behind the library where three single-wide trailers stood among some old apple trees. The trailers, owned by a local man, had affordable rents and were all occupied by older women. McNulty lived in the trailer in the middle with her grown son, who had mental illness. The front of the trailer was littered with trash. Several cats dug through the garbage bags looking for something to eat. Ulysses knocked several times before a woman in her seventies came to the door. "Yes, Sheriff?" she said.

"Hi, Ms. McNulty, may I come in?"

"I'm not dressed, Sheriff, can you come back?"

"We can talk from here, if that works for you," Ulysses said.

McNulty looked out her door and seeing one of her neighbors in her garden staring at them, she held the front door open for Ulysses. He went inside the trailer, which smelled strongly of cat urine and was stacked with newspapers, cartons, carboard boxes and overflowing garbage bags. She moved some material off a chair for Ulysses, but he preferred to stand. "My son is still asleep. Can you please talk quietly?"

"Ms. McNulty, do you know why I'm here?" Ulysses began. McNulty had thinning hair and blotchy skin and was dressed in an oversized bathrobe. Ulysses felt both pity and disgust, but he was determined to be respectful and kind if at all possible.

"Is Mr. Suazo going to evict me?" she asked in a whisper.

"No, that's not it."

"Are you going to make me give up my cats?"

"No. I'm here because of some calls you've been making about Rosemary Walker."

"How is Rosemary?" McNulty asked with a weak smile. "She's such a sweet lady."

"She's not very happy. You left her a voice mail message. She saved it. You were communicating threats, Ms. McNulty and that's against the law. And what you said isn't true. Mrs. Walker hasn't been stealing your water. You don't even have water rights."

"I'm sorry, Sheriff," she said, wringing her hands and starting to cry. "They made me do it. I didn't want to do it."

"Who made you do it?" Ulysses asked.

"I don't know his name. He wasn't a nice man."

"Did he pay you to make calls?"

"He said if I didn't do it he would hurt me."

"How much did he pay you?"

"Fifty dollars," she said with her eyes downcast, "but I only did it because I was afraid."

"How many calls did you make?"

"I don't remember, a few."

"Try to remember, Ms. McNulty. I know you called when I was on the Wishard call-in show, right?"

"Yes, and I called Bill Sykes a couple of times."
"Did you call the paper in Albuquerque?"

"Yes. But that's all."

"What about the call to Rosemary?"

"Oh, yes, that one too."

"What did this man look like?" Ulysses asked.

"He was big, shaved head. He had a little mustache."

At that moment her son came out of his room in his pajama bottoms, went to the refrigerator and opened it. "We're out of Pepsi, Mama," he said, scratching his stomach. He went and stood by his mother as if noticing Ulysses for the first time.

"Ms. McNulty, don't make any more calls, do you hear me? If you do I will issue you a citation and you don't want that. You would be arrested. So don't make those kinds of calls."

"What do I say to the man when he asks me?"

"Tell him I came by and told you it was against the law and you could be arrested."

"Okay, Sheriff. I hope he doesn't ask me again."

"If he does, call me at this number. And you can also file a complaint against him if you want." Ulysses handed her his card.

"I'd never want to do that," the old woman said. "That would be dangerous."

All the way back to the office, Ulysses kept smelling that house and seeing that woman and her son living in squalor. *I'll have Eli call Adult Protective Services and make a report on this situation,* Ulysses thought. *Maybe there is a way they could help them.*

When Ulysses arrived at work, Agent Tallichet and Eli were speaking in low voices at his desk. Zach was in the back room talking to Dakota about a 911 call and Angela was on the phone.

"Good morning, Agent Tallichet," Ulysses said. "How was yesterday?"

"It's not good news, Ulys," LizBeth said. "Mondragon is dead, murdered. And Raven Sandoval is missing. My forensic team is up there now."

"Come on in the office, you and Eli both. Did you get any clues as to the perpetrator?"

"The two BIA officers saw the man trying to bury Mondragon and can identify him," LizBeth said. "He shot at them and at us before he got away."

"From their description, I think it was Cody Parker," Eli said.

"Was there more than one perp?" Ulysses asked.

"Maybe," LizBeth said. "But we only had contact with one."

"If they kidnapped Raven do you think he'd still be alive?" Ulysses asked.

"I doubt it," LizBeth said. Eli shook his head.

"Did you track his phone?" Ulysses asked.

"It appears to be at the bottom of the Rio Grande Gorge."

"Now what?" Ulysses asked. "How are you going to find him?"

"I have no idea," LizBeth said. "I got a call from my boss telling me to come in and report to him on my findings. I have to drive down to Albuquerque."

"Eli, do you have any ideas about where we might look for Raven?"

"He has a girlfriend in Pilar. We could check with her. And what about that man that Angela found out about? Lassiter Kane? He's connected to Cody Parker. Or we could ask Senator Trujillo."

"I'm going to pay a call on Trey Cameron," Ulysses said. "I bet he knows where to find Cody Parker. And probably Lassiter Kane too."

On the drive to Trey Cameron's, Ulysses decided to check in with Stephanie. She'd not been in touch since the radio interview with Stu Wishard, which was unusual and worrisome at this point in the campaign. He thought she ought to know about the calls Jean McNulty had been making, especially to *The Albuquerque Journal*. He got her voicemail, so he left her a message. "Hey, Stephanie," he said. "Give me a call. I have a couple of things to talk with you about and I need my marching orders for the fundraiser tomorrow." He thought she might like the "marching orders" part as it implied he would take direction from her. He hoped she still wasn't still upset with him about how he pulled away and snapped at her when she was tying his tie.

Ulysses drove through Taos, north past the turnoff to Taos Pueblo, through the villages of El Prado, Arroyo Hondo, and Questa to where the Colorado Plateau stretched west from the Sangre de Cristo mountains out to the rift valley of the Rio Grande and toward volcanic mountains on the other side. Before long, he came to a turnoff and followed a series of turns indicated by the GPS through land that was mostly unpopulated. A few small groups of antelope grazed or rested in the high desert grasses. In the distance to the north, he could see the huge standalone dome of Ute Mountain, and farther to the northwest its twin, San Antonio Mountain, ancestral winter homes of the Southern Utes. When he came to a stout fence and a large "No Trespassing" sign, he realized he'd arrived at the Cameron property. He saw an empty guardhouse with a large camera mounted on its roof pointing toward the gate. Ulysses stopped the Expedition wondering what to do when the gate swung open automatically. He drove for another mile before he saw an imposing stone mansion situated near the jagged rift of the gorge, the home of Trey Cameron. The three-story house was surrounded by a plantation of dozens of large Pondarosa pines interspersed with Colorado Blue Spruce. Neither of those species would usually grow on the high, windy llano, but these appeared to be thriving. *Drip irrigation from a very deep well,* Ulysses thought. Next to the house was a large garage and across from it was an open bay building full of rafts, kayaks, ATVs, and racks loaded with hunting rifles and other long guns. A putting green shimmered in the midday sun as sprinklers watered it. Ulysses drove into the circular driveway where a marble fountain surrounded by blooming white rose bushes bubbled and splashed. Ulysses noticed Ramón Trujillo's shiny Lincoln parked off to the side of the house. *Lucky to find him here,* Ulysses thought. A trim man in black clothes with black hair grey at the temples and a dark mustache came from the back of the house and signaled Ulysses to stop. Ulysses rolled down his window.

"Hello, Deputy," the man said. "I'm Rowdy Eustace, Mr. Cameron's assistant. To what do we owe the honor of your visit?"

Ulysses got out of the car and shut the door. "Hello, Mr. Eustace," he said. "I'm Sheriff Ulysses Walker. I'm here to see Mr. Cameron." The wind blew through the big pines, scattering light and shadow on the groomed gravel driveway.

Rowdy stepped back and gave a deferential nod. "I'll see if he is available. What is this in reference to?"

"I'm investigating a murder," Ulysses said. "I have a few questions for him." He could hear children's voices from the other side of the house.

"Sir, please wait here." Eustace disappeared around the back of house.

Ulysses took off his hat and put it inside the car. He noticed another man in the same black uniform Eustace wore watching a monitor from the front gate camera. He wore a pistol in a holster on his belt. There was another uniformed man checking the gun rack with a clipboard. *This guy has a lot of security,* Ulysses thought. Eustace came back out of the house. "Mr. Cameron will see you," he said. "If you would please park your vehicle over in the visitor lot?" Eustace indicated the area where Trujillo's Lincoln was parked.

Ulysses was brought around to the side of the house and through an iron gate that led to a landscaped pool area, where two blonde girls were having a swim lesson with a young Asian woman. Above the pool was a ramada with a dining setup and red cushioned couches grouped around a low table. Trujillo and Cameron and another man sat there drinking coffee. Behind the well-stocked bar, a barman dried wine glasses with a white cloth. Cameron took no notice of Ulysses until he walked up the stairs to the ramada, then Trujillo looked up and said, "Good morning, Walker."

"Good morning, Senator Trujillo, Mr. Cameron." The other man introduced himself as Gilbert Herrera. The name sounded familiar to Ulysses. *Could this man be the new State Engineer?* Ulysses had heard plenty of scuttlebutt about Herrera's hiring, given he was from out of state and reputed to be beholden to big money interests.

Cameron offered Ulysses his hand to shake. "I'm sorry I can't stand easily to greet you," he said, indicating his bad leg with a tap from his silver headed cane. "My old injury is acting up this morning." Ulysses took stock of Cameron. He looked to be in his sixties and vigorous in spite of his disability. His tanned face was set off by a large aquiline nose, light blue eyes and black hair streaked with gray. He wore a seersucker blazer and linen trousers and an expensive-looking watch. He was also assessing Ulysses as if sizing up an adversary. A smile of comfortable superiority played across Cameron's patrician face. "Please sit down, Sheriff," he said at last. "What can I do for you? Would you like a coffee?"

"No, thank you, Mr. Cameron. I just have a few questions for you."

"Of course," he said. "Ramón, you can stay for this. Gilbert, if you don't mind, perhaps you could give us some privacy?" Gilbert stood up, bowed and walked toward the house.

"Do you have an employee named Cody Parker?" Ulysses asked.

Cameron chuckled. "It looks like the first question goes to you, Ramón."

Trujillo shifted in his chair and pushed his coffee cup away. *He's in trouble with his boss,* Ulysses thought. "Mr. Parker is my personal security," he said.

"Where can I find him?" Ulysses asked. "Is he here?"

Cameron looked at Trujillo with an expression of mild curiosity.

"He is not working today," Trujillo said.

"Recently Mr. Parker was seen entering tribal sacred land at Taos Pueblo. Do you know what he might have been doing there?"

"No idea, Sheriff."

"Is he a Taos tribal member?"

"No, I don't think so."

"Where does he live?"

"In Tres Piedras."

"Can you give me his phone number?"

"Yes. Why are you looking for him?"

"The FBI is investigating a murder that took place on Taos Mountain and Parker is a person of interest."

"Who was killed?" Trujillo asked.

"Delfino Mondragon. His apprentice, Raven Sandoval, who was with him on the mountain, is missing." Cameron stared at Trujillo, his bows lifting just perceptibly.

Trujillo shifted on his chair. "I know nothing about this," he said.

"Do you know any reason why Parker would want to harm Mondragon, Senator?"

"I do not. This is the first I've heard of it. It saddens me greatly."

"Do you have any information on the whereabouts of Raven Sandoval?"

"No, I do not even know that person." Trujillo adjusted his tie and wiped his mouth with a cloth napkin.

Cameron looked on with an expression of disdain. "Sheriff," he said, "what makes Cody Parker a person of interest in this matter?"

"I can't say at this time, Mr. Cameron. But I want to interview him."

"Well, I'm sure you can. You will be given his cell phone number. Sheriff, if that is all, the Senator, Mr. Herrera, and I have business to attend to."

"Mr. Cameron, I have a few more questions. Does a man named Lassiter Kane work for you?"

Again, Cameron chuckled. "Well, yes, he does, from time to time. Why do you ask?"

"Mr. Kane is a person of interest in the murder of Jeremy Diggs." A flicker of recognition crossed Cameron's face.

"Who is Jeremy Diggs?" he asked.

"I believe he used to go by Jeremiah. He worked for you at Big Hat some years ago."

Cameron laughed again. "It must have been a very long time ago, Sheriff."

"Mr. Diggs was murdered on Monday, near Vadito."

"I don't recall a Jeremy or Jeremiah Diggs being in my employ."

"Can you tell me where to find Kane?"

"He has an Airstream he parks in various places. I don't know where he might be at present."

"When was the last time you saw him?"

"He came to a staff meeting on Monday, I recall." Cameron said. "Wasn't he here then, Ramón?"

"Yes, that's right," Trujillo said. "We were all here for a staff meeting."

"Do you work for Mr. Cameron?" Ulysses asked Trujillo.

Trujillo cleared his throat. "No," he said. "I consult to Mr. Cameron."

"Is Lassiter Kane a member of your staff, Mr. Cameron?"

"He is, Sheriff. He has worked for me for many years."

"What does he do on your behalf?" Ulysses asked.

"Why do you ask?"

"We have had reports that he was involved in an incidence of domestic abuse and possible kidnapping."

Cameron seemed to relax. He laughed and shook his head as if in disbelief. "Domestic abuse! You came all the way here to investigate an incidence of domestic abuse?"

Ulysses felt his temper rising. He took a deep breath. "He is a person of interest in the disappearance of a young woman named Madeline Smith and her child. So tell me, what does Lassiter Kane do for you?"

"He is the supervisor of my security team," Cameron said. "And he does research for me."

"Is he here now?"

"No, he is not."

"Can you give me his cell phone number? I need to speak with him."

"Of course," Cameron said. "I'll instruct Rowdy to give you both Lassiter's and Cody's numbers." A tall, tan, blonde woman in tennis whites carrying towels came out of the house and spoke to the children in a foreign language. The children got out of the pool, and she wrapped them in towels. She waved to Cameron and then went into the house. "Are we done now? It's time for my lunch and I have another guest arriving soon," Cameron said.

Ulysses stood. "Thank you for your time and the information, gentlemen." When he walked out to the Expedition, Eustace came out of the house and gave him a piece of paper with the phone numbers he requested, then turned to greet another visitor who had arrived, an officious-looking man in a suit driving a green Suburban. The man got out and introduced himself to Eustace as James Halloran. *That's the new Forest Supervisor at Carson National Forest*, Ulysses thought. *Looks like Cameron has gathered his men to receive their orders.*

Angela was eating lunch in the break room when her cellphone rang. An anxious-sounding voice said, "Deputy, it's Cicely Duncan. Do you remember me?"

"Of course, Cicely. What's up?"

"Maddy Smith called me just now. She got away from her boyfriend and wants me to pick her up. But I'm at work and my boss won't let me leave."

"Where is she?"

"She hitchhiked to the café in Carson with the baby. She's there now. Can you pick her up? You can take her to my house. Mom said she could stay with us for a few days."

"Is he following her?" Angela asked.

"I don't know," Cicely said, "but she sounded scared."

"Okay, I'll get her. Text me your mother's phone number. You call Maddy to tell her to stay put. I'm on the way."

"I will, Ms. Romero, thank you," she said, sounding relieved.

Angela radioed Deputy Zach and told him she was going to Carson to pick up a domestic violence victim. She put on her vest and gun belt, checked her taser and mace and got ready to walk out of the office. Eli, who overheard the conversation said, "Are you sure you want to go out there by yourself?"

"It's not ideal, no. But the deputies are not available. Joseph has a court appearance, Zach is checking out a complaint in El Prado, and Mark is off. So I guess I don't have a choice."

"What if I ask Michael to come in and cover the front desk? I could go with you."

"I don't think Sheriff would approve," Angela said. "It's highly irregular."

"Can I radio Sheriff and ask?"

"Sure, go ahead, but I think I don't think he'll pick up. He's looking for a murder suspect."

"From what I can tell, Angela, so are you," Eli said. "Maybe the same guy, right? He's dangerous and this woman is running away from him. I don't think Sheriff would want you to go alone." Eli smiled as if to acknowledge he had the better argument.

Eli radioed the Sheriff but got no response. Then he called Ulysses' personal cell phone and left him a message about what he was doing and why. Eli got his gun and shoulder holster out of his truck and slipped on a jean jacket to cover the weapon. It was another hot and windy early afternoon but large cauliflower-like white clouds were gathering over the mountains, hinting at a thunderstorm. As soon as Michael arrived, Eli got into the passenger seat of the unmarked car and they drove off.

"Tell me what you know about Maddy Smith," Eli asked.

"I did a background check," Angela replied. "No arrests. She's twenty-three and was born in Silver City. She graduated from high school there and went to UNM but dropped out after two years. She worked for several years as a waitress at The Springs in Ojo. Her daughter, Willa, is sixteen months old. The father is a mechanic in Rinconada named Jared Renfro. Smith has an order of protection against Renfro but he denies abusing her. He said she has 'issues.' He also said she had a problem with oxy and may have relapsed. Smith reported being beaten up by her current boyfriend, Lassiter Kane, who is a person of interest in the recent murders. She's been living in a yurt near Carson, owned by Kane. Her friend, Cicely Duncan, knows nothing about any family in the picture. Maddy's been missing since Monday."

"How likely is it that she is being pursued by Kane?" Eli asked.

"I would say likely." Angela started to feel glad Eli was with her. In the heat of the moment she hadn't realized fully the danger they could be heading into—danger to them and also to the young woman and child they were supposed to help.

They crossed the Rio Grande Gorge Bridge and turned onto the upper rim road. The wind ripped across the high mesa and shook the truck, blowing a cloud of dust around them. They sped down an empty, potholed road.

"I'm not so sure it's a good idea to take her to Cicely's mother's house," Eli said.

"You listened to my whole conversation, didn't you?" Angela said.

"I couldn't help it. I am sitting right next to you!" Eli smiled again, a particularly attractive smile, Angela thought. "But yes, I did listen. Don't you think we should take her to the Women's Shelter? Wouldn't she be safer there?"

"I can't make her do anything. But I will offer her the Shelter."

They came into Carson and pulled into the Kit Carson Café and General Store, a well-kept white frame building with green trim, large windows, and a wrap-around porch. There were no other buildings nearby except the post office across the road. Angela and Eli parked in front of the café next to a handful of vehicles. A dry hummingbird feeder blew sideways on the empty porch. Inside, they were greeted by the owner, a man in his fifties, who was making pizzas. There were eight or ten tables in the room and about half of them were occupied with people eating lunch or drinking coffee and looking at computers. At one of the tables against the east wall of the room sat a slender young woman with a dark curly bob, red-framed eyeglasses, blue eyes, and freckles. She was holding a sleeping toddler and looked apprehensive as Angela approached her. Eli hung back, chatting with the proprietor.

"Are you Deputy Angela?" Maddy asked. "Are you the one Cicely called?"

"Yes," Angela said. "I can take you where you want to go. Are you ready?"

Maddy stood up and grabbed the quilted diaper bag that hung over her chair. The toddler stirred briefly but Maddy shifted her onto her shoulder and the child put her thumb in her mouth and went back to sleep. "Can you get Willa's car seat?" Maddy asked. Angela picked up the bulky car seat, but Eli came behind her and took it. Maddy was wearing torn blue jeans, worn blue sneakers and a black cut off tee shirt that showed her pierced navel.

"Do you have any other bags?" Angela asked.

"I couldn't carry anything else," Maddy said.

"Where was Kane when you left?" Angela asked.

"He was still asleep. He was out all night last night. I couldn't find his truck keys so I had to hitchhike. Nobody is driving on that road so early. It took me awhile to get a ride this way. That was the scariest part. Thinking he'd find me on the side of the road."

"Let's get you in the truck," Angela said.

With a great deal of effort, Eli managed to get Willa's car seat anchored safely in the pickup's back seat. Willa woke up and cried briefly but then settled down and Maddy was able to buckle her into her seat. She reached into the diaper bag and handed her daughter a squeaky toy, then climbed into the back of the truck with her child. "He could show up here," she said. "We should go."

"Do you think he followed you?"

"I never saw his truck. He might think I'd go to Ojo Caliente, not here. That's why I came here. But once he's checked around Ojo, he'd be sure to come here."

"Do you want me to take you into Taos?" Angela asked. "I can get you a bed at the Women's Shelter. It's nice there and would be safer than Cicely's mother's place." Maddy considered for a moment then shook her head. "No, I don't really want to go to a shelter," she said. "I'm afraid they'll mess with Willa. If Shelagh, Cicely's mom, is willing to have me that's where I want to go."

"Are you sure?"

"I'm positive. I don't think Las knows where she lives and she's good at protecting herself."

"Okay, well, let's go then."

They turned west toward 285 and then north into Carson National Forest according to the directions they got from Shelagh. The terrain was hilly and blanketed with juniper and pinyon trees. "Look there," Eli said, pointing to a huge bird at the top of a juniper, "a golden eagle." As they approached, the raptor took flight on widespread brown wings, showing the white spots on its flight feathers.

"I used to see that bird a lot driving back and forth from work," Maddy said. "This is one of his favorite places to perch."

"Probably gets lots of gophers and ground squirrels," Eli said.

"Yeah, and jackrabbits and mice," Maddy said. "And the occasional cat, unfortunately." Maddy offered a sippy cup of water to Willa, who was now fully awake and looking around with interest at her new surroundings.

After they'd gone about five miles on the first forest road, they turned on another dirt road that led northwest. That was when Angela noticed a truck was following them. In the heat glare she couldn't see much more than the plume of dust it created. She sped up. The road wound around a high rocky outcrop and down across a large arroyo. The car behind them had sped up also. "That truck is following us," she said to Eli.

"Yeah, I've been watching it. It was parked in the shade of a big pinyon right where we turned off."

"It's him," Maddy said in a quiet voice. "Can you hurry? We aren't that far now."

"I don't necessarily want to lead him to..."

"We'll be safest at Shelagh's," Maddy said. "Trust me. Don't slow down or stop until we get there."

"Okay, everybody, hang tight," Angela said and sped up out of the arroyo, the back fishtailing and a cloud of dust enveloping them. After three miles at this speed, they saw the drive to Shelagh's house, a battered 60's vintage Earthship with a satellite dish, bermed into the side of a big hill like a fortress. They came under an arch that said "Bar D Ranch," and had no-trespassing signs posted on either side. Kane's truck turned into the drive behind them.

"Pull around back. That's where the door is." Maddy said.

Angela's heart was racing as she drove the truck around the back and through a cattle gate that stood open with a padlock and chain dangling.

"Lock that gate," she yelled to Eli who jumped out of the truck. A woman came out of the door with a semi-automatic rifle at her side. Willa began to cry.

"Get inside," Shelagh yelled. Angela helped Maddy get Willa out of the car seat and they ran inside. Eli locked the back door. Shelagh moved to a gunport in one of the windows of the greenhouse that ran along the south-facing side of her house. "Stay back from the windows," she said. The truck pulled off the drive close to the south facing windows. Two men got out of the truck, both holding rifles. Shelagh poked the muzzle of her rifle through the gunport and picked up a bullhorn. "Get off my property or I will shoot," she said. Kane and Parker stood still for a moment. Kane lit a cigarette while Parker looked at something on the bottom of his shoe.

Kane said, "We just want to talk. We don't mean any harm." He took several steps toward the house. Shelagh let loose a burst of fire over his head. "Okay, ma'am," Kane said, raising both hands and smiling. He and Parker got in their truck and ambled down the driveway, with Parker giving them the finger out the open window.

On his way back to the office Ulysses listened to his voicemail. The first call was from Rosemary saying she'd just gotten back from the market and was going to take a nap before the children got home from school. She sounded tired and peevish. He felt overwhelmed with tenderness for his wife and dread toward the idea of a third baby, a confusing mix of emotions. He pushed aside his feelings and listened to his second message. It was from Eli. He told Ulysses that he was going to accompany Angela on a trip to pick up a domestic violence victim, who was fleeing from Lassiter Kane and possibly in danger. Eli said it was his idea to go, not Angela's and that Michael was coming in early to cover for him at the front desk. He said they'd check in with him soon. *Good call,* Ulysses thought. But how was he going to keep Eli as a secretary when every other day he was running out acting like a deputy? *I guess I'm just going to have to make him a deputy,* he thought. The final call was from Stephanie. In clipped tones she told him she had needed to take time off from the campaign after the radio interview but with the fundraiser happening tomorrow evening she was "back in focus" and needed to talk with him about some details. "Please call me when you get this and I'll be sure to pick up." As he turned into the office and parked in his spot, he called her back. She didn't answer.

After Kane and Parker left, Shelagh, a busty woman in her late fifties with a weathered face, introduced herself. "Make yourself at home," she said. "The toilet is just near the side door. It's a composter. Put some ashes in and close the lid when you are done. There's cold spring water in the fridge, but only open the door briefly. I'm low on propane. I'm going to check on Cicely. She's picking Nash up from the bus and coming home. I want to make sure there isn't any funny business from those two goons." Shelagh put her handgun in a shoulder holster, grabbed her AR, and headed out to her truck.

"Whew," Angela said. "I see what you mean, Ms. Smith. Shelagh is a force of nature. How long has she lived in this place?"

"I don't know. Cicely says they bought it for unpaid taxes. Shelagh makes good money now doing remote tech support for somebody and she's fixed it up pretty nice I think. I'd love to have a place like this."

Maddy sat in a rocker in the kitchen nursing Willa and drinking a large glass of water. Angela looked around the unusual house. The south-facing greenhouse overflowed with tomato, pepper and squash plants, trellised cucumbers, and lemon and fig trees, all bearing fruit. Overhead were heavy curtains that could be lowered at night to conserve heat. The bright kitchen's brick floor seemed designed to absorb solar gain during winter, but no sun currently fell on it, keeping the temperature cool. Garlic, onions, and herbs hung from the ceiling beams and shelves stacked with jars of rice, pasta, honey, beans and home-canned goods filled the back wall. The small dining room off the kitchen held a stationary bike and a cluttered desk with a headset, two computer monitors, and lots of blinking appliances. In the heat of the afternoon, the house was cool perhaps because the lower story living room and bedrooms were underground. When Angela peered into the dark living room, she saw a woodstove, plush rugs, comfortable couches and chairs, and a big television. The main and side doors were locked and bolted. There were gun safes both beside the main door and in the kitchen under a work table where a loaf of bread was rising in a covered stoneware bowl. The place felt like a cross between illustrations for *Mother Earth News* and *Guns and Ammo*.

Eli stood by the window that faced the road, watching the drive. Angela looked at his lithe body and handsome profile and felt the unfamiliar tingle of sexual attraction. Immediately she wanted to push the feeling away, as if it was dangerous. *Why not feel this?* she wondered. *What is the risk?* The pleasant feeling persisted. She turned her attention to the young woman in her care.

"Maddy, I wonder if you'd be willing to answer some questions for me?" Angela asked.

Willa pulled off the nipple to look at Angela and Maddy quickly covered her breast. "Let me change her diaper first," Maddy said. Out of the bag came a blanket, some wipes, and a clean diaper. Willa was tolerant of the quick change operation then trundled off to open cabinets on her level, looking for things to play with.

"Go ahead," Maddy said, poker faced. "What do you want to know?"

"How did you get to the Kit Carson Café?"

"I got a ride early on 285 but the man let me out at the turn. I stood there for a long while before a woman picked me up. She dropped me at the café."

"Why didn't you go to the yurt to get your car?"

"Las told me he'd taken it somewhere I'd never find it."

"When you called 911, you said Kane had pistol whipped you. Why don't you show any bruises?"

"I have a bruise but I guess it's faded." Maddy pointed to the bridge of her nose where Angela saw some discoloration. "My nose bled like crazy."

"Had he hit you before that?"

"Yes," Maddy said, with a deep sigh of irritation. "Willa, Honey, don't touch that, you could break it." The child stopped trying to pull a glass casserole dish off the shelf and started banging metal measuring cups together instead.

"Did he coerce you to come with him after you reported him?"

"He threatened to kill me, does that count?"

"Yes, of course," Angela said. *These questions make it sound like I'm not believing her. And I don't entirely believe her. Why is that?* Angela remembered the one time police came to her home when her parents were fighting and how the officers treated her mother like a suspect. Catalina hadn't told the whole truth of the abuse she suffered. She was too ashamed. So her father got off with just a reprimand, even though her mother had loose teeth from her father's hard slaps. For many years Angela had also felt ashamed of both of her parents, blaming her mother for being a victim almost as much as her father for being an abuser.

"Listen, Ms. Smith, I know these questions are unpleasant. But I have to ask them. I'm not blaming you for the situation you were in." *Really? I'm not?*

"It's okay," Maddy said. "You all ask those questions."

Angela cleared her throat and started again. "Where did he hold you and for how long?"

"His Airstream. Since Monday. He padlocked me inside."

"Where was it parked?"

"His friend Cody has a spot in the canyon not far from 285."

"Did he harm you there?"

Maddy thought for a moment. "He had me right where he wanted me. He could control me, make me have sex with him, cook for him, all of that stuff. I think he was pretty happy with the situation. But technically I think it was kidnapping and rape." *She's a pretty smart woman*, Angela thought. *How did she end up in her situation?*

"Did he harm Willa?"

"No. I would kill him if he hurt her." The girl gave Angela a hard look as if to emphasize the point.

"How did you get involved with Kane?" Angela noticed that Eli, still looking out the window, was listening to the questioning intently. *I wonder what he's thinking*, Angela thought.

Maddy stopped rocking the chair. She looked at Angela and then at Eli and then shook her head as if in regret. "I got injured at work," she said. "I was working a lot of shifts, trying to save up enough to leave Jared. I made good tips, but those trays are heavy. One day I was twisting to put a big tray on the stand and I wrenched my back. It was a re-injury, actually, from when I used to play volleyball in college. Then the doctor had prescribed oxycontin and I got in trouble with it. After I hurt my back at work I ended up relapsing. Las deals so that's how I met him."

"So you got injured at work but didn't go to a doctor?" *This sounds accusatory,* Angela thought. She noticed Eli looking at her.

"Look, I did go to a doctor, but I ended up relapsing anyway. Long story. I'm clean now." Maddy got a banana out of the diaper bag and peeled it. Willa turned her attention from the cupboards to the treat and crawled back into her mother's lap.

"Did you move in with him while you were using?"

"Yes. I needed a place to stay. As my father would say, out of the frying pan and into the fire. I wanted to get away from Jared but Las was much worse."

"So Jared was abusive also?"

"Yes, when he drank. Once he slapped me in the back of the head when I was holding Willa. That's when I knew I had to leave him, even though I hardly had any money." Angela found herself wanting to believe this young woman. She was smart and focused and an attentive mother in spite of the poor choices she'd made.

"Do you know anything about what Kane does for a living?"

"He works for an outfit called 'Wild West Development,' doing security. Has for a lot of years. He's a supervisor. But he has other connections too, with drugs and other stuff. None of it good."

Eli spoke up for the first time. "Did you ever hear him talk about somebody named Raven?"

Maddy looked surprised for the first time. "Yes, actually," she said. "Las and this guy he works with, Cody, were trying to find a guy named Raven all day one day. I don't think they found him, though."

"Why were they looking for him?" Eli asked.

"I don't know," Maddy said. "But Las was mad at Cody and threatened to kill him if he didn't find Raven. That night Las took off for a while and Cody also left. Cody forgot to padlock the door, so at dawn I escaped."

Eli looked at Angela. "Raven's still alive," he said.

"Ms. Smith, how long do you plan to stay here?"

"Not long," Maddy said. "I want to get my things out of the yurt and try to find my car. Can you help me with that?"

"Possibly. Where will you go then?"

"Back to Silver City," she said. "My dad says I can come home until I get back on my feet."

"Will Jared be okay with you taking Willa?"

"I don't plan to ask him," Maddy said.

"Why Silver City?"

"We'll be safer there than here," she said. "I need time to figure out what to do next, so I don't land up in another mess. Hey, I'm starting to worry about Shelagh and Cicely. They've been gone a long time."

"They are coming up the drive now," Eli said from his post by the window. "Nobody is following them."

Angela went out to open the gate for Shelagh's big truck to enter the back parking area. Eli followed her out. "Is it okay with you if I call Agent Tallichet and tell her what we found out about Raven?"

"Yes, definitely," Angela said. "And as soon as I debrief Shelagh we can go back to the office."

Chapter 11

It was quiet at Headquarters when Ulysses returned. Michael was covering for Eli at the front desk and Megan was working the 911 line. Everyone else was out. Ulysses went into his office and closed the door. He quickly ate lunch and then lay down on the couch and closed his eyes. His mind was restless with thoughts about Rosemary and what it would mean for them if she was pregnant. She'd wanted a third child since Monty was out of diapers.

Ulysses reflected on Rosemary's early life and why she was longing to have another child. She grew up in a conservative Mormon family. Her father ran a small dairy on 300 acres north of Provo that had been in the family for three generations. From the time they could walk, she and her siblings pitched in with the milking and feeding and the other unceasing work of the farm. As the youngest child of eight, Rosemary had been raised mostly by her older brothers and sisters, especially after her mother took a job as a kindergarten teacher when she was seven.

Not long after her mother went back to work, Rosemary was molested by a farmhand who'd worked for the family for many years. Her parents acted like they didn't believe her. They fired the man, though grudgingly. None of her siblings ever talked about what happened and until adulthood Rosemary always felt ashamed and somehow responsible for her trauma. She never told anyone about it, except a therapist she saw the year before they were married and Ulysses, after Amelia was born.

Rosemary graduated from Brigham Young University with a degree in early childhood education. Her closest sibling,

Calvin, just two years older, came out as gay the summer after Rosemary graduated and he moved to L.A. The way the church community handled Calvin coming out caused Rosemary to drift away from her faith. That fall, Rosemary left Utah for good. She moved from Provo to live with Calvin, breaking her engagement to a boy she'd dated since high school. Her parents did not accept her decision. They tried to forbid her to go, but they couldn't stop her. She was twenty-one and had been accepted as a substitute teacher in Orange County. Eventually, L.A. proved too urban for Rosemary and she found a job teaching second grade in Santa Fe. She fell in love with New Mexico. Once she met Ulysses Walker, at a Take Back the Night rally on the Plaza the first summer she was there, Rosemary knew she was home for good.

Although her parents finally accepted that Rosemary wasn't coming back, family relationships were strained by distances and by their increasing religious and cultural differences. Her parents, Foster and Maryanne Bell, rarely visited New Mexico. As dairy farmers, they were not people who travelled easily or well. Rosemary brought her own young family to Utah to see them, but often came home feeling sad and irritated at how little interest her parents and siblings showed in her or her husband and children during her visits. The fact that she had moved away made it easy to blame her for the chill. Their world—the farm, the church and their large, boisterous families—did not include her. Her parents never spoke of Calvin, nor did he visit. Rosemary's relationship with Calvin continued but became more distant when he moved to Hawaii just before Monty was born.

Rosemary and Ulysses had not used birth control for four years. Rosemary had experienced two miscarriages, the second of which, two years ago, happened at fifteen weeks. The loss plunged Rosemary into a depression. Ulysses was content with two children and dreaded another baby keeping them up at night and requiring so much, especially from Rosemary, due to his job. But he also felt Rosemary's sadness and disappointment when she miscarried. He knew they didn't have much more time.

Ulysses fell asleep and began to dream he was fishing on a quiet stretch of the Rio Grande on a summer day. Amelia and Monty were playing in the shallows and Rosemary was asleep on a blanket under a willow. Ulysses caught a huge fish and the children came running to look at it. The fish had a human face. It flapped around gasping for air with human lips. While he was holding it a bullet struck it and killed it. Suddenly bullets began to fly all around him coming from across the river. The children disappeared. Feeling desperate, Ulysses looked around, but couldn't find Rosemary. Then he woke up. He sat up and began to take deep breaths. The dream was definitely a nightmare. Was this dream a warning about his work or his family's vulnerabilities with a third child coming? Maybe it was just stress and nothing more. Before he could go much further with his dream analysis, Ray Pando was at his door.

"Did I catch you napping?"

"You did, Ray. I just had a terrible dream."

"What is with you and the dreams, my friend?"

"God knows. But this one…whew." Ulysses got up and drank some water.

"Maybe someone is trying to tell you something?" Ray smiled but Ulysses could tell he was serious. "You're investigating three murders. Are you afraid you'll be next?"

"Rosemary says I'm just stressed out. That's true enough," Ulysses said, taking another deep drink of water and changing the subject. "Hey, what brings you here?"

"I just met with Delilah Valdez," Ray said. "Her law firm is going to take our case. She says the firm is convinced the original letter I found is strong enough evidence that the Mora transfers should be reversed and Picuris should get its water back. It will likely be a long fight, but she thinks we might win. And she's got the firm on board. They're offering to do it pro bono."

"That's great news, Ray," Ulysses said, shaking hands with his old friend. "By the way, did you find out anything about the diversion dam that was damaged? Was it young men from the tribe?"

"Matt doesn't think so, Ulys. And he would know these things. He used to coach all the boys playing basketball at our gym. He says they'd tell him if they did it."

"Then who was it?" Ulysses asked.

"Jacinto Ramirez was right there to lay blame the moment we showed up to discover it. And there is the green paint on the tree. Maybe Cameron paid him to destroy the dam in order to get the acequieros riled up." Ray chuckled. "Of course, this is all speculation on my part, I realize. You would have to prove it. Maybe you should go check for a dent in that backhoe you saw at his place."

"Maybe I will."

After Ray left, Angela and Eli knocked on his door. They told him everything that had happened during their pickup of Maddy Smith, including the information that Raven was likely still alive.

"I called Agent Tallichet," Eli said. "She said she hoped to be back up here tonight."

"Okay, listen up, both of you. Angela, you can't take Eli out again instead of a deputy, not for any reason, right? We'd get in all kinds of trouble if something happened to him or anyone else because of him. So, until we get permission from Regulations and Licensing for him to fill in temporarily as a deputy, don't do it. It will be grounds for termination. Do I make myself clear?"

Angela and Eli exchanged a glance that Ulysses couldn't read. "Yes, Sheriff," they both said in unison.

Ulysses took a deep breath and continued. "Eli, go ahead and look into what's involved in a temporary deputy appointment— I'm pretty sure we can apply for emergency status. And find a temp who can step in to cover as secretary if you get an appointment. Oh, and by the way—don't forget the fundraiser tomorrow, you two. Four to six. You probably have to go early for a server class. Angela call Stephanie for the address, dress code, and time you should get there. And tell Dakota all of this, will you?"

Agent LizBeth Tallichet sat outside her boss Don Barkley's office suite waiting for his secretary to invite her into his inner sanctum. She was pretty sure she knew what to expect from this meeting. It would most likely be a reprimand for the way she'd handled the search on Taos Mountain, even though she'd followed the letter of every protocol for investigations on tribal lands. Except of course, she'd involved an employee of the Taos County Sheriff's Department. Even though LizBeth brought Eli Martinez along only to satisfy Barkley's demand that she be accompanied by a tribal member, she knew Barkley would object because of his distrust for "locals."

Barkley was old school FBI when it came to interacting with local police, tribal police, and county sheriffs. "The safest and best plan is to have nothing to do with them," the conventional wisdom said. "Leave them out of the loop even if you have to mislead them." LizBeth had other, more collaborative methods she learned from a former mentor during her early years with the agency.

Agent José Santistevan had taught her many things he'd learned during forty years working in the border regions of Texas, most of them helpful to her early career.

"In rural and remote areas, always play nice with the locals," he had said. "It will make your job easier and make you much more effective. Remember," the veteran said, "they live there. They know the place, people, la cultura. You have the same goals, mostly. And if they don't share your goals, you'll know it faster." LizBeth had found that José's words resonated with her to this day.

Barkley's executive assistant beckoned to her from the open door to his office. "He'll see you now, Agent." No smile from Michelle, a transplant from Oklahoma who either hadn't bothered to learn LizBeth's name or couldn't be bothered to be friendly. She went into Barkley's office and sat in an armchair in front of his imposing oak desk.

Barkley swiveled around in his chair to face her. "Agent Tallichet, how's it going?" He smiled briefly. "I heard you found you a dead Indian up on that mountain."

"Yes, sir," LizBeth said, shocked at the disrespect in his words and tone.

"We had a hell of a time getting the body out yesterday. Got caught in a gully washer on the way down. Too bad he couldn't have gotten killed closer to a road."

"I'm sure it was a challenge, sir. Could you ask for an expedited postmortem?"

Barkley waved away her request. "Will you tell me why you saw fit to bring a transgendered secretary along with you on your little mission?"

"Sir, Eli Martinez is a Taos Tribal member. You requested I find someone to accompany me and the dog team. Martinez was willing and able to accompany me and time was of the essence. We thought we might find Mr. Mondragon alive."

"But you didn't, did you? And your suspect got away." Barkley shook his head with displeasure. "And I have to explain to my superiors why you would bring a secretary who works for a sheriff we know nothing about along on a sensitive search operation, possibly jeopardizing it. I heard that shots were fired, is that correct?"

"It's in my report, yes, sir." She paused then said, "I have worked with Sheriff Walker before."

"Oh, yes, well my sources say he is not to be trusted."

LizBeth said nothing. She could feel her anger rising with an undercurrent of fear slithering beneath.

"And did you ever think what would have happened if your little secretary got shot?"

LizBeth, feeling there was no point, said nothing.

"Listen here, Tallichet," Barkley said. "I'm warning you. I don't want a big mess on my hands up there in Taos County. Trim your sails, do you hear me? When the forensics come back, I want you to check with me before you do anything, anything at all, beyond respond to what the forensics show. There are vital interests at stake. Is that clear?"

"What vital interests, sir?"

"That information is above your paygrade, Tallichet. You may have some rank among the agents in this office but I'm the boss. There will be severe consequences if you cross me."

"Yes, sir." LizBeth was now seething with rage but she kept her voice from betraying her. Her face was another matter. But Barkley wasn't looking at her and she doubted he'd notice, even if he were. "Can I ask you something, Mr. Barkley?"

"What now?"

"A young Taos Indian man named Raven Sandoval went up the mountain with Mondragon and is missing. I would like to go looking for him, sir."

Barkley shook his head and laughed softly. "It keeps getting worse," he muttered. "Do you have any leads that this boy is still alive?"

"I do. On my way here I received a call from Eli Martinez with information…"

"Eli Martinez again? Shit, girl. How did she/he get involved again?"

"Sandoval is a friend of Eli's. Anyway, Eli says Sandoval might be alive, hiding in the vicinity of Tres Piedras. I want to go looking for him tonight."

"Suit yourself, but like I said, keep a low profile. I don't want any local law enforcement involved and if you find him, contact me before you interview him. I might want him to be brought down here so I can supervise."

What the hell is going on? LizBeth wondered. *Raven is almost certain to have valuable knowledge about who killed Mondragon. Is there something Barkley doesn't want to come out? If not, why not?*

"Right, sir. Is there anything else?"

Barkley sat back in his swivel chair and rocked back and forth. He looked like he was about to spring a trap.

"Explain to me why you were inquiring this week into the failed RICO investigation against Wild West Development Company?"

LizBeth felt fear grip her. *Who told him about this?*

At that moment, Michelle knocked on Barkley's door. "Really sorry to disturb you, Mr. Barkley, but that call you've been waiting for is holding on line 1."

Barkley looked eager as he picked up the handset. "We'll get back to this later, Tallichet. Now, get along. We're done for now." He punched line 1 and said, "Hello, Laura."

LizBeth made her way to her car drained of emotions. She'd been treated with profound disrespect by Barkley, who'd revealed he was far more unscrupulous than she realized. It was completely appropriate for LizBeth to look into the RICO case and use the server to retrieve documents. Of course, giving copies to Sheriff Walker would be cause for a reprimand, but Barkley had no way to know about that. Still, Barkley must have someone looking at and reporting to him on her. But who? It could be any one of the loyalists Barkley brought with him from out of state.

She remembered José's surprising unwillingness to use some of the technology available to make his job easier. "Watch out for automated systems that track your presence, Lizzie. They exist so the powers that be can make sure you don't step on toes, especially theirs," he said. LizBeth committed to being more careful from now on. And what should she say about it when Barkley asked her in the future? Again, José's advice came readily to mind. "Always plead duty and honor first. No one can fault you for that. If you were trying to uncover a crime, say so. That will at least buy you time." Remembering José's advice made LizBeth relax. The man had survived really difficult times in his career before Hispanic people were well-established in the Bureau. And he'd retired on a good pension. The last she'd heard, José was living on the Gulf where he had bought a boat to indulge his passion for fishing.

LizBeth had come to New Mexico with a stellar record after four years in Texas. Her first years working out of the Albuquerque office made her reputation as a highly capable agent. She had lots of friends among the junior officers and was well-liked by her previous boss. But since Barkley's arrival, things had definitely changed. The mood in the office had turned paranoid in ways she'd heard agents in other locations describe. The new Congress didn't help with the way they targeted the FBI. In fact, LizBeth was sure that Barkley was empowered by key figures on the U.S. House of Representatives' Judiciary Committee, who wanted lax oversight for rich donors, corporations, and themselves. But surely they didn't want these people to be allowed to get away with murder? And if they did, they would have to do it over her dead body. LizBeth felt a chill run up and down her spine. *Could it come to that? I'm just being dramatic,* she thought.

As she drove toward Taos, LizBeth planned her search for Raven Sandoval. Eli had relayed information given by Maddy Smith that he had escaped. Where should she start? LizBeth decided not to use her duty phone and stopped in Santa Fe to buy a burner phone. On her way to Taos, she called Eli and Ulysses and left messages when neither picked up.

When Ulysses finally got Stephanie on the phone, she sounded cool and distant but focused.

"How's it going, Steph?" Ulysses asked. "We've only got five days to go before the election."

"Early voting is steady," she said, coolly. "According to one exit poll, you seem to be tied with Ruiz."

"Really?" Ulysses said, surprised. "I thought I was ahead."

"U, it always tightens up right at the end, you know that. And Ruiz is having a big shindig on Saturday night with 'Los Coyotes' and an open bar at the Local. He'll get a lot of attendance."

"How many folks do we have coming to ours?"

"Two hundred as of yesterday afternoon."

"That's very good, especially if it's the kind of crowd that contributes. How are finances holding up?"

"If we make $20,000, we can pay off all our debts."

"Is that realistic?"

"We'll see," Stephanie said in a brusque way that didn't make Ulysses feel optimistic.

"I'm supposed to give a talk, right? What should I cover?"

"I have a few notes on the hot button issues. Let's see—the cost of domestic violence to the community and families, homelessness and crime, and lingering confusion about clergy sex abuse and the murder of Archbishop Sullivan."

"Did you get this from a focus group?" Ulysses asked.

"Yes, I actually did."

"You're good," Ulysses said. "What about the whole constitutional sheriff deal?"

"We don't really know how that's polling," Stephanie said. "You might get a question or two about it, but I doubt it from our crowd."

"Anything else?"

"Well, there is one thing Kitty, our hostess, asked about that is so bogus I hate to mention it."

"Don't tell me. Rosemary misusing water?"

"Bingo. Some of her friends brought it up. If someone asks, you can handle it, but you might want to let Rosemary know so she isn't blindsided."

"What a bummer that she has to deal with this. But I'll tell her to be prepared. My mom will be there, too, because it's Monty's birthday."

"That's good. Can you get there about 4?"

"I'll do my best. And listen, Stephanie, I can't tell you how much I appreciate all you've done for me. Thank you so much."

"You're welcome," Stephanie said crisply and hung up. *She's still pissed*, Ulysses thought.

Ulysses checked his voicemail and found a call from LizBeth. He called her back.

"How'd it go with your boss?" he asked.

"Not great," LizBeth said. "But I'm in Taos now getting ready to go over to Tres Piedras to hunt for Raven Sandoval. Want to come along?"

Ulysses thought about it and realized he really needed to go home and help Rosemary get ready for the big weekend. It wasn't the right time for him to go on a missing person search on the far side of the county. "I can't this evening, LizBeth, but let me see if Angela is able to go."

"Don't you want to apprehend Kane and Parker?" LizBeth really hoped Ulysses would join her. Even though Barkley had expressly warned her not to involve local law enforcement, LizBeth knew she was dealing with two very dangerous men.

"I do and I will. But I can't tonight. I've got too much stuff to do before the fundraiser tomorrow."

"Oh yeah," LizBeth said, "I forgot about the campaign. Well, yes, I could use Angela if she's available."

"Let me check," Ulysses said. He looked at his watch. It was almost six o'clock. Angela would have gone home over two hours ago. "I'll call you back."

Ulysses called Angela on her cell and she answered right away. "Yes, Sheriff?"

"Agent Tallichet is going to look for Raven Sandoval. She could use a ride along. Are you able to do it?"

"Yes, Sheriff, of course. Where should I meet her?"

"Why don't you arrange it with her? She has a new phone. Here is the number to call," Ulysses said. "Listen, be careful out there. If you need more support, Joseph and Zach are on tonight. Or you can call me."

"Okay, thank you, Sheriff," Angela said. Ulysses could hear music and laughter that sounded like a party.

"Where are you, Deputy?"

"I'm at the Local with Eli. We were just finishing dinner. He got verbal approval for emergency deputization today. It's for sixty days, after which he'll have to jump through a bunch of hoops. But isn't that good?"

"Angela, have you been drinking?"

"I had a beer with dinner. I'm off duty, sir."

"Listen, Angela. This is a dangerous little outing I'm sending you on. I want you to take care of yourself. Clear?"

"Yes, Sheriff." Ulysses heard Eli in the background asking, "What's up, Angela?"

"Call me back when you know the plan with Agent Tallichet."

"I will. Don't worry, Sheriff. I've got this."

Ulysses got home just has Rosemary was putting dinner on the table, a homemade margarita pizza and salad. The children, unaccustomed to eating with their father, were excited.

"Daddy, Granny is coming tonight," Monty said. "And tomorrow is my birthday!"

Amelia said, "I made the salad tonight. It was so easy!"

Rosemary kissed him and offered him a glass of wine. She didn't pour one for herself.

"How was market today?" Ulysses asked, declining the wine.

"I sold out," Rosemary said. "So, pretty good! But three people asked me about the 'water controversy.' That's what they are calling it."

"Regular customers?" Ulysses asked.

"Yes. They thought it was ridiculous, but still they'd heard about it and were concerned enough to ask questions."

"What did you say?"

"I told them it was a politically motivated false rumor. That seemed to work."

"Did you get Mom's bed set up in the sewing room?" Ulysses asked.

"Yes, it's all good in there. Diana said she'd be here after the children are in bed. I got all the chores done, but maybe in the morning you can help me empty out the truck and set up for the party."

"Sure. I'll clean up from dinner and put the kids to bed. Why don't you take a rest while I do?"

Rosemary smiled and said, "I'll take you up on that!"

After the kitchen was clean and the children were in bed, Ulysses went into the living room where Rosemary was dozing on the couch. He sat down and put her feet in his lap, carefully removing her socks and starting to massage her feet. She woke up, and moaned with pleasure.

"I love it when you rub my feet," she said.

He gently massaged each toe and then rubbed the heels and ankles of one foot.

"How was your day?" she asked.

Ulysses decided not to tell Rosemary anything that would worry her. "Interesting. There is a lot going on with the investigations and the campaign is really heating up. A lot is riding on this fundraiser tomorrow. How was your day?"

"Long. But okay. I'm not taking the 'water controversy' personally. I'm just not even thinking about it. I have too much else on my mind."

Ulysses took her other foot and began to caress and massage it. "Like what?" he asked.

"I might be pregnant," Rosemary said. "I took a test and it said I am."

Ulysses was relieved she was telling him this rather than him having to ask. "I noticed you'd missed at least one period."

"I've missed two. I'm a little more than eight weeks along. It's early."

"Are you feeling okay?" During Rosemary's last pregnancy, she'd been nauseous for weeks.

"I feel pretty good. Just tired," she said. "No nausea. More like when I was pregnant with Monty and Amelia than the miscarriages. Ulysses, I know you aren't too keen on a third child."

"How do you know that?" Ulysses asked.

Rosemary laughed. "Because you've said it about a gazillion times."

"Yeah, but I keep doing what it takes to make one, don't I?"

She laughed again and sat up. "That just comes naturally, doesn't it?"

"Seriously, Rosemary. I've been involved in it as much as you. Okay, a baby wouldn't be my first choice, but I know how much you've wanted this. I'm sure I'll adjust to it."

"Adjust to it? That doesn't sound right."

"I'll love this baby when it comes as much as I love Amelia and Monty," Ulysses said. "And I don't think I could love them any more than I do."

"I just hope I can keep it."

"I know, honey. Are you going to tell anyone yet?"

"Lord, no," Rosemary said. "It's too early. I don't want anyone to worry. Do you want to tell your mom?"

"Let's wait a while," Ulysses said. "She's a world-class worrier. And I'm always giving her something else to worry about."

Rosemary squeezed Ulysses' hand as she stood up. "I think I'm going to turn in. Thank you for being happy with me about this baby, Ulys."

They heard a car pull up and Ulysses went to the front door to see his mother getting her overnight bag out of her car. He turned on the front porch light and went out to help her.

Chapter 12

When Angela got off the phone with Sheriff, she told Eli that she
was riding along with Agent Tallichet to try to find Raven.

"Do you want me to come with you?" Eli asked. "I have
permission now."

"No, I don't think it's a good idea. Sheriff said if I need back-up
I can call Joseph and Zach. Do you know anyone who might know
where Raven would go to hide?"

"I'll give you his girlfriend's number in Pilar. Hey, listen, stay
safe, okay? Wear your vest and don't do anything…"

"Eli, cool it, okay? I am a big girl. I can take care of myself." *I
hope he realizes now that I'm his senior officer and not some fragile
girl.*

Eli smiled and took her hand, causing her to soften. "I know
you can," he said. "I just want you to come back safe. I've gotten
kind of attached to you."

Angela was to meet Agent Tallichet at Headquarters in thirty
minutes. She raced home, fed Mr. T, closed the cat door to keep
him inside, changed her uniform shirt, and locked up. She arrived
at the office in time to get all her gear organized before LizBeth
showed up. As they were walking out the door, Angela's cellphone
rang. It was Eli.

"I got hold of Lorna Armijo, Raven's girlfriend. She said Raven
called her from one of the campgrounds up the road from her. He
sounded traumatized to her. He's headed her way on foot. She said
he told her not to go out of the house and to wait for him to get

there. I told her you two were coming. I'll send you a pin of her location. She's really scared."

LizBeth and Angela got into LizBeth's car and they drove south for thirty minutes through the canyon to the little village of Pilar, a settlement on the Rio Grande that was once an Apache village. It was getting dark and few cars were on the road. They passed one campground that was already full of tents and RVs, then crossed the river on a one-lane bridge and drove up a dirt road to where a tiny cabin stood in a grove of big spruce trees. There were no lights on in the cabin. LizBeth parked the car and they got out. Angela briefly saw an outline of a woman at the window, then a porch light came on. The door opened and a woman said, "Who are you? What do you want?" A dog wriggled between her legs and started to bark. LizBeth and Angela stopped about twenty yards from the house.

"I'm Agent LizBeth Tallichet, ma'am, FBI. And this is Angela Romero, Deputy Sheriff from Taos County. We're here to help."

"I don't need your help," the woman, who was young and looked multiracial, said. "I'm just fine. Please go away and leave me alone."

LizBeth whispered to Angela, "Someone is in there with her."

Angela replied, "Possibly. Or maybe someone threatened her."

LizBeth said, "Ma'am, can we come in and talk? You might be in danger and we want to keep you safe."

"No, no," she said, "Go away. Go away now." The dog, a large white pit bull, came out into the yard, barking aggressively.

Angela spoke up. "Ms. Armijo," she said, "We want to help find Raven, but we can't if you don't talk to us."

"I don't know what you are talking about," Lorna said, looking for a moment over her shoulder. "Get out of my yard, now!" Her voice sounded desperate.

"There *is* someone in there," Angela whispered to LizBeth. "What do we do now?"

"Yeah," LizBeth whispered. "I saw that little over the shoulder look." Then she yelled, "Okay, Ma'am, we're going to leave you alone. If you have any problems, call 911. Have a good night!" Angela and LizBeth walked back to the car.

"Are we just going to leave her there?" Angela asked. "She's a hostage, isn't she?"

LizBeth said, "Call Joseph and Zach and ask them to make a wellness check. Tell them what we suspect. We stand to do more harm if we try to barge in there and there's a shootout. They don't want her, they want Raven Sandoval. Let's focus on finding him."

The gibbous moon shone on the dark, rippling river as they crossed back over a one-lane bridge and headed upstream again. Parked at a little pull-out not far upstream from the bridge was a large late-model grey pickup truck.

"That's Kane's truck," Angela said.

Angela radioed Zach who happened to be not far away, in the canyon near Rinconada. She gave him all the information and the location. "Drive past the bridge a little, then turn around before you go across it. If you see a grey Dodge pickup parked upstream, the suspects are still there. Don't go in by yourself. Call Joseph and Sheriff before you do anything. These guys are armed and dangerous. If the truck isn't there, they've probably left. Go ahead and do a wellness check, get Ms. Armijo to safety, and gather any evidence that might be there. Agent Tallichet and I are going to try to find Raven."

"Be careful out there," Zach said. "Other thugs might be hunting for him too."

"We know. We will be. Out."

"Do you think Raven would be walking along the road?" LizBeth asked. "Or is there a trail he could go on?"

"The only trails I know about all lead away from the river, up to the rim of the canyon," Angela asked. "The easiest way to get down here is to walk on the road. But I'm sure Raven would be wary about being seen."

"Let's drive along the road first. Then we can stop in at the campgrounds and see if anyone has seen him."

"I'm worried about Lorna Armijo," Angela said. "What will they do to her?"

"The best thing we could do was go away from there," LizBeth said. *Of course there is a chance they could hurt or kill her,* LizBeth thought.

They drove along the narrow road that wound alongside the river in its deep gorge. If Raven was walking on this road, they would see him right away, as there was virtually no place to hide. Across the river, the walking would be arduous as there was no trail, just a succession of boulders and steep places with almost no place to stand. They drove for several miles, seeing no one until they arrived at the Taos Junction Bridge. From there, the dirt road left the river and became very steep as it climbed to the top of the mesa in switchbacks. They turned around before the bridge and stopped at the first campground, which was small with only a handful of campers. LizBeth rapped on the door of a Winnebago which was the only RV among tents. A man opened a window in his travel trailer and turned on an outside light. "Yes?" he said.

"Sorry to bother you, sir, but have you seen a man walking near this road? Small frame, Native American?" LizBeth showed her ID. The man shone a flashlight on the two women.

"No, we haven't seen anyone," the man said. "Is he dangerous?"

"No, sir. Were you outside before dark?"

"Yes. We just came inside about fifteen minutes ago."

"And you didn't see anyone?"

"Just the people in those tents," he said. "What is this about?"

"We are trying to locate a man who is missing," LizBeth said. "Thanks for your help."

"Good luck, Officer," he said.

LizBeth drove on to the next place, a wooded campground in a bend in the river. The campground was closed for repairs and the entrance was blocked by a chain. "Stop here," Angela said. "I know this place and it would be a good place to hide, especially because it's closed." LizBeth pulled to the side of the road where they parked and got out. "Follow me," Angela said. She led them past a group pavilion and onto a path to the river. They walked through high grasses and over driftwood, the swooshing and crackling of their passage covered by the sound of the river rapidly flowing down the canyon and lapping against the bank. Angela called out, "Raven? Raven Sandoval?

It's Deputy Angela Romero, Taos County. We're here to help. If you're down here, come out." There was no response. Angela walked closer to the water, feeling that someone was nearby. She started to call out again but the sight of a man crouching in the shadows among some willows startled her. The man, who was young and Indian, looked at her with a blank expression Angela had seen before on the faces of trauma victims. "Raven?" she said softly. The young man stood up. "Yeah," he said. "It's me." He was a small, slightly-built man with a close-cropped black hair and tattered clothes that were soaking wet. He was shivering and holding his right hand under his left arm. Pain showed on his face.

LizBeth came up behind Angela and Raven looked for a moment like he would run. LizBeth said, "It's okay, Mr. Sandoval. I'm from the FBI. We're here to take you to safety."

"Where are they?" Raven asked in a whisper.

"They aren't nearby," LizBeth said. "We're going to arrest them. But first we have to take you to safety. Come on to the car. I have a blanket and some food and water. You are injured. What happened to your hand?"

"The man cut off part of my little finger for a trophy."

"We'll take you to the ER and get that tended to."

"What about Lorna?" Raven asked. "They will go after Lorna."

"We have officers headed to her house," Angela said. "They are probably already there."

LizBeth found some energy bars, a blanket and a bottle of water for Raven and he got into the backseat for the drive back to town. Before they came to the bridge to Lorna's cabin they saw that Kane's truck was gone from its parking place in the pullout before the bridge. Across the river they could see the LED strobe lights of a deputy car parked in front of Lorna's cabin. Raven objected to going past without checking in with his girlfriend, but LizBeth convinced him the deputies would keep her safe and that they needed to take him back to Taos so he could get some dry clothes and medical attention for his hand. "Deputy Zach will get Lorna somewhere safe. You can see her in the morning," Angela said. Then she called Zach's cellphone.

Zach answered right away. "Is everything okay there, Zach?" Angela asked.

"Under control," Zach answered. "No sign of the perpetrators. Joseph should be here in ten minutes. We plan to follow Ms. Armijo to her mother's house in Rinconada when he gets here. I've completed a preliminary interview. I can share with you later."

"Okay, thanks. Please let her know that we have found Raven Sandoval and are headed to the hospital to get him looked at. See you later."

Angela told LizBeth and Raven the news from Zach and Raven appeared to relax somewhat hearing that his girlfriend was safe.

LizBeth called Lt. Manuel Quintana of the Taos Tribal Police and asked him to meet her at their headquarters later. "We're going to get his hand tended to," LizBeth said. "Get a hot meal and some dry clothes for him. He's had a hell of a time." LizBeth found that she had a secure message on her phone from the office. The postmortem on Mondragon was back, faster than she'd expected. Death from a blow to the head. *At least he hadn't had to suffer, she thought.* LizBeth would look more closely at the results as soon as she could.

After a long wait at the emergency department having his hand tended to, followed by warm clothes and food, Raven was too worn out to be interviewed. LizBeth took him to Mrs. Martinez's to spend the night and Lt. Quintana arranged for an armed guard to protect them. She promised to meet with him the next morning. In the meantime, Angela heard from Zach regarding his interview of Lorna Armijo. She said that two men broke down her door looking for Raven about dusk. They were wearing stocking caps and Halloween masks of the Lone Ranger and Tanto, which they never took off. The Lone Ranger did all the talking, adding sexual taunts to what he said. She told them that Raven had phoned her and he was on his way to Colorado, but they didn't believe her. When LizBeth and Angela showed up, he threatened to kill her if she didn't say what he told her to say. They fled fifteen minutes after LizBeth and Angela left.

At Trey Cameron's home, the outdoor lights were on and Rowdy stood guard at the front door. It was a clear night and the big pines swayed in a restless wind. In Cameron's walnut paneled office off the library, the atmosphere was tense. Ramón Trujillo sat at one end of a sumptuous leather couch looking frightened and miserable. He'd been called here after he'd already had several glasses of wine and had been about to go to bed. He was wearing a sweatsuit and his white hair was uncombed. At the other end of the couch sat Lassiter Kane, who was listening to music on earbuds, his legs crossed and his eyes closed. Cody Parker, who was expected, had not yet arrived. Cameron sat in his swivel chair with his back to Trujillo and Kane, looking at the day's stocks on his phone.

After a few minutes, Cameron swung around and spoke first to Trujillo. "Senator," Cameron said, "in the past week I've discovered that you mishandled the Forest Service leases severely. Because of your negligence, aspects of a lease are now in question. In the office of Governor Montaño, I learned that you are again under ethics investigation in the Senate where it is rumored by good sources that you are about to be censured. And today I learned that your man Parker is suspected of murder. There is an eyewitness to Parker being at the scene of the crime. My sources tell me that Taos tribal governor Jerry Quintana is about to expose you for bribery. Sir, you are a disgrace. You are no longer of use to me."

"Trey, please. I can explain all of this." Trujillo ran his hands through his hair. His eyes darted around the room for a means of escape.

"No, you can't explain, and I can no longer use you and I certainly can't protect you from any of this. You are going down, my man. You will be charged as an accessory to murder, bribery, extortion and more. And you know our deal. This is now entirely your problem, Senator. Do I make myself clear?"

"You don't understand," Trujillo said. "I negotiated on your behalf, always! I did as I was told. I cannot be held responsible for your decisions!"

Cameron shook his finger at Trujillo. "My decisions? You are responsible for your own bad, very bad decisions," Cameron said. "I warned you what could happen if you failed. And your man Parker has put us in an untenable position."

"How can you blame me for what he did? I didn't tell him to kill Mondragon. What have you done with him? He's not returning my calls."

"I will manage Parker from now on." Kane sat up at his point, took the earbuds out of his ears and started paying close attention.

"What should I do now?" Trujillo asked plaintively.

"That is up to you," Cameron said. "I suggest you hire a very good lawyer. And don't entertain any ideas about revealing any of our...agreements. That would be very, very dangerous for you." Kane looked at Trujillo and smiled broadly causing Trujillo to blanch.

"Now, it is time you to leave. I never want to see you again." "What about my compensation? You still owe me!"

"What compensation?" Cameron said, shaking his head. "I owe you nothing. You haven't fulfilled your contract. Now get out."

Trujillo, visibly shaken, got up and shambled out of the room, leaving Cameron alone with Kane. Cameron stood up and poured himself and Kane some scotch in crystal double old fashioned glasses. Kane sat up and took his glass.

"You sure showed him, Dad," he said. "He is such a fool, that man. And dangerous to us. Do you want me to take care of him?"

"Lassiter, you and I differ on when to take a life. You are ready to proceed on the first indication. I, on the other hand, prefer to wait until it is necessary. Which it definitely is not, at present."

"What would make you think it necessary?" Kane asked, taking a sip of whiskey.

"It's a feeling I get," Cameron said. "An inkling."

"Well, I think I take after you, sir," Kane said, leaning back on the couch pillows.

"The sheriff was here inquiring about some mayordomo who is dead."

Kane looked sheepish. "It's all good," he said. "It was a clean job."

"Again, though, was it necessary?" Cameron asked. He knew his son took pleasure in killing.

"I had an inkling he would talk," Kane said. "I have the same inkling about Trujillo."

Cameron shook his head regretfully. "You'll never learn," he said. "Your readiness to use violence will be your downfall. Even that girl you kidnapped, if she ever decided to go to the police you could go to jail for a long time. But do you let that stop you? No."

"She wanted to come with me," Kane said, smiling. "I didn't have to use violence."

Cameron stood up and looked out the window. "The weather is changing," he said. "I don't like this wind."

"No, sir."

"Lassiter, I am very displeased with you."

Kane sat up and put his glass down between his feet. "Sir?" he said.

"Why in hell did you allow Cody Parker to go after Mondragon alone?"

"Dad, he ran off. You know he chafes against my leadership or any leadership, for that matter. I didn't realize he was gone until the late afternoon."

"Because you were fucking that girl, Madeline Smith?"

Kane said nothing.

"Did you tell him to kill Mondragon?" Cameron asked, his back to Kane.

"I expressly said NOT to kill him. I said to threaten him, only. You know, to make sure he voted yes at the tribal council. Parker said Trujillo told him to kill Mondragon."

"Why is that?" Cameron asked. "If that's true, Trujillo lied to me."

"Parker said Mondragon had been at a meeting Trujillo held with Gilbert Herrera."

"What meeting?" Cameron asked with alarm in his voice.

"Evidently Trujillo met with Herrera and Mondragon last weekend and he referenced the bribes he was giving to approve something called a cross-basin transfer."

Cameron's face contorted in rage. "Why didn't you tell me this?" *Trujillo is going to ruin me by interfering like this.*

"Dad, I just heard about it yesterday," Kane lied. Kane took the last sip of his whiskey. "Don't worry, Mondragon is dead. That is one thing Trujillo had right."

"We could have paid Mondragon to stay silent. He had plenty of reasons not to talk. Now we are likely to lose the Taos water rights sale. This is a disaster."

"I know, and I am sorry. I should have got there sooner. I never expected even Cody Parker to be stupid enough to kill Mondragon. I also thought it would be better if I kept hidden while Cody threatened him."

"Parker must, of course, be dealt with as soon as possible."

"I've already taken care of it," Kane said.

"Good." Cameron poured himself another whiskey. "Parker would spill his guts if the feds caught up with him. What did you do with the body?"

"I buried it near Tres Piedras," he lied. Actually, Parker's corpse, the throat slashed, was in a body bag on the floor of Kane's Airstream. Kane hated hard work like digging a grave.

"And what about the Indian kid?" Cameron asked.

"Don't worry about him," Kane said. "I'll take care of him."

"You'd better," Cameron said. "You may be my offspring, but I brought you on board to be a professional. Now you have your dream job. Do it right."

"Okay, Dad."

"Call me Mr. Cameron from now on. I can't have people knowing you are my son. And you have to get over your sexual obsessions. You got distracted by that little girl with the baby, am I right?"

"Yes, sir. Maddy. She was a distraction. But she's gone. And don't worry, she won't come after me, or you. I made sure of that."

"What did you do to make sure?"

"The usual," Kane said, lying again. "Just like you taught me. I scared her good, but I didn't kill her!"

"That's better. Maddy was pretty, not trashy like your other women. But not submissive enough. In our line of work we need submissive women. Ones who are easy to control. Not little firecrackers like her."

"True enough. We always go after the little firecrackers, don't we? Like Mom. She was a hottie, wasn't she?"

"I'll never forgive her for what she did," Cameron said in an angry tone. "And you shouldn't either."

"I never blamed her," Kane said in a low voice. "Haven't you ever wanted to kill yourself?"

"Never bring that up to me again, do you hear? Remember, Shelly almost killed me in the process of killing herself."

Kane held out his glass for more whiskey, but Cameron shook his head and put the bottle away. The two men were silent for a few minutes.

"Can I move back to the property now?"

"You can move into the bunkhouse."

"With respect, Dad... Mr. Cameron, I don't want to be just another uniformed servant in the bunkhouse."

"Ah, yes," Cameron said, sneering. "You're better than them, right? To the manor born?"

"Not exactly," Kane said. "But I have my position as a supervisor to consider. I was hoping I could put the Airstream down where I had it last spring. By the edge of the gorge where you put in water and power?"

"Check with me when you've dispatched Sandoval and maybe I'll let you. But stay focused from now on. No more carelessness." Cameron turned back to the window and watched the big pine trees swaying in a fierce wind.

"I will, sir." Kane said. *What am I going to do about Sandoval? If Dad finds out he escaped I'll have no choice but to kill myself. Or him.*

LizBeth was up at dawn to prepare for her interview with Raven Sandoval. She'd gone to bed late after a long conversation with Dawa that caused her to lie awake for about an hour before she fell asleep. Dawa was a good listener and she asked all the right questions of her headstrong wife about her relationship with the Regional Director of the FBI, her boss, Don Barkley. At the end of the conversation, LizBeth realized she was on a collision course with Barkley, who she felt sure was protecting Trey Cameron. LizBeth wondered if a conflict with Barkley could land her in big trouble. Might she even be charged with something because of choices she made that her boss didn't like? She'd seen it happen to others. LizBeth made note to speak with her old friend in Washington, Raquel Bradshaw, deputy assistant Inspector General at the Justice Department. Raquel and LizBeth had met in high school and remained good friends in spite of years and distance. Raquel was trustworthy and could perhaps help her figure out how to navigate next steps.

LizBeth grabbed a quick breakfast at a drive-through and made her way to Taos Pueblo. Lt. Quintana met her at the door of the tribal police station.

The interview with Raven Sandoval was going to take place in the station's new interview room. LizBeth would conduct it by herself at Raven's request and Lt. Quintana would not listen in. Raven had expressed suspicions about the lieutenant being aligned with Senator Trujillo in the past. Lt. Quintana had no reservations about Raven's request. Since Mondragon's killing, he'd seemed eager to comply with everything LizBeth wanted.

"Good morning, Agent Tallichet," Quintana said. "Come in, help yourself to coffee. We have some empanadas too."

"Thank you, Lt.. How are things this morning?"

"Pretty tense," Quintana said. "A lot of people are reacting to what happened to Del and Raven. The rumor is out that the suspect in Mondragon's killing is Cody Parker. He is not a popular guy around here. And he's associated with Senator Trujillo. People are turning sour on Trujillo and this whole water rights purchase as a result."

"Isn't the council vote today?" LizBeth asked.

"It's scheduled for 4 pm. But my guess is that with Del's murder it will be postponed."

"That's good," LizBeth said. "Let things settle down a bit."

Raven came in and greeted LizBeth. He looked better than he'd looked the night before, having gotten medical help for his hand, wholesome food, and a decent night's sleep. LizBeth invited him into the room and oriented him to the interview and recording process. "Just answer the questions you're sure you know the answer to," she said. "If you don't know the answer, that's okay." Raven sat down and LizBeth began.

"Did Del tell you why he wanted to go up on the mountain?"

"First he told me he needed to think about what he was going to do with today's vote. I think he'd already decided to vote no, but he wanted to go over it all in his mind."

"Did he tell you about the threats made by Senator Ramón Trujillo if he voted no?"

"He told me that if he voted no, Trujillo said he would tell that the judges in the Native Artist Showcase had been bribed to select him as Native Artist of the Year. Del said that Trujillo would make it look like Del did the bribing."

"Did he tell you anything else?" LizBeth asked.

Raven held his left hand up and LizBeth saw that fresh blood had seeped through the bandage. "He told me that when Trujillo thought he was going to vote in favor of the water sale he was invited to a meeting Trujillo had with two government officials, where bribes were discussed. At least one of the officials took a bribe. Mondragon also took a bribe. He recorded the meeting on his phone."

"Did he play the recording for you?"

"No, I never heard it. He told me he had made an MP3 of the conversation and put it on a thumb drive. He gave a copy to his brother-in-law, who was killed, Mr. Valdez. Then he erased it from his phone and hid his thumb drive somewhere. He didn't tell me where. He said the recording was pretty incriminating to Trujillo, but he didn't want to use it unless he had to."

"Who were the two government officials?" LizBeth asked. *This could be a smoking gun if we can find it,* she thought.

"I can't be sure of their names," Raven said. "One might have been named Herrera."

"You say he gave the thumb drive to Antonio Valdez, correct? Do you know what Valdez did with it?"

"No. I don't think even Del knew what Mr. Valdez did with it. Del was paranoid that somehow Trujillo knew about the recording and would be coming for him. That's why he went up on the mountain—to hide until after today."

"Okay, let's talk about what happened on the mountain. What time did you two head up there?"

"In the afternoon. We set up camp before dark and Del went fishing. He caught a couple of trout for our dinner. I made a fire and we cooked and ate. That night we took turns on watch and sleeping."

"What about the next day?"

"Del fished and I sketched and cooked us some beans and rice to go with the fish in case he caught any more. Del was pretty quiet. He kept to himself. I did more sketching and took a nap."

"When did you get the idea that anything was wrong?"

"It was after dinner on the third day. It was dark. I took the first watch. I was staring into the fire and listening to the river and Del was asleep. I heard a twig snap and then suddenly Parker was in our camp swinging a shovel and yelling. It was so sudden I kind of froze. Del jumped up and Parker hit him hard on the side of the head. Del fell to the ground like a rock. Del never moved after that. I think that one hit killed him." Raven swallowed hard and went silent. He had tears in his eyes.

"Then what happened?" LizBeth asked.

"I grabbed my pack and ran down to the river and up on the other side. I had the advantage because I knew where I was going. I climbed up a big spruce with low hanging branches and hid. Parker came after me, but after a while, sometime after the moon set, he gave up and left. My phone was out of battery, so I couldn't call anyone. I dozed some in the tree but eventually I came down."

"Then what did you do?"

"I turned on my flashlight and started looking for a trail I knew about off the back side of that ridge that led down to another trail that ended at a road in about five miles. I couldn't find it."

LizBeth paused to make sure the recorder was picking up all the interview. It was. "Okay, go ahead. What happened then?"

"I was still up on the ridge when a man jumped me. He must have seen my flashlight beam. He rushed me and grabbed my throat. I thought he was going to kill me."

"Who was it?"

"A white man. I don't know his name," Raven said, shaking his head. "I never heard Parker call him anything but 'Boss.'"

"Then what happened?"

"He said he would take me down the mountain 'to a safe place.' I didn't believe him, so I left my backpack by a tree in case someone would find it and know I'd gone that way. It was so dark the man didn't notice. We went cross-country for a ways. He also had a flashlight, but it was tough going. Finally, we found the trail and hiked on until almost morning. When we got to his truck he told me he needed 'a sacrifice' for Del or some such bullshit. He pulled out a big knife and grabbed my arm. He told me to keep quiet and to stretch out my fingers on the metal tailgate of his truck. Then he chopped off the first joint of my little finger. I bled a lot and it hurt like hell. He put handcuffs on me and tied my feet and put me in the back of his truck. I don't remember much after that."

LizBeth stood up. Raven was sweating and holding back tears after recounting his trauma.

"Do you want a soda or something?" she asked him.

"Yeah," Raven said.

LizBeth stuck her head out and spoke to Quintana.

He brought two cold soda cans into the room and went back out. LizBeth and Raven flipped the pop tops at the same time.

"That was some tough stuff, wasn't it?" LizBeth asked.

Raven took a big drink of soda and wiped his mouth. He nodded.

"So let me get this straight. Parker killed Del, correct?"

"Yes. He hit him on the head. I think that killed him."

"And you never saw the other man near the campsite?"

"No. I think he was coming in off that other trail when he found me."

"Okay, let's go back to when you were in his truck. Do you remember anything about the ride?"

"No. But when we got to his campsite in Tres Piedras, he put me in an old, beat-up trailer that had broken windows and no door. He cuffed me to a post that was bolted to the floor. There was also a nice travel trailer right next to where I was. He had a girl in there and a baby, I think. I could hear their voices. I was there all the next day. He questioned me about Del's murder while he hit and punched me. Then he'd feed me, give me a drink, and let me rest. Then he'd start all over."

"What did he want to know?"

"I don't know. I suspected he would just kill me in the end, no matter what I told him."

"Was Parker there?"

"Not until the next evening. He told his boss he'd tried to bury Del's body but ran into the dog team and FBI. The boss whipped Parker with his own pistol and threatened to kill him."

Raven stood up looking pale and ill. "I need to go to the bathroom," he said.

"Okay," LizBeth said. "Take your time. Come back when you're ready."

While Raven was out of the room, Lt. Quintana came in and said, "Agent Tallichet, when you are finished here my brother, Governor Quintana would like to meet with you."

"Okay, is he going to come here?"

"He'd like you to come to his house. I can bring you there."

Raven came back in and sat down. "Can I go soon?"

"It won't take too much longer. Where are you going to go from here?"

"Over to Lorna's mother's house in town. She said I can stay in her garage apartment for a few weeks."

"Let's talk about how you escaped."

"The next night Parker came back. The man made him guard me. He gave him the handcuff keys and went back to his girlfriend. It was chilly that night. I was wide awake. My hand was hurting like hell. It was becoming infected. Anyway, Parker drank tequila and passed out on the floor right next to me. I managed to get the keys out of his pocket and uncuff myself. I ran out to the road and started walking. I hid from every car. There weren't very many. I didn't want to hitch because I didn't trust anyone. In the morning, I got to the Taos Junction Bridge and met some bikers. They gave me food and water and I found a bandana for my hand in one of the campgrounds. I hung out there and slept under a juniper tree until dark. I was headed to Lorna's when you and the deputy found me."

"So you never saw either man after you escaped?"

"No."

"Okay, Raven, that's all for now. Get some more rest. I may need to ask you more later."

On the same morning LizBeth was interviewing Raven, Ulysses woke up to the sound of his mother talking quietly with Amelia and Monty while she prepared their breakfast. It was early and Rosemary was still asleep, snoring softly. Ulysses stretched and slipped out of bed and into the bathroom for a shower. He got dressed in blue jeans and a tee shirt. When he came into the kitchen the children were at the breakfast table eating buckwheat crepes with whipped cream and strawberries from Granny's garden. "Happy birthday, Son," Ulysses said, kissing his eight-year-old on the top of the head.

"Can I open my presents soon?" Monty asked in a loud voice.

"Let's let Mom sleep. Once she is up and has had breakfast we can talk about presents." Ulysses gave Diana, who stood at the stove, a good morning kiss. "I'm going out to do the chores and start irrigating," he said.

He walked across the parched yard, past Rosemary's spring garden of lettuces, spinach, onions, kale, trellised peas and heirloom tomato starts, to the acequia headgate. The main ditch looked low, but at least there was some water there. Ulysses turned the wheel to lift the iron gate and water started to gravity-feed into Rosemary's garden, flowing down the rows to each thirsty plant. As he watered, he looked up at the mountains, which showed new green of aspen leaves across the middle elevations all the way to near the top. Spring was turning into summer and maybe the dry, windy conditions would change. Rain was not predicted, but then there was a 30% chance of showers in three days and a 50% chance after that. It was a good day for a birthday party and a fundraiser, a little cooler with a cloudless sky.

Ulysses fed the goats some hay and gathered a dozen eggs from the hens. He refilled their feeders and waterers and gave them some vegetable scraps. Just as he was preparing the grain for the goats, Rosemary came out of the house to milk. Ulysses felt relieved. He wasn't a great milker and Rosemary hated when he got cross with her "girls," which he invariably did when they wouldn't let down their milk. He fed the remaining wether from last year, who was so big he was almost able to jump out of his pen. The other wether was in the freezer. Ulysses tried not to think of its sweet face and rambunctious personality. It was easier for Rosemary, who grew up around livestock and had gotten used to their fates.

She was making quick work of milking Dolly, who typically let down easily and gave the most volume. She was due to be bred soon. Her other females, Margie and Bobbie, ate up their grain. They were both pregnant and not presently in milk.

"Are you going to be here for Monty's party?" Rosemary asked as she finished.

"I doubt it, Rosemary. I need to speak with Angela. She texted me that they found a man they were looking for down near Pilar. I should probably go debrief that with her."

"I'm so glad Diana is here. It was really kind of her to come. If you can't be here, I understand."

"Thanks for that. What's the plan?" Ulysses asked.

"Ten little boys will arrive at 11. Games until 12, then hot dogs, pizza, and lemonade, a piñata, open presents, and cake and ice cream. It will all be over by 1:30, so I'll have time to take a nap before the fundraiser."

"Stephanie said we should arrive by 4."

"Let's go ahead and give Monty his new bike. That way, even if you get called away you will have been here for the most important part."

Rosemary and Ulysses had selected a children's mountain bike for Monty and had hidden it in the garage. Monty knew all about it but still acted surprised when they brought it out from its hiding place. It was shiny and blue, his favorite color, had three gears, hand brakes, big knobby tires and looked very grown-up. Amelia, who had a similar bike in yellow, helped him adjust the seat and showed him the bike's special features. The two of them rode off down the long driveway together. Just then Ulysses' cellphone rang. It was Ray Pando. Rosemary went back in the house as he took the call.

"Hey, man, sorry to bother you at home so early," he said.

"No problem, Ray, what's up?"

"Somebody broke into our house last night while we were in Isleta at Clarice's sister's house."

"Are you and Clarice okay?"

"We're fine. We only just got home. Matt called us about six when he came by on his run and noticed our front door was open. We came right away. The place is trashed."

"Did they get anything? Like the original letter?"

"Hell, no. I have that document in a safe place, and nobody knows where it is, except me and Matt. But they sure enough broke a bunch of stuff and made a huge mess looking for it. Clarice is mad as a hornet."

"I'll come over and take a look," Ulysses said. "Maybe we can find some evidence of who did this."

"They left a note, Ulys. They said they were going to 'fuck up' whoever damaged the transfer apparatus up at Rio de la Presa. They are obviously targeting Picuris as the culprits."

"Okay, I'll be there in about thirty minutes."

Driving south to Picuris, Ulysses got a call from Angela. She told him what Zach had learned from Lorna Armijo about the two men and said that LizBeth would be interviewing Raven this morning around nine. *Things are really heating up with this case,* Ulysses thought. *Just in time for the election.*

Ray and Clarice were sitting in rockers on their front porch drinking coffee when Ulysses arrived. Clarice went inside to pour him a cup and brought out a bag of donuts from the Loving Oven in Española, Ray's favorites. Both seemed calmer than Ulysses expected. Ray stood up and shook Ulysses' hand.

"Thanks for coming, Ulys. After I spoke with you, I called LizBeth Tallichet. She was on her way to Taos to interview Raven Sandoval but said she'd send a forensic team. I also called Delilah and she is coming by. She should be here any minute."

"That's good," Ulysses said. "Go ahead and tell me what you know," Ulysses said, biting into a jelly donut. He'd missed breakfast and was hungry. The donut was fresh and delicious.

"One of Matt's war council guys did a check at midnight and didn't see anything, so it must have happened after that. He came around at six and saw the door kicked in. Nobody on the plaza heard anything, which makes me think it might have been around 4 am. Anything earlier on a Friday night or anything close to sunrise would have been heard. There weren't any tracks, though. The ground is too packed and dry. Come on and I'll show you the damage."

"I'll stay out here," Clarice said. "It's better for my blood pressure." Delilah had just pulled up and parked and she went inside with Ray and Ulysses.

Ulysses put on a pair of plastic gloves and examined the old wooden front door. The wood had split at the bottom where force had been applied, enough to break the lock loose from the jamb. Inside, to the left of the door stood a small antique secretary-style desk which had all the drawers pulled out and emptied onto the floor. "Those bastards took all my old bank statements and receipts." Ray laughed. "But they took my laptop, my external hard drive and a whole basket of thumb drives, too."

In the living room, the couch pillows were cut open and stuffing pulled out, as were the pillows on two side chairs. A television and sound system stood untouched. "They left my guns alone and didn't touch Clarice's jewelry. She has some expensive pieces, but they weren't interested in anything except papers and computer stuff."

"It's very much like what they did at Daddy's," Delilah said.

They walked into the bedroom where the mattress was also slashed open and clothes were pulled from closets and bureaus and strewn around the room. The kitchen had received the same treatment, with drawers pulled out and contents emptied.

"Show me the note they left," Ulysses said, and Ray pointed to a handwritten note on a scrap of paper that stood under a river stone paperweight. It said, "Keep your dirty hands off our presa. We're going to hurt you."

"I don't think this was done by acequieros from Mora," Ray said. "They want to make it look like the Mora folks are angry at us for damaging the presa, when all along it was Cameron's people. This note shows the whole thing was an excuse to search my house for something they really want."

"I agree. Do you think they were watching you?" Delilah asked. "They had to know you were out of town, I'm thinking. They were watching me when I was in Santa Fe."

"My guess is they've been casing my place for a while. It takes some cojones to do what they did. Seems like more than any farmers would do, even if water is involved."

"Cameron is used to getting his way," Ulysses said. "He's got a lot of money at stake to make this project work. He's had to enlist a bunch of bureaucrats to make this happen. I saw the State Engineer and the Carson National Forest Supervisor out at his house the other day."

Delilah said, "Arthur says Cameron just agreed to post a bond with the county and give money to upgrade roads to improve access for emergency vehicles. He says he'll add a lot of infrastructure as part of his development plan. These things make county commissioners happy, but it makes him sound desperate to me. He's also trying to get the Forest Service to overlook some problems with their leases."

Ulysses said, "Plus, he's got to keep the water from the Mora transfers and access more from Taos Pueblo on a cross-basin transfer. There could be a lot of ruckus if he doesn't have all the right people on his side. Highland Fling has to look like a boon for poor beleaguered Mora County. So he can't afford any glitches or leaked information that would interfere with the plan. And he can't afford to get tied to illegal activity. There have there been three murders: Antonio Valdez, Jeremy Diggs, and Delfino Mondragon, all three somehow connected to Cameron's little racket."

"They had to kill them because they couldn't bribe them," Ray said. "Antonio would never have accepted a bribe and I'm guessing he had some kind of information they didn't want him to have. Del was kind of sitting on the fence. I have a feeling he knew too much also. What about Diggs?"

"Diggs likely killed Antonio under pressure from one of Cameron's goons," Ulysses said. "That's the definition of knowing too much. Now we just have to figure out exactly what it was they knew."

After Delilah left to go home, Ulysses and Ray got into the Expedition and drove the few miles to the Ramirez property. As soon as they got there, they suspected Ramirez was gone. No truck to be seen and the child's swing was gone also. When they walked up to the house, there was no dog barking and from the front porch they could see through the windows that the front rooms were empty of furniture. The backhoe had been moved to a shed behind the house. Ray and Ulysses looked it over.

"Sure enough, a dent and a scrape," Ulysses said.

"Yep, paint is missing." Ray said. "Now it's on that ponderosa pine over near the diversion presa."

Ulysses took pictures of the backhoe and its treads, including new tracks from when it had been moved into the shed after a recent rain. "This is a slam dunk. Our vandal is none other than Jacinto Ramirez."

"And who is the paymaster?" Ray asked. "His cousin, the big rancher in Mora?"

"I'm not convinced Ben Ramirez would do this. According to Rita Wainwright, he's been unwilling to sell to Cameron. Ben's a land grant activist going way back and is law-abiding so far as I know. I think Trey Cameron paid Jacinto Ramirez to stir up all this stuff as a distraction. An attack on the presa to make everyone focus on the water rights dispute with Picuris, rather than Highland Fling. He may also have paid him to break into your house."

"Where do you think Jacinto Ramirez has gone?" Ray asked.

"Probably back over to Mora, where he's from," Ulysses said. "Maybe Cameron promised him a job in 'security.'"

"Sounds about right," Ray said. "Cameron's little racket isn't so little after all."

"I'm going to call the sheriff over in Mora and have him keep an eye out for Jacinto. We have enough evidence to arrest him."

LizBeth left her interview with Raven Sandoval and was escorted to the home of the Taos Governor Jerry Quintana by Lt. Manuel Quintana, the Governor's younger brother. It was a short drive from the historic pueblo to the newer, rambling one-story ranch house where the governor lived. Lt. Quintana said nothing on the drive over. LizBeth thought better than to ask what this was about, but she thought she knew. The murder of Mondragon had shaken the entire tribe and there were bound to be political implications. Quintana pulled into the driveway where two expensive new cars were parked. "Do you want me to come in?" Lt. Quintana asked. He seemed hesitant.

"I assumed you would. Yes, come on in."

Quintana said nothing and they both got out of the car.

Mrs. Quintana, a stout woman in her sixties, well-dressed, and wearing heavy makeup, came to the door. She didn't speak, just held the door open for them to enter. A young Anglo man in a suit stood up from a chair by the door. "I'm Jayson Jones, Tribal Governor Quintana's attorney." He sat back down.

The house smelled of cinnamon potpourri. Mrs. Quintana invited them to sit down on a spotless white couch. She went into the other room and LizBeth heard her talking with her husband in low tones. At last he came out, a short, stocky man of about seventy with grey hair in a single braid and many rings on his fingers.

"Agent Tallichet," he said in a deep voice, reaching down to shake her hand. "I have a few things to discuss with you." He sat in a chair opposite the couch. "Manny, you might want to wait outside. Or in the kitchen with Patricia." There was an uncomfortable moment as the brothers, one governor and the younger one the head of police, exchanged glances; then Lt. Quintana got up and went out to the car to wait.

Once he'd left, the governor said, "Ms. Tallichet, Senator Ramón Trujillo has offered me bribes on many occasions," he said. "I am interested in having immunity in exchange for my testimony against him."

"Sir, I don't know if you realize..."

Jones spoke up. "I've taken the liberty to draw up the terms of an agreement including a hypothetical set of testimonies my client might give and what kind of consideration he might..."

Agent Tallichet stood up. "We're not having this conversation, Mr. Jones. Now is not the time. Your client will be questioned regarding his involvement with Senator Trujillo. Once that happens, we can see if a prosecutor thinks immunity is indicated."

"Governor Quintana, was there anything else you wanted to discuss with me?"

The older man rubbed his brown hands and looked at his shoes. "Agent Tallichet," he said. "I don't believe that the source of money for the bribes was Senator Trujillo. I believe I can also implicate someone else. A Mr. Trey Cameron. I have information on him that would be very damning."

LizBeth saw an image of Don Barkley's fleshy, angry face. This was exactly the kind of information Barkley didn't want to come out. She felt an impulse to ask Gov. Quintana what he knew but decided to keep her powder dry.

"That is of interest, Governor. But as I said, now is not the time to discuss a plea deal. I'd like to interview you first. What about later this afternoon? Or do you have a tribal council meeting?"

Governor Quintana shook his head. "The council meeting has been postponed due to Del's death," he said.

Jones piped up, "I'll call you, Agent Tallichet."

"Use this number," LizBeth said, giving him the number to her burner phone.

I've crossed the Rubicon now, she thought. *I'd better see if I can get hold of Raquel.*

Ulysses was driving back home when his phone rang. It was Angela.

"Sheriff, I just got back from a call in El Prado. I thought you'd want to know this. Ramón Trujillo tried to kill himself. The Rescue took him to the hospital where he got medevacked to UNM in Albuquerque."

"Is he alive?"

"Yes, but barely, sir. Jazmine found him. He was in the garage. Carbon monoxide poisoning from his car."

"Did he leave a note?" Ulysses asked, shocked at the news.

"He did. Doesn't say much. But I got a picture of it. I'll text it to you."

"Thanks. Deputy, prepare an arrest warrant for Jacinto Ramirez, please. Make it for willful destruction of acequia property. I think he's in Mora, so... "

"I'll do my best, Sheriff. But I have to be at the fundraiser at 3:00 for a server class."

"Okay, ask Joseph to do it."

Ulysses got off the phone with Angela and called LizBeth, who picked up on the first ring.

"Hi, Ulysses, what's up?"

"Trujillo tried to kill himself this morning. He's at UNM in Albuquerque."

"Wow. Is he expected to live?"

"I don't know. He's down at UNM Hospital."

"It's been a busy morning, Ulys. Taos Tribal Governor Jerry Quintana just asked me for immunity to testify against Ramón Trujillo and Trey Cameron."

"That's good news. Are you going to deal?"

"I can't without the prosecutor on board and that means going through my boss."

"Does that mean that the water rights sales are off?"

"They postponed the vote because of Mondragon's murder."

"Did you send a forensics crew to Ray's?"

"They are there now. I just got off the phone with them. They found nothing, unfortunately. Professional job."

"It was probably someone working for Cameron. It looked to me like the same methods I saw at the Valdez house. They seemed to be looking for something, but we don't know what it could be. Delilah has a voicemail message from her father on the night he died indicating he had something really important to tell her. Something he couldn't leave on her voicemail. She thinks it is related to his murder."

"Maybe to Mondragon's murder also," LizBeth said. "The two of them met on the day Valdez was killed. Let me know if you find anything further on this. I may get a chance to interview Taos Tribal Governor Quintana this afternoon. If I do, I'm going to take all the information that I can, even though Barkley won't like it."

"Trujillo and Parker are going down and Cameron will do everything he can to keep from going down with them. Things could get pretty frisky around here."

LizBeth said, "I'm worried that Cameron will just get on his jet and fly away, maybe to Hungary, where his wife is from."

"I'm sure the jet's fueled-up and waiting at the airport. Do you have enough for a RICO case?"

"Possibly. But my old friend who works at the Justice Department warned me off going after it too vigorously if my boss is strongly opposed, until it's rock solid. It's one thing if a state senator from a little backwater like Taos County is put in the cooler, but a fat cat like Trey Cameron requires the white glove delivery. Problem is, he may get away to Hungary in the meantime."

"Don't we have an extradition treaty?" Ulysses asked.

"We do, but it isn't that simple. The government there is corrupt and could be convinced to slow-walk it, at least with a large enough bribe from one of his Hungarian cronies. And Cameron has dual citizenship, which makes it doubly complicated. It's better for us if it never gets that far."

"I have two people I can bring in who might be of help," Ulysses said. "Both members of the racket. Lassiter Kane, who we've got for kidnapping and aggravated assault, and Jacinto Ramirez for willful destruction of acequia infrastructure. I don't know if I could get Kane to turn state's evidence, but I might be able get Ramirez to do it. It's not much, but…"

"Well, it's something. My friend Raquel told me something interesting," LizBeth said. "Don Barkley and Trey Cameron are old fraternity brothers. The good ole boy network rides again."

"Well, I'd better go. I've got an election to win in two days."

"Yeah, and someone's trying to reach me on my other phone."

LizBeth saw that the call coming on her service phone was from Barkley. She let it go to voicemail.

Ulysses arrived home in time for a late lunch and nap before the fundraiser. The party was over, and Monty and Amelia had gone bike riding on the old Vedanta ring trail. His mother was resting in Paloma's old bedroom.

"There is some chicken salad on new garden lettuce in the fridge for you," Rosemary said, standing up from the section of garden she'd been weeding. "And I made some iced tea, nice and strong with lots of lemon."

They went inside the cool, dark house. "Looks like we might get some moisture in the next few days," Rosemary said. Ulysses could tell that Rosemary was making effort to be cheerful.

"How are you feeling?" Ulysses asked. He came over to hug and kiss her.

"A little tired but no real problems. Just don't squeeze me too tight. My breasts are killing me."

"How was the party?"

"Fun, I think. All the guests came and Monty was well-behaved. I wish the parents hadn't all asked me about the stealing water allegations. Every single one did." Rosemary shook her head in irritation.

"That just means that they trust you to tell them what's going on," Ulysses said. "What did you tell them?"

"I said, 'Ulys's opponents paid a poor woman in the neighborhood to make those calls. Someone who doesn't even have rights on our acequia.'"

"That's good, and what did they say in response?"

"They said they hoped you arrested her and that they were voting for you."

Ulysses hugged Rosemary again, more gently. "See? We are going to get through the next few days and then things will be much better." They stood still for a few moments, just holding each other.

"You better win, Ulys," Rosemary said. She took Ulysses' salad out of the refrigerator and filled a glass with ice for the tea.

"I'm going to win," he said, beginning to eat. Outside there was a low rumble of thunder.

"That sounds nice," Rosemary said, listening for more.

While Ulysses ate lunch, he told Rosemary about his morning, including the news about Ramón Trujillo's suicide attempt. Rosemary was shocked at the news. "How is this going to affect the election?" she asked.

"I was just wondering myself. I spoke with LizBeth on my way home and she's got some big news also, but I am not free to say anything yet. All of this is coming pretty late in the game. It could help us. But it depends on how the Ruiz campaign spins it."

"What does Stephanie think of it?" Rosemary asked.

"Stephanie has been kind of scarce lately," Ulysses said. He didn't want to provoke Rosemary with discussion of the unspoken falling out between him and his campaign manager.

"You should definitely talk to her about it," Rosemary said. "She might want you to do a news conference."

"That would be tricky," Ulysses said. His phone dinged with a text.

Rosemary said. "Do you want to give your phone to me while you take a nap?"

"You probably need a nap more than I do."

"Ulys, you take a nap every day. I hardly ever do."

"That is about to change."

The text was Angela's picture of the suicide note Trujillo had written. Ulysses struggled to read the handwriting and finally deciphered it and read the note aloud to Rosemary: "Jazmine, I am sorry. I have made mistakes that will soon be revealed. I cannot face the consequences. I am just too tired. Forgive me, Dad."

"That is a coward's way out," Rosemary said. "That's not very kind of me, but, it is true." She stood up and cleared the table, putting the dishes in the sink. Ulysses took her by the hand and the two of them went into their bedroom and closed the door, just as the children came up the drive to the house, talking about the ride on their new bikes.

"I've got this," Diana said, coming out of the room where she'd been resting.

Chapter 13

LizBeth went back to her motel room south of town with carry-out lunch. She called her wife, but Dawa had been summoned into the hospital and said she would see her in the evening. LizBeth ate and watched the midday news out of Albuquerque. The lead stories were a domestic violence homicide/suicide, a car crash on the Big I where interstates 40 and 25 cross, and the crisis in the child protective services state agency. Toward the end of the broadcast, there was a mention of State Senator Ramón Trujillo's death at UNM hospital. *I guess it must have been a more serious attempt than I thought.*

LizBeth turned off the television and her phone rang. It was Jayson Jones, the Tribal Governor Quintana's lawyer. The Governor was ready to talk. They set up a meeting in two hours, to give her time to get someone out of Santa Fe to assist and be a witness to her interview with Gov. Quintana. LizBeth's friend and colleague from the FBI, Agent Randy Douglas, agreed to come.

LizBeth drove to the tribal police station early and made sure the set-up for the interview room was correct. Lt. Quintana had selected Sergeant Eddie Gomez and Officer David Fresquez to cover for him and he left the office before his brother arrived. Inside the interrogation room, LizBeth had a chair for Randy, one for herself, as well as chairs for Tribal Governor Quintana and Mr. Jones. In the room behind the insulated glass there were chairs for Officer Fresquez and Sergeant Gomez. LizBeth checked that all the recording equipment was working and started writing down her thoughts on a legal pad. Fifteen minutes before the interview, she got a call from Agent Douglas on her burner.

"Where are you?" LizBeth asked.

"Still in Santa Fe. I don't know how Barkley found out you'd called me, but I've been ordered not to come. He's trying to protect one of his fat cat friends. Listen, I put a call in to the Field Office General Counsel and asked for information. Just wanted you to know. Be careful!"

"Is Barkley coming this way?" LizBeth asked, alarmed.

"No, that would interfere with his golf game."

"Well, thank God for that."

LizBeth decided to call Deputy Eli from the Taos County Sheriff's department. She was sure that Sheriff Ulysses would be okay with her requesting his help with an interview. Eli was just finishing up lunch with his grandmother. "Can you come help me with an interrogation?"

"Sure," Eli said, sounding happy to be asked. "When?"

"In fifteen minutes."

"I'll be there."

When Deputy Eli arrived, he was out of breath from running from the parking lot. "My grandmother sends her regards," he said. "She gave me some important information."

"What?" LizBeth said, taking him into the interview room and closing the door.

"She said she'd heard from Mrs. Quintana's sister that Tribal Governor Quintana had been having an affair with a woman named Melinda Yates. Turns out Melinda Yates works for Cameron as his housekeeper. I guess you'd call that a honeytrap? Trey Cameron threatened to expose the affair if Quintana met with you today. Yates called Mrs. Quintana about an hour ago."

"Wow, Eli, thank you for this. It might be very helpful."

At that moment, Tribal Governor Quintana and his lawyer arrived.

Governor Quintana was invited into the room and told where to sit. Jayson Jones sat down beside him. Sergeant Gomez and Officer Fresquez came in next and were shown their places behind insulated glass. Eli took his seat in the room with LizBeth. LizBeth, heart pounding with the realization that she was placing her career on the line with this interview, read Quintana his rights and oriented everyone to the interview procedure.

"How long have you known Ramón Trujillo?" LizBeth began.

"About seven years," Quintana replied.

"In what capacity have you known him?"

"First, when he was Sheriff of Taos County during my first term as Tribal Governor. He and I met once or twice to discuss how the structure of law enforcement in the county affected our sovereignty rights. He was always very supportive of the Pueblo, but emphasized how he really couldn't be of much help because our police interface directly with the federal police and FBI. When he became a state senator he showed interest in helping us get our casino up and running. He was really helpful with that enterprise."

"How was he helpful, Governor?"

"He introduced us to people who could look over our operations and make sure we didn't run afoul of either the Indian or New Mexico Gaming Commission."

"And did you run afoul of either Gaming Commission, Governor?"

"The New Mexico Commission, yes, but just one time. Ramón was able to untangle that for us."

"How did he do that?"

"I don't actually know, Agent Tallichet. You would have to ask our comptroller."

"What else did Senator Trujillo do for you, Governor?" LizBeth asked.

"After the Rimrock decision, he was interested in helping us profit from our priority water rights."

"Profit how?"

"By selling them to various entities interested in development who lacked sufficient water for their projects."

"And who specifically did Senator Trujillo want Taos Pueblo to sell water rights to?"

"A company called Wild West Development."

"Was the Senator a partner in this company? Or an employee?"

"Neither, to my knowledge. He described his role as a 'consultant' to Mr. Trey Cameron, the principal."

"How many acre feet of water did Wild West want to buy from Taos Pueblo?"

"They wanted 60 acre feet to start with, and an option for an additional 40 acre feet."

"That's a lot of water to sell, isn't it?" LizBeth asked. LizBeth knew about the 60 acre feet but nothing about the option for 40 more acre feet.

"It is. But the tribe could benefit greatly from selling it."

"How would the tribe benefit?"

"The sale would bring millions of dollars." Tribal Governor Quintana took out his handkerchief and mopped his brow. The interview room was hot.

"Was the sale of water controversial in the tribe, Governor?"

Quintana conferred in whispers with his lawyer. "Somewhat controversial."

"Were some tribal members in favor of selling and some not in favor?"

"That's correct."

"And you were in favor?"

"Yes, I was."

"And what about the tribal council? Was there opposition on the council itself?"

"Yes, some opposition. The transfer was complicated. Some thought that if it was rejected by the courts, the tribe would somehow be harmed. But I think they were just giving in to fear."

"How did you try to promote members to get on board with the plan to sell?"

"I explained the benefits to them. For example, we could build a state-of-the-art nursing home for our elders."

"Was that what the money would be designated for?"

"Not necessarily, that was just one idea. There were other ideas, like a community center for youth with job training, sports facilities and the like."

"How did Senator Trujillo sell the idea to tribal council members?"

"He met with us individually on a regular basis and offered encouragement to vote yes."

"What kind of encouragement?" LizBeth asked.

Again, Quintana engaged in a lengthy whispering consultation with his lawyer. "He offered material rewards for voting his way."

"What kind of material rewards?"

"Cash, predominantly."

"How much cash and where did it come from?"

Quintana, really sweating now, conferred again with his lawyer who stood up, and asked if a fan could be brought into the room. Sergeant Gomez spoke from the room behind the insulated glass. "I have just turned on the AC," he said. "It should get cooler in a few minutes."

"Could you answer the question, please, Governor?"

"I do not know where the cash came from or how much Trujillo gave out."

"Would you say that the cash benefits were large ones, like five hundred dollars or more?"

Quintana looked at his attorney and nodded. "He was handing out large sums."

"Did he offer you any cash benefits or goods and services in exchange for your vote?"

"I was already planning to vote yes."

"Did he give you any material rewards?"

"He gave me gifts from time to time. He bought my wife a new car. He paid for us to go to Hawaii last winter. And he helped us remodel our kitchen."

"Were these gifts in exchange for anything?" LizBeth asked.

"He and I were close friends over many years and he was a generous man."

LizBeth noticed Eli shaking his head in dismay at the Governor's answers.

"Are you aware of Senator Trujillo threatening anyone who he thought would not vote to sell the water rights?"

"Not that I am aware of, no."

"Did you know anything about a plan to expose Delfino Mondragon's award as Native Artist of the Year as fraudulent? Think carefully, sir, before you answer."

Quintana whispered to his attorney. When he turned to answer he said, "I plead the Fifth."

"Governor, do you know Cody Parker?" LizBeth asked.

"Yes."

"Did you know that he worked for Senator Trujillo?"

"Yes."

"Do you know if he threatened anyone on the tribal council?"

"He threatened Mr. Mondragon and his apprentice."

"Do you know why Cody Parker threatened Delfino Mondragon?"

"Trujillo thought Mondragon may have recorded a meeting the two of them had with Gilbert Herrera, the State Engineer." LizBeth took note. *Here is corroboration for what Raven told me this morning,* she thought.

"What kind of meeting, Governor?"

"A meeting where bribes were exchanged. I was not at this meeting. But I know that Senator Trujillo and his bodyguard became convinced that Mondragon had recorded the meeting on his phone."

"How did you find out about this meeting?" LizBeth asked.

"Mondragon told me about it before he went up on the mountain. He told me he had it on his phone and that someone else had an MP3 with the recording on it."

"Who was that?" LizBeth asked.

The governor shifted in his chair. "He wouldn't tell me," he said.

"Did anyone else know about the meeting?"

"Trey Cameron probably financed the bribes, but I don't think he knew about the meeting. He was also bribing these same officials."

"Were these bribes in some way different than those Cameron was making?"

"Trujillo told me he was setting up his own business relationships to operate separately from Cameron. He had some of his own projects he wanted to develop."

"But with Cameron's money?"

"I don't really know about that."

"And who did you tell about the recording?" LizBeth asked.

Governor Quintana shook his head, fear on his sweaty face. "No one."

"Did you tell Trujillo that Mondragon had gone up the mountain to consider his options?"

"I plead the Fifth," Quintana answered.

On top of accepting bribes, this man is an accessory to murder, LizBeth thought.

"Governor, did Trey Cameron ever offer you cash benefits for your cooperation with the water sale?" LizBeth asked.

"Not directly, no. But he was the source of Trujillo's cash."

"How do you know that?"

"I saw Cameron's assistant, a man named Rowdy, hand Trujillo envelopes of cash after some of our meetings."

"Did Mr. Cameron ever threaten you in any way?" LizBeth asked.

Quintana cleared his throat. "No," he said.

LizBeth stood up and went out. She summoned Eli and asked him to clear the entire interview space and go out himself so the interview could proceed privately while being recorded.

Then LizBeth went back into the interview room. Now only she and Quintana and Quintana's attorney were in the room, which was now icy from the air conditioning.

"Governor, did Trey Cameron threaten to reveal a secret to your wife about an affair you were having?" Quintana looked at his attorney, whose face showed surprise.

"How did you know that?"

"Just answer the question."

"Yes, he did."

"Why did he threaten you?"

"He thought I was getting cold feet about his enterprise. Especially after Mondragon was killed. He didn't want me to come to this interview. He didn't want me to expose him."

"What did he not want exposed?"

"That he was at the center of this whole thing. That he employed thugs. That he was engaged in bribery and extortion."

"So now you have exposed it, what can you expect?"

Quintana said nothing at first.

"I'll have to step down as tribal governor. I may face some charges…"

"That is correct," LizBeth said. "I am recommending to the prosecutor that you be charged with accepting bribes in the course of your official duties, extortion, and being an accessory to murder in the death of Delfino Mondragon. There may be further charges, Mr. Quintana, related to accepting bribes and conspiring to commit extortion." The old man wiped his face again with his handkerchief. "You will face arraignment in court. Until then you are free to go."

Tribal Governor Quintana stood up and walked out with his lawyer. Gomez and Fresquez, without saying a word, left also. Eli and LizBeth were in the room alone.

"Do you think he knows that Trujillo is dead?" Eli asked.

"Undoubtedly," LizBeth said. "It's bad news for him because now his co-operation is less valuable."

"What about a plea deal regarding Trey Cameron?" Eli asked.

"That might be a possibility. He may have some key information to add to a RICO case. It will be up to the prosecutor."

LizBeth went out to her car and began the long drive back to Albuquerque to see what she could find out about Trujillo's death. She looked at her service phone. Don Barkley had left her three voicemails and there was also a call from Raquel Bradshaw, with a voicemail.

The Walker household was a bit chaotic with everyone trying to get ready in time to walk out the door at 3:45. The children were cranky about having to dress up and Rosemary caught the mood, saying nothing fit her anymore. Ulysses took charge of cleaning Monty up while Diana and Rosemary dressed with Amelia in Paloma's old room. Finally, they all got into the car to drive to Kitty Austerlitz's estate. When they arrived and parked near the front, the caterers were already in the kitchen getting ready to serve gourmet hors d'oeuvres, while two bartenders prepared to serve sparkling water, local beers, New Mexico wine, and margaritas. Ulysses spoke to his staff—Angela, Eli, and Dakota—who had just completed their server class and were signing their temporary permits to serve alcohol.

The house was a huge, open-concept modern home with views of the Sangre de Cristo Mountains. Floor-to-ceiling glass doors stood open to invite guests from the minimalist steel and marble out to the flagstone patio ringed by a blue flowering creeping veronica. Dozens of white wooden chairs were placed among gas heaters surrounded by perfectly tended flowerbeds of native wildflowers in blues and whites, accented with boxwoods and red knockout roses. At the back was a stand of mature aspens trembling in the late afternoon breeze surrounded by plantings of native grasses that were gently waving. Beyond was an open meadow. Ulysses saw Stephanie and Kitty chatting under the aspens and walked over.

"What a beautiful home you have," Ulysses said to Kitty, a widow in her seventies with white hair who was slender, fit-looking, and wore a blue dress that matched her eyes. He reached out to shake her hand. "Thank you so much for hosting this party."

Kitty gave a friendly smile. "So glad I can do this, Sheriff. I really appreciate your work, especially the Women's Shelter. You are really helping the women who are most vulnerable."

Ulysses smiled and thanked her. Stephanie, looking her best in a fitted black suit, took Ulysses' hand when he offered it but only made brief eye contact with him. She looked anxious. "Thanks for being right on time, Ulys," she said. "I was just telling Kitty how busy you've been. And I'm glad you brought the family. How was Monty's birthday party?"

"A big success, thanks to Mom and Rosemary," Ulysses said. He looked over to where his wife sat near his mother. Rosemary looked uncomfortable in a green linen dress that was tight across the bust. Diana wore a pair of crisp white slacks and a yellow and white striped silk blouse. She had Amelia and Monty engrossed in a movie on her iPad. Ulysses caught Rosemary's eye and smiled at her. She smiled back at him and gave him a thumbs-up. Kitty excused herself to answer some questions from the caterers.

When they were alone, Stephanie said, "We are expecting 220 this afternoon and they will start arriving any minute. Do you feel ready?"

Ulysses took a deep breath. "I'm ready," he said. "I've got my speech good to go, here in my pocket." He patted the breast pocket of his dress uniform shirt. "You know Ramón Trujillo is dead, right?"

"I just heard. That could actually be good for us," Stephanie said. "Not to be ghoulish. Are you going to say anything about it?"

"I was planning on simply saying that he passed away. What do you think I should say?"

"Ulys, I don't feel good about where the Ruiz campaign is headed. I've been following social media and it's been getting darker and darker. Lots of personal attacks on you, your background, your family. They are starting to sound scary. Has Rosemary gotten any more threatening calls?"

"No. I'm pretty sure we got to the bottom of that. Hey, but thanks for monitoring social media. What should I say about Trujillo?"

"I think you should say, 'he was admitted to UNM hospital after a suicide attempt and the cause of death has not been determined. Our condolences go out to his family.'"

"You think I should disclose that?"

"You have every right to. It's already in the news." Stephanie looked around at the burgeoning crowd, many of whom were already holding drinks. "I think I told you that Ruiz is having a fundraiser at the Local tonight, unless they cancel it. My riding buddy, Barbara, is going to check it out. He's bound to say something about his father-in-law's death and I wouldn't be surprised if he somehow tried to blame it on you. Better to get out ahead of him, if only to this crowd."

"Okay, I guess that's politics, right?"

"It is. Plus, you are just sticking with the facts. You are not spreading innuendo and lies."

"Correct. Anything else?"

"One other thing, Ulys, and you aren't going to be happy about it."

"What is it?"

"Kitty showed me the RSVPs and I saw names on there that I hadn't expected."

"Who?"

"Trey Cameron and his wife."

"What? How did they get invited?"

"Kitty belongs to the same tennis club as Mrs. Cameron. She thought she'd be doing a good deed by inviting them, since they are so rich."

"Maybe they won't come." Ulysses and Stephanie were asked to move because a string quartet needed to set up where they were standing.

"Based on what I've been reading on Facebook, he'll be here. Just call it a feeling."

"I wonder if he'll ask any questions," Ulysses said, laughing.

Angela circled the room inside with a tray of prosecco flutes that were very in-demand. She took note of who was there that she knew and saw that it was a largely Anglo crowd. She might even say it was a bunch of newcomers, people with second homes, who came briefly during the spring and summer or to ski in the winter. Many considered themselves Texans rather than New Mexicans and might not even vote here. Why were they supporting Sheriff? *Because they are friends with Kitty,* she thought. *and she throws a good party.* She went back for more flutes and circulated outdoors. Here was a good contingent of Hispanic people, from well-to-do, aristocratic families who tended to be supporters of the arts and culture. A few people spoke to her, called her by name, and asked about Lorraine's health. And why do these people support Sheriff? *Because they know a criminal when they see one and the Trujillo/ Ruiz bunch are exactly that.* After handing out all the full glasses, Angela picked up empty glasses to return to the kitchen. The sky had suddenly become overcast and a breeze seemed to indicate a change in the weather.

When she came back from the kitchen with more wine, Angela looked over at Eli who was serving sparkling water and margaritas to a small group of people Angela identified as 'the artsy crowd' including several Indian artists. Eli seemed to know them and was chatting away, a little oblivious to picking up empties. The string quartet played a well-known classical piece. Angela looked at her watch. It was almost time for Sheriff to speak. She looked back at Eli and noticed him looking over her shoulder toward the door. He looked surprised. Angela turned toward the door and saw a well-dressed Anglo man with a cane and his much younger wife come in the front door. Eli approached Angela.

"What the hell is he doing here?" he asked. "Someone said that is Trey Cameron."

"I have no idea," Angela said, "but I guess he was invited." Kitty, the hostess, approached the couple and hugged the wife. She called to Angela to get them glasses of prosecco and then seated them on a couch next to Lex and Lori Sisnersos. Angela came by with her tray of bubbly wine and each took a glass. Lori and Cili began chatting. As she was walking away, Angela heard Cili Cameron say, "Would you like to play doubles with me on Monday?" *What a chummy crew,* she thought, feeling judgmental.

The hot hors d'oeuvres were coming out, which signaled that Ulysses would give his speech soon. There was a low rumble of thunder, prompting the crowd to look at the sky where a huge cumulonimbus cloud was looming behind the mountains. The servers circulated with their bowls of chips and salsa, plates, napkins, and trays full of delicious treats like Turkish meatballs with pomegranate sauce, figs in a blanket with goat cheese, and polenta bites with wild mushrooms. Primed by alcohol, the guests were loading up on gourmet treats that appeared to be abundant. Kitty was famous for the tapas and snacks at her lavish parties, something that might explain the turnout. The conversation had reached a peak of loudness when another peal of thunder caused people to stop and listen. Once the talk resumed, Ulysses and Stephanie came out and took the strategic position recently vacated by the string quartet. Kitty seated Ulysses's family on a couch nearby. The Camerons and Sisneroses were right across from them.

"Hello everyone," Stephanie began, "and thank you for coming and supporting Ulysses Walker for re-election as Sheriff of Taos County." The applause was louder and more sustained than Ulysses expected.

Stephanie went on to introduce herself and Ulysses' family and then handed the microphone to Ulysses and sat down next to Angela, Eli, and Dakota on a chair in back under the aspens.

Ulysses tapped the mike and the crowd grew quiet. "I just looked at my weather app and we should be good for about thirty minutes before we get rained on. So, I'll make this quick. First of all, thank you for your support. I know many of you have at written at least one large check and I hope you will write another before tonight is over!" Ulysses smiled; his blue eyes bright. "Because of you, we will end this campaign strong."

"This election really matters, my friends, to our quality of life here in Taos County. We have done more in the past four years to reduce crime, including domestic violence, sexual assault, homelessness and violence against women, than had been done in any previous administration. We've reduced street crimes and gun violence also, while increasing the diversity of our department and improving customer service for those of you who have to come into our office for any reason. We've increased gun safety classes, self-defense classes and outdoor safety awareness. But we have more work to do. In my next term, I will add an undersheriff and apply for funding to increase our number of deputies by 50%. We want to increase beds at the Women's Shelter and add GED classes and childcare support for the women temporarily housed there. And we will continue to enhance public safety throughout our county.

"Our opponents would do none of these things. They would cut funds for the Women's Shelter and refuse to prosecute laws they don't like, such as the Violence Against Women laws, under their so-called constitutional sheriff scheme. They are running a campaign based on untruths and innuendo to try to discredit me, my administration, and even my family. They must not be allowed to win. So please, if you haven't voted already, vote on Tuesday. And again, thank you for all that you do."

The applause was polite but sustained. "Does anyone have any questions for me?"

A woman sitting in the back asked what the Sheriff could tell them about Ramón Trujillo's death. "Was it a murder?" she asked. Ulysses found himself looking at Cameron's tanned face with its blasé expression.

"Senator Trujillo was found at his home this morning after a suicide attempt." There were expressions of shock and surprise. "He was medevacked to UNM Hospital where he died around 2:30 pm. Our thoughts are with Senator Trujillo's family at this time." A few more hands went up.

"What can you tell us about the death of Delfino Mondragon?" asked a man in the artist group.

"Since it took place on tribal land, Mr. Mondragon's murder is being investigated by the FBI. The agent in charge has a suspect who has not yet been apprehended."

"Why have you had so many murders recently?" Cameron's wife, Cili asked. She wrinkled her nose and shook her head as if she was talking about dirty socks. "It seems like there is one every other day! Could this be your fault, somehow, Sheriff?" She spoke in a flippant tone that her accent made sound flirtatious.

"We believe the recent murders are related, Ma'am, and we are working with the FBI to apprehend the culprits. Solving these murders and arresting the killers are partially my responsibility and I want you to know I take it very seriously. We are about to make some arrests very soon. I cannot say more at this time. Again, thank you, everyone, for coming and supporting our campaign. Enjoy some more food and drinks, but make sure you have a designated driver! Get home safe." Somebody turned on the house sound system to a recording of smooth jazz. People stood up and began to mingle with their friends.

As the guests were departing, Angela poured herself and Dakota each a glass of prosecco and they sat down at a table outside with plates of snacks. Eli joined them holding a bottle of mineral water. Angela watched Trey Cameron write a check and walk out, saying goodbye to Kitty and some of the other guests he knew by name.

"I thought Sheriff seemed a little off his game tonight," Angela said.

"You did?" Dakota said. "I thought he hit it out of the ballpark."

"He seemed, I don't know, wary, even a little paranoid. Not his usual confident upbeat self. It felt dark."

"It is dark," Dakota said. "Have you looked at social media? The haters are out in force. They really want Sheriff to go down. I'm actually afraid for him. There were all those lies they told about Rosemary. If anything would make you paranoid, that would. And we know his opponents were paying for those lies."

Angela nodded but looked unconvinced.

"Think about it," Eli said. "In the past week, there have been three murders and now a suicide. The Governor of Taos Pueblo is about to be indicted. Can you imagine a worse time to be up for re-election?"

"How did you know about the Governor of Taos Pueblo getting indicted?" Angela asked.

"The granny grapevine," Eli said. "More reliable that any newspaper."

"I hated to see that criminal Cameron and his wife sitting right up under Sheriff's nose while he was speaking. And then the trophy wife asked that obnoxious question." Dakota shook her head in disgust. "Do you think it could be *your husband's* fault?"

Angela finished her wild mushroom polenta and prosecco. "Shall we go?"

"Who is going to drive?" Dakota asked.

"I can," Eli said. "I didn't drink anything."

On the way out, they saw Rosemary talking with Cili Cameron near the door. Ulysses, Diana and the children were already in the car and Cameron sat in the back of a chauffeur-driven Mercedes, talking on his phone. As they got closer, they heard Rosemary say, "You have no business saying that to me, Mrs. Cameron. I think you've had too much to drink."

Cili, who was barefoot and holding her sandals by their long straps over her shapely bare shoulder, said in her thick Hungarian accent, "You are in way over your head, Mrs. Sheriff. Your husband is going to lose this election and there is nothing you can do about it. No matter how much money you raised tonight. You should go back to Utah."

"I wouldn't underestimate Ulysses Walker if I were you," Rosemary said. She turned her back and walked down the front steps toward the car as thunder rolled and the first raindrops fell. Then she stopped and turned around to look at Cili Cameron. "And don't underestimate me either."

LizBeth crawled into bed beside Dawa who was putting a delicious smelling lotion on her long legs. "How were things at the hospital this afternoon?" she asked.

"Oh, you know, the usual on-call stuff. Stroke evaluations, a motor vehicle hit a pedestrian, grim stuff, mostly. How about your day? Did you find out any information about that state senator who died?" Dawa put the cap on her lotion and started brushing her silky, black hair. LizBeth lay still, her mind racing from her day. *I should call Barkley back before the morning,* she thought. *Otherwise, I'm insubordinate.*

"Natural sequelae to his suicide attempt, apparently," she mumbled.

"Is something bothering you?"

"I went off the reservation several times today," LizBeth said.

"I could tell this was coming," Dawa said, brushing in long strokes. "I'm listening if you want to talk."

"I should probably call Barkley now, before I fall asleep."

"I'll save your place in the bed," Dawa said, smiling. LizBeth, wanting nothing more than to curl up next to her wife, got out of her bed and picked up her service phone.

Barkley's phone rang and rang but he didn't pick up and his voicemail was full. She'd had this experience with him before. *The guy isn't what you'd call a workaholic.* LizBeth looked at the clock and decided it wasn't too late to call Randy back. She used her burner phone. Randy picked up on the first ring.

"I'm glad you called," she said. "I've been waiting to talk with you. I had a long talk with our counsel today about your predicament."

"What did he say?"

"Kind of what you'd expect. 'Document everything, including your rationale for moving forward. If you are going to file a RICO, you will need lots of firsthand corroboration. And if you can prove any bias on the administration's part you should have that also.'"

"What kind of bias?" LizBeth asked. "Like that Barkley and Cameron were in the same fraternity?"

"More than that, I think," Randy said. "Have they met since Barkley took over last winter?"

"Good question. I can look into that…somehow, in my free time. What I really need is to execute a search warrant for Cameron's property."

"Yeah, but going after a search warrant will really throw down the gauntlet with Barkley. You'd better time it right and have enough ammo, if you know what I mean. Have you located Cody Parker?"

"No. The team they gave me combed Tres Piedras, Ojo Caliente and Carson yesterday but found nothing. No one was at his old campsite and no one in the neighborhood was talking about where he might have gone other than to say Parker had a family somewhere in the Oklahoma panhandle. Too bad. If I could nab him, I'd have this thing wrapped."

"He's bound to turn up," Randy said. "In the meantime, is there anyone else you could pursue?"

"Actually, there is. Another hired gun for Cameron. My friend Sheriff Ulysses Walker has a warrant for his arrest. His name is Lassiter Kane and he could be a key figure for both of us."

"Isn't the Sheriff pretty busy with the election?"

"I'm going to call him anyway and see if he wants to go hunting tomorrow."

"That's the spirit, LizBeth!"

LizBeth called Ulysses and they arranged to take Angela and Eli and go looking for Lassiter Kane first thing in the morning. "I'll ask Angela to get the warrants ready," Ulysses said.

Angela rolled over in bed and looked at Eli, who lay on his back, one brown, sinewy arm over his head, snoring lightly. She was a little mystified at what had happened the night before after the fundraiser. It had been several years since she'd been in bed with anyone, but she'd been aware of a deep attraction to Eli for a while. As they sat on her couch in front of a fire of piñon logs, they told each other more of their secrets and drank almost a whole bottle of wine. No doubt the wine played a role in her suddenly leaning over and kissing him full on the lips, even putting a little tongue into it. Not long after that they were shedding clothes on the way to her bed. Once there, Eli slipped off her pants and took his time giving her an orgasm like she'd never had, without ever taking off the rest of his clothes. Then they'd fallen asleep in each other's arms, a fact that displeased Mr. T, the cat who usually slept on the pillow Eli's head now occupied. Now T was standing in the doorway waving his tail back and forth insistently and meowing for his breakfast. Eli rolled over and pulled the covers over his head. Angela slipped out of bed, took a quick shower and got dressed in a fresh uniform.

In the kitchen, she made coffee and French toast and studied her feelings. Her first emotion was delight but it was followed quickly by guilt. As Eli's superior she had no business having sex with him. She also felt pleasure at finally having experienced a type of sexual satisfaction she'd always wanted to feel.

Angela had thought of herself as bisexual mainly because she'd slept with both men and women in college. But sometimes sex had seemed not worth the trouble. With men Angela felt that the actual act was over far too quickly or left her cold. With women, though she might feel pretty aroused, she'd never climaxed. She attributed her problem to "issues of trust" with both men and women, probably related to her father's physical abuse of her mother and her mother's abandonment of her. That was what a therapist had told her once, and it rang true at the time. *My issues certainly didn't pose a problem last night, though,* she thought. She had put the first piece of French toast on a plate when Eli came in, already dressed, his truck keys in his hand.

"I need to go home and change," he said. "I'll meet you at Sheriff's in about thirty minutes, okay?" He wasn't making eye contact.

"Here," Angela said, feeling awkward. "I poured you a to-go cup of coffee and you can take this first piece of toast."

"Thanks, Angela." Eli took the cup and toast and quickly kissed her cheek, then went out to his truck. "Don't be late," Angela called out. Immediately she wished she hadn't said anything. *This is why this can't go on,* she thought, *feeling irritable.*

Ulysses woke up before dawn and made a pot of coffee. He hadn't slept well the night before. In the middle of the night, he'd awakened from a dream about threats to a woman he loved. But he couldn't remember enough about the dream to know who the woman was. It didn't seem to be Rosemary.

Ulysses got dressed and took his coffee out into the front yard to watch the sun come up. LizBeth, Eli and Angela would be arriving in about an hour to go to Cameron's and try to arrest Lassiter Kane. Ulysses was pretty confident they would find him there.

Ulysses reflected on all that happened the day before.

Ramón Trujillo was dead, apparently from the effects of the carbon monoxide, which had led to a cardiac arrest. And, as Stephanie predicted, Ernesto Ruiz at his rally at the Local had blamed not only the "wicked, deep-state FBI" for harassing Trujillo with charges when he was only trying to help Taos Pueblo get the benefits they deserved, but he'd also insinuated that his father-in-law's death should be investigated as a murder, not a suicide. The rally spilled over into several drunken fist fights and the city police had to be called.

Stephanie said they'd raised $30,000 from the fundraiser, well over the break-even point. Cameron had written the biggest check, one for $7,000. When they spoke, Ulysses had instructed Stephanie to mail the check back to Cameron. Ulysses would never take Cameron's money, even if they needed it to stay out of debt, which luckily, they didn't.

LizBeth had called to report she'd arrested Tribal Governor Quintana, but that her team had not been able to find Cody Parker in the environs of Tres Piedras. Kane's Airstream was gone from the campsite Kane and Parker had used for months. LizBeth thought Parker was either dead or gone to ground in Oklahoma and that Kane was hiding out somewhere on Cameron's huge property.

As the light rose, Ulysses thought about Rosemary's interaction with Cili Cameron on the way out the door at the fundraiser. He felt pride at how Rosemary handled herself with a woman who was drunk and belligerent toward her. *Rosemary is always a class act,* he thought. But he worried about her vulnerability now with everything that was unfolding and her newly pregnant. Just as he was thinking this, she came up behind him and put her arms around him.

"You are up early for a Sunday," she said.

"I am," Ulysses said. "Want some coffee?"

"I have a cup of raspberry leaf tea," Rosemary said. "I'm going to miss my coffee for a while."

The sun peeked over the notch in the mountains where it rose at this time of year. The dawn chorus of birds began singing and the rain from the night before sparkled on the grass. Ulysses noticed that the light was on in Paloma's room. Diana was awake. She would stay one more full day and go home tomorrow. Ulysses was glad for her help, given all he had to do today.

Rosemary sat on the porch swing facing the sunrise. Long streaks of clouds that looked like flying saucers lit up pink and purple over the peaks. "Looks like heaven, doesn't it?" Rosemary said. "Want some pancakes?"

"I think it looks like an alien invasion. Let me help you with the chores first," Ulysses said.

"I got it, Babe. I'm going to go open the head gate and take my water just as soon as I wake up a little more."

While Rosemary watered and then milked Dolly, Ulysses took his gun out of the safe and got his supplies and ammo loaded into the Expedition. He poured a second cup of coffee and the phone rang. It was Delilah Valdez.

"Sorry to call so early, Ulys. I hope I didn't wake you?"

"Not a problem, Delilah, what's up?"

"One of the commissioners on Daddy's acequia, a woman named Cathy Rhodes, came by this morning with a lock box she found in the tool shed at the presa."

"A lock box? How did the commissioner know to give it to you?"

"Daddy had written 'Property of Antonio Valdez' on a piece of paper and taped it to the top. Cathy found it when she went into the shed to get a tool to shut down the presa before the rain last night."

"Was the lock the kind with a combination?" Ulysses asked.

"It sure was. I put in 1797 and it opened right up."

"What was inside?"

"Two things. One was an external hard drive, so we can recover items from Daddy's computer. The other was a thumb drive with an MP3 on it. The recording is of Trujillo enlisting support for a project in the Columbine Wilderness and giving bribes to the State Engineer and the Carson National Forest Supervisor. I guess he had a little side hustle separate from Cameron. The tape is clear and easy to understand. Unfortunately, in addition to the other two men, Uncle Del also can also be heard accepting a bribe."

"Don't worry about that, Delilah. Del had to take the bribe or Trujillo would know he was on the wrong side. He was trying to look like he was supportive of the whole scheme."

"I guess that could be. But at any rate, Arthur and I think the MP3 is valuable evidence. We also went over the external hard drive, which wasn't encrypted, and found some interesting documents."

"What kind of stuff?"

"Turns out Dad was researching Trey Cameron's past. He'd filed a batch of FOIA requests for documents related to Cameron's RICO investigation."

"I think I've seen some of those files," Ulysses said, remembering the files LizBeth had shown him.

"I don't think you've seen these," Delilah said. "Dad got these documents just five days before he died. He must have scanned them into his computer and then hidden the originals somewhere."

"What do they show?"

"The prosecutor at the time Cameron's RICO was dismissed was a woman named Nan Greene. Turns out, Greene was the attorney for Big Hat in the 1990s, working for Cameron's father back when her name was Coughlin. The younger Cameron and Greene managed to have a local irrigation group in Texas sell them surface water rights in return for cash to develop wells, which they were told would be more sustainable for growing organic cotton. Cameron subsequently sold the surface rights to an agribusiness consortium and made a pile of money. The local farmers drilled wells that turned out to be contaminated by Big Hat and Cameron knew it. The local farmers went bust and they've had to truck in water ever since to keep their little community alive. Last month, another prosecutor at Justice started looking into why Greene buried the RICO against Cameron and uncovered all this and more. It looks pretty bad for Greene and maybe for Cameron, too."

"That is big, Delilah. Have you spoken with LizBeth about it?"

"Not yet, but I will. I left her a voicemail to call me. I called Ray and told him about it. He thinks it might be a blueprint for what Cameron would do with water in Mora if his golf course doesn't work out. A kind of bait-and-switch. I wanted you to know about both items since they speak to the motive for killing Dad."

"It does. And also explains what they were looking for when they broke into his house. And Ray's. This is excellent news. Put those items in your safe at work. I have to go, Delilah. I'm going to make an arrest. I'll call you later."

Ulysses wolfed down some breakfast and put on his Kevlar vest. The team was assembled out by the garage ready for an early start. "I anticipate Cameron will try to resist us coming onto his property," Ulysses said. "But this warrant for arrest should make him stand down. And Angela was able to get a search warrant for his house. Still, we should be prepared. He has several armed men around him, in addition to Kane, and a whole arsenal at his disposal."

"Since you have the warrants, you be team leader, Ulys. We'll back you up," LizBeth said.

"Eli, since this is your first operation, stay back and watch carefully." Ulysses, Eli, and Angela got into the Expedition. LizBeth took her own car.

The peaceful morning on the high plateau belied the tension felt inside the Expedition. Light puffs of cumulus clouds dotted the azure sky and there was almost no wind. A few turkey vultures circled over the distant gorge. When they arrived at the Cameron gate, they saw an SUV parked there and that the security booth was manned. Ulysses recognized Rowdy Eustace. He pulled up to the booth and rolled down the window.

Eustace opened the sliding glass window. He was dressed in camouflage and wearing a Kevlar vest and wrap-around sunglasses. An AR-15 hung on the wall to his right and he wore a sidearm in a shoulder holster. Ulysses, also armed, got out of the Expedition.

"Good morning, Mr. Eustace. I have a warrant for the arrest of Mr. Lassiter Kane." Ulysses showed the warrant. He noticed an engine sound down toward the house.

Eustace reached a gloved hand through the glass and took the warrant, looking it over carefully. "Mr. Kane is not here," he said.

"We'd like to have a look around," Ulysses said.

"That won't be possible," Eustace said, placing his hand on his side arm. "Mr. Cameron's orders."

"Take your hand off your weapon," LizBeth said from behind Ulysses. "Step out of the booth, immediately." She came up to the gate holding an automatic rifle. There was a tense moment when Rowdy looked like he might not comply. Then he walked out of the booth and stood facing LizBeth and Ulysses with his hands up. Eli and Angela got out of the Expedition with their weapons and stood on either side of Ulysses. The engine sound grew louder.

Ulysses said, "As Sheriff of Taos County, my team and I have a right to enter this property with an arrest warrant. And we have a search warrant for the house as well. You are blocking our way. Is this a path you want to take?" Eustace looked around at the people arrayed against him as a helicopter appeared, flying toward them. It circled overhead. Ulysses could see Cameron in the back seat with his family. Cameron gave a jaunty wave and Rowdy waved back. *So that was the engine I was hearing,* Ulysses thought.

"Sheriff, you and your team can go on in now, if you wish," Rowdy said, relaxing and opening the gate.

"Give me your weapons first, Rowdy," Ulysses said.

"You can't take my guns," Eustace said.

"Yes, I can. You threatened me with them."

Eustace handed over his handgun and the AR.

LizBeth stepped away as two vans raced up from the house. The vans were full of Cameron's staff.

"I'm going to stop and search those vans," LizBeth replied. "And I'm going to arrest anyone who is taking documents."

The first van was full of women who identified themselves as the housekeeper, cooks, cleaners, a teacher, and a nanny. A few of the servants had small bags of clothes or backpacks full of their personal possessions. The second van held six security guards, none of whom were armed. Lassiter Kane was not among them. LizBeth searched the vans and Eustace's SUV and found no documents. She and Ulysses conferred and then allowed them all to leave.

"I'll take Eli and Angela and search the property for Lassiter Kane," Ulysses said as the vans drove off.

"I am going to the Taos airport to try to stop Cameron from leaving on his jet."

"Good luck," Ulysses said. "I'll tell you if we find Kane."

"Same to you," LizBeth said getting into her car. "I'll let you know if I am able to stop Cameron."

Ulysses, Angela, and Eli drove down the long driveway in silence, unsure of what they'd find. The fresh, clear morning made the approach all the more eerie. First, they noticed the smell of burning plastic and came upon a smoking burn pit that had mostly gone to ash. Then they saw the garage bays, open as if for inspection. Ulysses and Angela walked through each bay filming on their cellphones while Eli kept an eye out from the doorway. They noted two luxury cars and a military-style Jeep, all locked, and several trailers.

"Is there a back road out of here?" Angela asked.

"No," Eli said. "The property is kind of a peninsula surrounded on three sides by the Rio Grande Gorge. The land from the edge of the gorge to the river is Taos Pueblo land. The only way out is the road we came in on."

"Or the river," Ulysses said.

"Yeah, but it's the Box down there. Some of the whitest water around," Eli said.

"That bay there is the armory," Ulysses said, indicating a closed garage door nearest the house. As he started walking toward it, he held his weapon at the ready. Angela and Eli followed suit. "Lassiter Kane," Ulysses shouted. "I have a warrant for your arrest. Come out now with your hands up and no harm will come to you." Ulysses' voice echoed through the silence. A raven croaked overhead. They walked around the building to see if there were any other doors in the back, but there weren't. "No way to get in there," Ulysses said. "Let's go toward the house."

The front door was unlocked, so they opened it and walked inside. Sun poured in the front door to illuminate an ostentatious entry hall with a crystal chandelier, a walk-in fireplace where papers still smoked, and a larger-than-life-sized sculpture of an Indian woman holding corn in her hands. "That's one of Del's sculptures," Eli said. "It sucks that he has that."

They quickly cleared the formal living room which held thick pink and green Persian rugs, white leather couches, gold accent pieces, and ornately framed oil paintings of western landscapes. The kitchen, dining room, and library were also assessed to be safe. The library was full of cases that held expensive Indian pottery and leather-bound books. A long, narrow dining room faced the pool and western sky with floor-to-ceiling glass windows. Angela noticed that the dining room table was set with expensive porcelain plates, silver, and crystal as if ready for a dinner party. Ulysses led the way up a spiral staircase to the second floor where the master suite sprawled over most of the space, the rest occupied by two identical pink, princess-themed children's rooms with a shared white marble bathroom. A hallway led to stairs to a servant's quarters and back steps to the kitchen. The bedrooms were left in perfect order, with beds made and closet doors closed.

"It looks like Cameron expects to come back," Angela said. She peered into Cili Cameron's walk-in closet and noticed full racks of women's clothes. "I guess they really didn't have to pack. They probably have stocked wardrobes in all their houses." A safe stood open and empty. "She took her jewelry though," Angela said. "And probably a lot of cash."

Eli called from the hallway where he was looking out one of the huge windows that faced west. "Come look at this," he said.

Ulysses walked up and saw right away what Eli was pointing at—the flash of sun on metal. "That could be Kane's Airstream," he said. "See where it was driven over the llano toward the gorge?" The three of them looked at fresh tracks where a truck and trailer had been driven across the fragile soil.

"Maybe that's where he's hiding out," Eli said. "He could be pretty dug in down there."

"Yeah, but his truck is up here," Angela said. She pointed to a late model grey truck which was parked behind the pool wall, hidden among ponderosa pines. "Wonder why he parked up here?"

"Probably to make an easier get-away," Ulysses said.

Bullets shattered the glass in the largest window. Ulysses, Eli and Angela dropped to the floor.

"He's at his truck right now from the sound of it," Ulysses said.

"Should we go out after him?" Angela asked. "I wouldn't want to be trapped in this house if he got inside."

"Why not?" Eli asked.

"Because it is easier to kill at close range," Ulysses said.

Ulysses crept up to the window. "I can see him," Ulysses said. Kane shot again, shattering another window. Ulysses lay flat beneath it, careful not to cut himself on the shards. "He's set up with a scope. He can see the entire back of the house from where he is." Ulysses put his rifle through the shattered glass and fired several rounds. "I hit his truck," he said. "But now I don't see him." Ulysses fired at the truck tires, hitting two of them. "That will cramp his style."

Eli spoke up. "Do you still see him, Sheriff?"

"No. He's got cover from the wall around the pool. He's probably headed this way, though. Eli, keep your eyes trained on the pool area. He may try to get into the house through the back sliding door below us. Angela, I want you to watch the front through those windows on either side of the front door. Stay back from the glass. Either one of you, if you see him, shoot to kill."

"Where are you going, Sheriff?" Angela asked.

"I'm going outside to try to surprise him," Ulysses said. He crawled down the hall into the servants' quarters and came down narrow steps into the kitchen. Ulysses looked around at the big chef's kitchen with its sliding glass doors that gave out directly to the pool. This was not a safe place to stand or to exit. From above, he heard the rapid fire of Eli's semiautomatic pistol. *He's seen Kane*, he thought. *Now Kane will probably head to the front.* Sure enough, he saw a heavily armed man running past the sliding glass door toward the side of the house. Ulysses shot but missed, shattering one of the sliding glass doors. *Angela is exposed*, he thought. He turned from the kitchen into the dining room. Kane sprayed automatic weapon fire into the room, hitting the chandelier and shattering crystal everywhere. Ulysses fell to the floor near the door to the library. He heard Eli coming down the staircase. Eli yelled, "He's coming toward the front door!" Eli came into the dining room and stood, reloading his pistol.

"Get down!" Ulysses shouted. Eli dropped to the floor but Kane had fired at him, grazing his shoulder. Eli cried out in pain and shock and began to bleed from his wound.

"Cover me," Ulysses whispered. "I'm moving toward the front door now!"

"Sir, I see him," Angela yelled. She fired her service revolver in his direction. Eli shouted to her, "Hang on, Angela. Sheriff is coming!" Then the front door opened and Kane stood in the doorway, lit from the back. Ulysses took a shot at him but missed, shattering the glass beside the door where Angela was crouched. Quick as a snake, Kane grabbed Angela by her arm and put her body in front of his own. She struggled to escape, but he took her gun and shoved the butt into her ribs, knocking the breath out of her. "Don't shoot, Sheriff," Kane yelled. "Drop your gun, Deputy. You two put your weapons down and hold your hands high." Ulysses and Eli did as they were told. "If you threaten me, I will kill Ms. Romero here. If you let me go, I'll let her go when I'm done with her. It's that simple." Angela, sweating and wild-eyed said, "Shoot him, Sheriff, go ahead!" Kane slapped her hard across the face. Eli cursed under his breath in Tiwa. Ulysses said, "Eli, stay focused."

Ulysses spoke in a calm voice belying the panic he was feeling. "Mr. Kane, you should quit while you are ahead. Right now, you are facing relatively minor charges. But you are not going to escape. If you harm me or one of my deputies, even if you kill all of us, you'll be caught and you'll spend the rest of your life in jail. Or worse. So go ahead..."

"Sheriff Walker, hold up. You don't know me or who I am. You don't know what I'm capable of. Just do as I ask and let me and Ms. Romero go and I will release her unharmed. Or you can watch me shoot her and your Indian friend there before you can kill me, if you even can. You aren't much of a shot. Have it however you want."

Ulysses swallowed. "Where are you going, Kane? Do you want to take my car?"

Kane laughed, "Like I said, you don't know me, Sheriff. I can take any of the cars here, but I know exactly what that would set in motion. I have another plan."

"How come your boss didn't have room for you in his helicopter?" Ulysses asked. "Are you not important enough to him to take along?"

Kane's smile vanished. "That's it, we're done here." He grabbed Angela by the hair and started to drag her out the door front door, his gun at her temple. "If I see either one of you, I will kill her first, then you. Don't follow me. You've been warned."

Ulysses and Eli stood helpless as they watched Kane march Angela down toward the Airstream.

Chapter 14

LizBeth arrived at the airport just as Cameron's Gulfstream was beginning its taxi for takeoff. There was only one other plane on the tarmac, a private prop plane with a pilot, copilot, and two passengers inside. LizBeth jumped out of her car and ran into the small, empty terminal building and quickly located a door marked "Restricted, No Entry" that led to the air traffic control tower. She pounded on the door and shouted, "FBI, stop that Gulfstream!" The door opened and a short, stout, middle-aged man came out looking confused. He scrutinized LizBeth's FBI ID. "Come in here," he said, closing the door. Then he said to the other man in the room, "Bill, put a hold on the G6." LizBeth could see the sleek jet come to a stop and heard the chatter between the jet pilot and the control tower. Finally, she heard Cameron's voice say, "This woman you are talking with doesn't have authorization to stop me and my family. She has gone rogue. Call her boss, Don Barkley, head of the Albuquerque field office of the FBI. He will tell you I am correct." The stout official looked at LizBeth with irritation. "Ma'am, I'm going to have to call your superior. Mr. Cameron's flight plan has already been approved. Please step outside and wait while I do that."

LizBeth knew that a G6 could fly from Taos to Europe without stopping to refuel. After a few minutes, she saw the private jet taxi to speed and take off. Cameron was getting away. The official stepped out of the control room and told her that Mr. Barkley had approved the take-off. "You'd better leave now," he said, frowning at her. "I could have you arrested for interfering with aviation operations, but I think your boss will take care of that." He went back into the control room and locked the door.

LizBeth, frustrated and deflated, got in her car and called Ulysses. He didn't pick up. Then she called her friend Raquel at the Justice Department and got her voicemail. She saw a voicemail from Delilah Valdez, but felt she couldn't deal with it now. Not knowing what to do, she headed back toward Cameron's property.

When she arrived, no one was around. The place was ominously quiet. A few burn pits smoked. Sheriff Walker's Expedition was parked in the driveway and the house front door was open. Inside she saw signs of a firefight. There were bullet casings and blood on the floor of the entry way and in the dining room, and glass from the windows and chandelier littered the floor. LizBeth walked through the house with her gun drawn. She tried to piece together a narrative of what had gone down in the house, but it was incomplete. Outside, she found Kane's truck with two flat tires. *Where was everybody?* Hesitant to chance her two-wheel drive car on the soft, sandy soil, LizBeth walked along a trail toward the Rio Grande Gorge. It was hot and the UV was intense. Two red-tailed hawks circled high above her, riding the warm updrafts. She realized that there was no cover for her if a sniper decided to pick her off. She hoped a sniper wasn't set up near the gorge edge.

LizBeth felt alone and afraid, knowing she could be arrested for all she'd done, even though she had a strong rationale for every step she took. But she was also determined to see this through. She took a protein bar out of her pocket and started to eat it as she walked. She was nearing the edge of the gorge when she first saw a silver Airstream parked behind some standing rimrocks. Its door stood open, but it didn't appear that anyone was inside. LizBeth drew her weapon and ran toward a basalt boulder for cover. She called out, "FBI! Come out with your hands up!" No answer other than the scream of a hawk. She called out again and again she heard nothing. She approached the door and climbed the steps to look inside. The trailer was empty and stank of death. Clothes were scattered over an unmade bed. A computer stood open on the kitchen table. LizBeth touched the space bar. The browser was open to Pornhub. LizBeth came out of the trailer, walked to the edge of the cliff and gazed down into the rocky gorge. Hundreds of feet below her, the Rio Grande churned and frothed, making its way south. LizBeth took the steep trail toward the river. Halfway down to the river she noticed several turkey vultures perched in a big juniper. They flew away as she approached, and she saw what she thought was a freshly dug grave, the top covered with rocks. *I wonder who's in there?*

When she arrived at the river, she found a small boat house with racks for kayaks and rafts. Only the kayaks remained. *Had they gone down the river?* Unsure of what to do at this point, LizBeth began the climb back to the Airstream. She was thirsty and disoriented. She remembered what José used to say when she got discouraged: "Act invincible, muchacha! And soon you will see that you are!" LizBeth unscrewed her water bottle and drank several satisfying gulps, took a deep breath and then drank several more.

As she trotted back across the mesa toward her car, LizBeth began to formulate a plan. She needed to get help for Ulysses' team first and then she had to prepare her evidence for an FBI prosecutor. She was sure she had the makings of a RICO case.

When she got to her car, she listened to the long voicemail from Delilah Valdez about the new evidence Delilah had found, including a recording of a clandestine meeting with some of the principals they were investigating. Driving to a shady pullout off the Cameron property, LizBeth began to make calls. First she called Zach to tell him what she'd seen at the Cameron place, then Raquel Bradsher at the Justice Department to clue her in on the most recent developments, and Delilah Valdez to ask her to meet with her at the Valdez home later in the day. Delilah could help her walk through the status of her case and get it ready to submit to the prosecutor.

As soon as Kane and his captive disappeared down the trail to the river, Ulysses and Eli took off running toward the Airstream.

Eli's graze wound was still bleeding and his shoulder ached from the gash the bullet had made.

They went into the Airstream and refilled their canteens. Then they ran down the steep trail to the Rio Grande, which was roaring down among huge boulders. They arrived at a rack of kayaks and rafts not far from a launch built into the river.

"Have you run this stretch?" Ulysses asked.

"Yeah. It's rough. Have you?"

"I've never done the Box. I never felt confident enough."

"Let's take the raft," Eli said. "It looks like there is enough water for a big raft like this one. I'll pilot. You sit in front and push us off the boulders." He pulled the raft off its rack, pumped it full of air and checked it for leaks while Ulysses put their weapons in a dry bag.

"He's a good way ahead of us," Ulysses said. "Can we catch up?"

"Unlikely, unless we're lucky. Can Angela swim?" They both noticed helmets and life jackets on the ground under where a smaller raft might have been removed.

"I don't know," Ulysses said, "but I hope she's wearing a life jacket. And a helmet."

"Yeah, me too, but it doesn't look like it," Eli said. "I recall this section of the river. It's called the Airplane Turn. Down there is the Piano Hole. We have to avoid the big flat rock there in the middle. There are lots of hazards. I might need to get out from time to time and scout the runs."

"How is your shoulder?" Ulysses asked.

"It hurts," Eli said.

"Can you pilot the raft?"

"I have to," Eli said.

They both put on life jackets and helmets and climbed into the raft at the river's edge. Before long they were swept into rapids that carried them precipitously away. Ulysses remembered his dreams of being out of a boat in whitewater. *Here we go*, he thought, shuddering.

Down river Angela crouched in the front of a smaller, nimbler raft while Kane piloted them through a quiet stretch of water after a frightening drop over a large, flat rock that briefly submerged the entire raft. Angela, who was not a good swimmer and had no life vest or helmet, breathed to slow her racing heart. Even though she'd grown up in Taos, she'd never gone whitewater rafting before, nor had she ever wanted to. She recalled a college friend who had taken her mother on the Box where she fell off the raft, hit her head on a rock and drowned. It seemed like there was a swift water death like that every few years on the white waters of the Rio Grande. Angela braced herself for the next approaching rapids.

"We don't have time for me to scout this one," Kane said. He had a wild, excited look on his face. "I'm just going to wing it!" He was wearing both a life vest and a helmet.

Angela focused intently on her breathing. The water around her began to churn as the gradient dropped.

"If you fall out, lie on your back with your feet in the air and protect your head with your hands. If you get to the bank, then you are on your own!" Kane was furiously maneuvering, a blur of arms and oars. Angela began to pray, "Help me, Mother Mary," she said. She didn't really believe in prayer but it made her feel better. The rapids went on and on, water roaring. Angela held on, praying, and trying not to panic. "That was the Rock Garden, pretty girl," Kane said with a manic grin. "I aced it!"

They entered a brief stretch of calm water. Angela looked up at the sky and noticed storm clouds. Wind picked up from downstream, buffeting the raft and making it harder to pilot.

"Do you have a boyfriend, Ms. Romero?" Kane asked.

Angela didn't know what to say. "None of your business," she finally answered in a soft voice.

"The Indian guy?"

"That's none of your business," she said louder.

"Oh, but I plan to make *you* my business," Kane said.

I have to get away from this maniac. Angela looked at the bank and considered jumping out of the raft. She had no idea where she was, but with relative calm she thought she might be able to make it to shore. But would he follow her? Undoubtedly. She put the thought aside as another rapid approached.

"Here comes the Buzzsaw," Kane yelled. "I love this section!" They slammed into a rock and almost capsized, but Kane quickly righted the raft, and they continued down through torturous whitewater.

Eli and Ulysses passed through Powerline Falls, a huge drop that submerged the raft, soaking them both and filling the bottom of the raft with water. Ulysses used his long paddle to push them off rocks and Eli piloted expertly in spite of his wound. Ulysses looked for Kane's raft but saw nothing ahead of them. There were no commercial rafts on the river due to the coming storm. Winds from downstream slowed their progress.

"I need to get out and scout this next run," Eli said, coming to a stop on the west bank. He got out and looked at the stretch of water ahead. "It's a long rapid and it's technical—but here goes." They pushed the raft back into the flow and Eli negotiated a clean, safe run of the Rock Garden. As they came around a curve and into a long straight stretch, Ulysses saw Kane's raft ahead in the distance. Then they entered another rapids.

"There they are," Eli shouted. "I can see Angela. She's still in the boat." He navigated toward the swiftest part of the river, hoping to catch up. A loud thunderclap announced lightening overhead. "We are about two and a half miles from the Taos Junction Bridge," Eli yelled. There was a huge flash of forked lightning ahead of them and sheets of rain began to fall. "We really should get out if we value our lives," Eli said.

"We can't afford to do that," Ulysses yelled back. "Unless they stop."

"I know, but this is super dangerous, just saying." As if to add emphasis, lightning flashed again right overhead.

"I should really scout this next rapid, Sheriff, but if I do, we'll lose time."

"Eli, let's take our chances. I'm afraid if Kane makes it to the Taos Junction bridge much before us, we may never see Angela again." They'd already lost sight of Kane's raft in the narrow, winding canyon.

The rain came down hard, foreshortening their ability to see and causing both men to shiver with cold. Ulysses barely noticed the thunder and lightning. In the flood of adrenaline, he felt almost no fear. *I'm not as afraid now as I was in my dreams,* he thought. Eli worked frantically to keep them from hitting a huge rock ahead of them, but they careened into it anyway. When they crashed Ulysses fell out of the raft and was swept over a six-foot drop in turbulent water. He was sucked into a hole on the other side of the rock and came up gasping for air. Eli and the raft came to his right and Eli called out, "Swim for shore!" but it was all happening too fast for Ulysses to make it to the bank before they were in another intense rapids. He struggled to keep his legs and head up and off the rocks. A short distance ahead, Ulysses could see Kane's raft. It was trapped under a snag on the west bank. He tried desperately to get out of the rapids and into the calmer water near shore. *Where was Kane?*

"Look!" he yelled to Eli, who couldn't hear him. As he struggled out of the swift, deep water, he ended up close to Kane's raft which was badly deflated and overturned in the water. There was no sign of Angela. He remembered his dream of being worried about a woman he loved. *Angela. A woman who was like his little sister.* Eli was able to maneuver his raft out of the swift water and near the bank.

"Do you see her?" Ulysses yelled, touching bottom with his feet at last.

"No," Eli answered. "I don't see Kane either."

Just then they heard gunfire.

Eli got down from his seat at the back of the raft and jumped into the river as bullets spit into the water around him. Eli had moved into a series of eddies. Kane shot at them again. Ulysses approached the raft from underwater, pulled out the dry bag and struggled ashore with it over his head. Eli came up to Ulysses and got his gun. "Take cover," Ulysses said to Eli, "He's up above us, behind those three rocks. I saw a muzzle flash."

"I see him," Eli said, taking a shot.

Ulysses said, "Run up that hill and I'll cover you. We have to find Angela."

Kane continued to shoot at them. Bullets hit their raft and Ulysses could hear the leak hissing. He checked his ammunition. He had two thirty-round magazines. Eli ran up the hill in a crouch while Ulysses put down lots of fire. Kane stopped shooting and then Ulysses saw Angela scrambling up a steep, slippery incline far above them, obscured by sheets of rain.

After the Buzzsaw section, Kane hit a big rock that squatted in the middle of a Class v+ rapids. The raft spun from the impact, throwing Kane's helmeted head into a sharp edge. Then the raft capsized. Angela was tossed into roaring whitewater. When she came to the surface, she had lost sight of Kane. She had swallowed a bellyful of water and her heart was pounding. Their raft tumbled downstream empty before being sucked into a snag.

Angela tried to lie on her back to keep her feet from getting trapped between the rocks, a sure way to drown. Praying, she allowed the swift current to carry her, knowing she could be dashed into a rock at any time. Somehow the water bore her away from the central torrent and close enough to shore that she could paddle herself into shallow water. Gasping for breath, she looked around and saw no one, so she climbed out of the water. She ran up the steep bank as fast as she could go. Rain had made the muddy ground very slippery. Lightning flashed around her and heavy rain washed over her shivering body. But the relief of escaping together with being on land propelled her up the flank of the gorge. *I know where I am,* she thought. *I can do this. Thank you!*

Angela thought she was near the Vista Verde Trail, one she had walked once before with a girlfriend from college. The trail ran along a rocky shelf of land that jutted out above a steep drop to the river a few hundred feet below the basalt cliffs and rimrock at the top of the gorge. This area had been a wintering shelter for the Comanche people who used it to pasture their horses after summers hunting buffalo on the southern plains. The dirt road to Carson wasn't far from the trailhead.

The long climb to the trail left her exhausted. She hadn't eaten anything since breakfast and it was now early evening. Soaking wet from the river and the rain, she was shivering uncontrollably. She heard gunshots below her. Was Kane shooting at her, or were Sheriff and Eli nearby? Angela realized that without her weapon there was nothing she could do but save herself.

The rain began to diminish but the sun remained hidden behind heavy clouds. Angela felt at risk for hypothermia if she stayed still to avoid Kane. She decided to keep moving, hoping the trail would end at a parking area just off route 567, the road to Carson, which was what she remembered.

Angela moved from rock to rock at first, finally coming out into the open at a wet weather pool where bighorn sheep had come to drink. A ram and four ewes looked up, startled, then bounded to the rocks behind the pool as she approached. They stood gazing at her with their strange eyes as she passed. No one else was on the trail. It wound through open country, passing some volcanic rocks with petroglyphs. Angela heard more distant gunfire. Although she wasn't sure she knew exactly where she was, as she moved farther away from where she parted ways with Kane she began to feel less afraid of seeing him lurking around the next turn. After about forty-five minutes of walking, she came up a rocky hill and saw the parking area in the distance. With relief she ran toward it. As she drew closer, she noticed that except for one SUV the lot was empty. She dropped to the ground and looked closely at the car below her. It was one she thought she'd seen before. The man in the driver's seat was Rowdy Eustace.

Deputies Zach and Mark had responded to LizBeth's call with a flurry of efforts, none of which yielded effective results. They tried to get the river operations team at Dixon's Volunteer Fire Department to undertake a swift water rescue of Angela, Eli, and Sheriff, but were informed that as unarmed volunteers the Fire

Department couldn't be part of a law enforcement operation. Then they drove to Cameron's property, but were unable to determine who, if anyone, had actually gone down the river. They lost some time looking at a fresh grave, afraid it could hold one of their friends and wondering if they should exhume the body. Finally, they decided to drive around to the Taos Junction Bridge, a trip of at least forty minutes, to see if that would give them any information. Later, they drove through Carson and decided to stop at the Kit Carson Café to see if anyone had seen Kane or any of their colleagues.

Cicely was in the market buying supplies when they came in. When she heard the deputies asking after Angela, she approached them.

"Hey, guys," she said, "what is up with Deputy Angela? Did you say she might be in danger?"

"Who are you?" Deputy Mark asked in a guarded tone.

"I'm Cicely Duncan. I live not far from here. Angela helped us when my friend Maddy Smith was in trouble."

Zach said to Mark, "I've heard about this. What she's saying is true." Then to Cicely Zach said, "Have you seen Angela today?"

"No. Is she missing?"

"She and Sheriff and another deputy went down the Box after a suspect," Zach said. "That was several hours ago."

"What suspect?" Cicely asked. "Lassiter Kane?"

"We can't say, Ms. Duncan," Mark said. "But if you haven't seen her, we should be moving on."

"If she's with Lassiter Kane you'd better find her," Cicely said. "He's a killer."

"That's what we're trying to do," Mark said. "Come on, Zach, let's get going."

She watched them get in their truck and pull out of the parking lot, turning toward Ojo Caliente.

Cicely paid for the supplies and got in her car, feeling angry and afraid. All the way home she worried about Angela. When she arrived, her mother opened the gate for her to park and then let her into the house. Nash, Cicely's little brother, was eating an early dinner at the kitchen table. Cicely put down her bags and told Shelagh what she'd learned at the Café.

"Where were they going to look for Angela and Eli?" Shelagh asked.

"It seemed like they didn't have a clue," Cicely said. "They turned toward Ojo Caliente."

"If Angela and Eli went down the Box, they couldn't have made it all the way to Carson by now, not on foot," Shelagh said. The older woman paused for a moment. "Unless they are still on the river, they should be looking for them on the roadside."

Shelagh put her hair in a ponytail and put on a Kevlar vest. She went to her stash of weapons and got a rifle and pistol. "You say here with Nash, Cicely," she said. "I'm going to look along the road. With these clouds it will be dark soon."

In spite of the mud, Eli climbed rapidly up through the rocks trying to catch up to Angela. Kane, under fire from Ulysses, stayed hidden. Ulysses thought Kane was lower, closer to the river, but when Kane peeked out to shoot, Ulysses saw Kane was higher than he thought, among some rocks about halfway up to the shelf where the trail was. Somehow, while Ulysses was shooting, Kane had managed to move up the mountain without being seen. Ulysses saw Eli moving rapidly toward the shelf. The young man was dangerously close to where Kane was hiding. Sure enough, Kane began to shoot at Eli who had to scramble to get cover. *Was he hit?* Ulysses had a sick feeling he might have been.

The wind had picked up and was gusting around Ulysses, turning the evening chilly. Ulysses prepared to advance on Kane. To his north was a fissure in the gorge that provided enough cover for him to get to the shelf. Once there, he could come around above Kane and perhaps surprise him. He moved to his right and scrambled up a treacherously steep incline as fast as he could, as the wind roared around him. There were no shots fired in his direction. With his weapon over his shoulder, he climbed hand over hand. He pulled himself onto a ledge that hung out over the river far below and tried to catch his breath while he looked around. Kane was nowhere to be seen. However, just to his south, behind a massive rock, he saw Eli's feet poking out.

Rather than yelling into the wind, Ulysses ran toward Eli. Kane saw him and fired but missed. Kane was now behind some rocks about twenty-five yards from Eli, near the cliff's edge. Eli fired back at Kane, which filled Ulysses with relief. *He is alive.* However, when he arrived at the rock, he saw that Eli was seriously wounded in the thigh.

"Really glad to see you, Sheriff," Eli said, breathing heavily and shivering.

"Same here," Ulysses said. He looked at Eli's thigh and probed a bit with his hand. Eli groaned deeply. "Doesn't look like it hit your bone or femoral artery. But it isn't good."

"No, not good," Eli said.

"Can you roll a bit and let me look at the back of your leg?"

Eli leaned over for Ulysses revealing the large, bloody hole where the bullet exited. The sight of the exit wound troubled Ulysses even more. Eli was losing a significant amount of blood. Ulysses looked out from behind the rock and fired a couple of rounds toward where he thought Kane was. Then he took off his belt and applied it as a tourniquet to slow the bleeding. Ulysses felt so much adrenaline that he wasn't cold, even though his clothing was soaked and his skin was covered in gooseflesh.

"I need to kill this son of a bitch," he said.

"Yes, Sheriff, kill him or he will surely kill us."

"You stay here. Don't move." He reloaded with his last ammo clip.

Ulysses, full of rage and purpose, ran from behind the rock, firing his gun toward Kane's hiding place and yelling at the top of his voice. He arrived at the rock without Kane firing a shot at him. Ulysses looked all around for his adversary. *Did he get away?* Then Kane emerged from behind the rocks, hands up.

"Fucking gun jammed or I'd have killed you, Rambo," Kane said.

For a moment Ulysses was unsure. *Was this some kind of trick?* He looked over his shoulder toward Eli and in that moment, Kane jumped him, knocking his rifle away toward the cliff, slashing Ulysses with a knife hidden in his right hand. He cut Ulysses' arm inside the elbow. Ulysses threw his shoulder at him and knocked him to the ground. He jumped on Kane and punched him hard in the throat. Kane sputtered and swiped toward Ulysses' neck with his knife. Ulysses backhanded him in the face and pinned his knife hand while looking around for his gun. Before Ulysses saw it, Kane struggled loose, and sliced at him again, cutting deep into Ulysses' torso under his arm. Startled and in pain, Ulysses fell back. He saw his rifle lying in a muddy puddle near the cliff's edge. Kane pushed him off his body, and stood, swinging the large knife side to side. He backed up and tripped over Ulysses' rifle. A look of triumph spread over his face. He stooped to pick up the weapon, grasping it at last. But as he lifted it, his feet slipped in the mud and he began to fall backward. Kane's eyes locked with Ulysses' as he waved his arms trying to right himself, the rifle falling from his hands and clattering over the cliff. In a moment of horror, Kane recognized his fate, his face contorting with fear. He fell off the ledge, a sheer drop of more than a thousand feet. Ulysses heard his screams and saw him tumble head over heels, hitting rocks that hardly slowed his fall until he landed face down in the Rio Grande.

A dark, familiar feeling of emptiness came over Ulysses. The wind whipped around him. Overhead, a faint blue sky began to appear as the clouds were swept away. His mind closed on Lassiter Kane's face the instant before he fell. *Another image I'll remember the rest of my life,* Ulysses thought.

Ulysses ran back to where Eli lay in the mud and wind. Eli's face was blanched and his lips were blueish.

"Hey, man, mind if I snuggle up with you?" Ulysses asked. "We're both fucking freezing."

"Sounds good to me, Sheriff," Eli said. Ulysses laid his body over Eli's to shield him from the cold. *What am I going to do now,* he wondered. *And how long does Eli have?*

It was dinnertime when Ray, Delilah and Arthur met at the Valdez home to discuss the information they'd found in Antonio Valdez's lock box. LizBeth was expected but had not yet arrived. After the rain stopped, the spring evening had turned limpid with rainbows and pink sunset clouds. Ray arrived first and he and Delilah reviewed their plans to file a lawsuit to stop the Mora diversions, while Arthur, who loved to cook, made pasta primavera with garlic bread and salad and opened a bottle of wine. No one was aware of the raid at the Cameron compound or the dangers currently facing Ulysses and his team. Delilah had only exchanged voicemails with LizBeth that day.

Ray asked, "Has Cameron made it out of the country? Or do you know?"

"I know he took off from the Taos Airport, but that's all I know," Delilah answered. "Hey, listen, I'm going to go ahead and make LizBeth a plate. You two eat before it gets cold. I wonder what's keeping her?"

"Do you think she's in trouble with the FBI for trying to stop his flight from Taos?" Ray asked, serving himself some pasta.

"She could be, but I don't know," Delilah said. "LizBeth said there were people at Justice who were now suspicious about Cameron's activities."

"In big agencies like the Justice Department, the right hand often doesn't know what the left hand is doing," Arthur said, pouring himself a glass of wine. "Do you know if they are favorable to LizBeth putting together a RICO case against Cameron?"

"LizBeth left me a message this afternoon saying she'd told her contact at Justice about the charges against Taos Tribal Governor Quintana, and the contact knew about the ongoing investigation into Nan Greene, Cameron's old buddy. But the contact didn't know anything about Greene's connections to Big Hat and the Camerons. Now she does. So, yes, RICO is back on the table."

LizBeth's car pulled into the driveway. She came into the kitchen looking sunburned, windblown and anxious. Delilah gave her a plate of pasta and poured her a tall glass of water.

"Have any of you heard from Ulysses?" she asked, sitting down and chugging her glass of water.

"No," Ray asked. "When did you hear from him last?"

"This morning, right before I went to the airport to try to stop Cameron's plane."

"Where is he most likely to be?" Delilah asked.

"Somewhere down the Rio Grande is the best I can figure. If they are still on the river."

"Do any of them have river experience?" Arthur asked. "That's the Taos Box down there."

"Eli used to work for Far Out Adventures," LizBeth said. "And I think Ulys can hold his own in a kayak. But I don't know about Angela."

"But why would they go down some of the whitest water around?" Arthur asked.

"There was some kind of shootout in Cameron's house. Maybe there was a chase, I couldn't say. But it looked like somebody took a couple of rafts down the river." LizBeth was shoveling in food if she were starving. Delilah refilled her water glass. "I spoke with Zach Wright sometime after lunch and filled him in on what was going on. He and the other deputies were going to mount a search. But I haven't been able to get hold of them since."

"Wait a minute. How did Ulysses get a raft down to the river?" Ray asked, sounding confused and alarmed.

LizBeth said, "The perp they are chasing has an Airstream at the edge of the gorge on Cameron's property and there was a sizeable rack for kayaks and rafts down at the river just below it," LizBeth said, wiping her mouth. "Evidently our perp is a real river rat."

"With an emphasis on the rat part," Ray said.

"That's right," LizBeth said. "Anyway, when I got there it looked like two rafts were gone."

"What time was that?" Ray asked.

"Around midday," LizBeth said, "Before that huge thunderstorm."

"So, they were on the river during the storm?" Ray asked.

"As far as I know they may still be on the river," LizBeth said. "I'm really worried about all three of them." She looked at her watch. "It's seven now. I'm going to call the State Police. They need to get a helicopter out there." LizBeth stood up from the table and took out her phone to make the call. Just then, Ray's cellphone rang. It was Rosemary, worried about Ulysses. He hadn't checked in.

Angela shrank back behind some rocks as Eustace got out of his SUV and spoke for a few minutes on a cellphone. She was pretty sure he hadn't seen her earlier. She found a large standing rimrock to hide behind and tried to make a plan but couldn't figure out what to do. Meanwhile, Eustace locked his truck and walked toward the trail head with an automatic weapon in one hand and night vision binoculars in the other. Eustace passed within a few feet of where she was hidden and started down the trail. Angela worried that Eustace would find Ulysses and Eli and even the odds against them. They would not be expecting him so he would even have an advantage. *But without a weapon, what can I do?* Feeling confused and overwhelmed, Angela made her way stealthily in the gathering dark to the parking area and the steep, rocky, dirt road that led toward Carson. After about a mile of walking she began to cry from frustration and exhaustion. She felt so helpless. *I think I'm suffering from hypothermia,* she thought. Then she saw a truck coming toward her and quickly ducked behind some rocks.

Shelagh Duncan had been driving up and down 567 as wind cleared the sky of clouds and the sun dropped toward the western horizon. The rain had settled the dust and the chilly evening was quiet with no vehicles on the road. After driving on backroads for an hour, she'd seen no one. Even though she was starting to lose hope of finding Angela, she decided to drive one more time to the Taos Junction Bridge. Just as she rounded the corner on the mesa top and started into the gorge, she saw someone run behind some rocks near the road. Shelagh pulled over and got out. "Angela," she yelled, "if it's you hiding back there, it's me, Shelagh Duncan, Cicely's mom. Come on out, I can take you to my place where you'll be safe."

Angela ran out from behind the rocks and the two women embraced. "Get in the truck," Shelagh said. "Wrap up in that blanket there in the back. Let's get you out of there."

"No, we can't," Angela said. "There are killers out there and they are stalking Sheriff and Eli. I have to stop them."

"You are in no condition to stop anyone," Shelagh said. "Get in the truck and wrap up in that wool blanket." Angela climbed into the truck and did as she was told. She was trembling but managed to drink water from a canteen and eat two protein bars Shelagh gave her. "Do you have any dry clothes in here?'"

"No. But like I said, you can't go after anyone. You are in no shape to do that. We are going to have to trust your sheriff and Eli to take care of themselves."

"Listen," Angela said, "I hear a helicopter. Do you hear it?"

"Yes," Shelagh said, "I see it, too, look!"

The helicopter, a unit from the New Mexico State Police, was flying up the gorge from Pilar, shining lights down to the river, lit by the moon in an almost cloudless sky.

"I hope they have some idea of where to look," Shelagh said, looking through night binoculars. "There are three officers in there. That's good!"

"Listen, Shelagh, trust me. One of the killers has his truck parked at the Vista Verde Trail parking lot, just right down there. When this guy sees this helicopter, he's going to try to get back to his car. If we go now, maybe we can apprehend him."

"Okay, Angela. I'll drive you down there. I'm well-armed and I've even got handcuffs in here if you want to arrest him."

The two women drove down the road with lights off and pulled into the parking area as the helicopter flew over them headed upriver. They waited in the dark to see if Rowdy Eustace would show up. Sure enough, after a few minutes he emerged from the trailhead, running. Shelagh jumped out of her truck and yelled, "Drop your weapons or I'll shoot. And I ain't kidding."

Eustace, surprised, put his rifle and night vision on the ground and held his hands in the air. Angela ran forward and handcuffed him.

When Ulysses saw the helicopter approaching, he ran out from the rocks and started waving his arms. The helicopter approached and an amplified voice said, "Get on the ground, facedown. Now!"

"Officer down," Ulysses yelled, as he dropped to his knees, hands over his head.

Ulysses, facedown and shivering, heard the helicopter land. A man came running toward where Ulysses lay and yelled, "Identify yourself!"

"Sheriff Ulysses Walker of Taos County. Deputy Eli Martinez needs immediate transport."

"Really sorry, Sheriff Walker, we didn't know who was who down here."

"Sir, take my jacket." He handed Ulysses a light quilted jacket. Ulysses put it over his right shoulder because his right arm and side were bleeding from knife wounds.

"Don't worry about the blood, sir," the stater said. He ran back to help his partner load Eli onto a stretcher. Ulysses walked alongside the stretcher. Eli was semi-conscious.

"You were really brave back here, Deputy," Ulysses said. "Hang in there. You are in good hands."

Eli nodded. "Thank you, Sheriff," he said, taking the hand Ulysses offered.

The man who'd loaned him his jacket said, "We've reached your deputies and they are on the way here to get you. They should be at the parking area in about fifteen minutes. They can take you to get that arm stitched up."

"Thank you, Brother," Ulysses said. "Get my man to a trauma center as soon as you can."

"We will, Sheriff Walker. Don't you worry."

Chapter 15

The morning of the election, Ulysses woke up before daylight. His right arm and side, where he'd received dozens of stitches from knife slashes, were throbbing. Rosemary was sleeping deeply, snuggled against his back, so he didn't want to move and wake her up. He lay there and thought about taking another Percodan. He hated how those pills made him feel.

The last two days had been a blur. After the fight on the mesa Eli was medevacked to UNM. Zach kept Ulysses informed about Eli's progress. After receiving blood and having surgery to remove bullet fragments, Eli's condition moved from critical to serious; he was expected to recover fully but would remain in the hospital for the time being.

Ulysses had been transported to St. Vincent in Santa Fe, where he stayed overnight, receiving stitches for his knife wounds and treatment for hypothermia.

Shelagh had given Angela hot tea with milk and sugar and put her into a warm bath before giving her dry clothes and driving her home. Angela, though sporting some nasty bruises, was feeling okay. On Monday, she had held a debrief for staff at Headquarters regarding the events at Trey Cameron's property and on the river. On Ulysses' advice, she'd given a local press conference where she revealed that Lassiter Kane had kidnapped her at gunpoint and subsequently fallen to his death in the Rio Grande Gorge after a struggle with Sheriff Ulysses Walker. Ulysses had watched his deputy handle the press with skill while he sat on the couch at home, his injured arm in a sling. *She's already doing the job of undersheriff pretty damn well,* he thought.

LizBeth had also met with the press and sent Ulysses a link to the video to watch. She handled some difficult questions exceptionally well. She announced the arraignment of Taos Pueblo Governor Jerry Quintana on charges of bribery of a public official. When LizBeth didn't announce accessory to capital murder among Quintana's charges and stated that the governor had implicated the late Senator Ramón Trujillo and Mr. Trey Cameron, a local businessman who had fled the country, as the source of bribes, Ulysses knew there must have been a plea deal. When asked if she was going to be reprimanded for trying to stop Cameron from fleeing on his private jet, LizBeth chuckled. "I don't think so," she said. "But we shall see." *Looks like LizBeth has her mojo back,* Ulysses thought.

Ulysses sent the deputies to search Kane's Airstream and exhume whatever was in the grave nearby. He wanted to go himself to supervise despite being in pain and foggy from opiates, but found he needed another day of rest. When the team arrived at Cameron's, another team from the FBI field office led by LizBeth was already there combing through the house and outbuildings, tagging and boxing evidence which they loaded into a van.

Angela informed Ulysses about their work at Kane's Airstream, where they found boxes of methamphetamine, cocaine, and fentanyl. In one custom cabinet they had to break open, they found Kane's trophy collection: two ears and three fingers, one still sporting a turquoise ring.

Angela had Mark and Joseph dig up the shallow grave to reveal the corpse still recognizable as Cody Parker. The stench of decomposing human remains made everyone gag as they loaded the cadaver with its hideous wound back into a body bag for transport to the morgue in Taos. Angela had taken the rest of the day off, leaving Zach in charge. She went to Albuquerque to visit Eli.

It was starting to get light. Ulysses could hear Amelia and Monty arguing upstairs. Now that they were out of school for the summer, Rosemary would have them all day, every day until they started attending the patchwork of day camps she'd been able to arrange for them. Rosemary groaned and rolled over, awake.

"What is your day like, today?" Rosemary asked her husband as she threw back the coverlet and got out of bed.

"Stephanie says I should visit a few of the polling places, but I can't face that just yet. I plan to go into the office to work. I want to clear my head and doing paperwork helps for that. After the polls close, I'm going to the office to be with everybody and watch the returns on TV. It should be over by about eight o'clock. What about you?"

"Bobbie is ready to kid so we'll be at home all day in case she goes into labor. The children will have to entertain themselves. If she delivers, we'll come in for the party."

"How are you feeling?" Ulysses asked. He got out of bed.

"Surprisingly well," Rosemary said. "If you had asked me on Sunday, it would have been a different story. But I'm starting to figure out that days like that are part of my destiny as long I'm married to you. Want some coffee?"

"I do," Ulysses said. "Thank you for understanding me, Rosemary. I'm sorry it's so hard that I'm in law enforcement."

"I'm feeling like you will be in law enforcement for at least four more years," she said with a smile. She stood up and gave Ulysses a gentle hug, careful of his wounds.

"We'll know tonight," Ulysses said.

Stephanie brought pizzas, beer, and brownies to Ulysses' office right before the polls closed and all the deputies except Eli, including the 911 staff and the campaign volunteers, gathered to hear the outcome of the election. She also brought a copy of the *Taos News* that had a front-page headline, "Sheriff Catches Kidnapper by Running the Box." Below the fold was another headline, "Tribal Taos Governor Implicates Senator Ramón Trujillo and Businessman Trey Cameron in Bribery Scheme."

Ulysses, his arm in a sling, had a bad case of election night jitters, but everyone around him was confidently upbeat. He wished Rosemary were there.

Deputies Zach and Joseph came to the party after delivering Kane's body to the morgue. Zach said, "That's two days in a row we had to deliver a cadaver to Dr. Vigil. He wasn't happy at all. Oh, and he gave us the DNA results on the cigarette butts and the shovel—traces of Lassiter Kane on both." Angela was late arriving, having driven the arrest warrant for Jacinto Ramirez to the sheriff in Mora County.

Before all the pizza was eaten, Rosemary and the children arrived announcing that Bobbie had given birth to a doe and that both nannie and kid were doing fine. The TV announced that Ulysses was the projected winner. By the time they'd finished the brownies, the race was called for him.

"Congratulations, U, you just got another term. Be careful what you ask for," Stephanie said. Ulysses hugged her. "Thanks for all your help, Stephanie. I couldn't have done it without you."

"You know you'll have to get someone else to run your campaign next time, right?"

"Right," Ulysses said, feeling the deep relief of knowing that would be almost four years from now. "I'd never expect you to do it again. But you did a wonderful job."

Ulysses kissed and hugged Rosemary. "It's over," he said.

"Oh no," Rosemary said with a laugh. "It's just beginning again."

Epilogue: Eleven months later.

Ulysses and Rosemary's third child, a daughter, Frances, was three months old when Rosemary threw a party for Ulysses' work colleagues, some of whom hadn't met the baby yet. It was a cool Sunday in May, perfect for strawberry shortcake and iced tea and being outdoors in beautiful spring weather. Ray and Clarice, LizBeth and Dawa, and Angela and Eli were the guests.

After everyone had their chance to adore the baby, who had Rosemary's curly red hair, sky blue eyes and ready smile, they settled down to talk shop while Rosemary sat on the swing nursing Frances and supervising Monty and Amelia, who were serving the refreshments. Frances, after filling her tummy, fell asleep in her mother's arms.

"Congratulations, Angela, on receiving your appointment as Undersheriff!" LizBeth said.

"Thanks, LizBeth. I'm really happy with my new job. And Sheriff is already working me hard, training our three new deputies."

"You aren't training Eli, are you?" Clarice asked. "That would be awkward given your relationship!"

"No, she's not training me," Eli said, smiling and taking Angela's hand. "I start the FBI training program in the fall," Eli said. "I'm still working with Sheriff on some special projects though."

"What kind of projects?" Clarice asked.

"Mainly focused on upgrading our tech and teaching Sheriff about surveillance and investigation using computers," Eli answered.

"How is the recovery with your leg, Eli?" Ray asked.

"Good, sir, thank you. I'm pretty much healed up. I have a wicked scar and some weakness in that leg but no lasting problems, I hope. I did a lot of physical therapy and feel almost back to my old self. What is happening with the Picuris Mora transfers case?"

"Delilah has been working hard for us," Ray said. "We go to court for voir dire in three weeks. I'll keep you posted once the trial is underway. We think we have a strong case. LizBeth, what is happening with the Cameron case?"

"We finally successfully extradited Cameron and he is awaiting trial in federal court in Albuquerque under RICO indictments. Jerry Quintana, the former Taos Tribal Governor, has given some damning evidence on a plea deal. They are both out on bail awaiting trial. We don't expect any developments until probably the end of the year, but our prosecutor is confident. Of course, Cameron has a whole array of high-priced lawyers, so it won't be a slam dunk. Still, we've charged him and a number of his associates—including Gilbert Herrera and James Halloran—with participating in organized crime, including murder, extortion, bribery of public officials, and a lot more. Jacinto Ramirez was charged with breaking and entering and destroying a water presa, which is a capital crime here in New Mexico."

Dawa laughed at her wife's joke. "LizBeth is throwing the book at Cameron," she said. "She gathered so much evidence, I don't think he can get away this time."

"We found an interesting bit of information last week during the legal discovery," LizBeth said. "Turns out Lassiter Kane was Cameron's son, born to a teenager who was the daughter of one of his father's employees at Big Hat, a girl named Shelly Kane. She was sixteen when Kane was born."

"Is she still alive?" Angela asked.

"When Kane was about twelve, Shelly was killed in a single car accident where she ran off the road and down a steep embankment," LizBeth answered. "Cameron was a passenger in the car and sustained the injury that caused him to lose his left leg below the knee. Shelly left a suicide note making it clear she

260 · C. R. KOONS

intended to kill them both. Lassiter came to live with his father but he was in and out of juvie until he became an adult. He always worked for his father but Cameron never claimed him publicly as a son. Kind of sad, really."

"What ever happened to your boss, Don Barkley?" Eli asked LizBeth.

"Unfortunately, he is still in the FBI, but he was sent to the field office in Jackson, Mississippi and then demoted to deputy director. I don't think he is too happy about it."

"Did you suffer any repercussions for your tussle with Barkley?" Ulysses asked.

"Not really. In fact, I'm up for a promotion. I could be in charge of all operations from Santa Fe north in three months. If I get the job, that is."

Amelia and Monty came around with seconds on strawberry shortcake and refills of iced tea.

"Ulys, I heard that Lorraine Baca died last week," Ray said.

"Yes, quietly, in her sleep. When her nephew came by to take her to a doctor's appointment, he found her. He said she looked peaceful. The funeral is tomorrow at Our Lady of Guadalupe at 11 o'clock. Angela and I are going."

Ray said, "That's good. Maybe I can make it too."

"Everybody in town will be there," Angela said.

"On a lighter note, things have settled down enough that Delilah and Arthur are finally getting married next month at the Valdez home. Should be a good party," Ray said. "And Clarice and I just got our insurance claim and bought all new furniture!"

"Rosemary, where did you and Ulys get the name Frances from?" Clarice asked. "It's sweet and old-fashioned. Is it a family name?"

Rosemary held her finger to her lips, not wanting to wake the baby. Ulysses answered, "We just like the name. It means, 'the free one.'"

"And it's gender neutral," Eli commented.

Ulysses looked around at his friends and colleagues and felt grateful for each one of them. Since the Cameron case, no other big, dangerous cases had come his way. For almost a year the Sheriff's Department had been relatively quiet. Ulysses even took three weeks of parental leave after Frances was born. He knew he couldn't count on things staying so quiet forever, but he was grateful for this moment, nonetheless.

The End

Glossary

Acequia: An ancient irrigation system established by Spanish settlers in the Southwest to make surface water available for irrigation in arid areas of low rainfall but abundant snow fall.

Acequias are a series of ditches including the main ditch, "acequia madre" and supporting ditches, "laterals." Acequias maintain water rights owned by their members, landowners who live on the ditch and irrigate crops, orchards, and pastures. Acequias are governed by their by-laws and the laws of the state.

Acequieros: People who participate in or advocate for acequias and acequia culture.

Arroyo: A dry watercourse that flows during times of heavy rainfall only.

Bordos: The sides of the acequia (the banks).

Bosque: Literally "woods." The riparian area on either side of a river or stream.

Comisión: An elected body which manages an acequia, consisting usually of a president, vice-president and secretary-treasurer.

Comisionado: An elected member of the comisión. Comisionados must be landowners with water rights on the acequia. They work as volunteers.

Desagüe: Literally, "drain." Infrastructure, including head gates and ditches, which allows the acequia to be emptied or drained back into a river or stream. Desagües are used to manage or cut off flow when needed due to heavy rainfall or to make repairs.

Diversion: Infrastructure created to direct the course of water away from its natural course in order to irrigate acreage.

Earthship: A passive solar home typically made of natural and recycled materials that makes use of renewable energy sources and smart design to meet most if not all heating, cooling and power needs.

Flume: A raised culvert on a permanent support for conveying water across an arroyo.

FOIA: Freedom of Information Act.

The Lab: Los Alamos National Laboratory. Also called LANL (La'-nul). LANL is a major employer in northern New Mexico. It was the site of development of the atomic bomb and continues to be involved in nuclear weapons research and manufacture.

Land Grant: During colonization, the conveyance of acreage to individuals or groups by someone in authority, such as the Spanish King, to promote settlement.

Llano: A treeless plain or plateau.

Mayordomo: A parciante hired by the comisión to manage the physical ditch and distribute water shares. Also called the "ditch boss."

Mesa: An isolated hill bounded on all or most sides by steep escarpments. A mesa stands out from the surrounding countryside.

Mora Transfers: Three significant diversions of water from creeks to flow into the Mora watershed rather than toward the Rio Pueblo/Rio Embudo watershed. The diversions, which date from the 1800s, transfer water by means of ditches and diversion dams and use contours to take the water from the natural western flow toward Picuris Pueblo and downstream irrigators, to the eastern slope toward irrigators in Mora County. As much as 10% of the natural water is thus diverted from one watershed to another.

Pala Power: Literally "shovel power." The power of acequieros to manage and make decisions for their acequias.

Parciante: A landowner who has water rights on an acequia.

Paper Rights: Water rights that have been transferred away from the original water source. Paper rights may be transferred from one watershed to another, although it is legally difficult to do this without a compelling reason. Water rights typically go with the land itself.

Patos: Ducks. Acequia de los Patos would be translated to Acequia of the Ducks.

Peon: A measure of how many acre feet of water is owned. From the Spanish word for day laborer. In the past, each parciante was supposed to provide day labor annually as needed during projects equivalent to the number of peones of water attached to their land.

Perfecting the Right: When an entity has used water to which they were not originally entitled by right, after a period of time they can be adjudicated to actually own a right to that water. The term for that adjudication is "perfecting the right."

Presa: Infrastructure, essentially a dam, that allows an acequia to take water from a watercourse into its acequia structures. Infrastructure can be as simple as rocks in the river, which can be moved by hand, or as complex as a concrete structure with a large iron head gate that can be opened and closed by a wheel. A presa is also called the "point of diversion" because it is where the acequia diverts water from its watercourse.

Priority Rights: Water rights given priority of use by the time when use of the surface water began at that point of diversion. Older priority rights have more leverage in maintaining their water use when disputes arise. The oldest priority rights usually belong to Indian tribes.

Repartimiento: In acequia culture during times of water shortage, the process by which acequias that share the same water source apportion the water in order to "share the shortages."

RICO: Racketeer Influenced and Corrupt Organizations Act.

Transfer of rights: The legal process of moving the water rights from one parcel of land with rights to another which either has no rights, or a smaller right, on the same acequia.

About the Author

C. R. Koons is the pen name for Cedar R. Koons who in addition to the Sheriff Ulysses Walker series has published nonfiction, *The Mindfulness Solution for Intense Emotions* (2016 New Harbinger) and poetry, *Bourbon and Branch Water* (2023 Kelsay Books) as well as numerous academic chapters and research articles. A retired psychotherapist and consultant, Koons lives in the village of Dixon, New Mexico where she writes, serves as an acequia commissioner, gardens, raises chickens and plays in a marimba band. She is married to the photographer Edward Scheps and they have four children and four grandchildren.

Printed in the USA
CPSIA information can be obtained
at www.ICGtesting.com
JSHW031243180224
57477JS00005B/22

9 781684 921539